RISE OF CITHRIA

THE CHOSEN

by

Kris Kramer, Alistair McIntyre, Patrick Underhill

Book 1 of Rise of Cithria

SHAWN, THANKS FOR READING OUR BOOKS
HOPE YOU ENJOY!

Shaun,
Hope you enjoy the books or the series!

PUBLISHED BY:

www.the4threalm.com

This book is a work of fiction and any resemblance to persons, living or dead, or places, events or locales is purely coincidental. The characters are productions of the author's imagination and used fictitiously.

Cover artwork by Marek Purzycki

http://igreeny.deviantart.com/

https://www.facebook.com/pages/igreeny-Graphics/123983141043597

The4threalm.com

The authors of this work are part of the4threalm.com, a group of writers who work, edit, critique and publish collaboratively. They would like to invite you to see more of their work, along with that of several other talented people, at the site below. And be sure to participate in the discussion. The4threalm.com is nothing without its readers!

http://www.the4threalm.com

Prologue

When the Thandaran Empire arrived five centuries ago, they found an untamed, fertile island called Andua. As with every other new land they discovered, the Thandarans subjugated the Anduain people, including the old races of elves, nuathreens and firbolgs. They renamed the island Caldera, and colonized it with their own citizens. Over time, the Anduains and their culture diminished, retreating to the west, into the oldest, most remote areas of the island imaginable. They were hunted, and persecuted, but they endured, and they kept their stories and history alive for centuries, until the moment finally came when the Thandarans left the island, retreating to their besieged homeland far across the sea.

With no Thandaran army to keep the peace, the island fractured. The east, under the control of former Thandaran nobility, remained Caldera. The west became Andua once again. And lurking across the narrow sea to the north was the land of Bergmark, home to fierce havtrols, opportunistic dwarves, and magic-wielding humans. War broke out, leading to chaos, death and destruction… until Damhran, grandson of a Thandaran clerk, ascended to Caldera's throne.

Damhran rallied the Calderan forces to victory after victory, eventually claiming most of the island, staying the hand of

Bergmark, and forcing Andua into a tenuous peace. From his home in Corendar, the capital city of Caldera, Damhran presided over an era of prosperity unprecedented in the history of the three realms. But resentments and rivalries simmered below the surface. Damhran's peace strained, but held for almost forty years – until the day the Century Star appeared.

The Century Star grew bright in the sky, and then faded away, as it did every hundred years, and its arrival triggered prophecy, introspection, and devastation. Damhran saw the star as a sign that his time as King had run its course. A young Anduain warrior named Darren believed that the star signaled the rise of his people. In Bergmark, however, the star coincided with a tragedy, as a volcano erupted, destroying the dwarven kingdom and covering the lands of Bergmark in fire and ash.

War came once again. Damhran retired, passing the throne to his son, who was ill-prepared to handle it. Darren ascended the throne of a new Andua, and he rallied his people to the cause of freedom as their King. And the people of Bergmark, with no lands left to sustain them, invaded the island, looking to claim greener pastures.

For seventeen years now these nations have fought, trading lands, glory, and lives. The balance of power has shifted back and forth among them, but none of the three kingdoms has managed to strike a blow decisive enough to claim a final victory. But times are changing. Bergmark's fierce yet ageing armies have slowly dwindled in numbers, and Andua's forces have suffered several notable defeats. Caldera, long under siege, is at the brink of victory.

But old enemies lurk beneath the surface, waiting for the right time to strike. The three kingdoms, weakened by decades of war, are at their most vulnerable. The fate of these lands, and their people, is at stake.

A new war is coming.

Caldera

Chapter 1

"Coward! Coward!"

The word stabbed at Aiden, like the point of a knife in his back. The mob of children had gathered at the edge of Alvarton's market, where the uneven stone paths turned into a worn, grassy road. They chanted the word over and over, as if singing a verse in some cruel playground song. He walked away as stoically as he could manage with a beaten cloth sack slung over his shoulder and the hood of his worn, frayed red cloak pulled low over his face, hiding what everyone already knew to be there. He hated coming here for this very reason. If he could afford it, he would have sent someone else to pick up his food, but he barely had the money to feed himself. That meant he had no choice but to suffer through this lonely, humiliating ordeal every time his pantry emptied out. The kids would taunt him loudly, the adults would scorn him silently, and he would try to get through it all fast enough that none of the local toughs would think to provoke a fight.

By now, the adults knew him on sight. His sturdy Sotheran build and the fact that he owned only one dingy old army cloak always gave him away to the locals. They rarely said anything to him, though, at least not to his face. As long as he had some spare coin to spread around, the merchants in Alvarton would take it.

They'd wait until after he left to call him the Coward, or the Wolf Cub, or whatever new nickname had made the rounds in the pub. The children weren't so forgiving.

The fat, freckle-faced son of a woman hawking bread had recognized him, and it had taken only seconds before he'd scampered off to tell the other village children that the Coward was back. He only had time to buy bread, a small wheel of cheese and a cheap flagon of wine before they began congregating in the center of the market, pointing and laughing. As soon as he had left and moved onto the east road, they'd gathered at the edge of the town center, near the mile marker, taunting him.

"Coward! Coward!"

No matter how many times he heard that word, the sting never lessened, and neither did his fear that this would be his fate for eternity... to be mocked by children until he died of old age, worthless to his people and to his kingdom. Blood rushed to his face in shame, as it always did when he left this place, and the brand on his left cheek grew hot. He rubbed it absent-mindedly, a rough-edged 'C' burned onto the side of his face. He'd tried growing a beard to cover it up but that only made it more noticeable since the hair around the brand didn't grow. Not that it mattered. By now, everyone in this part of Caldera knew who he was and what he'd been. He ignored the sounds of thrown rocks landing harmlessly on the ground behind him, and trudged along the path, hoping only to get home without incident. The sun would be up for another two or three hours, which was roughly how long it would take to reach his small home in the hills. Once there, he could throw off his clothes, eat a meager dinner, drink some cheap wine, and try to forget about his fate for a few precious minutes before falling into a merciful, drunken stupor.

Unfortunately, an incident seemed to be coming his way.

Aiden saw it out of the corner of his eye - the smooth silhouette of a hooded bandit lurking in the thick woods to his right. Whoever he was, he was cocky, because he followed far too closely for someone who should value subtlety and stealth. Aiden kept his hood low and his gait steady, trying not to tip off his pursuer that he could see him darting from shadow to shadow. The bandit made no noise, which suggested some skill at stalking prey, but he apparently thought Aiden's hood blocked his vision because he was far too careless about keeping his profile low. Aiden gritted his teeth. It was only a matter of time before the bandit attacked, looking for an easy target on a secluded road, and Aiden had no weapon, and thus no way to defend himself. He'd taken to leaving his sword at home to avoid even more raised eyebrows when coming to town. Had he brought it, he could have taught this bandit a painful lesson about stalking a former armsman of the Sotheran Army. But with no sword, he'd be at the bandit's mercy if he didn't have a good plan.

The clop of hoof beats caught his attention, and he turned to see two horse-drawn carts moving onto the road behind him. Merchants, leaving the Alvarton market for the day. They were catching up quickly, so he moved over to let them pass. The first one had an older man and woman up front. Brin, he thought, based on their style of dress. Probably refugees staying near the Silver Hills, like himself. The man held the reigns of his horse loosely, and a few empty sacks lay scattered in the back. The second cart was driven by a younger man, Artoran probably, with a woman and two small children in the back. A few sacks of food lined the back of the cart, either wares they hadn't sold, or that they'd picked up for their own use. Aiden kept his head down and let them go their way, hoping none of them recognized him or cared to see his face. But he knew salvation when he saw it, and he picked up his pace to stay in sight of the merchants as long as possible.

A surreptitious glance toward the woods revealed no sight of the bandit, who had likely decided to be cautious now, at least until the carts pulled away and left Aiden alone again. He wondered if he could hail them down and ask for a ride. In most cases they'd probably let him, but if he tried to hide his face from them they'd get suspicious. If he didn't... well, he couldn't take any more disapproving looks today. He decided he'd just walk faster, instead. The carts were already pulling away from him at a pace he couldn't hope to match, but he could keep them in sight long enough to dissuade the bandit and send him back to Alvarton for easier prey. If he'd thought the Goddess still listened to his pleas, he'd have prayed for her help to keep them close. He only wanted to get home without trouble.

Had he sent any prayers, they would have been answered. A man appeared from the edge of the woods ahead of the carts. He wore a black, hooded robe that hung to his feet and covered his face, like Aiden, only his was in far better shape, with a decorative blue and silver trim along the edges. He walked to the middle of the path and waited, facing the oncoming carts. For a moment Aiden thought this might be his mysterious bandit, but he seemed too tall, too broad, too menacing.

The carts slowed as they approached the stranger.

"You there. Step aside," the older man in the lead cart called out, annoyed at having his trip home so blatantly interrupted. The stranger casually pulled back his hood and flung his cloak off his shoulders, revealing a man close to Aiden's own age, rugged looking, with tanned skin and long blond hair, and a short beard with braids in it. He wore drab gray clothing covered by well-worn chain mail, and he gripped a long-handled hammer in his right hand. Aiden caught his breath. This man was no resident of Caldera. This was a Bergsbor, an invader from the land of Bergmark, standing before them in full battle garb. A Warshield.

He raised his hammer to the sky. Aiden instinctively reached for his belt, remembering with a silent curse that he still had no weapon.

The Brin couple recognized the threat almost immediately. Anyone from the county of Brinwall knew the look of these Northmen, who'd ravaged their borders for years. The old woman screeched in terror, and the old man tried in vain to get his horse to turn around, all while the Warshield shouted an ancient chant to his gods. Without warning, a bolt of lightning crashed down into the front cart with a deafening crack, splintering it into two pieces and

11

sending fragments of charred wood flying about the path. The Brins were thrown clear in opposite directions while the horse whinnied in panic, yanking at its collar. The mother in the second cart screamed, while her husband tried unsuccessfully to turn his horse around.

This isn't possible, Aiden thought, his body frozen in shock. Warshields can't summon lightning from the sky.

The Bergsbor turned to the old man, holding his hammer out in front of him, both hands wrapped around the handle. Tiny bolts of blue lightning crackled dangerously around him. The Brin slowly lifted his head off the ground, blinking as if stunned, but conscious enough to realize the Northman was approaching him with murderous intent. He held his hand up, pleading for his life. The man's wife, who had recovered more quickly, also screamed out for him to stop. Both of their pleas were ignored. The hammer came down, crashing into the Brin's shoulder and crushing his chest. The second blow followed immediately, caving in his head. The old woman wailed at the sight of her dead husband, and the Bergsbor turned to her and raised his hand. A smaller, thinner bolt of lightning arced outward from his palm, striking her, and knocking her flat to the ground where she writhed silently.

"Alfrith! Here!" The Artoran woman in the second cart held a sword up to her husband, shouting at him to take it, while trying to scoop up her two children with her other hand. Alfrith struggled with his horse before reluctantly taking the sword, just as the Northman turned his attention to them.

"Get out of here!" Alfrith yelled back to his family. He gave up trying to soothe his terrorized horse and stepped down from the cart to face the approaching Warshield. He held the sword like a stick, completely unsure of himself, and he shuffled his feet, backing up so he could keep his distance from the Northman. Alfrith's wife jumped off the back of the cart, which rocked dangerously as the confused horse tried to pull free, and dragged the two children out. The Warshield, showing remarkable quickness, darted forward at Alfrith. One swing of his hammer was all it took. The weapons collided, knocking the sword out of Alfrith's hands, sending it skidding across the ground out of reach. The Northman followed with a roaring bellow that sent a shockwave radiating out from his body, kicking up dust and dirt in all directions and knocking Alfrith off his feet.

Aiden took a step back without thinking, only now realizing that he'd watched the whole scene play out in front of him as if he were just a spectator. As if he were the coward everyone thought him to be. This was battle. This was what he wanted, what he'd been denied for two long years. But he hadn't expected to be thrust into the middle of it, deep inside his own kingdom. He had no weapons or armor. He stood little chance against a fully armed Warshield, if that's even what this enemy was. But he also knew that if he let this man slaughter everyone here today, then he deserved that coward's brand on his cheek. He deserved to be mocked and scorned.

Coward... coward...

Aiden squeezed his hands into fists, feeling a strength in his body that had been dormant for years. This wouldn't be the smartest decision he'd ever made, but he wasn't looking for smart. He was looking for brave.

So he dropped his pack and charged.

The Warshield stood over Alfrith and held his hammer high. He didn't seem content to smash the man's skull, however, because he began chanting his spell again, the one that destroyed the first cart, and would no doubt flay this poor man's skin from his bones. Aiden ran at a full sprint toward the discarded sword lying on the ground, hoping to distract the Warshield long enough to save Alfrith. The Northman's eyes darted up, and he seemed to realize that the Calderan lying prone on the ground wasn't his immediate priority anymore. He turned toward this new threat, just as Aiden had hoped, and as he shouted the last words of his chant, Aiden changed direction in mid-stride and threw his large body at the Northman instead of the sword. He hit the Warshield in the stomach with his shoulder as lightning cracked loudly into the empty ground behind him.

The two of them tumbled into the dirt, rolling over each other until the Warshield kicked up his knees, flinging Aiden away to his left. He followed that up by swinging his hammer sideways, but Aiden grabbed the handle, preventing the blow from having any real force. Aiden pushed off the hammer and rolled sideways into a crouch, then leapt toward the discarded sword, grabbing it with his right hand. He was back on his feet in an instant, facing off against his enemy, who'd also regained his footing, and held his own weapon menacingly. Aiden swung the sword, testing its weight and balance, and he knew right away it was junk. The edges were dull, the blade slightly crooked, and if hit in the wrong spot, it would likely snap in two. He might as well have been holding a blunt stick.

Well, Aiden thought, if the sword couldn't handle parrying blows from a giant hammer, then the answer was simple – don't parry. Be aggressive. Aiden steadied his stance and his breathing, and took the fight to the Bergsbor. He swung carefully and deliberately at first, keeping his enemy at a distance while he thought of his next tactic, because now he worried the sword wouldn't even pierce the Northman's chainmail armor. He never had a chance to find out, though. The Warshield grew tired of the duel, raised his hand to the heavens and let loose another small bolt, like the one he'd used on the old woman. The magic coursed through Aiden's body, making his muscles twitch violently and then tense up until frozen in place. Aiden fell to the ground like a toppled statue, unable to do anything except stare up at the Warshield, who grunted at him in annoyance before heaving his hammer back and over his head. Aiden was trapped. He could feel the first sensations of his body loosening up, but it wasn't fast enough. He wouldn't be able to avoid the crippling blow in time.

He would die, painfully – that is, until an arrow clipped the Warshield's ear.

The Northman cried out angrily and grabbed the side of his head, looking around for the arrow's source. Aiden used the extra

15

seconds afforded to him to roll clumsily out of the way. He stood up awkwardly, fighting against his reluctantly loosening muscles, ready to fend off another attack. But the Warshield didn't come for him. He was too busy scowling at something over Aiden's shoulder. Aiden followed his gaze, seeing a young man in a black cloak standing in the middle of the path holding a nocked bow, aimed right at him. The bandit. Aiden almost laughed before realizing he was in the way, so he ducked to the side. The bandit fired another arrow that glanced off the Warshield's left shoulder. It didn't penetrate the armor, but the Warshield narrowed his eyes at this new danger. He turned to Aiden and snarled, then ran into the woods along the side of the path. Aiden hesitated, wondering if he should chase after him with no reliable weapon. But his decision became moot when the Northman vanished. Once he reached the shadows of the trees, he disappeared into thin air.

Aiden froze. That was impossible. He'd seen that ability before, but only from highly trained assassins. They called it fading, and it was their most closely guarded secret. And as far as Aiden knew, they hadn't shared it with the people of Bergmark. He backed away, suddenly afraid for his life. He turned to the bandit, feeling the need to have an ally nearby, only to find him leaning over to pick something up off the ground. Aiden almost called out to warn him, before realizing what exactly the brigand had picked up. Aiden's pack. With his food, and his money, and his wine. The bandit threw it over his shoulder. He saw Aiden looking at him so he smiled back and gave a quick wave, then ran off into the woods where he vanished himself.

Aiden stood there in disbelief. Both of them could fade. Both of them had assassin training. What had he stumbled into?

He scanned the road around him. Alfrith and his family had escaped, running as fast as they could back to Alvarton, leaving their cart and horse behind. The old man from Brinwall was dead, and his wife lay still only a few paces away from her husband. The horse from their cart had pulled free of the wreckage and was galloping the other direction, dragging parts of the harness behind. Aiden was alone, and he knew he couldn't take that Warshield if he came back, not with this flimsy excuse for a sword. He squeezed the hilt in frustration. He knew this feeling, the rush and the wild uncertainty of battle, both of which he'd been so effective at harnessing. He laid out his options before him, and he found the one that made sense. He hefted the crooked blade in his hand and ran into the woods. The sword was useless against the Northman, so he wouldn't use it on him. Instead, he'd find the arrogant little bandit who thought he could steal from a highly trained soldier. If he was lucky, he'd not only retrieve his pack, but maybe a little bit of his pride as well.

Chapter 2

A iden crashed through the woods like a lumbering bear, pushing aside low branches and trampling the brush under foot. He hadn't run like this in over a year, and his body did its best to remind him of that fact. His legs burned, his chest was tight, and his breaths came fast and shallow, but he didn't mind. Fighting that Warshield had reawakened something inside, something that had been slumbering ever since being forcibly branded by his own countrymen. Tonight, for the first time in two years, Aiden felt like a warrior again, and he wasn't about to waste that feeling by accepting his fate and trudging back home. No, tonight he would show his fellow citizens of Caldera that he was no coward.

He made enough noise to rouse the entire county of Artora, but that was his plan. Aiden had trained as an armsman, not a bandit, which meant his skills were best utilized in an open, face-to-face fight, not in tracking someone who could disappear into thin air. So Aiden gambled that by making as big a ruckus as he possibly could, the bandit might come to him instead. He'd already shown his overconfidence earlier. Plus, you didn't take on someone who could fade in a wide open space. A thick forest with plenty of brush would help even the odds.

It was a calculated risk, though, because his current direction would take him toward the river. Any minute now he would be within shouting distance of the relocated goblin settlements nestled along the riverbank, and he didn't want to attract any curious hunting parties if he could help it. Not to mention that these woods were home to more than just goblins, if you believed the stories. And with night approaching, the dangers became even worse. He needed to finish this soon and get back to safety, before he stumbled into even more adventure.

The crack of a branch made him stop, and he looked around carefully to see if his ruse had worked. It took a few moments to get his labored breathing under control, but once he did he stood completely still and silent, waiting to see if the bandit had taken the bait. The sun had dropped low in the sky by now, making the shadows in the forest long and dark. Plenty of room to hide in for a thief. Hopefully this one felt safe enough to stalk a clumsy, lumbering oaf, and would maybe even show himself before launching a few arrows.

"You really should learn to be quieter, old man."

The voice came from behind, maybe a dozen yards back. He debated turning to face him, but decided instead to stay still. He wanted the bandit to feel like he was in charge.

"And you, boy, shouldn't take what isn't yours."

"Curious words coming from a man with an arrow pointed at his head. Drop your sword."

Aiden didn't want the bandit to do anything rash, like shoot him in the back. He also wanted him to feel comfortable enough to get a little closer. At this distance, Aiden was a sitting duck. A skilled archer could get two or three shots off before he could close the distance, and that's only if the first shot didn't kill him. He needed to close the gap to around three or four paces before he could make his move. But he could be nonthreatening and still have a little bit of fun.

"I don't think I want to do that."

The bandit chuckled under his breath. Aiden heard a couple of soft footsteps.

"You do what I say and you don't have to die today."

"I will do nothing you tell me to do, unless it includes retrieving my things."

This time the laugh was loud and haughty.

"Well, aren't you a brazen old man? A little thick in the head, too, because I don't think you understand just how precarious your position is right now."

"Explain it to me, then. Use small words."

Another footstep. Aiden grinned. Almost there.

"I have an arrow pointed at the back of your neck," he proclaimed, a little too grandly. Aiden suspected that this bandit was more concerned with putting on a show than actually killing people. "All I have to do is let it fly and you'll probably die before you even have time to feel it pierce your skin. It won't be as painful a death as

I normally like to hand out, but it will be fast, which will save me from having to hear you moan in agony. Now drop your sword."

Another small footstep, and Aiden decided this was probably his best shot. He held the sword out to his right, holding the hilt between his finger and his thumb, letting the blade dangle over the ground next to him. He let it hang for a moment, purely for show since the bandit seemed to enjoy that, then dropped it. The blade hit the ground, digging into the dirt a bit, before tipping over.

"There's a good man," the bandit said.

Aiden heard a couple more footsteps, so he glanced over his shoulder. He could see the bandit at the edge of his vision, shrouded in shadow, standing about four paces behind him. More importantly, he'd lowered his bow slightly, thinking his prey had been disarmed. In reality, Aiden secretly slipped the palm-sized rock he'd been holding in his left hand this entire time into his right.

"Now, why don't you kick that sword away?" the bandit asked. "Just a bit."

Aiden moved his leg back, as if to do what he'd been told. Instead of kicking, though, he planted the leg a half step behind him, then spun around to his left, launching the rock at the bandit. The bandit realized the danger too late, and as he twisted his body to avoid the rock, he ended up moving his right arm into its path, where it struck him just below the shoulder with a thud.

He cried out and pulled his arm in, letting go of his bowstring and dropping the arrow he had nocked. Aiden charged, covering the space in three quick bounds. He leaped at the cowering bandit, who used his longbow to defend himself, but Aiden grabbed the bow and twisted, prying it free from his hands. The bandit deftly slipped away and pulled a long sword out with his left hand, while Aiden, still clutching the bow, hurried back to pick up his own sword. The two stood a few yards apart, their weapons ready, sizing each other up.

This was the first time Aiden had been able to get a good look at the bandit, and his early impressions about him seemed to be right. He looked young, late teens perhaps, with a mop of wavy, tangled black hair on his head, the hint of a beard on his face, and deep-set black eyes. His light-brown skin was natural, not tanned like Aiden's, and he suspected that at least one of the boy's parents was Movri. He wasn't especially tall, and his build seemed slight, but he'd just shown himself to be quick and nimble on his feet. After sizing up the boy, though, Aiden got the impression that he'd been well-born, despite his dubious parentage, and had only recently taken to the life of a bandit.

"Well, this is an interesting turn," the bandit said finally, breaking the silence.

"I don't want to hurt you," Aiden replied. "I just want my pack returned to me, along with everything that was inside when you stole it."

"I saved your life. This is just payment." The bandit motioned with his head to Aiden's pack, slung over his shoulder.

"I don't much like those terms," Aiden moved a step closer, "and I don't recall agreeing to them."

"You could agree to them now."

"Or, I could drag you to Corendar and watch them hang you for banditry and theft."

"Really?" The bandit smiled at him, but it was the kind of smile someone gives just before they knife you in the stomach. "So they take the word of a coward at face value these days? I'll have to remember that if I ever get such a lovely brand."

"I am no coward," Aiden said, his tone as serious as he could make it.

"Your face says otherwise."

"A brand doesn't make it true." Aiden suddenly wondered why he needed this thief, of all people, to believe him.

"Ahhhh. Is this a sore subject?" the bandit mocked. "Or are you just afraid to talk about it?"

Aiden pointed the sword at the bandit. "You are playing with fire, boy."

"Ohhh, now I'm the one who's scared."

Aiden held the longbow out in front of him with both hands, ready to snap it in two.

"Just how attached are you to this thing?"

"Okay, now wait a minute," the bandit said, suddenly serious. "Let's not get hasty here. We can be civil about this."

"Can we?"

"How about a trade?" The bandit slipped Aiden's pack off his shoulder, and held it out gingerly with his right hand. His face scrunched up in discomfort. "My bow, for your pack?"

"So you can point it at me again?"

The bandit shook his head in frustration. "Well, then we're at a bit of a standstill, aren't we?"

They stood in silence, staring at each other, although their stances were less aggressive now.

He's right, Aiden thought, but not about the impasse. He couldn't go back to Corendar. Even if he felt like dragging this boy all the way back to the city, there was no guarantee that anyone would believe what he had to say, or care about it even if they did. For every city guard he spoke to, he was just as likely to find someone willing to pay a bounty as he was to find a former soldier who'd knock him on his backside for betraying his people with cowardice. He'd even run into guards once who wouldn't let him into the city and he certainly couldn't bear dealing with that embarrassment again. No, the bandit was right. This brand would keep a lot of doors closed to him unless he had something better to offer them than an alleged thief.

Like perhaps a Warshield.

Aiden held his breath as a plan formed in his head.

"What's your name?" he asked.

"What's yours?" the bandit replied, his voice even haughtier than normal. "Or should I just call you Coward?"

"My name is Aiden," he said, keeping his tone calm and cool. "I'm from Sothera, just outside Solstin. Now tell me yours."

The bandit cocked his eyebrow. He pressed his sword hand against his sore shoulder, rubbing it. Aiden quietly hoped he could still use that arm well enough to handle his bow.

"I am the Owl of the Shadows, the Eagle of-"

"Your real name," Aiden said, cutting him off. "Not some bandit title you made up to scare the poor folk."

The bandit sneered at him, then looked away in annoyance. He stared up at the trees nearby, probably thinking up a lie to tell him. Aiden didn't care. He'd use any made up name he was given if it helped him achieve his goal.

"Finias," he said finally, and Aiden was surprised because he actually believed him.

"Well then, Finias. You did save my life, and I'm ready to agree to terms of repayment."

"You are? What terms?" He looked interested now.

"Your service. To me. And mine to you."

Finias huffed in disbelief. "Are you mad? What would possibly make you think I'd agree to that?"

"I want your help to kill that Warshield."

Finias stared at Aiden blankly for a long moment before finally replying, "No."

"Did you see what he did when he ran away? He faded. Disappeared into thin air. Warshields don't do that. You can, obviously. But not him. Something isn't right about this."

"I think it's you," Finias said. "You said it yourself. Warshields don't fade. So you must be mad."

Aiden grunted. "I saw it with my own eyes, and you would have too if you'd been paying attention to him instead of my belongings."

"Why should I believe a story like that?"

Aiden held his arms out in exasperation. "Why would I make up a story like that?"

"Because you're mad!"

"What will take for you to believe me?"

Finias shrugged. "How about if he proves it? That's it. I'll believe it when I see it happen. Wait, maybe I will see it happen, because he could be right here watching us, couldn't he?" Finias turned left and right, looking dramatically into the shadows nearby. "Here, little shadow Warshield. Come out and play with us, because I know you're watching, aren't you?"

Aiden shook his head. "Whether you believe me now or not, it makes no difference. I just need your help to find him and kill him. That is the bargain."

"This is silly. You're insane. And I have no idea why you'd want to drag me down into your crazy little world."

"Because I can't find him alone."

"Then go to the guards."

"The guards will know soon enough. But I need to find him first. We need to find him."

"Why? Why me?"

"You have assassin training. I don't care how, but you do. So who better to track a man with similar skills?"

Finias had no response to that, so Aiden stepped forward and continued his argument.

"Listen to me. You don't think that if we brought in a Warshield who'd slipped past our northern defenses, killed two Calderan citizens, and was capable of fading, we wouldn't get something in return? Whether you believe me or not, you should at least be smart enough to know that there will be a reward for him, a reward we don't get if the guards find him first."

Finias thought about that for a long moment. Finally, "I want my longbow back."

"I want my belongings back," Aiden countered.

"Well, Aiden, now you're finally making some sense. Fine. I agree with your poorly-thought-out little plan. I get my bow, you get your pack, and then we shall find ourselves a Warshield and make some gold in return."

Aiden stepped forward to stand in front of Finias.

"Don't agree just yet. Before you bind yourself to me, and I to you, you must understand that this is serious. If you break your oath to me, then I will have little choice but to find you and kill you. And because of this brand on my face I'm unable to serve in the army or get any decent work. So I have nothing but time to track down dishonest bandits to the ends of the earth." Aiden held out his hand. "So now.... do you agree?"

Finias let out a short chuckle. "See, now I know you're insane. But gold can cure many ills, or so I've been told. I agree."

Finias reached out and shook Aiden's hand, and they both smiled, although Aiden knew in the back of his mind that they were smiling for very different reasons. He had no time to linger on that thought, though. A recognizable popping sound filled his ears, only moments before a cloud of crackling blue energy pounded the forest around them, shaking the trees violently and tossing both men to the ground. Aiden slid sideways until he hit the trunk of an oak tree, a gnarled root jabbing into his back. He groaned, then lifted his head, blinking away the disorienting fog. He looked around, trying to make sense of what happened, only to see his best chance at salvation standing at the edge of the clearing, a mere ten paces away, wearing worn chain armor and carrying a long-handled hammer.

The Warshield had found them.

Chapter 3

Aiden scrambled to his feet, looking for cover amongst the splintered trees surrounding him, but his sluggish body resisted his every movement. He'd been the victim of Warshield magic before, but nothing as formidable as what he'd seen from this one. His muscles were numb, and the forest around him had been ravaged. But he was still alive, and as long as that held true, he could fight back.

"Move!" he yelled, although the word sounded more like a garbled moan. Aiden ducked behind a tree, then glanced back to see Finias still on his back, staring in shock at the Warshield. "Move!" he shouted again, and this time Finias responded, rolling over and darting across the clearing to his own hiding spot. "Here!" Aiden tossed over the longbow, which Finias snatched out of the air with his left hand.

The sky rumbled and Aiden ducked back behind the tree as another lightning bolt slammed into the ground between them, shaking the trees and rattling the branches so violently that hundreds of leaves and nuts fell to the ground. Aiden turned back to Finias, who had sheathed his sword and pulled out an arrow. Finias gave Aiden a nod followed by a roguish grin, and then disappeared into thin air, fading into the shadows so he could sneak up on the Warshield. That left it to Aiden to keep their enemy distracted.

Aiden shook his head, partly in disbelief, but mostly at the fact that he'd have to play the bait against this monster. He squeezed the hilt of his sword, took a deep breath, and then charged.

He dodged left and right through the trees, always keeping something between him and the Bergsbor, to make it more difficult for him to target his spells. It proved to be a fortuitous tactic as the Bergsbor raised his hammer to the sky, and a crackling blue bolt struck the tree just behind Aiden, splitting it down the middle. The shockwave sent Aiden stumbling forward before he awkwardly regained his balance and pressed on. The Warshield held his hammer out, ready for melee this time. Aiden remembered his no-parry strategy from their last meeting and decided it was still a good idea, so when he finally got close enough to attack, he made sure he was the aggressor. He feinted a high swing, then switched into a low thrust. The Warshield bought the feint and raised his hammer up, allowing the sword to go into his midsection – where it bent as soon as it hit armor. Aiden pulled the sword back to see a curve in the blade that might have snapped it in two had he thrust any harder. He didn't have time to be upset, though, because the Warshield swung his hammer outward in a wide arc, aiming straight for his Aiden's head. He waited as long as he could before finally dodging to his left, his heart skipping as the wind from the swing brushed by his cheek.

Aiden held the bent sword out in front of him, having no other defense for the back swing that was sure to come. Luckily, Finias appeared from the shadows behind the Northman, holding his bow up and pulling back an arrow. The relief must have been clear on Aiden's face because the Warshield noticed his gaze and turned to see Finias readying his shot. Aiden ducked away – in case Finias missed – but they were both surprised when the Warshield disappeared into thin air.

"Whoa," Finias said. His eyes went wide, then darted all about. He lowered his bow in disbelief. He'd mocked Aiden only moments ago for claiming the Warshield could do this, but there was no denying it now.

"Watch out." Aiden looked around frantically. "He's still here, we just can't see him."

"I know how it works," he replied, backing away and raising his bow again.

Aiden put the bent sword into his belt and reached down to grab a large, club-shaped branch lying on the ground nearby. Not a great option, but it was thick and sturdy, and he felt safer with the branch in his hands than he did with that ridiculous piece of iron. He swore to himself that if he got out of this alive, he'd have that sword melted down one day and re-forged into something useful – like a spoon.

Suddenly, the Northman reappeared a few yards to Finias' right, and Finias responded by yelping in surprise and ducking away to his left. He scurried toward the nearest tree and faded. Aiden charged once more, yelling taunts to get his enemy's attention, but the Warshield faded again before he could get in range, leaving Aiden standing alone amongst the trees.

"Show yourself!" he yelled out in frustration. "Fight me!"

He waited, but got no response. He stood silently, listening to the sounds of the forest around him. Fading was a skill based on magic that tricked the eyes, but not the ears. If he concentrated, he could hear the footsteps of both Finias and the Warshield. Especially the Warshield, considering all the armor he wore. A gentle wind rustled the leaves nearby, making it hard to pick out distinctive noises, but he thought he heard the crinkle of leaves to his right. He moved in that direction, hoping to get lucky by stumbling into one of them. Fate must have been with him, because he heard a twig snap in the same area, behind two clustered trees growing around each other. He stopped again, listening, and choosing exactly where he would throw his body.

Without warning, the Warshield appeared several yards to Aiden's left, charging toward the same trees. He shouted as he reached them, releasing another spell that caused everything around him to tremble. Finias appeared, falling backward from his hiding spot, his fade broken by the tactic. The Bergsbor sidestepped the trees and raised his hammer, looking to crush the young bandit's skull.

Aiden lunged forward, and the Warshield twisted his hammer around, knocking the branch away with the edge of the long handle. Aiden pressed the attack, swinging again and again, each blow knocked away expertly by the Northman, but distracting him enough to let Finias pop up and sprint away, getting distance between him and the two warriors. For the hundredth time Aiden wished for a better weapon, or any weapon for that matter. Between the bent merchant's sword and this tree branch, he'd barely put a scratch on his enemy. And he'd thought to kill this thing?

He remembered a lesson he'd learned from a trainer in Solstin, a former armsman and spearman named Graff, who'd lost his hand in one of the early battles of the war. Graff, despite his bitterness at having to stay behind and train others instead of fighting himself, always harped about using your environment to gain an advantage. Solstin was surrounded by marshlands to the east, which were full of shallow pools that proved useful in slowing down an enemy's advance if you situated yourself just right. Aiden didn't have any shallow pools handy, but there was a river close by - a dangerous environment for someone wearing armor.

He had to refocus his thoughts as the Warshield quickly countered a parry by bringing his hammer forward in a thrust toward Aiden's belly. Aiden sidestepped, but he felt the edge of the hammer's iron head brush across his torso. Fortunately, that allowed Aiden to swing high and smack the Warshield square on the side of his head with the branch. The Warshield stepped back and swung out angrily, exactly as Aiden had hoped. He backed away, drawing the Bergsbor after him. When he saw that he had his attention, he turned and ran toward the riverbank.

"Stay with us!" Aiden yelled to Finias. "And shoot him!"

"I'm trying!" Finias fired off a shot that just missed the Warshield's shoulder, striking a tree nearby instead. He grimaced with the effort, then shouted back. "In case you forgot you hit me in the arm with a rock!"

Aiden crashed through the trees, glancing back every so often to make sure the Northman stayed in pursuit. Eventually, the forest thinned out and he reached a narrow clearing that edged up against the river. He spotted a small batch of clay huts about fifty yards down the bank that a clan of goblins called home. Calderans in the past had been notoriously prejudiced against non-humans, one of many reasons why elves, dwarves, firbolgs, and a host of other races fought so readily against them in this war. But some Calderan lords had recently made token measures to rectify that, including providing land to the Garzhak goblins. The Garzhak once lived in caves and forests in the southern edges of the county, and raided farms for livestock and supplies. But Lord Amus Enrik, who owned the land south of Corendar, including the town of Alvarton, had decided to solve two problems at once, by giving the Garzhak land near the river. Hidden away by thick woods, they could hunt and fish in peace, and leave southern farmers alone, provided they paid taxes, which they surprisingly managed to do most of the time.

The Warshield, carrying forty pounds of armor and weapons, had fallen behind a bit, so Aiden had enough of a lead to do what he needed to do. He ran for the village, shouting like a mad man. At first, only one curious goblin poked his head out the front door of his half-sized hut, watching in confusion as Aiden came charging down the riverbank towards him. But as soon as the goblin squealed out a warning, eight more appeared from their own huts, brandishing weapons and shields. Garzhak goblins were small creatures, the tallest coming up to a man's waist, with thin, sinewy arms and legs under leathery, faded green skin. They had long, thin faces and long protruding noses, with small bug-eyes peering out from a prominent forehead. They weren't strong, but they were quick and fierce, and dangerous when attacking as a group. They used swords and spears for hunting and fighting, and while a goblin sword would be little more than a dagger for Aiden, their sturdy hunting spears would be strong enough to pierce a Warshield's chain armor.

Aiden ran to the closest spear-wielding goblin. The creature tried to stick it in his gut as he approached, but Aiden easily sidestepped the thrust, grabbed the spear and yanked it out of the goblin's hand. The goblin shrieked at him, but Aiden ignored it and kicked him in the chest, sending him tumbling away. Several more came running toward him, yelling at him in their gibbering nonsense that passed for a language, and he immediately targeted the one carrying a big shield. He glanced back to see the Warshield stop in the clearing between the village and the tree line, raising his hands to the sky. Aiden had only seconds to get that shield before things became much more complicated. He charged through the four goblins trying to flank him, parried a sword strike with his spear, then grabbed the edge of the goblin's shield tightly just as the sky above them roared.

Blue energy crackled in the air around them as lightning struck the space just behind Aiden and the goblins. Aiden stumbled forward onto his knees, while the four goblins around him were thrown in four different directions, including the one with the shield. Aiden kept his grip on the edge of that shield, though, so when the goblin landed, he threw himself forward and prodded the creature away with the butt of his spear. The goblin, terrified of the lightning, abandoned the shield and ran back to the village, where dozens more of his people watched with a terrible fascination. Aiden slid his left arm through the loops on the shield and hefted the spear in his right. He stood in the middle of the goblin village, feeling like a true warrior once more, and with a renewed sense of vigor, he charged forward.

The Warshield called forth his lightning again, but Aiden was ready for it this time. He hit the ground, rolling forward as the bolt pounded the earth behind him, sending the awestruck goblins back into their homes. Aiden found his feet and lunged forward with his spear, forcing the Northman to duck to the side. He responded with a wide swing of his hammer, and Aiden leaned back to avoid the blow, but the heavy iron head caught the edge of the wooden shield, breaking off a small chunk with a loud snap. An arrow whizzed by the Warshield's head, and they both turned to see Finias standing at the tree line. The Northman ignored him and swung at Aiden again. Aiden leapt back, then used the Warshield's long backswing to his advantage. He jumped in close, trying to hook the Northman with his shield arm and hold him in place while he jabbed him with the spear. The Northman pushed him off, and then shouted his bellow again, trying to knock Aiden off his feet. The cagey armsman was prepared for that, though. He widened his stance, which helped him hold his ground against the buffeting wind.

Another arrow flew by, this time clipping the Warshield on the side of his hand. It didn't pierce the armor, but he definitely took notice this time, and visibly contemplated breaking off to attack Finias instead.

"Don't scare him!" Aiden shouted, not taking his eyes off the Warshield. "Kill him!"

Aiden lunged with the spear, trying to keep the Warshield focused on him. The Warshield parried away the attack, but he didn't follow up with one of his own. He'd obviously decided to stay on the defensive now, which would make things difficult if Finias couldn't hold up his end. Aiden stepped forward with a feint to the Northman's head. He leaned away, so Aiden thrust the spear again and again, each time seeing it smacked away by the hammer or simply sidestepped. Aiden, frustrated by the change in tactics, decided to gamble. He feinted low, going for the legs, and deliberately lowered his shield to leave an opening for a counterattack. The Warshield hesitated, but took the bait. After dodging the feint, he raised his hammer and swung down. Aiden quickly raised his shield and prayed it would hold.

The wood cracked in two as the hammer hit the shield, and Aiden's left arm flared in pain, but he had the opening he needed. He leaned in and thrust the spear down, digging it deeply into the Warshield's thigh. The Bergsbor cried out, and yanked his leg away, freeing it from the spear, but Aiden just spun around and thrust the butt end of the spear into his gut, sending him staggering back, clutching his stomach with one hand and his leg with the other. Aiden sensed the advantage now. He strode forward, determined to end this with another feint and thrust, only this one would be fatal. He hefted his spear up and decided that this time he'd be aiming for the heart.

Suddenly, an arrow stuck into the Warshield's neck. His head jerked back and his eyes went wide. He dropped his hammer and clutched at his throat helplessly as blood poured out of the wound. Aiden turned to see Finias readying another arrow. He raised his bow, pulled the arrow back slowly, and after a moment's hesitation, let it fly. The arrow sailed across the clearing and pierced into the skull of the Northman. The momentum of the impact carried him over, toppling him onto his side, dead before he hit the ground.

Aiden stood next to the body and stared at his vanquished enemy. Blood poured from his throat, but there was no movement, no breathing, no nothing. Aiden let himself take a deep breath, reveling in the knowledge that it was done. The Warshield was dead, the old Brin couple – and who knows who else – were avenged, and they could take the body to Corendar and claim their due reward. He smiled, exhausted, and turned to look at Finias, expecting to see the same. But there was no smile, no sly expression, no flippant remarks. Instead, Aiden saw a young boy, still in his teens, with a look on his face that he'd seen a hundred times before on the battlefield.

He had the look of a man who had just taken his first life, and who realized that there was no going back.

Chapter 4

Aiden and Finias spent almost an hour carrying the Warshield's body back to Corendar. As the looming city gates came into view over the horizon, Aiden tried hard to suppress his anxiety. He feared this place, Corendar, the capitol of the Kingdom of Caldera, because he couldn't hide himself there. The gates would be manned, the streets patrolled, and the pubs filled with soldiers, all of whom would recognize the mark on his face. No matter where he went, he'd find men and women eager to make him suffer for it. Going to a place like Alvarton, a quiet little hamlet only a few miles down the road, was vastly different. Small towns like that would be populated by farmers and craftsmen. They would scorn him, and make fun of him, but they wouldn't take the brand as an affront to their own honor.

But today was different. Today he would be returning a hero. He'd killed the Warshield that had murdered two Brin merchants on the east road from Alvarton, and he'd brought the body with him to claim his due. Technically, Finias provided the killing shot, but they'd fought him together, and Aiden had been the one to push them both into the battle. Their reward would be gold, which would please Finias, and honor, which would please Aiden. Tonight would be the beginning of his road back to respectability, and maybe even to his former place in the army, fighting for his lands in the great

Uprising. He hated those who'd branded him, and who had spurned him since, but he loved his kingdom, and he desperately missed fighting for it. After tonight, he'd be one step closer.

After killing the Warshield, Aiden made peace with the goblins by trading his food for some rope. Normally, it would have been a terrible deal - rope wasn't that hard to find - but Aiden wanted the goblins to leave them alone while they tied up the body and carried him away. And it allowed him to keep the spear. They'd used the rope to create two crude harnesses, one for the Northman's shoulders and one for his feet. Aiden carried one end by looping the shoulder harness rope over his shoulder, while Finias did the same with the Northman's feet, and the two of them slowly lugged the body, still wearing the heavy chain armor, out of the forest and back to the road.

Finias barely spoke the entire trip back, which seemed out of character. Quiet and introspective weren't qualities Aiden would have used to describe the boy based on their short time together. Aiden made one attempt at conversation shortly after reaching the path to Alvarton, asking Finias what he'd spend his money on, but the boy had responded with a terse, distant, "I don't know." Aiden suspected that he knew what troubled him, though, so he let him be. They'd both just survived a battle that they were lucky to win, not to mention one they shouldn't have been in to start with. Now was as good a time as any for introspection.

The sun had finally set when they reached the outskirts of Alvarton. The market was empty by now and everyone had returned to their homes. One old man sat on a chair outside his small, stone house, and he watched the two of them curiously as they trudged slowly along the road just east of town. Aiden wondered if word had gotten back to them about the Warshield yet. If the merchant family had run back to Alvarton, then they would know, but he expected a few guards to be wandering around if that were the case. Except for this old man, the streets were empty, and the old man never left his chair, nor did he say a word as they passed by.

Alvarton sat in the shadows of the giant city of Corendar. After leaving the village all that remained of their journey was a straight stretch of smooth, paved road bounded on either side by a row of inscribed Thandaran columns that led right up to the south gates of Corendar. The tall, grey stone walls and thick oaken doors were formidable, though they'd never been tested. The city had never been attacked. Even with the war inching into Brinwall in the north and the Red Hills to the west, the gates still stayed open. No one in the county of Artora, which Corendar loomed over from its spot at the top of Croll Hill, had any fear of battle coming to them. Artorans were naïve by necessity, caught up in the politics of nobility ever since the death of King Damhran. That was no matter, though. All Aiden cared about was finding at least one who thought a dead Northman was worth a bounty, and would take him off their hands, which his sore and aching legs would appreciate.

Four guards stood at the gates ahead, dressed in the regal red and blue livery of Caldera, though like most soldiers in the kingdom, their cloaks and shields were in the style of their home county,

Artoran crimson in this case, specifically the Army of the Dragon. Despite their majestic attire, however, none of them actually looked to be interested in doing their jobs and keeping an eye on things. Three stood in a bunch, talking and laughing, while the fourth leaned against the wall, staring at the ground, trying to keep his eyes open. But when they saw Aiden and Finias approach, carrying a body no less, they perked up. Even the sleepy one became wide-eyed as they all gathered to watch the travelers approach their station.

One of the guards, probably the watch leader, walked up to them before they reached the actual gate. Like the others, he wore a chain shirt with an iron helm, and a red robe over his shoulders fastened together at the neck with a silver brooch in the shape of a dragon's head. He held up his gauntleted hand and looked curiously at the Warshield.

"What is this?" he asked.

"This is the Northman," Aiden said, keeping his head down. He had his hood on, but that wouldn't help him much if he looked the guard in the eye. "The one that killed some merchants outside Alvarton."

The guard stared at the body, then at the two of them, then back at the body.

"You killed him?" he asked suspiciously.

"Aye." Aiden nodded back toward Finias. "We both did."

The guard stepped closer, to get a better look at Aiden, who fought the urge to look away. Hiding his face would be too obvious, so he let the guard stare at him. His eyes narrowed when he saw the brand, and though he said nothing, Aiden could feel every thought going through his mind. He'd come to know them all by now. Finally, the guard turned away and held up his hand to the others.

"You two," he pointed at the two closest to him, then motioned to the Warshield, "take this to the Palace."

The two guards jogged up and took the rope harnesses from Aiden and Finias, who eagerly slid them off. Once they had the body secured, the watch leader motioned them through the open gates, and then past the watch towers on either side of the main road. Another guard appeared to take Aiden and Finias' weapons, and once they relinquished those, they followed a few steps behind the watch leader, careful to stay close, while not seeming too excited about their coming reward.

The guards led them about a hundred paces into the city, past the row of inns, taverns and craft shops lining the street near the gates, then turned east onto the curved path that led to the Grey Palace of Corendar City, where King Thaine Trannoch ruled the kingdom. Thaine, by most accounts, was a good man who'd salvaged the kingdom after King Damhran's death and the disastrous turmoil that followed. But even though Thaine had ruled the land for nearly fifteen years, it was Damhran whose legacy still adorned the walls of the city. Dragon banners lined the walkways or hung from arches over city streets, and a statue of his likeness stood proudly in the fountain at the city's main crossroad. Most of the kingdom had moved on after Damhran's death, an event that had fractured the kingdom and led to the current wars with Andua and Bergmark, but Thaine, a former general under Damhran, saw himself as merely a caretaker of this great kingdom. A man waiting for another leader to step up and take his place. He'd been waiting for fifteen years.

Aiden caught himself admiring the city as they walked along the wide, cobblestoned streets. He'd been here plenty of times before, but after avoiding the place for two years, or more accurately, being unwelcome, he had a new appreciation for the architecture, the people, the grandness of the capitol. The cathedral-like Church of the Resurrection loomed to his left, towering over the entire southern half of the city. A small group of priests, in their immaculately pressed white robes, crossed the road ahead, leaving their duties at the church to return home for the night. They all turned as they did, staring at Aiden, Finias, and the guards in obvious disapproval, but none of them bothered to stop and investigate any further why these men carried a body through the streets.

Just past the church they took a right down another wide path, where a row of expensive carriages waited in line to enter the wide wooden gates of the Esterwick, the walled-off section of the city where lords and nobles from afar kept their city residences. One of them had decided to host a party tonight, and the carriages likely held wealthy lords and ladies from all over Artora, eager to mingle and be seen. For a moment, Aiden wondered if they'd pass through that gate, something he'd never done before, and announce their victory to the assembled nobility. But as they walked past the carriages, Aiden realized how foolish that notion must be.

Shortly after the Esterwick gate, the road curved to the left and led straight to the southern walls of the palace. As they approached the entrance, the watch leader slowed and motioned the guards carrying the Warshield to go ahead. He pointed to a stone bench nearby and looked at Aiden and Finias.

"Wait there," he said. That seemed odd to Aiden. He'd expected that they'd be there when the body was brought in, so they could be properly recognized. Aiden nodded without protest, though, and sat down, watching anxiously as the guards disappeared through the iron gates. Finias seemed a bit more agitated by having to wait, shaking his head in annoyance. After a moment, though, he joined Aiden on the bench.

They sat in silence, each of them lost in their thoughts. Aiden tried to keep his expectations low. He knew deep down that his life wouldn't completely turn around overnight, but he still wondered what this might mean for him. It was hard not to want the last two years to just disappear. He missed his old life dearly, and he wanted it back more than anything, but he had to temper himself. The most he could honestly expect from this was a small reward and maybe some kind words, or a proclamation at the most. The brand wouldn't go away – at least not without some priests willing to go to a lot of trouble – but he hoped that killing this Warshield would at least start the process of healing his reputation, just enough to lessen the burden and the shame he felt when people saw him. He wanted so much more than that, but for tonight, he was willing to accept less, a lot less, as long as he knew things were headed back up for him.

"So," Finias began, breaking the silence, "just how big a reward do you think this is worth?"

Aiden shrugged. "I don't know. I would guess at least a few gold. Each."

"That's it?" Finias seemed disappointed. He thought about that for a few moments, then, "That seems low."

"Perhaps." Aiden glanced over at the boy, who stared at the ground, all of his frivolity and arrogance gone. Aiden barely knew him, but he was certain that this wasn't the same man he'd met a couple hours ago. He wondered again about his initial impressions of Finias, and he became more and more convinced he'd been right on every count. "You've never killed a man before, have you?"

Finias looked at him in surprise, and then quickly turned away. He forced a laugh. "You can't be serious. Have you forgotten how we met?"

"You're right." Aiden nodded slowly, faking thoughtfulness. "I apologize."

"As well you should."

"Tell me about it, then."

"About what?"

"The first time you killed a man."

"You don't believe me?"

Aiden shrugged.

"Of course I do. I just want to hear the story."

Finias pursed his lips in thought, then flicked his eyes up at the armsman. "You first."

"Fine." Aiden leaned back and crossed his arms. "I'd been in the Sotheran Army all of three weeks when they sent me out on my first patrol. We were to garrison one of the advance forts northwest of the Red Hills, in preparation for a raid force coming out shortly after us. Before we got there we were ambushed by Thorns." Aiden chuckled as the memories of it came back to him. "They hit us from behind, and if one of us hadn't been keeping a close eye on our surroundings, it would have been over fast, because Thorns are vicious. They go into a fight with no expectation of coming out alive. Fortunately, we survived. In fact, it was a spectacular battle... and it's the most vivid memory I have of my time in the frontiers."

Aiden sighed, remembering the details of that afternoon. The clanging of swords on shields, the sting of sweat running into his eyes, the heat from a blaze of fire cast by one of his wizard allies, and the smell of smoke afterward. He wanted to feel it all again.

"Anyway," he continued, "we fought back and forth for a while, neither side really able to take the advantage, and of course all I did was stand there looking like an idiot. That's all you do your first few times. You try not to screw up what your mates are doing. Eventually, another patrol group found us and we managed to turn the tide and slaughter the Thorns. I'd contributed almost nothing to the fight, but I saw one of them trying to run away, which is strange in hindsight. So I pulled out my crossbow, chased after him, aimed for his head – and ended up shooting him in the calf instead. He stumbled, so I ran over there and pulled out my sword."

"He tried to fight back, but he was already hurt pretty bad, and I was too eager to prove myself, and I wanted to make up for not doing enough earlier. So I killed him. I did my duty and I drove my blade right through his gut, and he died. But, I realized afterward that I'd seen something in his eyes just before. It wasn't fear. I don't think he was afraid for his life." Aiden glanced at Finias. "I think he just wanted to get away and go home, and he was sad that he couldn't. That I was taking that from him. For a long time I wondered if I would have held my blade if I'd recognized that sooner. If I would have just let him go." Aiden let his voice trail off.

"And?" Finias said, filling the void. "Would you?"

"No." Aiden finally responded. "I wouldn't."

They were both quiet for a long moment.

"So, you remember it all that clearly?" Finias asked. "The whole thing?"

"You never forget it," Aiden said, and then flinched when he realized what he was telling his young companion. Finias was an excellent shot, but he'd obviously never killed anyone before tonight. And he certainly didn't need anyone telling him that he'd relive that moment for the rest of his life. He wondered if that's why Finias was out here in the woods in the first place, and not putting his talents to use in the war. Maybe he'd never had it in him before now.

"So, you want to hear the story of my first kill?" Finias asked.

"No," Aiden said, no longer feeling the urge to push the boy into a lie. "You can tell me later."

Several long minutes of silence passed before they finally heard voices approach from the other side of the palace gates. They glanced at each other apprehensively, then watched the doors, waiting. When they finally opened, the watch leader stepped through, along with five additional guards. Aiden wondered if they were an escort of some kind as he and Finias both stood and took a couple shuffling steps toward them. The watch leader stopped in front of them and held out his hand.

"Here's your reward," he said, dropping some coins into Aiden's hand first, and then into Finias'. "Now go home, and say nothing of this to anyone."

Finias looked at the coins curiously. "This is five silver."

"Yes it is," the watch leader responded with a stern tone. "Is that a problem?"

"I should think so," Finias said, his voice rising. "How is killing that thing only worth five silver?"

The watch leader scowled and stepped forward, standing as menacingly close to Finias as he could. The other guards became restless, too, and Aiden watched two of them rest their hands on the hilts of their weapons.

"I think you should take your money, keep your mouths shut, and go home, before we decide that even five silver is too much for the likes of you."

Finias stared back at him, either choosing not to back down or not realizing how dangerous the situation had become. They were in an empty street, at dusk, surrounded by guards who'd just cheated them of their rightful reward. One misstep, and they could end up in prison, or dead.

Aiden put his hand on Finias' shoulder. "Come on." Finias glared at him, but luckily allowed himself to be pulled away from the confrontation. The two of them walked back down the street as the guards stood their ground and watched them leave. Aiden led Finias back around the corner, trying not to look back, while Finias couldn't help but glare over his shoulder constantly. Once around the corner, Aiden stopped, closed his eyes, and shook his head.

"So what do we do now?" Finias asked, annoyed. "We can't let them throw us out like that. They took the reward for themselves! That's why they kept us outside."

There would be no recognition. There would be no real reward. No one would know what he'd done and no one would even bother to believe him if he tried to tell them. The coward's brand might as well be a liar's brand now. Killing the Warshield had become the guards' victory tonight, not his, and any dream he might have had about turning things around, any little glimmer of hope he still held on to, had now drifted away in the cool evening wind.

"Well?" Finias asked.

All of this had been for nothing, Aiden realized. Nothing.

"Say something, you lunk. What do we do?"

"We do nothing," Aiden said quietly. "This was a mistake."

"What? Nothing?" Finias shook his head in disbelief. "I didn't spend all evening chasing down some killer Bergsbor just so I could be robbed. Where are you going?"

Aiden walked away, back down the path they'd taken to get here. He stopped and barely glanced back at Finias, too ashamed to even look him in the eye.

"I'm going home," he said, and he continued down the path to the gates.

Alone.

Chapter 5

iden trudged along the narrow, tree-lined dirt path that led to his house in the woods south of the Silver Hills. The sun had set long ago, and the forest had completely surrendered to darkness. The trails out here could be a dangerous, twisting maze even in sunlight; in the dark they were just short of treacherous. But Aiden knew this one intimately, and he could wander it without thinking and still make it home in good time. And that worked out well for him, because he wasn't thinking about where he was going. He thought instead about where he could have been.

All he'd wanted was hope. A glimmer of it, even. Just enough to let him know that the Goddess hadn't completely forgotten about him, or that she wasn't playing a cruel joke with his life. He'd wanted little from tonight, just enough to prove to everyone that he was a better person than what his brand showed, and he didn't even get that. He had nothing left. Nothing to strive for. Nothing to live for. But he'd always kept on, persevering through all of his trials, waiting for the moment to arrive where he could take back his life. He was sure that moment had come tonight. And he'd let himself believe in it, only to see everything yanked away from him at the very end. He hated himself for that, for thinking he was more than a useless, cowardly old soldier.

The path faded back into grass and the trees around him opened into a small clearing where he could see the moonlight shining down on the roof of his small house. A shack, really. It was a single room, with enough space for a bedroll, a small table, a stove, a cupboard and some shelves. No one would ever call it fancy, or even quaint. But it kept the rain off and the wind out, and it was remote enough that few people ever bothered him. The wood was old and bent, and the roof constantly needed repairs, but Aiden didn't mind since it gave him something to do when he grew tired of feeling sorry for himself.

A bark greeted him from the darkness, and a moment later a skinny, gray-haired dog wandered up to meet him, tail wagging.

"Hey, Bastion," Aiden whispered, holding his hand out for the dog to sniff, then scratching absentmindedly behind his short, scruffy ears. Bastion was an old hunting dog that once belonged to a Grunlander nearby who'd died of old age. He'd found Aiden shortly after that and decided he liked it well enough around here that he'd stay for a while. Aiden couldn't afford to keep him well fed, but he didn't mind having the company some days so he gave him what he could and let him chase off the rats. The dog was far past his prime, partially deaf, and rarely did anything except lie around and watch for forest critters to run by, but Aiden didn't care. He had someone to talk to who didn't care about the brand on his face, and that was enough for him.

Aiden stepped inside, threw off his cloak, dropped his pack on the table, and leaned the goblin spear against the wall, while the dog followed him in and settled down in his familiar spot near the stove. He fished for the lantern sitting on the cupboard, lit it and then kneeled down near the foot of his bedroll to unlock the heavy iron chest nestled in the corner. Inside the chest were all of his weapons and armor from his time in the wars. At the bottom, face down, was his shield, with his armor pieces stacked up neatly on top. Lying on either side were two swords, one long, used for open field fighting, the other short, used in the brutal shield walls. He frowned at his weapons and armor, wishing he'd had them when fighting the Warshield. But really he wished for any chance to use them again. He pulled out the bent merchant's sword hanging from his belt and tossed it into the chest. He closed it and locked it, then laid down on his bedroll, letting out a long, slow sigh. All he wanted was to clear his mind and go to sleep, and hopefully forget everything that had happened tonight.

But he couldn't forget. He never did.

~~~~~

This one's for you, father. I hope you drown in it.

Finias lifted the heavy mug of ale and drank, sucking it all down in one long gulp after another. It tasted suspiciously watery, but he didn't care. He sat alone at a small table in the back of Ye Merry Mug, a loud, raucous tavern on the corner of Fountain Square, near the east gates of Corendar. He'd been here almost an hour, his instincts helping him keep a low profile while watching the Artorans, Sotherans, Venrians and even a Movrisian or two drink, sing, and laugh all around him. Finias wasn't here to get drunk with them, though. He'd come here because he needed to be around other people. He wanted to peer into someone else's life and not have to think about his own.

"One more," he said to a passing barmaid, a pretty young woman with dark hair, who looked so flustered that Finias suspected she was new. "And some of that Arley's ham."

No matter how intently he watched the other denizens of the tavern, though, he had trouble escaping from the day's events. He wanted to whack that fool Aiden across the face with his mug for getting him riled up to his cause, only to walk away after getting cheated. Those guards were nothing more than thieves playing dress up, and they should count themselves lucky Finias wasn't the type to hunt them down in their sleep. But those were small, unimportant things. What really troubled him tonight was the Warshield.

The man was dead by Finias' own hand. He'd aimed for his neck and head, fired both shots, and those arrows hit exactly where he'd wanted them to hit. There was no mistake. It didn't happen by accident. He'd killed him because he wanted to, and now he couldn't stop seeing the Northman's body in his head, arrows protruding from his neck and skull, blood everywhere. But the worst part of it all, what had him sitting in this tavern drinking watery ale, was that he wanted to be sick about it, but he wasn't.

I did it because it had to be done, he thought. I did the right thing.

He needed to believe those words, even though they felt hollow. He thought back to Aiden's story of his own first kill, that Anduain Thorn. He'd told Finias that he didn't have any mercy for him, even after seeing in his eyes his last desire. That was duty, though, right? Aiden was a soldier, in a battle, and he'd killed someone who had been trying to kill him just moments earlier.

He'd done the same thing here. Just like Aiden. He'd been a soldier, and tonight his battle had been stopping that Warshield. He wasn't a murderer. Not like his father, and his brother. Not ever like them. He was a soldier. At least for one short night.

His rumination was interrupted when he realized someone had approached him. Finias looked up and saw a middle-aged man with long, graying brown hair standing nervously at the other end of his table. He wore dirty, frayed, woolen robes, dark green, very similar in style to a Resurrectionist war priest, the kind who fight with the armies, and he leaned on a thick wooden walking stick. He guessed the man had fallen on hard times lately, because he looked to have lived a very rough life. In fact, he'd have thought him a beggar if beggars were allowed in the taverns. The man raised a fidgety hand in greeting, and Finias nodded back but didn't say anything. The priest, or whatever he was, looked like he wanted to sit down in the extra chair, but then stopped himself awkwardly and looked to Finias for permission. Finias nodded, slightly amused now that the ale had begun to kick in, and the man sat down.

He fidgeted nervously in the chair, and kept leaning forward as if about to say something, only to change his mind at the last second and look away at the crowd of patrons instead. This happened five times before Finias decided he couldn't take it anymore.

"I don't have any coin for you," he shouted over the din of several Artoran soldiers singing at the next table. He knew they were Artoran because of the song, which celebrated the dragons of old, and the chaos they had sown. It was a song he'd heard more than once growing up. The old man muttered something back that no one could possibly hear.

"What?" Finias said, leaning closer. The disheveled priest seemed uncomfortable, and he scanned the crowd again before finally leaning in closer.

"I'm not a beggar," he said, just loud enough to hear.

"Then who are you?"

"I'm Riordan," he stammered. He looked around carefully, as if his revealing his name might get him in trouble.

"Riordan?" Finias asked, and the man nodded, and then scanned the crowd again. He was awfully fidgety, either constantly wringing his hands or rubbing his face. His erratic behavior made Finias wonder if he might be sick or maybe just crazy. Finias raised his drink in greeting. "Well met, good man."

"I-I saw you," he said, stammering. "With the Northman."

"Aye?"

"You killed him?" he asked. "You and–and–and the other man?"

"Yeah." Finias gave Riordan a fake smile. "But I've been told that I can't really talk about it."

"You're in danger," Riordan said in a loud whisper.

"What?"

"You're in danger, here," he repeated, louder. "I have to talk to you, outside."

Finias narrowed his eyes. "Why?"

"I want to help you."

Finias drummed his fingers on the table, and stared at Riordan, who didn't flinch this time. He hadn't expected this, to be accosted in the middle of a pub by a crazy man who looked like he'd woken up in a barn after an all-night bender. And he certainly didn't follow men like that out into the street at night. But he had to admit, he found himself intrigued by whatever this priest had to tell him.

"Sure. What the hell," Finias said. He took one last gulp of his drink and stood up. Tonight had already been dangerous, thrilling and completely unpredictable, so the chances were pretty good by now that the rest of it would be fairly mundane. Besides, he was willing to throw his reservations aside for a little while if it gave him something else to mope about besides his own life. Either that or the ale was a lot stronger than he'd first thought.

"No. Not the front door," Riordan said. "The back. We should go out the back."

Even more foolish, Finias thought wryly, but he followed Riordan anyway, through the crowds and out the tavern's back door. The door led into a narrow, dimly lit alley crowded with wooden crates and boxes, small piles of hay and trash, and linens hanging from windows. At first glance it seemed empty, but there were too many hiding places to be sure. Finias smiled at how completely stupid he was being, and how little he cared. Still, he had just enough self-preservation in him to at least let his hand rest on the hilt of his sword. Casually, of course.

"You're in danger," Riordan began cautiously, also scanning the alley.

"You mentioned that already. From what?"

"From them!" Riordan pointed vaguely off in the distance. "The men you gave him to."

"The guards?"

"No. No, not just them." Riordan looked around again, then lowered his voice almost to a whisper. "The people at the palace. The King and his councilors."

Finias wondered if Riordan was crazier than he initially thought. "The King is after me?"

"Not him. Not exactly. It's his men. They don't want anyone to know about *them*. About what you found. They're keeping it all a secret. That's why you and your friend are in danger."

"Uh huh." Finias nodded slowly, curious about where this might be going, while trying not to laugh at the absurdity of it all. "A Warshield wanders by Alvarton of all places, kills people in broad daylight, and that's supposed to stay a secret? Sounds like they have their work cut out for them."

"Listen. You have to listen to me," Riordan said, nearly pleading. The look on his face clearly told Finias that he was formulating his argument as he went along. "I did what you did. I found something like you did, and they threw me in a dungeon for it. For three months!"

"Three months? Wow. For finding a Warshield?"

"No. No, not-not exactly. It wasn't a Warshield. It was... something, though. And they threw me in jail for it. For warning them!"

Finias made a show of looking up and down the alley. "You don't look like you're in jail right now."

"I escaped! I got out, because... because I have to fix it."

"I think, Riordan, that maybe you need to go home and get some sleep."

"No! No sleep. No, I-I-I need to fix this. And I need help. From both of you."

"You too, huh?" Finias shook his head, his curiosity quickly turning to boredom. "Do I have a sign over my head that draws you loons in from all over?"

"I'm not a loon," Riordan said slowly. "Listen. The Warshield... he-he wasn't just a Warshield was he?"

That struck a chord, and Finias eyed the old priest carefully. "What do you mean?"

Riordan smiled. "I'm right, aren't I? It was one of them? A tenebrous?"

"A what?" Finias stepped closer to Riordan, suddenly taking this conversation much more seriously. "Start making some sense."

"It's what I call them. They're Bergsbor, Anduain, or even our own Calderan brothers, but they've forgotten who they are. They fight together, against all the rest of us and they share their abilities. They're not of the three kingdoms, nor of the three Paths to the Goddess, so at first I thought they were seculant. Outside of the Three. But now I realize that they're hidden from the faith. They're veiled, by someone. Someone who's decided to send them after us."

Finias frowned. The man was loony, but at least he'd been correct about him being a priest. The barrage of Resurrectionist terms signaled as much. Unfortunately, Finias hadn't been raised in the faith, so he didn't understand any of it. All he knew about Resurrectionists was that they worshipped a goddess, and the number three. "How do you know this? About the Warshield?"

"I told you. We found them, in the north first. But now they're here."

"Who is 'we'?" Finias asked. Riordan was slow to respond.

"My friends," he said finally, but he looked away from Finias as he spoke. "My friends and I found them."

"Where are your friends, Riordan?"

"They're dead. Like you will be soon."

Finias struggled to focus, and push past the effects of the ale so he could make sense of what he'd heard. This story could all be in Riordan's head, even his supposed friends. But he seemed genuinely distracted by the thought of them, and he'd known about the Warshield's ability to fade. Well, not that specifically, but enough to know that this Warshield was somehow different.

"This is my fault," Riordan said to no one in particular. "I found them first, and I told them about it. Now they want to keep it a secret so they can use it, but you know now." He looked at Finias with scared eyes. "Now you know."

"Who exactly is coming for me?"

"They're not stupid." Riordan continued as if Finias hadn't spoken. "They let you think everything is normal, then they come and take you in the middle of the night." He looked up at the night sky. "Nights like this."

"Riordan, look at me." Finias grabbed the priest's shoulders. "Now, let's just suppose all of this is true. What do you suggest we do about it?"

"You have to let me help you fix this," Riordan said, finally looking Finias in the eye.

"Okay. How do we fix it?"

"We have to find your friend," he said. "We need him too. We can't do this alone."

Chapter 6

"Something moved over there." Riordan pointed to the south, his hand shaking. Finias followed the gesture to see a patch of darkness between two small houses at the southern edge of Alvarton. He frowned, hoping Riordan's tick was just nervous tension, and not an illness that made him spin outlandish stories.

"I'll check it out," Finias grumbled as he jogged away.

The two of them had spent their evening knocking on doors, waking everyone up in the hope that someone here would know where Aiden lived, or could at least point them in the right direction. Riordan was adamant that they needed his help to save them from the trouble they were in, though he hadn't been clear about why. Finias would have been happy with just leaving the man a note here in town, warning him of some vague danger coming his way, because what good was a cowardly old soldier to them at a time like this? In fact, if Riordan hadn't been so eager to find him, Finias would have suggested they move on without him, especially since locating him had proven to be especially aggravating.

They'd woken people at eight different houses so far, each more irritated by the intrusion than the last. One especially angry old man yelled at them for a good two minutes before Riordan calmed him by apologizing profusely. The worst part, though, was that they all knew who Aiden was – the Coward from the Silver Hills – but no one could be more specific than that in describing where he lived. They just pointed off to the west and expected that to be enough to track down one man in the hills in the middle of the night. When pressed for more information, one of the villagers told them, "He lives in the woods, you crazy buggers. It's not like they number the lots out there," and that had been the most useful information they'd received so far.

Finias huffed in annoyance as he approached the two houses, despite his natural instincts to stay quiet. He stepped delicately on the soft grass, keeping his keen eyes focused on the darkness, looking for any sign of movement. Finias knew what signs to look for, and despite Riordan's protestations, he'd seen none of them tonight. He reached the edge of the first house and peeked around, scanning for movement. An oak tree stood proudly in the grass behind the two houses, a few of its branches swaying in the gentle breeze. But other than the rustling leaves, nothing moved. If someone was following them, they were damn good at it. So good, in fact, that it strained credulity.

"Nothing," he said as he walked back. Riordan nodded while anxiously rubbing his hands together, his walking stick resting in the crook of his arm. Once Finias reached his side again, the priest took a deep breath, as if steeling himself for something, and then stalked off toward the next house. Finias rolled his eyes in disbelief and followed. They'd been here an hour since leaving Corendar, and Riordan had already sent him off four different times to check the shadows or to investigate a noise. Even worse, Finias had let him do it each and every time. It was his own fault. He'd let himself get dragged out here on nothing more than a whim, a distraction to keep him from other worries. But the novelty had worn off. And he still hadn't determined if he was indulging a stark raving lunatic whose claims of death and danger around every corner were just delusions of an old man and his ale.

"Is this how they got you?" Finias asked while the two of them walked slowly toward the next house. "Sneaking up on you in the middle of the night?"

Riordan nodded. "Fadeblades. I was at an inn in Corendar. The King's Chamberlain arranged for us to stay there the night we came back from... from finding them. That night, fadeblades snuck in and took me in my sleep."

Finias pursed his lips. He knew fadeblades well. They were men and women trained in the art of stealth, poisons, and death. They were spies and assassins, mostly, and they were not to be trifled with if you could help it. They were also a convenient boogeyman for someone who may not be entirely sane.

"That's why we had to stay in the city and not at the palace," Riordan continued. "People had to see us. They had to see me go into my room there and never come out, to keep suspicion off the King's men. To everyone there, I probably just left in the middle of the night. Or I snuck away, or went mad, or whatever other rumor was spread to keep suspicion off the King's men."

Riordan told an incredible tale. Claiming to be taken in the night by fadeblades sounded like a story children would tell to scare each other, not a priest several years past his prime. Maybe he really did go mad and he'd just made the whole thing up. It was only a passing thought, one of several he'd had tonight about this crazy little jaunt, but this one at least jogged his memory, reminding him that he didn't know many of the details about this endeavor. Details he should have asked about much sooner.

"What did you call that Warshield, earlier? A tenebrous?"

Riordan nodded. "I take it you're not Resurrectionist?"

Finias shook his head. "My father considered religion a sign of weakness."

"Ah," Riordan said, frowning. "A shame. Tenebrous are those who walk in the shadow, obscured from the light by something, or someone."

"Sounds appropriately ominous."

"Actually, it's quite literal in this case. Those men and women, including that Warshield, don't quite know what they're doing. They've had a spell cast on them that changes their reality, like a dream that takes them over. It's domination magic taken to a powerful extreme."

"So they're being controlled by Andua?" Finias asked, trying not to laugh at Riordan's inclusion of yet another scary enemy. Dominators were elven wizards who'd mastered a form of magic that let them attack the minds of their opponents. Like fadeblades, they were not to be trifled with.

"Andua isn't the only realm with domination magic. We use it, too."

"You mean sentinels use it. And those people are a strange lot."

"I can relate," Riordan smiled. "I'm one of them."

Finias furrowed his brow. "You? A sentinel? You expect me to believe that?"

"You've heard of the Warhounds?"

Finias' eyes grew wide, and he grabbed Riordan's arm, stopping him mid-stride.

"You're *that* Riordan? The leader of the Warhounds?"

Riordan smiled again, only this time it felt forced. "I was that Riordan. I'm not exactly the same man I was ten years ago." He started walking again, forcing Finias to hurry up alongside him. "And I was never the leader. That would be Andreas, who would be quite upset to know that there existed a Calderan who didn't know that."

Finias fell a step back, letting Riordan take the lead. He had a million questions, but he kept his mouth shut, mostly because he wasn't sure he'd believe any of the answers. The Warhounds were considered one of the elite lance companies in Caldera, a group of twelve Sotheran soldiers under the direct command of the Earl of Sothera, who funded their efforts. The Warhounds, like only a few other companies in this war, were legendary in their exploits, having single-handedly stopped the advance of a Bergsbor army in Astrovia with their miraculous defense of an aging outpost, and forcing an

Anduain army to retreat after decimating their supply lines with harrying hit-and-run attacks. This couldn't be the same man who'd been part of that. Finias narrowed his eyes. Maybe because it wasn't. He bit his lip in annoyance. He had to keep reminding himself that he'd met this man in a tavern.

"Now that I think about it, you haven't told me where we're going," he asked casually.

"Away from here," he said. "Away from anyone who might be coming after us."

Finias rolled his eyes. "That's vague. I'm sure you've considered a more specific location?"

Riordan's gaze subtly shifted from scanning their surroundings to looking at the ground. "We need to go northwest. Past the Red Hills. They can't find us as easily out there."

"Ahhh. Past the Red Hills." Finias nodded in mock agreement. "You're right. Hiding in a war zone is much safer."

"We'll have Aiden with us."

"Oh, of course. Him. That should keep the mighty armies of Bergmark and Andua at bay. One soldier." Finias chuckled. "You know he's been branded a coward, right?"

"Is he?"

Finias shrugged. "The large brand on his cheek says he is."

"His brand says he is?" Riordan smiled at his own question, which unnerved Finias because he hadn't yet seen such a relaxed expression from him. "You fought with him, didn't you? What do you say?"

Finias smiled back, ready to retort, but he found himself strangely silent instead. The priest was right. He'd seen Aiden in battle, fighting the Warshield, and there had been no hint of cowardice there. To be honest, if Aiden didn't have the Coward's Mark on his cheek, Finias would have never thought him one.

Riordan glanced at Finias knowingly. "Aiden will do his best to protect us. It's who he is." He walked on toward the next house, no doubt expecting Finias to just follow along. To his own surprise, he did, wondering again who this strange old man was. This eccentric old loon who spent one minute seeing monsters in the dark, and the other acting the wise, soothing grandfather. Maybe Riordan was crazier than Finias realized. Either that, or he was far, far smarter.

~~~~~

It took some doing, but they finally found their way toward what they hoped was Aiden's house. A small stone fort sat on the hill just behind Alvarton, and one of the guards on the night watch had a friend who'd once served with Aiden many years ago. He'd heard he lived out past the homesteaders in the woods just south of the Silver Hills. He pointed them in the right direction, and once on their way Finias was able to navigate the paths through the forest with ease.

Before leaving the fort, though, Finias asked the guard why Aiden had been branded. Riordan's words had stirred something in him, and now he was curious why a man who seemed to be such a formidable warrior, and who'd fought in the Uprising for years would end up a coward. The guard shrugged and said he'd heard that Aiden deserted his men during a fight out in Andua. Finias grunted at the lack of specifics, but he didn't press for any more details, even though he knew there had to be more to the story.

It took them roughly an hour of trekking through the dark paths before they reached the homesteaders, a collection of hundreds of shoddy huts and shacks scattered amongst clearings in the woods. The homesteaders were a community all their own, backwoods hunters and farmers, small-time traders and thieves, outlaws and people just looking to get by without interference from Calderan law. This area was remote and hard to get to, so guards rarely came out this way, and tax collectors and census takers had long ago given up trying to get money or information from anyone out here. The homesteaders ignored the Crown's laws and made their own, respecting their neighbor's privacy and reason for being out here, but demanding enough common sense to not prey on each other. This was where the forgotten people of Corendar lived. And, of course, Aiden was beyond even them.

After stopping for directions at a campfire surrounded by rowdy, late-night revelers, they slipped past two small groupings of shacks and took the first west-leading path they found. The trail was narrow but navigable, despite the scarce moonlight streaking through the forest canopy. The branches hung low, however, forcing them to duck under and around every dark shape that jutted across the path. The slower pace only added to Riordan's anxiety, though, making him even jumpier now than he was in Alvarton. And that had the effect of pushing Finias even closer to his breaking point.

"There's someone over there." Riordan pointed at the space between two trees in the distance, then became aware that he was pointing and pulled his hand back, pretending to play with his sleeve.

"No, there's not," Finias replied sourly, not even bothering to look.

"There is," Riordan protested. "I know I saw someone this time."

"Okay," Finias said, not stopping.

"Shouldn't you go check?"

"No."

Riordan jogged up alongside Finias and leaned close, whispering. "That could be them! They could be here!"

"Well, that would be awful for you."

Riordan stopped, a look of shock on his face. "Don't you care about this? Don't you care about what happens to us?"

Finias sighed and turned back to the priest. "You know what I think? I think the only thing moving in the darkness is you. I think you're so bloody fidgety that your head shook and you thought it was the world around you."

Riordan frowned, but he said nothing, so Finias stalked off. Neither said a word for several minutes, and Finias did his best to enjoy the quiet. Until Riordan interrupted it once again.

"You've given up, haven't you?"

Finias shook his head. "I haven't given up. I'm here, aren't I? I'm still walking down this path, in the woods, in the middle of the night, surrounded by a darkness full of everything... oh, except fadeblades stalking us for the King." Finias slapped a branch out of his way. "No, I certainly haven't given up."

He continued down the path, leaving a stunned Riordan behind. It was a long moment before he finally heard the brisk footsteps of the old man trying to catch up.

"They're guarding a treasure," Riordan said furtively. "Where we're going."

"And I bet it's fantastic," Finias responded sourly. "With mountains of gold and jewels."

"I'm telling you the truth. It was down there. Down... where we found them. Where we found the tenebrous."

Finias stopped and hung his head. He didn't know why he kept entertaining these notions, but for some reason this old man knew what he liked to hear. "Okay, then. What kind of treasure?"

"You have to understand something, first. It's tainted treasure. Some of it. It's surrounded by shadow. You have to understand that."

"Understand what? It's still treasure, right? How do you taint gold?"

Riordan's face belied his desperation. He was painfully incapable of hiding his feelings. "I have to be careful, Finias. That's why I haven't said where it is. If everyone knew where the treasure

73

was, they'd go looking for it, and they wouldn't understand – no, no, that's not right. They wouldn't want to understand that they'd be walking into the same trap we did."

Finias considered that for a long moment. "Is that where we're going, then? Are we going back to the treasure? It's out past the Red Hills?"

"Yes," Riordan said after a short pause.

"But you won't say where it is?"

He shook his head. "I can't. Not yet. I'm sorry."

"Because it's too dangerous to know that?"

"Yes."

Finias laughed. He'd had enough of this. "Well, of course. That would be too easy."

"I told you, I have to be careful."

"Then why tell me that? Why not just say we're going to a cave somewhere to kill another crazy Warshield?"

Riordan took a deep breath. "Because I need your help. And because I don't know yet what motivates you more. I don't know if you care more about money or about honor. About yourself, or about doing what's right."

"What is that supposed to mean?" Finias said sharply.

"What do you care about, Finias? That's an important question, because with the trouble we're in now, I need for you to care about this. Or we're going to die."

Finias was left speechless at this old priest's condemnation of him. Of course he cared about what they were doing. He wouldn't be out here if he didn't, right? He wouldn't have walked out of the tavern, or left the city or spent all night waking up cranky old villagers if he didn't feel like he was doing something important. He didn't do anything unless it was important, unless he truly cared about it. And he was tired of being played for a fool.

"You know what I think? I think you're a crazy old man!" Finias said, his voice rising. He shook his head and started pacing around in a circle. "How did I even let you talk me into coming out here? I was drunk, that's why. Stupid, Finias. So stupid. All you've actually done is tell me stories and point at every little sound in the dark like it's some bogeyman coming to get you. A sentinel... you're just a beggar, or worse. Or – or maybe you're a madman seeing nightmares from your time in the wars. That's what you are. That's all that you are. And I'm done listening to you."

Finias stood there for a moment, expecting Riordan to break down and plead with him, but the priest wasn't looking at him. He was staring over Finias' shoulder, unable to even look him in the eye.

"You're wrong," Riordan said.

"No. I'm not," Finias replied, a little more harshly than he'd intended.

Riordan reached into the flap of his robe, pulling out a short sword that Finias hadn't known he had. Instinctively, Finias reached for his own sword, thinking that his off-balance companion had fallen completely off his rocker. Riordan, still not looking at him, pointed calmly at the trees behind Finias. "Then who are they?"

Finias turned, expecting more shadows in the dark, or made-up monsters. Instead, he saw several well-armed men appearing from the trees, men who didn't look like simple homesteaders out protecting their property. They wore expensive armor, their weapons – axes, swords and knives – were already drawn, and they'd spread out along the path, surrounding the two of them. It was at that moment, as Finias drew his own sword, that he realized his terrible mistake. They'd been followed and he, of all people, had missed it. He'd been careless and emotional, everything his father taught him not to be, and now this unending nightmare of a day had thrown another obstacle in his path.

He only hoped he lived long enough to learn his lesson.

Chapter 7

L uckily, the dog woke him up.

Aiden stirred from his sleep to hear Bastion scratching at the door and whining, desperate to get outside. The old dog usually slept through the night, only rarely waking him to go out. And even on those nights when he did want out, he would make it clear with nothing more than a lazy whimper and a tired gaze. Tonight, however, he tried to get out like Death itself prodded him.

"Hold on."

Aiden groaned as he climbed up from his bedroll. In his groggy state, the events of the prior evening seemed distant and vague, for which he was grateful. But the longer he was awake, the faster those brutal memories would return, and he may never get back to sleep. So he hurried to throw the door open, let the dog out and then fall back to into bed, before the horrible details of his life seeped back in to his consciousness.

Before he could reach the door, though, Bastion's whining turned to barking. Loud, aggressive barking at something on the other side. Before he could shush the dog, the door slowly cracked open on its own. Surprised, Aiden backed away and leaned against the wall on the hinged side of the door, waiting to see who was brazen enough to come into his house, unannounced, in the middle of the night. Bastion did the same, staying near Aiden and well away from this intruder, but still barking like his life depended on it. The door closed as if being slowly pushed, but Aiden saw nothing in the darkness. Slits of moonlight streaked in through a few wooden slats in the roof and from the south-facing wall, providing only the barest hint of light. It was impossible to see any kind of detail, but Aiden could make out shapes and edges, and he knew where everything in the room should be. But even with all that, where he'd expected to see a person standing, there was nothing.

That's when he groaned. Finias, Aiden thought.

Somehow the boy had found out where he lived and had come here to finish what he'd started on that road outside Alvarton – stealing his belongings. Aiden was in no mood for games, though, so he decided to teach the boy a lesson. He didn't want to hurt him, not really, but he did want him to know that he'd gone too far this time. He grabbed the spear leaning on the wall next to him, and swung it out in a wide arc, aiming low for the shins. The spear struck something hard – his ankles, Aiden thought – and a figure appeared from the darkness, his fade broken by the impact. He toppled forward to the ground, having been caught in mid-stride by the blow.

Aiden firmed his grip on the spear shaft and jabbed the point down at the intruder's neck, fully prepared to give the young bandit a tongue lashing. Now that he had him lying prone on the ground, though, he hesitated. He could only see a vague outline, but the figure below seemed too short and bulky to be Finias, and the clothing he wore wasn't right. Aiden tapped his bare toes against the man's leg and felt what was unmistakably some kind of hardened leather armor.

His stomach turned. This wasn't Finias, and it wasn't some random burglar. The man lying prone on the floor of his home was a fadeblade. Questions flooded his mind, fueled by panic. Why would an assassin sneak into his home at night? They didn't break into houses to steal; they did it to kill. Quickly, silently and without mercy. What had Aiden done to warrant a death sentence? He pushed the spear against the man's neck, making it clear that the smallest jab would pierce his throat and kill him. Aiden knew from years of experience that you didn't play nice with fadeblades, because they certainly wouldn't play nice with you.

"Who are you?" he asked, ignoring the still-barking dog.

The man said nothing. Aiden pushed down on the spear just enough to see him squirm a little bit.

"You either talk to me, or you die."

Aiden swore he saw the man smile in the darkness, and he wondered what could possibly make him so confident. Bastion's barking had become incessant, past the point where he could think clearly. He looked over at the dog, about to yell at him to be quiet, but he saw that the barking wasn't directed at the man on the floor like he thought. He barked instead at the open space to his left, in front of the door. In front of the open door.

Aiden froze. Another fadeblade had come inside.

Adrenaline surged through his veins as he realized he had no time to waste. He swung the spear out again, wide to his left, and clipped the second fadeblade in the arm, breaking his cover. He'd been in the process of leaping out of the way when he got hit, leaving him on the far side of the room, which gave Aiden enough space to bring the butt end of the spear back down onto the first man's head, cracking him in the skull and knocking him senseless.

The second fadeblade leapt forward. Aiden barely managed to move out of the way, bringing the spear up to parry one of the two daggers the assassin no doubt held. He still couldn't see much. He had only a general awareness of movement, and a sense for when and where he would be attacked. That was enough to handle the first few seconds of this fight, but wouldn't keep him alive much longer than that. He lunged forward with the spear, missing, then jabbed two more times, both of which were parried away. Aiden swiped the spear sideways, forcing the fadeblade to keep his distance until Aiden could figure out his own plan of attack.

A burning, wickedly sharp pain flared through his leg, and he turned to see the man he thought he'd incapacitated jabbing a small knife into his calf. Aiden grunted, refusing to let them hear him scream, and brought the butt end of the spear down again, hopefully knocking him out this time. The second assassin used the opening to pounce across the room, his daggers flying out in wide arcs. Aiden used the spear like a staff and brought it across his body, trying vainly to defend himself. He knocked away one of the daggers, but the other dug deep into the side of his chest. This time he let out a howl.

Aiden was sure he would die. The blade had struck him just under his left arm, aimed for his heart no doubt, and for a disorienting moment he wondered if this was the last thing he would feel in his life. His leg was on fire, his chest wracked with pain, and the burning weakness of the poisons coating the two blades coursed through his body. His strength would fail at any moment. His knees would buckle, and he'd collapse to the ground and die, lonely and forgotten.

He instinctively twisted away from the pain and the dagger came free with a sharp tug. Aiden had suffered many injuries in his time in battle, and as soon as that dagger came out of his chest, he realized what had happened. Instead of piercing his heart, it had stuck in his rib. By chance or by fate he was still alive, although by the slimmest of margins. The poison might still finish him off, but he could still fight, and if he was going to die, then he would at least take these assassins to hell with him.

The assassin hesitated after pulling his dagger free, waiting to see if he'd done enough damage to Aiden to finish him off at his leisure. But that hesitation would cost him. Aiden lunged forward now, not with the spear but with his body, using the spear only to keep the daggers at bay. He reached out with his left hand and grabbed the fadeblade's armor at the shoulder, slipping his fingers under the seams around the neck. He dropped his spear and pulled his enemy in close, using his raw strength to spin him around and wrestle him into a bear hug, keeping his arms pinned. The struggle, and Aiden's momentum, knocked them both off balance and they crashed to the ground, the fadeblade taking the brunt of the fall. Aiden did everything he could to keep the furiously squirming smaller man in his grasp. He grabbed the man's right wrist, then pried the dagger in his hand loose and it fell to the wooden floor with a thud. Once he did that, he kept the other arm pinned as best he could and wrapped his free arm around the fadeblade's neck, fully intending to choke him to death.

The assassin fought for a while, pushing and twisting, trying to break free of Aiden's grasp, but it was of no avail. His last gasp at life was a weak stab at Aiden's leg with his other dagger, which broke the skin but little else. Aiden ignored the pain and squeezed the life out of the fadeblade, using all of his anger and pain to fuel him. He didn't let up, not even when his assailant – now his victim – stopped moving. Not until he was sure he was dead. Only when he felt the body go limp in his arms did he finally stop.

Aiden let go and rolled away. His chest heaved from the exertion, though whether from the poison, or just the normal rigors of battle, he didn't know. He lay there for a long moment, catching his breath, trying unsuccessfully to ignore the pain from his wounds. He wondered if he could be content with dying now. His attackers were dead, or at least they would be when he could stand and finish off the other one. He'd been victorious, but he didn't want it all to end with a few bodies rotting away in this shack out in the middle of nowhere. Who would mourn him? Who would even know what he'd done tonight?

The dog barked again, and he tensed, immediately worried that a third assassin had come. But when he stopped to listen, he realized the dog had barked at noises coming from outside. Noises that sounded like more fighting. He stood up slowly, groaning, and leaned on the wall alongside the door to gather his strength, then pulled open the door to see what other trouble had found him.

Illuminated by moonlight, three men fought each other fifty yards away, straight down the main path to his house. Two of them were lightly-armored, with no standards or recognizable badges of association, mercenaries most likely, fighting an older man wearing dingy robes and holding a sword and a stick. The mercs were fairly young, and in good shape, but their older opponent held them at bay with a variety of efficient parries and clever use of his environment, dodging between and behind trees and skirting around exposed roots and thick brush. He moved like a man who'd known combat for a long time, like many of the experienced old soldiers of the war, who only became so because they'd learned that survival was paramount.

The old man held out his hand and a flash of light brightened the forest. The two mercenaries staggered back, suddenly blinded for a few crucial seconds. Aiden blinked away the disorientation, which didn't affect him as much at this distance, and realized that he wasn't seeing just a soldier, but a priest. Priests were more than just religious figures. They were also healers, drafted into the war effort to fight with and protect Calderan soldiers, a task some of them took to more readily than others. As Aiden watched this one duck, dodge and spin away from the attacks by the mercenaries, he was reminded of a priest he'd once known. A priest who had watched over him, and helped him learn what it meant to be a soldier of Sothera, and of Caldera.

The same priest who now fought in front of his house.

Aiden's eyes grew wide when he recognized the face of Riordan. Riordan of the Warhounds, one of the few men in that storied company who'd been a friend to him. Aiden shook his head in awe as the magnitude of this moment hit him. This was more than chance. And far more than just dumb luck. The events of the last day were nothing short of destiny, a long overdue response to every prayer he'd ever made. There was no more doubt now that the Goddess had finally, and truly, called to him, daring him to take back his life.

Aiden hurried as fast as his failing strength would allow him to the chest in the corner. He opened it and pulled out his long sword and then dragged his shield out from under the stack of armor that lay on top of it. He hefted the shield on his arm, tightening the straps just enough to feel snug. He held his sword in his hand, feeling comfortable with the weight and balance. He smiled. He'd just survived a brutal assassination attempt, he was wounded in the leg and chest, poisoned, and getting weaker by the minute. But he had a friend outside who needed him, a friend who'd come to find him, a friend he wouldn't fail.

He limped out the front door and down the path in front of his house, banging his sword on his shield as he did. The mercenaries, who until now had been held at bay by Riordan's magic and defense, backed away in surprise. They'd probably expected to see two assassins walk out of that house, not this stout armsman who should be dead by now. Aiden glared at them, sizing them up as decent enough fighters, but they were confused by Aiden's appearance, and slow to adjust.

"Aiden," Riordan said, smiling at him as if nothing untoward was happening. "Think you could give me a hand here?"

Aiden watched as the two mercenaries backed away, not sure who they should worry about more.

"It would be my pleasure," Aiden replied with a smile. He hefted his shield up and charged into the fray.

Chapter 8

Aiden ripped his sword free from the mercenary's belly, and he watched with heated satisfaction as the man dropped his brightly polished hand axe, clutched his wound, and fell to his knees. He'd be dead in moments, but that wasn't fast enough for Aiden, so he plunged his sword down into his enemy's shoulder, cracking his collar bone and wrenching out a chunk of flesh. A scream permeated the remote, desolate hills around Aiden's home as the mercenary collapsed to the ground, where his shrill wailing quickly turned to loud, preening groans.

Aiden was about to finish him off when he heard a loud thud behind him. He turned to see the other mercenary crumpling lifelessly to the ground, his head misshapen from a cracked skull. Riordan stood over him, his sword held ready, but slowly coming down to rest now that he'd finished off his own assailant. Aiden looked around, just to make sure no one else had come for them in the dark. When he was sure they were alone, he thrust his sword through the first mercenary's throat, silencing him forever. He pulled his sword free and held it tight in his hand, reveling in the frenzy of battle. He grunted at the dead man lying on the ground, one of victory and of satisfaction. Only then did he lower his guard and allow himself a sly grin as he limped over to his old friend.

Before he could say anything, though, Riordan held up his hand, scanning the forest around them. Aiden stopped, squeezing the hilt of his sword anxiously, listening for the sound of movement nearby. Bastion finally came jogging up the path from the house and when Aiden saw him, he motioned the dog off into the forest. That old hunting dog had just saved his life twice tonight with his ability to sniff out assassins – a skill he didn't know the dog had – and Aiden hoped he'd be able to do it a third time. Sure enough, as soon as the dog started running off into the trees he stopped, sniffed the air, and barked at something to Aiden's left. He turned, and as soon as he did, he heard the telltale creak of groaning wood, the sound a bow makes when stretched. Aiden immediately brought his shield up as a man appeared from the shadows only an instant before letting fly an arrow. It clipped the upper edge of his shield, right in front of Aiden's heart, and bounced sideways off into the bushes. Before Aiden could react, though, a second arrow flew out, this one from behind, flying just over his shoulder, and striking the first bowman directly in the center of his chest.

Aiden ducked to the side and spun around. He expected another attacker, but instead saw Finias standing about a dozen yards behind him, his bow in one hand and a second arrow already in the other. He gave the boy a crooked smile, but Finias didn't see it. He was completely focused on the now staggering archer. He coolly nocked that second arrow, pulled back the bowstring, aimed for his target, and fired at the man's chest, sending him flailing backwards into the brush, moments from death.

Aiden let himself breath again, and when he saw Finias glance over at him, he nodded to the boy, glad to see him again despite it all. He turned back to Bastion, and sent him off into the trees, to flush out any other nearby attackers. The dog bounded off through the underbrush, sniffing the ground.

"What about the other one?" Riordan asked Finias, breaking the silence.

"He got away," Finias said darkly.

Riordan nodded glumly and walked over to Aiden, where he began examining his wounds. Aiden immediately turned his head, mostly by instinct, trying to keep his brand out of sight. He wasn't sure if Riordan had already seen it, but if he had he showed no sign of it, instead staring inquisitively at Aiden's knife wounds. "It's good to see you again, Aiden. Although I wish our circumstances weren't so dire."

"I should say the same." Aiden's battle high was fading now, the pain and fatigue coming back quickly. He felt his strength wane, and he decided he needed to sit down before he fell. He limped over to a tree stump, with Riordan following, and sat with a painful groan.

"Let me take care of those wounds." Riordan kneeled down next to him. "Which one is the worst?"

Aiden tugged on the bandage around his leg. "This one," he said with a sigh. "I think I'm poisoned, too. There were two assassins in my house. One of them is dead. The other... might be. I don't know."

Riordan turned to Finias. "Can you go in and check? We might need one alive, so we can question him."

"Hold on," Finias said brusquely. "I'm not doing a bloody thing for either one of you until I'm sure I'm not being lied to."

Riordan looked at Finias, surprised, as did Aiden.

"You two know each other." Finias pointed accusingly at Riordan. "You didn't think to mention that sometime in the last few hours?"

Riordan calmly turned back to Aiden's wounds and slowly pulled away the cloth of his leggings. "I should have, I suppose," he began, "but I didn't feel safe. I thought I'd made that clear."

Finias shook his head in disbelief. "I don't know what to believe about you anymore. You were right about the assassins, but you lied about knowing Aiden. You've been acting crazy and paranoid all night, but now... now you're about as calm as a corpse." Finias slung his bow back over his shoulder. "What are you? A liar, a mad man, or someone who's just done a really good job at making me the fool?"

"I'm a man in trouble, Finias. Just like the two of you. Great trouble, as I think I've just proven. And I assure you that I'm no less scared for my life now than I was before we were ambushed. These men," he motioned to the bodies around them, "will not be the last ones we have to defend ourselves against."

"What's going on?" Aiden finally asked. He could sense the tension in the air.

"The King wants us dead," Finias remarked. "Haven't you heard?"

Riordan looked down at the ground and sighed for a long moment. Finally, he looked up at Aiden, and he saw the brand on his face, but Aiden couldn't tell by his blank expression what he thought of it. For the first time in a long while, though, he truly felt ashamed. This was the first time in the two years since his effective banishment that he'd come face to face with a former comrade in arms, a man he respected, with the mark of a coward plain on his cheek. He wanted to look away, but he knew that would only make it worse. So he forced himself be strong and to look his friend in the eyes.

"Finias," Riordan began, "would you please check Aiden's house and see if anyone is alive? We need to learn what we can from these men while there's time. After that, I will tell you everything. I promise."

Finias stood his ground for a moment, no doubt bristling at being told what to do, but he relented and walked away. "There's rope on the side of the house there," Aiden said, calling after him, but Finias gave no sign that he'd heard him.

"You were stabbed in the chest, too?" Riordan asked, looking up at the wound under Aiden's arm. Aiden nodded, and Riordan began rubbing his hands together. He chanted something under his breath, then he gave a quick wave of his hand and Aiden saw a flash of light appear in the priest's palm. Riordan quickly put his hand over Aiden's leg wound, where the light at first spread out over his leg and then quickly retreated back into the wound. Aiden gritted his teeth as he felt the telltale sting of a priest's healing magic coursing through his leg, repairing the torn flesh through a magic they called Restoration. He knew nothing about how it worked, only that it did, and he was grateful for it tonight. But as wonderful as healing magic could be, it did strange things to a person's body while repairing it, uncomfortable things that some people just never could get used to. But it would keep him alive to fight another day, and that's what Aiden focused on while trying to fight off his nausea.

The effects were apparent in seconds, and Aiden felt his ripped leg muscles pulling, rolling and stretching as they worked to find each other once again. Riordan let his magic do its work and he moved up to the chest wound, and Aiden steeled himself for the next round of healing. The whole thing was familiar to him, and he remembered quite vividly the last time Riordan had kept him alive like this. They'd been defending the fort outside the town of Whitecap, in the southern reaches of Astrovia, from an invasion by Bergsbor forces almost three years ago. Aiden took an arrow to his shoulder, and Riordan had found him in the chaos of that battle, pulled the arrow out, and healed the wound. It had been only a few months after Aiden left the Warhounds, finding it impossible to get along with their commander, Lord Andreas of Devrin. He didn't feel bad about that, since few people were able to suffer that arrogant bastard, but he did miss many of his other comrades in that unit, Riordan included. In fact, his time in the Warhounds had been both incredibly frustrating and completely exhilarating. There were few other groups of soldiers serving the kingdom of Caldera who'd achieved the same level of success as the Warhounds, and the day Aiden had been invited to join them was one of the proudest of his life. He spent only a year with them, and Andreas had pounced on his every little mistake, but he'd learned and experienced more in that year than all the other years of his life combined.

"This one will take care of the poison," Riordan said calmly. "Just close your eyes and relax."

Aiden did as he was told, although it was hard for him to ignore the queasy sensation. His eyes were closed, but he could tell when Riordan cast his next spell, because he felt a wave of cold flow through his body, making him feel numb for an instant as the magic cleansed his blood of the poison. It was over as soon as it began, and as his body warmed up, he felt better, and stronger. The magic had worked, and once his leg and chest muscles finished their incessant tugging and stretching, he would be ready to fight again in minutes.

He heard the door shut behind him, and he glanced back to see Finias walking up the path toward them.

"They're both dead," he said.

"Are you sure?" Aiden asked.

"The one you left alive poisoned himself. He had a vial in his hand."

"Why in the Goddess's name would he poison himself?" Aiden wondered aloud.

"To keep his secrets," Finias said.

Riordan stood, and looked at the darkness around them with a resigned scowl.

"So now what?" Aiden asked.

"Now, you tell us everything," Finias said, staring at Riordan. "Everything."

Riordan nodded, then slowly started pacing around in the small clearing. "I'll start at the beginning, then."

Finias leaned against a nearby birch tree, watching the old man intently.

"I'm part of the Warhounds, a lance company in the Sotheran Army. At least I was. It seems there aren't many of us left. About three months ago, we were part of a patrol group scouting Teekwood Forest. We'd heard rumors that King Darren was trying to hide an Anduain army in there, preparing for an attack to break the cease-fire. We spent days looking before we finally found them, but unfortunately, they found us, too. We fell back, but they sent out groups to cut us off in the woods, before we could escape and report back. So we took refuge in the Endless Caves. But some of the Anduains followed us down."

Aiden knew of the Caves but he'd never been inside. They'd been discovered many years ago after a violent earthquake, crude, underground tunnels, with entrances in Teekwood, the Red Hills, and even Astrovia. But only recently had any serious exploration been done. Two years ago, an explorer, braving the war, broke through a rubble wall in the Astrovian caves to discover even more tunnels, some of which connected to the Teekwood ones. Some now said all the tunnels were connected, and that they stretched even farther and deeper than anyone had realized.

"We went deep into the caves as those Anduains chased us, staying just far enough ahead of them to think we might have a chance. But, we ran into a dead end, and had no choice but to turn around and fight. And so we did. And against numbers greater than our own, we held our ground. Until..." he paused, then cleared his throat. "You see, the caves are unstable. There are constant tremors down there, and our fighting set one off. A bad one. Parts of the walls collapsed around us. And just as things started to turn bad for us, Tholstan," Riordan glanced over at Aiden as he said the name, and Aiden nodded back, remembering his friend fondly, "found a crack in the wall large enough for us to escape through. So we retreated through the crack, and found ourselves in a tunnel that sloped dangerously down into the depths of the world. Under normal circumstances we'd have thought twice about going down there, but we didn't have a choice this time. Another tremor came, threatening to crash the entire tunnel down around us, so we went down, for a long time we went down, and when we finally came to the end we found ourselves in a place so deep below the earth that even the Goddess doesn't know about it."

Riordan paused for a long moment, looking absently at his feet. The silence stretched uncomfortably, and Aiden noticed the tremor in Riordan's hand.

"And?" Finias asked, breaking the silence.

"We were in a large tunnel, with smooth walls that looked... deliberate. The Endless Caves are just tunnels, rough and dirty. But not this. This looked like the walls of a building, a structure. Perhaps," he paused, "an underground city. The walls are carved, with hard corners, like hallways, or rooms. All of them crafted like they were meant for someone to live within them. But it also felt primal, and dark, like it was connected to the bowels of the world. The air itself was heavy with some terrible magic. It felt like we were walking amongst the souls of the dead down there."

Riordan's hand made a flittering gesture while he talked, which caught Aiden off-guard. The priest had always been unflappable. No matter how desperate the battle or the stakes, Riordan kept everyone else calm and focused. Now, Aiden watched a man he'd known as the rock of the Warhounds seemingly lose his cool.

"There were some rooms along the side of the tunnel," he continued, glancing over at Finias for a moment, "and that's where we found the treasure. There were small mounds of gold and jewels packed into the corners of the rooms, swept over there like trash. There were also dead bodies. Most had been there for years, but there were some who couldn't have been dead more than a few weeks, maybe even days. We found rotted food, cases of ale and wine, little charms and mementos, like something you would carry around to remember your family or someone you loved.

"I remember examining one of the bodies, trying to figure out how long it had been down there, when we were attacked. There were only a few torches lit, so it was dark and confusing, but the first thing I saw was a firbolg. I naturally thought those same Anduains had caught up to us. But then I saw a havtrol next to him. Everyone started yelling that Bergsbor were here now, too, and we were fighting another group as well, but I realized that they weren't fighting each other. They were fighting together, against us. That, in itself, was strange, but then I saw Calderans amongst those ranks. And when I saw that, when I saw our own countrymen fighting with them..." he shook his head and gave a short laugh.

"We managed to move the fight back out into the main tunnel, thinking that our only option was to escape back the way we came, but when we got out into the open, we saw three strange-looking men in the back lines. They weren't fighters, though. They were short, hairless, with pale skin and eyes that seemed unnatural. They wore these heavy, dark red robes, and they stayed back, chanting in some old tongue I've never heard before. It took me a moment to realize their chanting was actually magic, a spell, like the kind a dominator would use, or even a sentinel, but I couldn't see yet what effect it was having."

"And then suddenly one of them let out a scream, and these people, these tenebrous as I've come to call them, they backed away. We thought that was our opening, our chance to escape, so we started falling back." He paused again for a moment, remembering. "Some of us started falling back."

"I remember looking behind us as we ran, and I saw two of our own, Leesin and Henry, just standing there, like they'd forgotten where they were. I stopped to go back, to get them, and that's when I saw that those men had started chanting again, and staring right at those two. And I knew, at that moment I knew they were doing something to them."

Riordan sighed. "Then it started happening to the others. One by one I saw men I'd fought alongside for years just drop to their knees. Or stare at nothing. It was like their souls had been pierced by this magic, and it was..." he trailed off again, and Aiden thought he almost saw a smile on the old priest's face before he blinked and started talking. "I grabbed one of them, a woman named Haylin, and she just looked at me like she'd never seen me before. I thought she'd been dazed somehow, that maybe the magic was disorienting them, so I grabbed her arm and tried to drag her back with us, but she pulled away from me. And then she turned her sword on me. Whatever magic these people were using, they'd turned our own people on us in moments, making them think we were the enemy.

"I don't remember much detail after that. I was hit by something, and everything went black. I only remember waking up back in that passageway, the long sloping one, with Andreas and Tholstan dragging me along behind them. We'd escaped in the confusion somehow, just the three of us. No one else made it out. We spent a day trying to navigate those tunnels and escape the caves without being seen. And then it took another five days after that to get back to Corendar, where we reported what we found to the King's Chamberlain, and some of his councilors. We spent hours with them, describing everything we saw down there in as much detail as we could remember. And later that night, we were sent to an inn in town." He glanced over at Finias. "And that's where the fadeblades captured me, and I spent the next three months in a dungeon under the city."

"You were imprisoned?" Aiden asked. "What for?"

Riordan frowned. "My guess is they want the treasure, to help pay for this war. The King and his men want to keep this a secret, so they can find it, before everyone else learns what we saw. And in the meantime, people will be hurt, killed, or captured by these things. All because of greed. Someone is down there, and they are dabbling in very dark magic, and creating an army to protect them. The King either knows about this, and he's letting people die because of his greed, or he doesn't know and it's his ignorance letting this happen. You two found that Warshield outside Alvarton. That means these tenebrous are starting to spread out into the world. Their numbers are growing, and it will only get worse."

Aiden suspected he already knew Riordan's plan, but he asked anyway. "You want to go back to the caves?"

"I have to, Aiden. I need to find out what happened to my friends down there. Our friends. I need to save them."

"But what about Tholstan? And Andreas? They could still be down in that dungeon."

Riordan let out a long, heavy sigh. "They weren't in that dungeon. I don't know where they are, but I suspect that Andreas isn't spending his time in shackles right now."

"What do you mean?"

"The King's men need someone to show them how to get back to where we were. Andreas is a shrewd man, Aiden. If he sensed that things were about to go bad, he'd be the first to ensure his own survival."

Aiden's jaw nearly dropped. Andreas was an arrogant, self-serving bastard, and a glory hound of the worst kind, but even he had some sense of honor, especially to his men. The Warhounds were successful because Andreas had been smart in his recruiting, and even if his personality was ice cold, he was loyal to those he trusted, like Riordan, who'd been with him since the beginning. Aiden may have hated the man, but he could at least admit to himself that there was no way Andreas would betray Riordan. At least not willingly.

"Then we better get moving," Finias said, and both men turned to look at him, surprised. Finias just shrugged back at them. "We either go out there and take our chances, or we stay here and hide for the rest of our lives." Finias looked at Aiden. "I know some of us are good at that. But I'm not. I want to fight."

"You think I don't?" Aiden replied, harshly.

"I know this is sudden, but I came to you, Aiden, because I know you will always do what's right," Riordan said. "I don't know what's happened to you lately, and I'm sorry I wasn't around to help, but I do know you would never do anything to hurt or abandon your friends. Andreas was not fair to you, I know, but I have to believe you still have some compassion left for the others."

Aiden looked down at the ground, shook his head and just laughed.

"After everything that's happened tonight, you think I'm just going to sit around here and wait for more of them to show up?" He gestured toward one of the mercenaries lying lifeless on the ground nearby. "No. Something more important than we realize is happening here. The Goddess brought us together, my friend, and She did it for a reason. And I, for one, can't wait to see what happens next."

"Good." Riordan smiled, a look of relief on his face. "Then let's not waste any time. It's about five days to the caves. We should leave tonight."

Chapter 9

"I could fix that for you."

Those were the words that Riordan spoke to him yesterday. The words that still haunted him today.

Aiden stood at the eastern edge of the market that dominated the field just south of Trenant Keep, waiting nervously before his first foray into the battlefield in years. He leaned on a wooden support pole holding up one corner of a large pavilion, trying not to be noticed, an easy enough task in this crowd. The market was full of merchants and vendors from all over Caldera, looking to sell their wares to the hundreds of soldiers that passed through the fortress every day. Large multi-colored cloth tarps and tents were stretched out on poles all over the sloping, grassy field, with dozens upon dozens of men, women and children hawking food, clothing, specialized weapons and arrows, mementos, armor-adornments, charms, and whatever else they thought they could trade or sell.

The whole market area lay in the shadow of Pauk's Hill, upon which the fortress of Trenant Keep stood. This location, in the northernmost reaches of the Red Hills, provided Caldera easy access to Teekwood Forest and Terlgow, the nearest regions of Andua, as well as Astrovia, a once-beautiful Calderan county that had been devastated by war and mostly overrun by the Bergsbor. The hill also provided a fantastically strategic vantage point that allowed scouts on the keep's central towers to see almost to the tree line of Teekwood in the north, a good seventy miles away, as well as the foothills of the Caelmont to the west. No army could sneak up on this fort. Massive walls extended from the outer fortifications to the east and west, sloping down the hill and then veering south to eventually form a semi-circle. The walls were easily as tall as ten men, thicker than four or five standing abreast, and made from a magically endowed dark-gray granite that some claimed was harder than arcite, the metal used in the most expensive weapons and armor in the world. No effort had been made to complete the circle, however, because the west wall ended at a cliff overlooking a forty-foot drop, and the eastern stopped at the edge of a small lake that fed into a marsh far on the other side. Similar fortresses had been built at Rose Hill and Lyranton, both farther east, in Brinwall, but they paled in comparison. Outside of Corendar, Trenant Keep was the largest and most defensible structure on the entire island.

Aiden rubbed his eyes, trying to look casual even though he felt anything but relaxed. Two strenuous, life-threatening battles, followed by two and a half days of hard travel, had taken their toll. His eyes drooped, his shoulders sagged, and after waiting around nearly half an hour for Riordan to purchase supplies for their trip, he'd become irritable as well. About a dozen large wool and cloth blankets hung from a rope tied across one side of the pavilion, and Aiden had positioned himself so that they blocked him from the view of most of the market area while he waited. He wore his familiar red cloak, the hood up over his head, and hanging just enough to cover part of his brand if anyone happened by. He had his old armor on underneath the cloak, battered and dented, but it felt comfortable and familiar on his large frame. His wolf's head shield was strapped to his back, his sheathed sword hung from his belt and he'd even brought the goblin spear along with him, thinking it good luck. Bastion sat quietly at his feet, watching the crowd lazily and every so often gnawing the fleas on his haunches. Finias had been waiting with him, but he'd grown tired of standing around and wandered off some time ago, leaving Aiden alone with his thoughts.

"I can fix that for you."

Riordan had told him that yesterday morning, as they left the town of East Barret. He referred, of course, to Aiden's scar, which he hadn't mentioned up to that point, although the townspeople they passed on their way out weren't quite as polite. Two women carrying baskets of vegetables whispered to each other and laughed while an older man herding a few sheep into town stared incredulously. No one said anything out loud, but they didn't need to. No words could add to his shame. In the midst of that indignity, Riordan's statement had caught him off guard, and Aiden didn't know how to answer at first. Any priest could use healing magic to remove most scars. Aiden knew this already, but he also knew that anyone who tried such a thing on him would end up banished themselves. He could have gone to a healer out amongst the homesteaders, or some of the more unsavory types that were part of the Corendar underground. They would have done it for a price. But they were unreliable, Aiden didn't have the money anyway, and going to someone like that, even in secret, would have completely shattered his already fragile sense of honor and respect.

"No," he said. "It's nothing."

"Trying to be noble?"

"No. I just… I don't want the trouble."

"It would take me all of five minutes."

"You'd ruin your reputation," Aiden replied hastily.

"My reputation?" Riordan nearly laughed. "I just escaped from a dungeon. I'm being hunted by fadeblades. Somehow, I think fixing your brand would go unnoticed amongst all the rest of my problems."

Aiden desperately wanted to take him up on his offer. He was ready to drop his pack, his weapons and shield, and just sit on the ground like an anxious little boy while Riordan used his talents to make his humiliation go away once and for all. But he knew better. Removing the scar wouldn't remove the last two years of his life. He wanted things set right, and this didn't feel like the way to do that.

"Maybe later," Aiden said, though he didn't really mean it. "When this is over, maybe then."

Riordan nodded. "Agreed."

He'd agonized over that decision ever since, and there were several times throughout the day he'd almost pulled Riordan aside to do it, just so he didn't have to keep thinking about it. But something held him back. Self-respect perhaps, although it felt more complicated than that. Maybe he was afraid of what would happen next, how he would face the people he once knew, and that seemed even more daunting than this journey to the caves. Ultimately, the reason he'd settled on yesterday, and still felt sure about today, was that he hadn't earned it. He didn't want to get rid of the brand just so he could run away and start over in some new land across the sea. No, he wanted to go back to his old life. He wanted to be a soldier. He wanted to fight for his kingdom, and he couldn't do that unless he earned the right to have that brand removed, in the eyes of everyone else in the armies of Caldera. Hopefully, this little journey would bring him that opportunity.

Since arriving at Pauk's Hill, he'd done his best to keep his mind off his own troubles. The battlefields were a terribly harsh place, where distraction or introspection would get you killed. So he kept himself occupied by remembering all of the little things about this place he didn't realize he'd forgotten. Sights, sounds, and smells he'd taken for granted before, but now he drank them in like a parched man who'd stumbled upon a stream. The sound of heavy footsteps and metal clanging as armored soldiers marched about in the regal red and blue livery of Caldera. The screeching of sword and axe blades being sharpened on a pedal-spun grindstone. The smell of new leather and the oils that tanners used to soften it. In the past all of this had just been in the background for him, but not today. Today he wanted to experience every last bit of it. He was happy to be here, and anxious to get out into the front lines, where he'd always felt like he made a difference. He wanted to remember as much of this as he could, and enjoy it in case he had it all taken from him again.

"I know you normally wouldn't do it, but we're ready."

Aiden turned at the sound of a woman's voice nearby. He found her only a few yards away, a short, thin little waif, barely out of her mid-teens, with long blond hair pulled back into a ponytail by several golden clasps. Her face was round, and her eyes were deep-set and blue. She was pretty, and she carried herself like a woman much older than she appeared. She wore the dark blue cassock of a wizard, with the brown vestments that symbolized her specialty in earth magic. Aiden suspected she'd stolen that robe from her mother, because she was far too young for anyone to believe that she'd mastered any of the magical arts. She walked in lockstep with a decnar, a soldier who typically commanded a unit of ten men, Aiden's own rank before joining the Warhounds. He was slightly older than Aiden, fully armored in worn and dented plate mail, and with a look on his face that suggested he'd already had enough of this girl.

Following both of them was a young man, roughly the same age as her, though quite a bit taller and broader, wearing various pieces of palatine plate armor that looked fancy enough, but had never seen a single day of battle. The polish was too perfect.

The decnar shook his head and waved her off gruffly. "Not today, girl. You'll have to find someone else."

"But we're ready!" she exclaimed, sounding a little too much like a child. She must have realized that because she quickly regained her composure. "I promise you we are."

The decnar stopped and turned to her, towering over her small frame. "I already have a bunch of kids to take care of out there. I don't need two more. 'Specially not ones who look like they should be playing with dolls." He punched the boy right in the center of his plate hauberk, not too hard, but it sent the would-be palatine stumbling back a step with a look of surprise on his face. The sergeant shook his head again and walked off, while the girl looked at her companion with embarrassment.

Aiden turned, hiding his smile. That conversation had been a familiar one for him. Children pretending to be soldiers, coming to Pauk's Hill intent on proving themselves in the war without having any idea of the horrors that waited beyond those walls. It was all glory and adventure to them, but to the hardened veterans, it was something else entirely. If they were smart, those two would grow tired of their begging and go home where it was safe, before someone made the mistake of taking them out to their deaths.

Riordan arrived several minutes later, to Aiden's relief, and they looked through the provisions he'd purchased. Aiden had given him his reward money, all of which Riordan had just spent on a little bit of dried food, water skins and blankets. It was a meager collection of supplies, but it would be enough to get by for a few days. Hopefully, they would be able to scavenge more from any fallen foes, which was how many good soldiers made a comfortable living.

"Our best chance of survival is to find a fight," Riordan chuckled. "I always loved that irony."

"We'll be fine," Aiden assured him. "All we need to do is stay near the outposts and get to the docks. Once we're on the ferry, we'll be safe most of the way to Teekwood. Getting from the east end of that forest to the west will be the worst part."

"Yes it will," Riordan said solemnly.

Aiden paused, realizing with some embarrassment that he was acting the leader around a man far more qualified than him. "I know I haven't been out there lately, but I'm guessing things haven't changed that much in the last two years."

Riordan shook his head. "No. Nothing's changed. That's the unfortunate part. Thorn patrols will be our biggest problem. With only three of us, we'll have a hard time defending ourselves against them."

"Playing in Teekwood was never easy," Aiden said, adding a lighthearted smile. He saw movement out of the corner of his eye and turned to see Finias approach. Good, he thought, eager to finally get moving, though that relief was quickly tempered by the fact that the young man and woman he'd seen earlier were following the archer.

"What are they doing here?" he asked carefully, his smile disappearing.

"They're coming with us," Finias said.

"No, they're not."

Finias cocked his head, taken aback. "Yes, they are. I invited them."

"You invited them?" Aiden didn't want to make a scene, but he could feel his temper rising. "To what? To join us on a death march? They're children!"

Finias smiled back at him, bemused. "How old do you think I am?" he asked, and Aiden realized his mistake. Finias was likely only a year or two older, but he carried himself in a way that made him seem more aware of the world. He seemed more adult than his age should allow. "Besides, they want to help. They know the risks, so why not bring them? Five is still better than three, right?"

"Not when two of them should still be playing with dolls." Aiden purposely used the same insult the decnar had. He wanted to make sure it sunk in.

"I'm having trouble understanding why this is a problem for you, especially after you chased me down and wrangled me into this in the first place. This one," he pointed to the girl, "is a wizard, and this one," he tapped the boy's armor, "is a palatine. However limited their actual skills may be, we could use both of them, and any little help on our grand adventure should be welcome."

Aiden clenched his fist and grunted. It didn't feel right to let these two tag along, but he also didn't feel like arguing about it with Finias, who had already proven himself stubborn and headstrong. "Fine. Bring them. But their lives are in your hands." He turned to the young man and woman, who seemed reluctant to say or do anything that would upset anyone more than they already were. "And you two. What are your names?"

"I'm Katarina," the girl said. "Kat," she added.

"Malcolm," the boy said quietly. "Her brother."

"Kat and Malcolm." Aiden said, nodding. "I don't know what Finias told you, but this is no game. Once we're on the other side of those walls," he pointed, "you two will say and do nothing unless I or Riordan tell you it's okay. We're not getting killed because you two have never been in a fight."

Their faces blanched but Aiden didn't care. Better to be harsh with them now and make sure they knew what they were getting into, than to regret doing it after they died from making a stupid mistake. He also hoped he could scare them into backing out, but Malcolm only nodded, and Kat, after a moment's hesitation, followed suit.

"You, you're a wizard?" he asked Kat, who nodded. "Where's your escort?" Kat pursed her lips in worry, obviously not prepared for that troublesome little rule.

All Resurrectionist priests practiced various forms of healing magic, but other types of magic were considered heretical and outlawed in Caldera. Wizards, and the magic they practiced, were deemed a necessary evil, especially in light of the war. Anduain and Bergsbor mages were dangerous and powerful, and Caldera had no choice but to literally fight fire with fire. However, because of the terrible temptation of magic, everyone trained as a wizard had to have an escort, specifically one who could keep them under control.

To do that, the Resurrectionists came up with another necessary evil, and trained some of their priests in domination magic, a specialty of Anduain dominators. These priests, called sentinels, were assigned to keep an eye on the wizards under their purview, and to take any measures necessary to pacify the wizards if they ever showed signs of using their magic for anything other than wartime activities.

"My brother is a palatine–" Kat began, but Aiden shook his head, cutting her off.

"That doesn't work. Palatines are only trained to ward magic, not to keep wizards from turning into tyrants. Luckily for you, Riordan here is a sentinel. So he can twist your brain."

Kat looked at Riordan in surprise, and Riordan responded with a cautious smile. "I promise to go easy on you, my dear."

"Do you have food and supplies?" Aiden asked, and Kat nodded vigorously, pointing to Malcolm's small leather pack.

"See?" Finias said, holding out his arms in a grand gesture. "Everything works out perfectly." Aiden shook his head at Finias and walked off. Finias scowled. "I'm not the one bringing a dog into the frontier."

Aiden ignored the comment. He walked around the edge of the pavilion toward the north end of the market, the others following him in a line. A worn, muddy path snaked up the hill, leading to the south gates of the keep, which stood open, a small company of swift-emblemed Venrian soldiers standing guard. He motioned Riordan forward, wanting a priest to lead them through the fortress so fewer eyes would be on him and the brand he tried to keep covered. The guards nodded them through, saving their stares for Kat instead of his partially-covered face. Maybe she wasn't completely useless.

A wide courtyard awaited them just past the gates, leading to the inner keep ahead. Catwalks circled the interior of the walls, allowing defenders to see over the top, and two giant wooden staircases stood at the east and west edges. Some men congregated near the weapon storehouses in the corner, and a small group of robed casters, men and women, chatted near a tailor who was busy repairing the tears in a robe. Riordan took them left, where the courtyard wrapped around the western edge of the inner keep, cutting around to the other side, where they'd find the north gate. He stopped halfway around, though, and took them all about twenty paces to his left, toward a giant rune-inscribed stone with two small pillars standing on either side. The Soulstone.

Aiden and Riordan approached it instinctively, conditioned to do so after countless trips into battle. It stood as tall as Aiden, and was almost as wide at its base. The circular rune carved into its front glowed with a faint bluish hue, and two high-ranking priests of the Church stood on either side, watching Aiden and his companions as they approached. Aiden went to the stone first, keeping his head down in only partially feigned reverence, and he placed his hand on the stone. When he did, one of the priests – an older man with a long grey beard and a disinterested expression on his face – stepped forward to place his hand on Aiden's. The priest chanted something under his breath and the blue glow grew bright for a moment, then faded.

"For the glory of Caldera, my son. Praise be to the Goddess," the priest said in a monotone voice as he pulled his hand away.

"Praise be to the Goddess," Aiden repeated, and stepped away as Riordan came forward to repeat the process.

The Soulstone was a powerful magical relic, and the prized symbol of the Church of the Resurrection. The Goddess herself created the first Soulstone, used to temporarily capture part of a person's soul so that they could be resurrected. Dozens of men and women died in battle nearly every day. But by releasing a soul fragment to the stone before leaving the fortress, the priests of the Church could restore you to life, provided your body was returned to the stone within a reasonable time, usually within a day, and that it wasn't damaged beyond the care of healing magic.

But there was a catch. The process of releasing and regaining a portion of your soul – dying and being brought back to life – was incredibly taxing, and most people could only handle a resurrection two or three times before they started undergoing terrible changes. Too many resurrections and people began losing their memories, seeing their bodies break down, or even going insane. Because of this, most soldiers were forcibly retired from any kind of active combat after their third resurrection, although there were always a few who managed to sneak through until they reached five or six. Aiden himself had only been brought back once, after dying during a failed strike on Grunland. It was a terribly traumatic experience.

But he'd known soldiers who had been resurrected four or five times, and none of them was the same person they'd been when he first met them.

Once the other four touched the stone – Finias was noticeably hesitant to do so for some reason – he let Riordan lead them across the courtyard and around the inner keep to the north side of the fortress, toward the outer gates. He tried to push down the excitement as they approached the giant iron portcullis that stood between them and the entrance to the frontier, where all his best years had been. Memories flashed before him of walking through that gateway into a land where only your weapon, your shield, and your wits kept you alive. He'd been part of countless battles out there, defending keeps and outposts, destroying towers, roaming the countryside with his comrades, claiming narrow victories and suffering crushing defeats. Even though some days had been better than others, in the grand scheme of things every moment had been worth it because Aiden knew he had been lucky. Not everyone was able to find their true calling in life, and he'd found it, and lived it, for a decade. Now he was only moments away from going back, and he wanted to relish every moment before fate conspired to take it from him again.

Riordan nodded to the guards manning the gate, and one of them signaled the two in charge of operating the winch that raised and lowered the portcullis. They turned the heavy winch and the portcullis slowly creaked upward, as did Aiden's excitement. He didn't even wait for it to open completely, slipping under as soon as he had enough room, and then walking down the short stone hallway that led through the open outer gate. Outside, a sloping trail led down the hill, away from the massive walls, and Aiden stopped, staring at the vast, rolling landscape before him. For a moment, a brief moment, Aiden forgot everything that troubled him. He didn't see the several dozen Calderan soldiers patrolling the grounds around him, or the powerful wizards and archers manning the walls above. All he saw was his home.

And that's when he knew for sure that he'd made the right decision. He needed to lose his Coward's brand with a clear conscience, and he'd never been more sure that this journey, this fateful trip to Teekwood, or wherever he ended up, was a test to earn back his honor and reputation. Riordan meant well with his offer, but it was a temptation, an easy way out, and that's not what the Goddess had intended. She had greater plans for him, and right at this moment Aiden had never felt more confident about his future, and everything that would come with it. He would pass his test, he would reclaim his honor, and he would once again stand with the armies of Caldera, as he was born to do. And it all began out here.

Chapter 10

F inias crouched over the fadeblade lying on the floor of Aiden's shack, holding his hand next to the man's mouth and nose. This one was likely dead, but he'd learned from an early age to be thorough when dealing with assassins, because they made their living by convincing people to lower their guard. He dutifully went through all the tests he'd been taught to do – feeling for a heartbeat, even a slow one, checking for breathing, even jabbing a knife point into the palm of the hand. This guy had passed all of them, which meant he was either dead, or really good at pretending.

He moved to the other body lying motionless on the floor, and reached out to check his breathing. As soon as his hand touched the man's nose, the fadeblade jerked away, and reached for something on his belt. Finias grabbed the man's wrist with his right hand, snatched a dagger from his own belt with his left, and held it to the assassin's throat.

"Don't move," he whispered. The man kept still, but that meant nothing. Finias knew he was only biding his time until he could strike. He glanced down, expecting to see the dim outline of a dagger in the man's hand, but instead the moonlight illuminated a small glass vial. Poison. He'd been reaching for a way to end his own life.

At first Finias was tempted to let the man take his poison and die. It would be one less assassin to worry about. But then he realized that this was his chance to take back some control. Everyone else kept secrets from him, maybe now he could finally find out something that the others didn't know.

"You want to die?" he whispered. "Fine. I'll make a deal with you. You answer one question for me, and I'll let you take your poison and die honorably." Finias felt the man's muscles tighten in his grip, no doubt expecting some kind of trick. "Or, we can fight. And if we fight, I'll break that vial and then I'll gut you with this knife. My friends outside will hear the noise, come in here, and tie you up. You'll be tortured for a while until we get our information. Either way, I get what I want. The only question is, do you get what you want?"

Neither of them moved for a long moment, and Finias worried that the assassin might be mulling over his options. So Finias decided to put his offer in perspective.

"Remember, if you're found with that poison on your lips, your bosses will know you died without revealing anything. If you die with rope burns on your wrist, they'll have to assume otherwise. And I know what kind of leverage they keep on men like you."

Another long moment passed, and Finias worried that he'd get nowhere with this one. He prepared to knife the man before the fadeblade's body finally relaxed, and he nodded his consent.

"Smart man," he said, not relaxing his own grip - he was still dealing with an assassin after all. "Now who sent you? And I want names."

"I don't know who sent us," he replied in a hoarse voice, "only who paid us."

"Who, then?"

"Caelis."

"Caelis?" Finias repeated, making sure he'd heard right. "Cutter Caelis? He hired you?" Finias could feel his chest tightening uncomfortably. Caelis was one of Caldera's most notorious fadeblades, known both for his prowess, and for his questionable sanity. His nickname was self-explanatory, and it had inspired an untold number of partially true stories about what he did to his victims. Finias had met the man once as a child and even then he'd known immediately just how dangerous he was. But even with his savage reputation, it wasn't Caelis he feared. "Does that mean... do you know who I am?" he asked breathlessly.

The assassin just smiled back at him. "That's more than one question, Finias."

~~~~~

Finias let his arm hang over the front side of the ferry's hull, feeling the water spray up as the small waves crested into the bow. Troubling thoughts filled his mind, so much so that he'd barely slept the last two nights, but being out here on the river seemed to calm him. He couldn't explain why, but he loved the water, especially the open sea. He'd spent very little time near water growing up, but he felt like it called to him whenever he saw it, beckoning him out onto its endless oceans, where he could get lost in a larger, less crowded world. When he first left home, he thought about getting a job on a trade ship and sailing away from the three kingdoms and their wars. He could have left everything behind if he'd ever had the guts to start his life over. He'd never done it, though. At first he figured he was just too scared, but that was only part of the reason. As much as he hated admitting it, Caldera was his home, and he bristled at the notion of leaving before he'd proven his worth to everyone who doubted him. Of course, the last two days had left him wishing he'd run away when he had the chance.

After leaving Trenant Keep, they'd traveled northwest to Hannerkeep, an outpost that overlooked the Lemais River. The Lemais flowed north from the Red Hills into the eastern edges of Teekwood, the vast forest where they would find the entrance to the caves that Riordan and the Warhounds had discovered. They secured a ferry at the Hannerkeep docks to take them about half the distance to their destination. Any farther would be dangerous, and expensive, so they would have to walk the rest of the way and hope they didn't run into any serious trouble. All three kingdoms were under a ceasefire, and had been for almost two years now, but that only kept the main armies from engaging each other. Nothing stopped smaller groups from acting on their own, a practice that had strained the ceasefire to its breaking point. Each kingdom had been waiting for one of the other two to attack, hence the Warhounds scouting mission in Teekwood a few months ago. For some, the fact that they'd had relative peace for two years was a miracle in itself.

The ferry slowly drifted downriver with Finias and his four new companions. Aiden and Riordan sat near the front while Kat and Malcolm kept to the back next to him. Bastion sat on the floorboards at Aiden's feet, his tongue hanging lazily out of his mouth. Finias had spent the last hour of their journey trying to occupy himself by watching the shore and surveying in his mind all the spots with good cover for an archer. They were currently passing by a long stretch of cedar trees on the east shoreline, and he wondered how many other archers had hidden there to take shots at ferries as they moved back and forth along the river. He swore he'd heard someone loose an arrow shortly after they left the docks at Hannerkeep, but he never saw the arrow or heard it land. The short wooden barricades on each side of the ferry would block a direct shot, and he doubted there were many archers out here with the skill to drop an arrow on them from above, but he'd still spent much of the trip watching for good hiding spots. Partly for his own edification, and partly because he was worried about who might be following them.

Caelis and his small army of hired goons would be a problem for them. Caelis was vicious, cruel and unpredictable, which was why he'd been so effective for so long, and Finias could only imagine that he'd hire assassins in his own image. But he wasn't clever. He'd made a solid reputation out of being impetuous and rash, which made him hard to deal with, and an ineffective leader. Caelis was a soldier, and even though most of the commanders in Caldera found him impossible to control, there was one man Cutter Caelis would listen to, one man he respected enough to follow. Varusinian Vardakin. Varus the Dragon. One of the most feared and reviled fadeblades in the history of Caldera.

Varus was a cunning and vile man, who liked to study his opponents. He enjoyed finding their weak spots, so he could strike fast and hard, giving them no chance to defend themselves. And unfortunately for his targets, those weaknesses could be found in more than just armor. More than likely it would include friends or family, emotional weaknesses, as he called it. Varus was not above destroying everything his victims held dear. In fact, he probably delighted in it. Caelis may have hired these men, he may have handed them the money, but Finias was positive that Caelis still got his marching orders from Varus. And if that's who now pursued them, then the stakes of this mission had changed drastically.

"They're under a spell?" Kat asked, shaking Finias out of his thoughts. She was responding to Riordan's long monologue explaining why they were going to the caves, but it wasn't just her question that got his attention. Her voice constantly drew him in, partly because he couldn't quite identify it. It had a sing-songy quality that she kept trying to hide. It immediately pegged her as being raised in a noble house, though why she would hide that was a curious question. But he liked her voice. He liked hearing her talk. He found her to be especially pretty, though he hadn't quite decided

121

what he thought of her assertiveness, even though that's what drew him to her earlier. He'd seen her pleading her case outside the keep, she was about his age and very easy to look at, and he really did want to help her. He certainly knew how it felt to have everyone doubt you. Or to try to force you down another path.

"Yes," Riordan replied calmly. "And because of that spell, they think we're their enemies. And they will try to kill us because of it."

"Our own people?" she said with disbelief. Upon meeting her and Malcolm, Finias had only mentioned that they were undertaking a mission in Teekwood. He hadn't felt the need to explain much more than that because they'd been so eager to go, Kat especially, which technically made it her fault for not bothering to find out just what she had agreed to.

"Surely we can't fight our own people?" Malcolm asked, in what was probably the second time Finias had heard him say anything. His voice was deep and regal, another clue to noble upbringing. In fact, he hadn't noticed before, but he sensed the hint of an accent, one that placed his childhood in Venria, perhaps. Is that where they'd grown up? An even more interesting question, though, was whether or not they'd owned Movri slaves.

"You can if they start fighting you," Aiden said, watching the shoreline. Like Finias, he'd only been half paying attention to the story.

"But if they can't control it, then wouldn't you be murdering them?" Kat asked, although it was less a question and more an accusation.

"You'd rather they murder us?" Aiden quipped. Kat turned to her brother in frustration, but all he could muster in return was the same worried look he'd had on his face ever since leaving Pauk's Hill.

Finias cringed at the sound of that word. Murder. He could still see himself firing the two arrows that killed that Warshield. He could see his body falling lifelessly to the ground. He remembered carrying that same, ridiculously heavy body to Corendar, and being unable to look anywhere but at the two wounds in the man's head and neck. He'd never killed anyone before that moment, despite years of prodding from his father, and he feared what would become of him if it ever happened. Now it had, and he didn't feel different, but still he worried. He worried, because those images in his mind were fading. He expected to have that moment ingrained in him forever, but he was already having trouble remembering all of the details. Finias had spent every moment since then expecting to be sick, to be ashamed, hoping for any kind of physical response as retribution for that act. But he felt nothing. No remorse, at least none that he didn't try to fabricate himself. No guilt. Nothing.

"I know it's strange," Riordan said, "but we're going there to help them. And we'll do what we can to avoid them. But you must be ready to do your part."

"I don't know..." Katarina's voice trailed off, but no one else on the ferry cared to fill the silence, and they continued north with little discussion. Finias thought he would be glad to have quiet, but he soon wished people would start talking again, about anything, just to get his mind on something else. He was tired of worrying, tired of feeling angry, and most of all he was tired of running.

They reached the Medwain outpost about an hour later, a thick, stone tower on the west bank that stood about three stories tall. As the ferryman steered the boat closer to the docks, Riordan explained the dangers that lay ahead once they disembarked. From Medwain they would travel a few hundred paces farther north, to a bridge that spanned a narrow section of the Lemais River. He wanted them on the east bank, which would be a little bit safer to travel for a group their size. That meant they would have to move north from the docks across a dangerously open stretch of riverbank before they could cross the bridge. A small hill dotted with clumps of trees overlooked the west bank, and Anduain and Bergsbor archers liked to hide in those trees and look for stragglers moving back and forth between the docks and the bridge. And that's exactly what a small, ill-equipped group of five was out here. Stragglers.

"Don't dawdle." That was Aiden's only advice.

The ferry finally reached the dock where a small contingent of five soldiers greeted them, having already seen their approach. The ferryman threw a rope to the dock master, who caught it and used it to pull the boat up alongside the near edge of the dock. Aiden stepped up first while holding Bastion under one arm, followed by

Riordan, and Finias noticed that both men kept a watchful eye on that hill to the west. Kat went up next, then Malcolm, and Finias reluctantly climbed out last, almost immediately missing the gentle rocking of the waves.

"How are things today?" Riordan asked the dock master, a young man wearing woefully inadequate leather armor. He had a patch on his chest with the outline of a falcon, which marked him as Astrovian.

"Been quiet out here for a few days now," he replied. "Feels a bit eerie if you ask me. You headed north?"

"Aye," Riordan said. "To Teekwood."

The dock master raised an eyebrow. "The wood's a different story. Lotta noise up there. Had some swifts come down yesterday saying trackers are crawling all over that place." Aiden and Riordan shared a frown at that news. The dock master looked the five of them over and then shrugged. "So good luck."

Riordan smiled weakly, then followed Aiden onto the grassy riverbank where they both waited. Kat and Malcolm hurried after, but Finias lingered, watching the horizon carefully. He didn't like being out in the open while surrounded by so many hiding spots. A thousand pairs of eyes could be watching him and he wouldn't know. Bastion barked at the air, and Finias pulled his bow off his shoulder as a precaution, feeling a kindred sense of unease with that mangy beast. He reluctantly followed the others toward the bridge.

They were just shy of halfway there when Kat spoke. "There's another fort up ahead, right?"

"Yes," Riordan said. "It's called Annsmoor Keep, although that's a generous description. Barn might be a better term."

"I think that maybe when we reach Annsmoor," she began, slowly, "we can just try to help with the defense there. I appreciate the trouble you've all gone to today, and I know not everyone would have done the same. But I'm not sure my brother and I should be involved in all of this."

Finias knew exactly how she felt. She was in over her head and wanted to get away.

"I think you would be doing more for your realm by stopping what's down in those caves, than simply waiting at Annsmoor for the ceasefire to end," Riordan said.

Kat just stared at the ground. "I'm sorry."

"So you're running away," Finias said. "Like children."

"What?" Kat seemed offended by the notion.

"You wanted to prove yourself, right? To show you two could do this? Well, here you go." Finias held his arms out, motioning to the land surrounding them. "You don't always get to pick your fights, right Aiden?"

Aiden glanced back at him curiously before nodding. "Right."

"Well this is your chance. It may not be the one you wanted, or hoped for, but this is it. What we're doing is important, and we're going to need help. But what we don't need is two little kids who run away at the first sign of trouble."

126

Kat's mouth opened in surprise, but no words came out, while Malcolm's eyes grew wide at the suggestion. They may have been used to people much older than him chastising them, but having someone their own age call them out was a shock. But that's what he wanted. He hadn't known it at the time, but when he'd decided three nights ago to go through with this plan, he'd made a decision to stop running and hiding. He realized that now. Maybe it started as youthful defiance, or arrogance, but he'd been able to think it through now, and he'd decided this was the path he wanted to take. He would face his demons head on, and he didn't need anyone holding him back. These two needed to decide if they were ready to back up their claims, or if they were going to run back to Trenant with their tails between their legs.

"You listen here, you–" Malcolm began, but he never got a chance to finish. A small dark globe raced at them from the west, and Finias twisted away just as a silent explosion of blackness enveloped them. The wave of energy scattered around him, the touch cold to his skin. He spun around to see Riordan, Kat and Malcolm lying on the ground, recovering their senses, while Aiden crouched, hefting his shield up, facing the hill to the northwest. He followed Aiden's gaze to see an army.

Anduains streamed over the hill, human mostly, with a few small groups of elves and nuathreen. All of them screaming in rage, defiance or just plain bloodlust. Finias pulled out his bow and reached for an arrow. All he could think of was to attack, to fight back, but there were too many. He didn't know who to aim at. A mob poured over the hillside, coming right at them, and all he could see was his death.

Chapter 11

"**M**ove!" Aiden's command boomed in Riordan's ear as a strong hand grabbed his arm just under the shoulder, hauling him up off the ground. He was dazed and his vision blurry, but he didn't have to see clearly to know what had happened. He recognized the magic of a dominator. Luckily, it was a glancing blow, and he came to his senses quickly, but Aiden was right. They needed to move before their luck changed.

"Back to the tower!" Aiden shouted those words over and over, and Riordan followed without thinking. His vision cleared as they ran south, back the way they'd come, and he turned his head left and right to make sure no one had been left behind. Kat and Malcolm ran on either side of him, and Finias trailed a step behind. About a hundred paces behind the young archer, however, were dozens of Anduain invaders streaming over the hill, with a single, brazen elven dominator leading the charge.

Riordan heard a clang to his right, and he turned to see Malcolm stumble forward from the force of an arrow that must have glanced off his shoulder. He held out a steadying hand, and Malcolm regained his footing then gave a quick nod of gratitude. Several more bolts of magic flew wildly around them, exploding into flashes of black dotted with silver, like patches of the night sky. An arrow whistled as it sailed just over his head, and a magical bolt hit a tree a few paces to his left, causing bark and splinters to spray out. Kat let out a muffled scream, and Riordan slowed to make sure she was okay. Her eyes were wide and her face had turned white, but physically she was unhurt, so he grabbed her arm and dragged her along. He moved by instinct now, staying low, moving fast, creating space and giving his enemies little to no target. He'd done this for over twenty years, and he didn't even think about it anymore. He did feel fear, but it wasn't from the Anduains. He feared not making it back. He was afraid that after all this time, so close to returning to the caves, he could be stopped almost within sight of his goal.

They reached the tower, where two spearmen waited on either side of the oak double doors, armored in full chain with spears in one hand and shields in the other, each gripping the large iron handle of one door. They waved Riordan and the others into the tower.

"Close the doors!" Aiden shouted as they passed through the entryway. "Anduains are attacking from the west!"

The two guards stepped inside after them and pulled the doors shut with a thud. A stocky younger man, probably in his mid-twenties, met them inside. He wore the uniform of a decnar, chain armor topped with a plate hauberk, covered with a red and blue surcoat with a fox emblem. The man looked almost as scared as Kat. "What in the Goddess's name is happening out there?" he demanded. Two other men waited behind him, an archer and an armsman.

"There's an army outside. Anduain," Aiden said, trying to catch his breath. "They came over the west hills. Did your men see their approach?"

The decnar looked confused. He turned to look at the archer who just shook his head. "No. We didn't see anything."

"You need to get this door barricaded and get the archers and casters up top fast. Where's the centnar?" Aiden shouted, asking for the man's commander. The decnar opened his mouth to respond, but then he saw Aiden's brand, uncovered now that Aiden's hood had blown back during the run to the tower. A look of disgust swept across his face, and Aiden must have realized what happened, because his tone suddenly changed. "Where is your centnar?" he asked again, calmly.

The decnar still seemed flustered by the events. "He's at Annsmoor," he said, but he looked at Riordan now. "We had a wizard arrive some time ago, hurt, and he went to fetch a priest."

"You're in charge, then?" Aiden asked.

"I am," the decnar stiffened. "I'm decnar Alder, of the South Brigade, Army of the Falcon. I serve under Lord Harrel. I'd take care to remember that. Especially you."

Aiden noticeably tried to compose himself. "Decnar Alder, the signal fire needs to be lit–" Aiden stopped when he heard a shout from above. The men up top had apparently seen the Anduains approaching.

"I don't need you to tell me how to do my job out here," Alder said to Aiden.

Riordan felt his patience wearing thin. If they didn't hurry, they'd be dead, and this soldier, as well-meaning as he may be, would be a barrier to that if he didn't let experienced people take charge.

"Decnar, my name is Riordan, of the Warhounds. I served under Lord Andreas of Devrin, the grandson of the Earl of Sothera. Do you know who that is?"

Alder said nothing at first. His face showed that he knew those names, though whether he believed Riordan or not he wasn't yet sure. The roars of encroaching Anduains outside reminded everyone of their predicament, though, and Alder shook his head quickly. "Of–of course, sir. I know of you."

"Then do me this favor. Consider everything this man says," he pointed to Aiden, "as a command coming from my own mouth. Do you understand?"

Alder said nothing, his incessant blinking the only clue to his consciousness. Riordan grew more frustrated by the second. Finally, "Him, sir?"

"Did you not hear me the first time?" Riordan said sharply, trying to sound as imposing as he could. It wasn't natural for him, but time was of the essence. He was too close now to let anything else slow him down.

"Yes, sir. I did."

"Good. Then get your men ready to defend this tower." His hand started to shake and he instinctively clenched it into a fist.

"Yes," Alder said, flustered. "Of course. Umm–"

"Get your archers to the top of the tower and light the signal fire," Aiden said. "Everyone else needs to stay down here and barricade this door with anything that moves. You," Aiden grabbed Malcolm's chest plate at the shoulder, "stay with me." Malcolm nodded and moved next to Aiden, looking lost. Aiden turned to Riordan next. "Can you check up top?"

Riordan nodded and headed for the stairs. "Finias. Kat. Follow me, please," he said, and they both eagerly moved up the stairs behind him, although Kat still seemed shaken by the ordeal. Riordan had been here many times before, and he knew the place like the back of his hand. The tower consisted of three levels, the bottom floor, which housed a small barracks and stable, a mid-level floor where the centnar's quarters and a storeroom could be found, and a top level, basically a roof surrounded by stone battlements. The stairs were built into the walls, wrapping around one half of the floor on its way to the next. The second floor stairs only went to a landing halfway up, though, where a ladder reached up to a wooden panel in the ceiling that opened out onto the roof.

"Excuse me, sir," Alder said, suddenly appearing next to Riordan as they approached the second floor landing. "You're a priest, aren't you?"

"I am."

"I was thinking," he began, "that you could look at the wizard who showed up earlier. He's in bad shape, but if you could heal him, he could help us here."

"Of course, where is he?"

"He's in the centnar's quarters." Alder motioned behind him. "It's the room we just passed."

"Certainly," Riordan said. "After I find out what we're up against."

After climbing the ladder, they stepped onto the roof. The battlements circled the edge, with wide embrasures, or crenels, between them. The crenels allowed archers and casters to attack from above while also providing some cover. Two archers stood near the edge, each wearing full studded armor covered by red and blue livery, firing arrows down onto the Anduain invaders. They glanced at the newcomers and nodded to the decnar, but continued their assault unabated. Riordan led Finias and Kat to the edge of the wall and peered down through the closest opening. He saw around fifty Anduains below him attacking the front of the tower, while three times that number seemed to be moving down the slope of the hill toward the bridge that led across the river. This was no small force. This was the beginning of an invasion.

Riordan leaned back and let Kat and Finias take a look. "Careful," he said. "Don't linger, or else they'll get a good shot at you." Kat quickly stepped back, but Finias took his time, carefully gauging the enemy. An arrow bounced off the stone next to him and everyone nearby ducked. Riordan backed away from the edge, and then motioned to the battlements nearest him. "You two should set up there. I'll try to be back shortly to check on you. Finias," he said, and the young archer looked at him. "Try to keep an eye on Kat."

Finias smirked, then pulled out his bow. "She'll be okay."

Riordan walked back to the ladder, but as he turned he saw something that made him stop in mid-stride. To the east, across the water, stood a man that hadn't been there a moment ago. He was short, bald, with pale skin and dark eyes, and his mouth moved, but Riordan couldn't hear his words, nor did he need to. Riordan blinked, and the man disappeared, but his hand started shaking, and he quickly shut his eyes, trying to fight off the urge to run as fast as he could to the spot where the heretic had been standing. The urge was powerful, so much so that he feared what it might be doing to him. He felt his eyelids flicking open and closed, shuttering like hummingbird wings, and his legs lost their strength. He reached out to the ladder, to steady himself, but it wasn't there.

He stood in a vast wheat field. It was his field. His farm. He saw the brown timbered house where he lived off in the distance, and three children, his children, playing in front. He smiled, and walked back to them, so he could scoop them up in his arms, and kiss each one on the cheek. He hoped his wife was inside, preparing dinner, and then they'd all eat and–and... He slowed his pace, confused. He couldn't remember his wife's name. He struggled, thinking it was just on the tip of his tongue, but nothing came to him. Maybe his oldest son would remember. But now the boy's name was gone from his memory. As were the other two. He couldn't remember anything about them now.

A blast of magic hitting the battlements shook him from his dream, and he nearly stumbled forward reaching for the ladder. After steadying himself, he looked around, and noticed that everyone was still exactly where they'd been. Everything had happened in an instant, just like it always did. He quickly hurried down the ladder and once he reached the landing below he took a deep breath. His waking dreams were far less frequent now than when he'd been a captive, but it was still jarring when he came back to reality. He heard a noise above and saw Alder following him down. He waited until Alder reached the landing and then they walked down the stairs to the second floor.

"Why did your centnar go to the keep?" Riordan asked, feeling the need to say something. "Why didn't he send someone instead?"

"We've had problems getting men and supplies from other outposts. He wanted to go himself so he could yell at someone about it."

"Terrible timing, I'd say."

"Of course, sir."

"The wizard is here?" Riordan said, pointing to the door at the bottom of the stairs.

"Yes, inside. That's the centnar's quarters."

"I'll check on him. Go back down and tell everyone what we saw."

"Right away," Alder said, and he bounded around the corner and down the next stairwell. Riordan heard an explosion outside the walls as he reached for the door handle – dominators and wraiths trying to attack the doors, he presumed – and he cursed his luck for running into a marauding army of Anduains just as he'd almost

136

made it back to Teekwood. His agitation turned to anger, and his mind raced back to those three months he'd spent in a dungeon, alone in the dark, and how he'd bided his time until he could make it back. All of that was about to be wasted, thanks to some terrible, terrible timing.

Inside was a meager office, with a simple wooden desk sitting in front of a small window slit, some maps arrayed on the walls, an empty armor stand in the corner to his left, and a wooden cot to his right. A disheveled man with long, stringy white hair lay asleep in the cot, facing the wall, wearing purple robes covered in mud and dirt. Riordan stepped close and leaned over to examine the man's wounds, but he found no obvious ones. In fact, this wizard seemed to be more malnourished and exhausted than injured.

"Wake up." He patted the wizard's arm, trying to wake him gently, although the fact that he'd slept through the commotion up to this point meant he might need to resort to rougher tactics. Surprisingly, the wizard's eyes flittered open, and he turned to face the priest, who was now kneeling on the ground next to him. Riordan had initially thought this man was a bit older than him, due to his white hair and haggard appearance, but now he thought him younger, probably around his own age. In fact, as he stared at the gaunt face before him, he started to realize that he recognized the man under the dirt and mud.

And Riordan smiled, for he knew that fate had struck again, just as it had when he witnessed Aiden on the streets of Corendar. This was no ordinary wizard. The man he saw lying before him was his friend and fellow Warhound, lost to him in the caverns on that fateful day three months ago.

"Landon?" he asked, hoping he wasn't imagining this, too.

The wizard slowly looked up at him, his eyes squinting, then opening in surprise. "Riordan?" he whispered, staring back as if wondering himself whether this was a dream. "Is that you?"

Riordan gave his old friend a hug. "It is. I'm here."

"I can't believe I found you," Landon said. His voice was hoarse and raw, like he hadn't spoken in some time.

"Found me?" Riordan was surprised. "How are you even here? I thought you were still down in those caves."

"I was. I..." his voice trailed off and he seemed lost in thought. Then, "I escaped. I'm not sure how."

Riordan heard a loud thump from below, and he grimaced. The Anduains had a ram up on the door, and they would break through in moments.

"I'm going to heal you, Landon. Are you hurt anywhere?"

Landon thought about that for a moment, then shook his head. "I'm tired," he said.

"I can fix that." He began casting a spell, one that would return some life to his weary friend. He'd barely started, though, before guilt tugged horribly at his soul. He wanted to go back to where his friends were. That's what he told Aiden and Finias. But he wasn't going there to save them, no matter how much he pretended that to be the case. He couldn't tell them the real reason, not until they saw it for themselves, and they would, soon. But he'd been able to accept his lies up to this point because he thought the Warhounds were already beyond saving. He thought they were either dead, or in a place they didn't need rescue from.

But now, seeing Landon here, he knew there really was a chance to save everyone. And that went against everything he'd hoped for the last three months. If he'd made it out, the others could, too. And the idea of that tore him apart inside.

"Landon, we're going back to the caves," Riordan said, the lie coming naturally to him by now, "to save the others."

"I know," Landon said quietly. "That's why I'm here."

"What?"

"I don't know how I escaped, but I know who helped me. He saved me, Riordan. He sent me to find help." Landon smiled.

"Who did?" Riordan asked.

"King Damhran," Landon said reverently. "He's returned to save us all."

Chapter 12

Malcolm waited anxiously at the foot of the stairs as the tower door – and the tower itself, he thought – shook violently from the ram's impact. The Anduains pounded the door from the outside, sieging the tower as the first step in an apparent full-scale invasion. Malcolm tried to settle his nerves at the thought of being thrown so abruptly into war. He knew what would happen. He remembered the stories his uncle told him about keep and tower sieges and the bloody room-to-room combat that entailed once the door came down, and he wanted to be ready. He counted the seconds between each strike of the ram, using the monotony of it to keep his mind occupied and calm against the threat of death looming over everyone in the room. Counting was a trick his uncle had taught him as a child, and Malcolm stuck to it as a way to honor him. It helped him focus, whether during sword-training drills, working on his footwork, or any of the other mundane chores his uncle had insisted he perform as part of his training. He'd tried to get his sister, a far more excitable person, to try it herself, but she thought the notion silly. He wondered if she still thought so now.

"Hold!" Aiden shouted, as he, decnar Alder, four armsmen and two spearmen pushed up against the interior of the door. They'd barricaded it with a thick wooden beam that sat on metal brackets, as well as a shelf full of chain and leather armor pieces, two wooden chairs, and a bench. Malcolm would have helped, but there was no more room at the door, and Aiden had told him to wait here, so he would wait here. He was scared. He could admit that to himself. Who wouldn't be in a situation like this, with an army waiting outside those doors, ready to slaughter everyone inside? But he also felt proud, because he'd discovered in these last few moments that he was more worried about living up to his uncle's expectations than whatever might be on the other side of that door. Despite his inexperience, he would rather fight than run away. And if he was to die today, then at least it would be as a warrior, and not a scared little child playing pretend, which he knew was how everyone thought of him.

The door shook again, and Malcolm heard a loud crack in the wooden beam. "They're almost in!" Aiden shouted. He backed away from the door and picked up his shield, which had been lying on the ground nearby. "Form a shield wall high up on those stairs! You," Aiden slapped a nearby armsman on the shoulder. "Go up top and tell them to get down here. We need everyone in the stairwell!" The armsman jogged past Malcolm and up the stairs. The rest of the soldiers followed, but they all stopped about halfway up, where the stairs disappeared behind the walls of the second floor above them as they wrapped around the inner wall. They hefted their shields and formed two lines, three men wide, with shields overlapping. This was where they would make their stand.

Aiden sent Bastion, who'd been sitting at the base of the stairs, up to the second floor with a quick shout and a nudge in the dog's backside. Then he picked up his spear, also lying on the ground, and handed it to Malcolm. "Here," he said. Malcolm took the wooden shaft, a little underwhelmed by its meager quality. "It's a goblin spear. It's not much to look at, but it's brought me luck so far."

"What do I do with it?" Malcolm asked, not understanding why he couldn't just use his sword.

"You stand behind me in the shield wall, and you use that spear to gut anyone who gets close. Keep your shield on your back for now, and hold that thing with two hands. Then just jab it over my shoulder as hard as you can." Aiden held his fists together and made an overhand stabbing motion. "If they get past me, you drop the spear and use your sword instead, because that thing's useless in the front line."

Malcolm nodded and followed Aiden up the stairs, then took his place in the line just behind him. Malcolm's uncle had told him about fighting in the shield wall, how the enemies were close enough that you could feel the heat of their breath and smell the sweat on their face. It was the place where warriors were truly born, he'd always said, and Malcolm felt his stomach turn at the thought. The two men on either side of him were close in, shoulder to shoulder, and he felt cramped in the narrow space, but he wouldn't let them down. He held the spear up high and waited for the inevitable battle to come.

"If you're a palatine, then you've learned your battle chants, right?" Aiden asked, barely glancing back.

"Yes."

"Good." Aiden took his place between the two other armsmen in the front line. "Now would be a great time to use them."

Malcolm nodded. Aiden reminded him of his uncle. They carried themselves with the same authority and they both had a boldness about them that made Malcolm think they were always in control and never afraid. Malcolm had adored his uncle, as had his sister, and losing him had been a blow neither of them had truly recovered from. But even though he was reticent at first to go through with this trip, he felt sure he could serve with a man like Aiden.

The tower shook again, and this time the pounding was joined by a roar of Anduain voices, followed by a cacophony of screeching and crashing below. From where he stood, Malcolm could only see the area of the bottom floor where the stairs reached the ground. But he knew what had happened as soon as he saw sunlight pour into the bottom of the stairwell. Shadows danced on the ground below them, and Malcolm gripped the wooden spear shaft tightly. The Anduains were in the tower, and he would be face to face with them in seconds.

Now was the time to make his uncle proud.

~~~~~

Kat had never been more terrified in her life. She'd curled up in a ball behind one of the battlements at the top of the tower, making herself as small as possible and hiding for dear life. Arrows whistled over her head constantly while black and red magical bolts crashed into the stone around her, sending pieces of rock skittering across the roof. A stone platform, about waist-high, stood in the center of the tower roof, supporting a giant stack of wood that was now covered in flames, a signal for the neighboring towers and keeps that they were under attack. Kat desperately hoped that a Calderan army was nearby, and that they'd seen that signal fire and were on their way already. She knew it wasn't likely, but right now that hope was the only thing keeping her from losing her composure and embarrassing herself, or worse, fainting.

Finias crouched to her left, at the next battlement, calmly firing arrow after arrow at the Anduains below and only casually moving or dodging away from return fire. She wondered how he could do that so easily, so unafraid. He couldn't be that much older than her, but he carried himself like he'd been fighting out here for years. His cold, dark eyes showed no fear or worry at all. Meanwhile, she was so completely petrified that she couldn't even muster the courage to peek out from behind the wall to see how many enemies were attacking. She felt the trembling vibrations that shook the entire tower, and wondered for the eighth time how much longer it would be before they broke the door down and started pouring in. And that, of course, made her wonder how her first real trip past the walls had gone so badly, and so quickly.

Kat was a wizard. Perhaps not a fully-trained one, but she was a wizard nonetheless, capable of using the earth itself to attack her enemies or defend her allies. But all she could do right now was flinch at every nerve-wracking whine, pop, rumble or hiss around her. Kat closed her eyes and tried to concentrate on her progressions. Her abilities were mostly defensive in nature, providing support to those around her, and her uncle had helped her devise a set of progressions, skill checklists basically, to go through in different situations. She could imbue melee weapons with tiny bits of earth that made them more jagged, or she could sharpen blades to help them penetrate armor. She could lighten the weight of the heavy metals those weapons were made of, allowing their wielders to swing them faster. She could even create a flimsy magical barrier that would sometimes protect against a sword strike or an arrow. All of those spells were far more useful to the men defending below, though, like her brother, and she wished she'd thought of that before coming up here.

She had some other spells, though, ones that might at least distract the Anduains below, which would in turn give Finias and the other archers here on the tower a few better shots. But she'd need to see the Anduains to cast those spells, and that meant leaving the protective confines of this battlement for a few precious moments. She swallowed and counted to ten, taking a deep breath at each number, another trick her uncle taught her, then slowly moved toward the edge of the battlement. She hoped to find someone near the edges of the crowd, away from the other casters and archers.

Even better would be finding one that wasn't paying close attention to the tower roof. She just needed enough time to concentrate without getting killed.

Just as her eyes reached the edge of the stone, however, an explosion rocked the tower behind her. Kat ducked without even thinking, fearing the worst, but as soon as she realized she wasn't hurt she turned to see the crossbowman to her right lying on the ground a few feet from her, clutching his arm and gritting his teeth in pain. She couldn't see a wound, but she knew he'd been injured because blood slowly seeped through his chain armor near the shoulder. Her first instinct was to grab him and pull him back against the wall, or maybe to the ladder, but her body wouldn't cooperate. Stepping away from the battlement meant exposing herself to the enemy below, and just giving them a second could be enough to get her killed. She needed to do something, though. She'd gone through too much to get here. She needed to prove herself. But even though Kat knew all of this, she couldn't make herself leave that wall.

"The door's coming down!" Kat heard a shout, and turned to see another soldier on the ladder, poking his head up through the roof panel. He disappeared a second later and at first she didn't know what to do, but when she saw the other archers around her packing up their bows and arrow bags, she realized that everyone was leaving the roof. One archer ducked over to the injured crossbowman and helped him up to his feet, and Kat felt disappointment welling up inside her as someone else helped him to safety. She needed to get back inside, where there were walls and a roof that could protect her. But now her conscience balked at the thought of looking like a useless failure by scurrying off the roof before the others. So she sat still and waited as everyone else grabbed their gear and moved down the ladder. Everyone except one.

"Finias!" she shouted. "Come on!"

He either didn't hear her or he was ignoring her, because he hadn't moved from his spot, still firing away with a look on his face that suggested he enjoyed this. Kat held her breath, then lunged away from the battlement, toward the ladder. She refused to crawl on the ground, even though it was safer, and for once her will dictated her actions instead of her fear. She quickly stepped down a few rungs of the ladder, and relished the protection she now felt with stone walls around her, but when she glanced back at Finias, she saw that he still hadn't moved.

"Finias!"

He slowed his assault just long enough to glance back at her in annoyance. "Go! I'll catch up!"

Kat almost heeded him and stepped down the ladder to safety, but then she thought back to the injured archer, and she knew she couldn't just run off and leave anyone else to their fate. She'd failed during a critical moment, and she needed to make up for that. A loud crash came from below mixed with a roar of Anduain cheers, and her stomach twisted again. The door must be down. Her brother was down there, and he needed her help. There was no more time to be indecisive.

"Finias!" she screamed at him as she climbed back up onto the roof. "We have to go! Now!" She lunged toward him and grabbed his arm, intending to pull him back toward the ladder, but what happened next was lost to the blackness that suddenly overtook her.

~~~~~

Riordan stared blankly at his old friend, lying weakly on the centnar's cot, and wondered if he'd found him after all this time, just to see him lost to madness.

"Damhran is dead, Landon," he explained, like a parent would to a child. "He died almost twenty years ago."

Landon shook his head. "I saw him. He told me he was in trouble. He said he needed help."

"You saw him... in a dream?" Riordan asked hopefully.

"No! No, he was there. I could – I could touch him."

Riordan sighed heavily. As a sentinel, he'd learned spells that muddled the mind, but not any that reversed such a state.

"Let me heal you. It will help you relax, and clear your mind. You'll feel better."

Landon smiled weakly and laid his head down. "He told me others were coming, Riordan. I knew it was you."

Riordan smiled back as he started casting his spells. "I'm glad you thought so." A question came to him just then. "What about Andreas? Or Tholstan? Did you see them, too?"

Landon closed his eyes and grimaced as Riordan clasped his left hand and let his healing magic course through the Wizard's body. "No. Are they still down there?"

Riordan tried to be careful with his answer. He wanted to know if either of them had been spotted going back to those caverns, to help prove his suspicions, especially about Andreas. But he didn't feel the need to get Landon caught up in his worries until he knew it to be true. "They escaped with me."

"Are they here, too?"

"No. " Riordan shook his head. "It's a long story." Riordan pulled his hands away and watched as Landon opened his eyes and slowly lifted himself up. His strength seemed to be returning quickly, Riordan noticed, and his eyes were clear and alert. He sat on the edge of the cot and rubbed his face.

"How long was I down there?" he asked.

"About three months."

His expression didn't change at first, but then understanding slowly seeped in and Riordan saw surprise on his old friend's face. "Are you sure?"

"I am," Riordan nodded.

"It didn't feel that long."

"It did for me," Riordan whispered, thinking back to his captivity. He heard muffled shouts outside the door, and the sound of armored footsteps running by, and he knew the significance of that.

"What's that noise?" Landon asked. He looked around the room as if he'd just realized where he was.

"Anduains are attacking. Sounds like they're almost through the door." Riordan raised an eyebrow at his old friend. "If I remember correctly, this is the kind of situation where your talents are quite useful."

Landon stared at one of the maps on the wall nearby, though he seemed to be looking through it rather than at it. "How was I gone that long?"

"I don't know." Riordan was suddenly jealous of Landon, envious of the fact that he'd not known the passage of time during his ordeal. But that only steeled his resolve. Once he returned, he could do the same, and his pain would be forgotten. "Do you remember your dreams?"

Landon looked confused at that question. "What dreams?"

"You don't remember what you dreamt of down there?"

"I, uh... " he began. His eyes darted back and forth, as if remembering something, but then he blinked and snapped out of it. "I don't really remember much of anything. I don't even remember sleeping. But I must have, somewhere down there."

"But you remember Damhran? Alive?"

"I do," he nodded, not looking at Riordan. "That wasn't a dream, Riordan. Everything that happened down there is still hazy. But I remember that at least. He came to me, and he told me I would be the one to save him. Me, Riordan." Landon shook his head at the thought. "He said I'd find help, and I have. So now it's up to us to do what comes next."

"What comes next?" Riordan asked carefully.

Landon stood up slowly and groaned, stretching his sore muscles. Riordan stood to help him, but the wizard waved him off. "I'm going to go kill some Anduains." He smiled then grabbed Riordan by the shoulders, suddenly confident in his demeanor. "And then we're going to save Caldera."

Landon opened the door and walked out. Riordan frowned. His entire plan had just become much more complicated, and he worried how it would affect those around him. And what he might have to do if they wanted to stop him.

~~~~~

Somehow, Finias knew it was coming before it even happened. His arrows weren't especially effective against the heavy armor of the Anduains manning the ram, so instead he'd been aiming for the casters and druids in the back lines and watching in amusement as they scurried about for cover while he picked them off one by one. At first, he'd only been trying to push them back by aiming for their legs and arms, or to incapacitate them to keep them from firing back. But that had been a bad idea. The Anduains were smart, and by leaving them alive, they'd been able to plan a counterattack. They moved out of range, or changed their targets, or slipped out of his line of sight, all to distract him or to lull him into thinking he was winning. And just when Kat tried to pull him back, they had moved in and attacked his position en masse. He saw the barrage of bolts and arrows coming from the corner of his eye, and he'd been able to dodge the brunt of it as the battlement exploded around him, but a chunk of stone hit Kat in the head, and she fell to the ground in a heap. Bad luck on her part, he figured.

Finias leaned over and checked her breathing, and was relieved to find that she still lived. But her hair was matted with blood, and she'd need Riordan's help very soon. He knew how dangerous a head wound could be and he didn't want to take any chances. He looked back and saw that the battlement he'd been hiding behind was half-destroyed anyway, and he counted himself lucky to not be dead right now. He wiped the sweat from his forehead with his sleeve, then leaned over to pick her up, intending to carry her down to the lower levels. As he leaned over, though, he saw blood on his sleeve. He wiped his forehead with his hand this time and confirmed that he was also bleeding. He hadn't felt the wound at first, but now the side of his head throbbed, and it was getting worse. Suddenly, he stopped worrying about his injury, or even about Kat. The only thing he felt now was anger. He wouldn't let these Anduain invaders come to his lands and take a piece of him or of anyone else. Not now, not ever. He grabbed his bow again, leaving Kat lying unconscious on the roof behind him, and leapt over to the next battlement.

He peered around the edge and saw that most of the Anduains had rushed inside the broken door, but several of the casters and healers had stayed back, their arms moving frantically as they worked to keep those in front of them alive. They probably thought they'd killed him with their attack, but he would prove them dead wrong.

He loosed arrow after arrow at the attackers below, and while a few missed their mark, most did not. One pierced a nuathreen in the leg, just below the hip. Another caught a human in the center of his chest. Then he struck an elf in the neck, who dropped to the ground, writhing about and clutching his throat. Finias reveled in the moment, no longer concerned about the bloodlust he'd feared his whole life. It came naturally to him now, one arrow after another. Suddenly, he was a hunter, perched on the high ground, and everything below him was prey.

He found another elf, a wraith he thought, dressed all in black, black robe, black cloak, black boots, waving his arms about maniacally in his casting motions. Finias fired an arrow and watched it strike the mage's chest, near his right shoulder. The elf spun away, clutching at the arrow, and started to run away clumsily, but Finias would have none of that. He fired again, this time striking the calf, and the elf fell to the ground. Finias ducked back behind the battlement, and pictured his next shot in his mind. The killing shot. He pulled the arrow out, nocked it, then stepped back over to the crenellation and fired. The arrow found its mark, puncturing the elf's throat at an angle that caused the bodkin to exit from the back of the head. The elf stopped writhing and Finias smiled at how easy this was for him.

He aimed for another target, a human tracker, who wielded a bow just like him. The tracker fired an arrow at Finias' position, but he ducked back as it sailed over the tower. Finias peered back around to see the tracker running away, trying to get out of range. Finias aimed for his legs, hoping to cripple him like the mage, but the tracker made that a moot point when he stopped. Finias glanced just ahead of him, noticing movement in the trees behind the Anduain forces, the same movement that now prompted the tracker to back away. Finias watched him turn and run to his allies, shouting something in warning, only to get cut down by an axe in his back. The tracker dropped to the ground, still alive, barely, and Finias watched as a new horde of enemies emerged from the shadows of the forest to finish him off, mercilessly.

~~~~~

The firbolg warrior stood inches from Aiden's face, laughing at his prey.

The firbolg were impressive people. Taller than humans, usually by a hand's width, and strong, like the havtrols from Bergmark, but with an agility that their size belied. Firbolg, being one of the old races, had always been Anduain in spirit, but they'd been apathetic about efforts in the last few centuries to break free from Calderan influence. That is, until a Calderan army slaughtered most of their people while returning from a failed attack on Andua at the beginning of the Uprising. Now, the remaining firbolg had not only joined the war, but they'd become some of Andua's fiercest warriors, cutting down their enemies with savage glee. They killed Bergsbor and Calderan alike, but they saved a special hatred for anyone who wore the emblem of the wolf, because it had been a Sotheran army, led by the Earl himself, that had nearly destroyed their people. And unfortunately for Aiden, this particular firbolg had seen his cloak, and ever since breaking through the tower door, he'd made a point of trying very hard to kill the overwhelmed armsman.

They pressed together in a clash of shields and armor, Andua's soldiers trying to push up the narrow stairwell and the Calderans trying to push them back down. Aiden strained against the raw strength of the firbolg in front of him, their shields locked together, their faces both desperate and angry. This one seemed to be their leader, shouting to the others around him to push forward in their language, the old Anduain tongue adopted by the west. His armor, polished and expensive, had the scratches and dents earned by many battles.

"Push!" Aiden shouted, and both lines of defenders took a coordinated step forward, albeit a small one, the second row shoving against the backs of those in front. The clanking of armor plates smashing into each other echoed through the stairwell, but the Anduains held strong, using their greater numbers to keep the Calderan defenders in place. Aiden saw the firbolg's eyes dart up, then his head suddenly tilted to the side as a spear jabbed over Aiden's right shoulder, missing the firbolg by inches.

Good try, Aiden thought. Malcolm had actually injured the first man who ran up the stairs to engage them, a human who'd barged into Aiden's shield only to take a spear into his arm. The Anduain fell back, replaced by the firbolg, but Aiden had been surprisingly impressed by Malcolm at that moment and was glad to have him at his back.

The firbolg roared a command of his own, and the Anduain front line, supported by three more behind them, pushed up, and Aiden had no choice but to back up almost two steps. He was out of practice, his strength wasn't what it used to be, and now his muscles screamed at him from the exertion. But he couldn't give up now. Not unless he wanted death. A spear jabbed in under his shield, missing his legs, and Aiden responded by awkwardly hacking his own sword over his shield at the Anduain on his right. The blow struck armor, but it didn't have enough force behind it to pierce the metal. Aiden cursed, wishing he had an axe instead, a much more useful weapon in a shield wall than a long sword.

"Push!" he yelled again. The Calderans surged, and again they gained only inches of ground. The firbolg yelled, and the Anduains pushed them back up another two steps. They were running out of room in the stairwell fast, and Aiden's only backup plan was to retreat to the roof, where they could hopefully cut off attackers as they came up the ladder. That would work for a while, at least until the Anduains rained siege weapons down on them, or just razed the entire tower, destroying it, and them with it. The curved stairwell made it difficult for the Anduain casters and archers to get a good shot at the defenders, so they could hold here for as long as they could push back, but if no reinforcements showed up soon, they wouldn't survive this ordeal.

A crossbow bolt clanged off the helmet of an Anduain infantryman in the second row, and Aiden glanced back to see that the archers from above had moved in behind them. The second and third rows of Anduains raised their shields to provide cover for those in front, and a call went up in the back lines that no doubt warned those behind that archers had arrived. Suddenly, a barrage of magical bolts hit the walls to Aiden's left, as the dominators began counterattacking. The explosions were small and glancing, but the armsman closest to them, the one protecting Aiden's left side, fell back trying to take cover, a huge mistake. Another firbolg had pushed up to the front line, and he knocked the armsman off balance, sending him sprawling backward against the line behind him. Aiden twisted, partly to cover his now exposed left side, and partly to pin the other firbolg against the left wall before he could cut down the fallen defender. The firbolg leader opposite him sensed the disorganization and pressed in, holding his sword high as he readied to strike.

Aiden had been in enough shield walls to know that this one was moments from collapse. If that happened, he would die, as would everyone else in the tower. The second firbolg had almost pushed past him, his sword low, ready to gut the fallen armsman like a pig. The only thing holding him back was the confined space and Aiden's jostling with his shield. But every twist to his left gave the leader a clearer shot at him, and he couldn't hold them both off at once, while also avoiding tripping over his own man. He had to make a choice. He could either pick a target and commit, hoping the rest of the defenders around him could compensate until the fallen Calderan was back on his feet, or he could try to defend against both firbolgs, and surely fall himself in the process. So he gambled, and faced up against the leader, knowing that the Goddess had not taken him this far just to see everything fall apart again. He just hoped that the men to his left could somehow protect themselves, and him.

Fate was indeed on his side, as suddenly Malcolm threw himself forward into the gap, hefting his large shield in one hand and the spear in the other. The spear was useless at this point, but Malcolm either didn't know that, or just plain forgot to drop it and switch weapons. Either way, Aiden could breathe again knowing his left was covered. The boy blocked the firbolg's sword with his shield, seemingly by accident, and used his own considerable size to keep the snarling enemy at bay. He straddled the fallen armsman, who tried to crawl behind the palatine and get back on his feet. Somehow, Malcolm's strength and balance made the whole maneuver, as dangerous as it could have been, look easy.

More good luck came as Aiden heard a strangely familiar voice shouting behind him to make room. He chanced a glance over his shoulder to see a ragged-looking wizard moving through the cramped mass of soldiers at the back, with the posture and grace of someone accustomed to situations like this. Aiden's eyes grew wide as he recognized another old face from his past – the Warhound wizard named Landon, who smiled when he saw Aiden in front of him. Landon deftly moved between the armored men around him and stood just behind the armsman.

"Duck," was all he said.

"Get down!" Aiden yelled as he crouched, holding his shield up to cover his head. Blue and white light suddenly flashed out above him in waves, and Aiden felt the air in the stairwell grow instantly cold. Landon's magic was designed to emanate from his own body, pulsing outward as a powerful defense mechanism. The magic froze living skin, causing incredible pain, and even though it only hit those he deemed as enemies, Aiden never liked being too close, just in case Landon made a mistake. The Anduains closest to them screamed out in pain, patches of their skin hardening and turning blue. They fell back, front lines pushing on back lines, trying to escape the stairwell and the blasting cold. They retreated back down to the bottom level in a disorganized mess, giving the Calderans some breathing room, though that wouldn't last long.

"Reform the lines!" Aiden stood up and watched the retreating Anduains cautiously. "Hurry!" The Anduains were already regrouping at the bottom of the stairs, fresh soldiers moving to the front while the injured ones moved back to let the Anduain healers tend to them. Except that firbolg. He stood at the base of the steps, watching Aiden, and Landon, menacingly.

"I'm surprised to see you here," Landon said, behind him.

159

"Been a lot of surprises the last few days. You need to step back, though. That entire army will be looking for you first when they get regrouped."

"Right." Landon slipped back behind the second line and waited amongst the archers in the back. Malcolm stood anxiously next to Aiden, still holding that spear. Aiden shook his head and took it from him.

"Use your sword now." Malcolm nodded quickly and pulled his long sword from its scabbard. Aiden reached over and gave him a friendly pat on the shoulder, trying to calm his nervous energy. "You're doing well," he said, and Malcolm nodded again.

The firbolg roared his commands from below, still staring at Aiden like he'd just seen his next meal. The Anduains rallied around him, ready for another push, and Aiden hoped his men had enough strength left to keep holding them back. If they stayed here in the stairwell, at some point they would get overrun and cut to pieces, so Aiden had to judge the strength of everyone around him, to make sure they could fall back before that happened. He looked at his fellow defenders in the stairwell, and he saw Calderans who were weary, bruised and scared. Their breath came fast and heavy, and sweat poured from their faces, but Aiden could tell they had enough in them for more. He could judge a fighter, a true warrior. That had always been a gift of his, and he knew these men weren't ready to give up yet. Even Alder, who stood behind him and to his right, looked eager for a fight, his eyes wild and a small hint of satisfaction on his face.

Suddenly, a horn sounded outside the tower and the Anduains stopped in confusion, peering behind them. It took only seconds for them to notice something amiss, and they quickly retreated from the stairwell and ran back out the tower door. Aiden heard shouting, blades clashing together, and the whine of powerful magic outside. He cautiously stepped down to the base of the stairwell to find an empty bottom floor. The doors were cracked open, damaged beyond any kind of quick repair, so there was no point barricading or even closing them. The sounds of combat were louder now, so Aiden moved to the open door, holding his hand up to keep everyone else back, and peered out from inside the tower.

He saw chaos outside. The forces of Bergmark were here now, streaming out of the forest behind the Anduain lines, and also veering east, toward the bridge. They must have been in the area and caught wind of the Anduain attack, deciding to take advantage by attacking the smaller Anduain tower force first. The horn had been an Anduain trying to warn his allies that a new enemy was on the field, because now more Anduains charged across the bridge far in the distance to meet the incoming Bergsbor forces. In the field just outside the tower firbolgs, elves, nuathreens and humans fought havtrols, dwarves, and their human slaves all for the right to eventually wipe out the small force of Calderan soldiers defending this tower.

"Bergsbor are attacking!" Aiden heard Finias' voice and turned to see him coming down the stairs with Kat over his shoulder.

They were both bleeding from head wounds, though Kat was unconscious.

"What happened?" Malcolm rushed over and they laid her down on the steps, Riordan leaned over to take a look at her wound.

"The roof exploded," Finias said.

Riordan ran his hands through Kat's blood-matted hair, examining her head. "It's fixable," he said finally, "but not here." He turned to look at Aiden, who quickly understood.

"What does that mean?" Malcolm, who had held up well in the shield wall, was now losing his temper. "What do you mean not here?"

"Carry her," Aiden told Malcolm. "We'll heal her somewhere else. We're leaving this tower."

"What? Why?" Alder stepped forward. "We held them off. We can do it again until reinforcements come."

"No, we can't. No matter who wins that fight outside, they'll still outnumber us ten to one. Probably more." Aiden glanced back outside, gauging distances to the tree line to their south. "If we don't leave now, we're dead."

Silence throughout the room affirmed Aiden's assessment.

Alder stepped up next to Aiden, looking outside carefully. "Then how do we escape with two armies fighting right outside?"

"We pray," Aiden said calmly. "Then we run."

A chorus of silent, curt nods followed, and Aiden knew there was no time left to waste. Malcolm lifted his sister into his arms while Finias held out his bow, an arrow already nocked. Riordan and

Landon, longtime veterans of these wars, stood together and shared a knowing look. Decnar Alder rallied his men behind him, spearmen, armsmen and archers, some injured, some exhausted, but none ready to give up. And Aiden stood in front of them all, ready to lead them out to safety.

He thought back to three days ago, to a time just before finding that Warshield on the road outside Alvarton, before meeting Finias and then finding Riordan outside his door. He'd been convinced then that this life was over, that his time in battle had come and gone. Yet here he stood, in a broken tower, with a small group of defenders looking to him for leadership, looking to him to keep them alive, despite the scar on his face. He didn't understand how he'd gotten here, but he was glad for it, even with the specter of death looming over them. This is what he was, what he'd been born to do. He had his second chance now, and he wasn't going to let anyone who counted on him down. Not now, not ever.

"We'll swing around the left side of the tower and go south, into the trees. If we get split up, we rally on the far side of the woods, at the other end of the plateau." He paused. "Hopefully all of us."

Everyone nodded in agreement. Aiden held up his battered shield, sheathed his sword, and grabbed his lucky goblin spear. One day, he'd have to replace it with something a little sturdier and sharper, but not today. Today, he wanted something in his hands he trusted, that he felt comfortable with. He patted his thigh, rapping the armor loudly, and Bastion emerged from behind the legs of the nearby soldiers, tail wagging, completely unaware of what he was about to get himself into.

"Let's go," he said to the dog, and charged out the door into the fray.

Andua

Chapter 1

The wide stone corridor rumbled underfoot, causing a trickle of small rocks from the ceiling in some places, a burst of cloudy dust in others. Ancient walls displayed what were once expertly crafted symbols from floor to ceiling. The worn markings had cracked and split over the years, the meanings now indecipherable to all but the most dedicated archeologists. In these dark days, most travelers at these depths underground paid the carvings little heed.

A young woman sat on what she discerned to be a useful pile of rubble: the remains of a fallen statue older than her ancestors. Her recently acquired armor still felt weighty and ungainly on her slight frame. A bright sword hung sheathed on her belt and a wooden shield lay at her feet as she rested her weary head against the artfully engraved wall.

Eilidh closed her eyes and tried to relax her shoulders, overly tense from supporting the heft of her new protective wear. The scale hauberk had only a few scratches and dents from the previous owner, but the chest piece was far from appealing to the eye. Her companion had given it to her the previous week, gleeful to provide such a fancy gift to his beloved.

She had smiled and accepted the token graciously, as well as any upstanding lady, at least one in the first couple of months of a courtship. Inwardly she still balked at the grotesque display of a raging bull's head etched in crude relief in the center of the hauberk. Where Ruaidhri had salvaged such a hideous thing, Eilidh couldn't guess.

"Beggars can't be choosers," her mother had said, glad to finally have her daughter out of the family's small cottage in Bristaen. Eilidh had thought the old woman had only meant the ugly armor, but perhaps not.

Behind her resting head, the sound of Ruaidhri's mace resonated along the wall. A cry of delight indicated another conquest. Eilidh loved this young soldier that she'd met only months ago. They were destined for each other: the unstoppable warrior and his lovely companion. She smiled and stood up stiffly, anxious to see the result of Ruaidhri's latest battle.

A look at her chest reminded her of just how bulky and unattractive her armor was, but functionally it was far superior to the leather jerkin it replaced. Her father had told her not to worry about the armor sagging on her slight frame; he'd promised if she filled out anything like her mother, finding any clothing too large would be a difficult task. A matriarchal slap to the back of the head had promptly silenced him and elicited raucous laughter from her older brothers.

Her brothers still hadn't met Ruaidhri, mostly because they spent so much time out on patrol, but they were not too happy that she spent her time with a man who seemed to spend too little time in active duty. In fact, the last time she'd seen her brothers, the conversation hadn't ended well.

"He's teaching me how to fight. That's something neither of you ever took the time to do," she'd retorted angrily before stomping off outside. Spending time in nature always soothed her soul.

Unfortunately, she'd spent much of her time recently in the damp caverns under Teekwood, the immense forest that covered most of northeast Andua and formed part of the natural border with Caldera. She'd absorbed Ghrian's light all the way to the caverns, but now the glow had started to wane, slowly affecting her usually spritely demeanor. But she was with the love of her life, and that mattered most.

They'd traveled together from her small village, Bristaen, up through the outer edges of the immense forest. In the midst of endless trees, Ruaidhri had led her into a great clearing. In the center of the clearing stood a large rock formation, and around the rocks extended a man-made fortification. The few guards present had ushered them through without so much as a second glance, obviously recognizing her companion as a valiant Anduain soldier. That wasn't hard to do considering he wore full military dress: a dark blue tunic displaying the silver tree of Andua, and matching blue helmet, cloak, and shield. And under it all lay tightly linked chainmail, which protected most of his body, arms, and legs from slashing weapons. Ruaidhri insisted he practice his martial skills in the same attire he'd wear in combat with the enemy.

Despite the tensions surrounding the recent truces with both Caldera and Bergmark, the guards had slouched at their posts and paid little heed to the forest surrounding them. Ruaidhri had muttered something under his breath as he led Eilidh past the sentries, but she'd been too preoccupied with their destination to catch it. A small tunnel cut into the rock fortification had led them down into Teekwood Caverns, where Ruaidhri promised Eilidh would learn to fight. His own example set the bar rather high.

The dismembered carcasses of two cave spiders the size of wolfhounds lay sprawled on the tunnel floor. Ruaidhri stood over them, grinning like a small boy through streams of sweat emanating from under his shiny helmet. Eilidh's heart leapt at the sight of him. He was so amazing. What a strong man! Not one, but two spiders at once! She couldn't dream of achieving that level of valor.

"It's your turn again, sweetheart," he called to her.

Eilidh didn't know what she would do without his constant encouragement. She certainly didn't get such edification from her family, so she would probably be a mere housewife instead of a soldier-in-training if not for Ruaidhri. Having said that, the idea of staying at home and taking care of this man did sound nice.

She quickly dismissed that notion. The housewife of such an active warrior would never rest easy. No, it was far better to train in order to march against the Bergsbor and Calderans by his side.

"Okay," she replied cautiously as she unsheathed her cheap blade. She'd stolen it from a goblin in an abandoned mine two months ago, so it was a bit short, even for her. A smith had sharpened it recently, but she could tell it was time to revisit the craftsman again for repairs.

The tense moments before a fight always terrified Eilidh, no matter how many times Ruaidhri coached her through them. She'd defeated many monsters during her training, but she knew that her love chose targets far easier than ones he would choose for himself. He was so patient, so understanding that she couldn't vanquish the same foes he could.

Having Ruaidhri at her back gave Eilidh a small boost of confidence as she shuffled down the narrowing tunnel. Magical torches placed at regular intervals illuminated her path while casting eerie, flickering shadows all around. Even her own shadow bounced before her in a spastically unnatural dance.

"Eilidh, keep your eyes up. You won't know what's ahead if you stare at your feet."

Now at full attention, Eilidh pressed on, faster now, her shield and sword feeling lighter as the adrenaline coursed through her veins. She focused on the more positive aspects of combat. Ruaidhri had explained that although she was weaker than he, with time she would be able to swing her sword tirelessly, unrelentingly, fearlessly. These words echoed in her head now as she heard a cave spider growl in the gloomy shadows between two of the torch lights.

She charged the sound, shield held just high enough that she could still see over the top, already bracing for the large spider leaping at her.

Then she slid to a sudden halt.

Cave spiders don't growl.

The enormous bear roared, charging at Eilidh from a hidden alcove in the shadowy section of the wall. The monster stood taller than any man, with shoulders more than double the width of Eilidh's. A fearsome rack of claws appeared in the firelight, careening towards Eilidh's head. Before she could even raise her heavy wooden shield in defense, the mighty paw rebounded off of a wall of dirt that shot up from the earth in front of her. The wall shattered, sending dark shards in all directions.

Now staggering back to the wall, the black bear looked up in confusion at this small human who'd magically deflected his tremendous blow. Eilidh couldn't believe it either and stood stunned, failing to capitalize on the bear's lack of balance. Perhaps sensing her hesitation, the beast roared and rushed her again, crashing its claws against her shield, violently throwing her small form towards the tunnel wall. She took the impact with her shoulder. A jolting pain seared across her back. Now down on one knee, she looked to the ground in horror as a terrible shadow played out the bear's next attack.

Stones buried in the dirt nearby instantly formed a barrier curving up over Eilidh's head. A roar of frustration filled the tunnel as the earthen shield absorbed the latest onslaught with a crash. As the broken rocks rattled off the wall behind her, a sudden weariness overtook Eilidh. The realization that this fight was far more difficult than any she'd ever encountered started to sink in. Why didn't Ruaidhri help her?

Obviously he knew that she could win alone.

With a burst of strength from her legs, Eilidh leapt at the recoiling brown mass and slammed her shield into its exposed gut. The large beast banged against the opposite tunnel wall in a daze. Eilidh rushed forward, blade drawn back. Her foe's eyesight steadied in time to see her nicked sword drive solidly into its throat, pinning the thick neck against the wall.

The gush of blood spewed out in a red stream above Eilidh's head, leaving a splatter on her lowered helmet; it had sunk forward on her forehead during her final thrust. The pair stood frozen in time. The wheezing creature's life drained slowly from its ruptured neck as Eilidh held the sword in place, staring at the ground, not wanting to see the damage.

"Finish it quickly, Eilidh," said the voice of reason beside her.

Knowing the meaning of the words, Eilidh twisted the sword in the beast's throat and yanked it free, stepping aside to avoid the teetering bear. It collapsed in the middle of the tunnel, facedown, blood pooling around its head.

Eilidh also collapsed, falling onto her backside clumsily. Shield and sword dropped to the stone floor. Her head hung low, her whole body momentarily exhausted. At these depths she seemed to recover from strenuous physical activity far slower than out in the forests near her home, but she could already feel her strength slowly returning.

Ruaidhri's hand rested on her shoulder as he crouched next to her.

"That's the way we kill, my love. They shouldn't suffer more than necessary. This is their home, and they will defend it against us."

Eilidh nodded and then looked to her companion. "I couldn't have done that without you, Ruaidhri."

He smiled broadly and stood up. "I think you did great on your own. Looked like you learned a new trick, too," he said. "How did you do that, anyway?"

"Do what?"

"Create that shield out of the dirt. That was amazing."

Eilidh accepted his outstretched hand and let him lift her to her feet. "I'm not sure I did anything. It just happened."

"Have you always been able to manipulate earth like that?"

"No, I really don't know what happened," Eilidh insisted.

Ruaidhri winked. "It's okay, my love. You don't have to share your secret with me, but it's not like you're practicing fire magic; no one's going to come drag you away."

"There's no secret, Ruaidhri. I really don't know how it happened."

His smile faltered just a touch. "You can build walls out of dirt, you can heal wounds," he said. "Have you ever thought that you might be better suited for the druids?"

She punched him in the arm, stinging her fingers inside her gauntlet. "How can you say that? I'd have to leave you."

173

"Maybe—"

"Maybe *nothing*. I'm not going to Arbreldin, Ruaidhri. The Tree doesn't call to me. I came here with you for a reason. I want a blue cloak, not silver."

Ruaidhri drew her close and engaged her as intimately as their armor allowed.

"Whether the Tree of Rebirth calls to you or not, its power is in you," he said gently.

Eilidh avoided his deep, bright eyes.

"I want to fight, and not be some druid sequestered away to pray to Ghrian and her Tree all day." She rested her head against his chest. "I'm just not cut out for that life."

Ruaidhri lifted her bloodied helmet and tossed it aside. His hand caressed her wavy red hair softly.

"Not all druids live under the Mountain, Eilidh," he said, referring to the mountain covering the giant Tree of Rebirth. "Many train in Arbreldin and then join the fight against Caldera and Bergmark."

Eilidh looked up at his face.

"That makes sense, I suppose." She gently stroked a deep scar in Ruaidhri's cheek. "Soldiers need someone to take care of them."

He laughed, but it echoed into silence as the two continued to hold each other.

"I must tell you, sweetheart. That was brilliant. Killing a huge bear so early in your training is no small feat. You have the spirit of a soldier in you."

Eilidh pushed back smiling. "Not yet, I don't."

Ruaidhri blushed, as any chivalrous soldier should.

"Oh, I didn't mean to embarrass you, my love," Eilidh said, reinstating their embrace.

Her fighting partner withdrew from her. Eilidh cursed herself inwardly for being so forward. Ruaidhri wasn't some promiscuous Thorn; he was a soldier of Andua. They held themselves to a much higher standard than she'd just implied. Now it was her turn to blush.

"Let's continue the training, Eilidh," Ruaidhri said, moving down the passageway.

Eilidh absently gathered her simple, dome-shaped helmet off the ground and then stood, still as a statue, mortally embarrassed by her mistake, so consumed with her own thoughts that she didn't pay heed to the increasing rumble under her feet and in the walls around her. The first of the ceiling bricks had started their descent to the floor when Eilidh snapped out of her trance, just in time to see Ruaidhri turning back to her, a look of concern spreading rapidly across his face.

The trickle of falling rocks grew into a torrent before either of them had taken more than two steps towards the other. The ground rocked violently enough to throw Eilidh from one wall to the other, never allowing her to regain her balance. She crashed to the

175

floor and tried in vain to get back up as the stones filled the shrinking void before her. The earthen cascade roared, deafening Eilidh and scattering her thoughts like leaves before a gale.

As the floor settled, Eilidh surged to her feet and, to her dismay, observed a solid rock wall where a clear view of her love had just been.

She thrust both hands onto the large stones and cried, "Ruaidhri!"

No response.

Eilidh looked around feverishly, panic rising, a grim realization setting in.

She didn't know the way out.

Chapter 2

With the dust still settling around the cave-in, light from the torches created an eerie, powdery aura throughout the hallway. With such limited visibility, Eilidh could barely make out the body of the fallen bear just a few yards in front of her. The ground trembled again. An aftershock. The falling particles of debris swirled in response.

Stepping carefully through the orange-lit dust clouds, Eilidh focused on the task at hand. She had to find another way to Ruaidhri. Surely he was seeking a path to her, also. In fact, she knew that was precisely what her brave Ruaidhri would do, so she needed to return the favor.

A sharp and sudden intake of breath caught Eilidh by surprise, reminding her that she'd been holding her breath in panic. The dirty air clogged her throat and brought on a coughing fit that echoed loudly in the quiet tunnel. The dust fled from her face as she coughed out its brethren.

At least the cave spiders will know someone's still alive in here, Eilidh thought gravely.

Traversing the unstable hallway proved precarious. With each painstakingly careful step, the chance of finding a weak spot in the floor always loomed. On more than one occasion, Eilidh's boot cracked a floor tile, causing her heart rate to soar instantly. One wrong move could spell death for her, plummeting her into some hidden abyss formed by the quake.

"Optimism would be nice at a time like this," she muttered as she stepped over a decent-sized fissure in the ground.

At the end of the hallway, Eilidh faced her first decision. Should she go left or right?

Ruaidhri had led her all the way down, so she admittedly hadn't paid nearly enough attention to their constant twists and turns through Teekwood Caverns' maze-like tunnel system. Both of her options looked very similar and offered no hints as to their identity. Eilidh moved a little ways down each hallway and looked back towards the entrance to the tunnel where the cave-in had occurred.

A missing wall tile sparked a vivid memory. Yes, she'd noticed that missing tile because it disrupted a grim picture of a priest sacrificing an unlucky victim over a flaming pyre. Not exactly what she would consider a work of art, but the image had etched itself into her brain well enough. Hope welled up within her. She would find a way out of this labyrinth, as long as her memory stayed sharp.

She stopped suddenly.

"Find a way out?" she asked of no one in particular. "A way out? No, I have to find Ruaidhri!"

Already Eilidh had lost sight of her true mission. She had to find her love and not just selfishly save herself. She scowled, staring down at her feet, her cheeks reddening with an embarrassment displayed only for herself. Even the floor before her seemed to glow bright crimson, the cracked tiles sharing her shame.

The red shadow before her feet slowly separated in front of her, half moving to the right and half moving to the left. Eilidh tilted her head curiously, embarrassment forgotten. What was this?

Eilidh knelt and reached out a hand to the rightmost half of the shifting red glow. The color continued its slow path to the edge of the floor and started to ascend the wall at a slow creep. When her hand touched the patch of crimson, a dark shadow from her right hand stretched out to the left.

She froze, eyes each as wide as a hunter's moon.

The source of the red light was behind her.

As if reading her mind, the red glow rapidly shot up the wall and then began a quick downward descent. Eilidh twisted around to see an enormous havtrol bringing down a red flaming sword towards her head. An enemy of Andua had snuck up behind her while she pouted! Instinctively she reached out a hand and closed her eyes, foregoing all of her training, praying for a quick death.

"I'm sorry, Ruaidhri," she whispered.

Eilidh opened her eyes, befuddled to still have that ability.

The havtrol was running away, chasing after its giant sword as it clattered loudly down the dim tunnel. Pebbles and dirt splattered all around her.

Of course! Her magical shield had saved her again. The havtrol's wicked blade had rebounded off of the earthen wall with enough force to wrench it from its hands.

She clambered to her feet and drew her cheap sword, its weight giving her mind some peace. This havtrol obviously had even less combat experience than she did; she hadn't dropped a weapon in over a fortnight.

Eilidh rushed down the tunnel after what she suspected must be a berserker of Bergmark. How the bastard had snuck up on her, she had no idea. Thankfully the havtrol's gaudy choice in weaponry had given it away.

Truth be told, Eilidh had never actually seen a havtrol before, but this one matched all the descriptions she'd heard in stories. The brute was simply enormous; Eilidh doubted she reached the middle of its chest. Huge hands displayed monstrous claws, and the features of the ugly face looked unnaturally wrong. The monster had no cloak, and wore only simple armor that covered the key parts of its body.

Now Eilidh's confident footsteps alerted the berserker, who'd bent down to retrieve its wayward sword. Its arms flexed to the size of Eilidh's waist as it lifted its weapon. The havtrol leered at Eilidh and then disappeared before her unbelieving eyes. She ground to a halt and slowly walked backwards, bracing herself, readying her shield.

Ruaidhri had told her that assassins trained heavily in the art of concealment, learning to magically blend into their surroundings. But berserkers were not assassins, especially not this graceless, clumsy havtrol. Yet her eyes didn't lie. The havtrol had vanished, and now she couldn't allow it to get behind her, providing it an easy target.

As the blurry, shadowy shape of a havtrol materialized a few paces in front of her, she thanked the Tree that this creature hadn't mastered its strange art quite yet. She rushed forward. The overly confident berserker, caught off-guard, took the full brunt of her shield right in the face.

The havtrol lost its balance as its concealment failed completely. Now in plain sight, the berserker reached a hand up to its broken nose, paying far too much attention to the damage done and not near enough to the damage yet to come. Eilidh raised her shield and lunged at her enemy once more, making solid contact with its unguarded torso.

The pair toppled to the floor, with Eilidh straddling the havtrol's thick waist as it tried in vain to gain any leverage to swing its oversized glowing sword. Despite her foe's vigorous twisting and grunts of rage, the moments passed fluidly and ethereally for Eilidh. Maintaining her powerful position seemed effortless as she drew back her sword and stared into the blood-soaked face.

The writhing fury beneath her stopped as the havtrol's eyes accepted the inevitable. Typically known for brute strength and unrivaled fury, the mighty berserker's face revealed nothing in its defeat to a small human. Eilidh drove her blade straight through the havtrol's throat as it stretched out an arm in protest, mouth gaping in dispute.

Blood pooled in the berserker's throat and spilled over the corners of its open mouth as its head wrenched back in momentary agony. Remembering Ruaidhri's words, Eilidh turned the blade sharply and withdrew her weapon, leaving a ragged hole. The havtrol's life streamed forth. After a single drawn-out convulsion, her foe's body flopped lifelessly and remained still. Its eyes stared horribly into nothingness.

Eilidh had never killed a true enemy of her nation. She'd slain wild animals and a few wandering spirits within her own lands, but never a citizen of Bergmark or Caldera. Now a berserker lay dead at her hands. She'd spilled the blood of one of the Bergsbor.

And with this step she'd become a defender of Andua, just like her brothers, just like Ruaidhri. Apparently this *creature* hadn't heard about the ceasefire arranged by King Darren and the Bergsbor ruler. Too bad.

The calm sensation in her bones gave way to a powerful rush of adrenaline. Her hands shook so much that she had a difficult time cleaning her sword on the havtrol's brown cloak. Without anyone to tell her otherwise, this seemed like the most logical way to cleanse her soiled weapon.

The exhilaration thrilled her. Never before had she felt so alive. This kill had purpose; it had meaning. This *thing* had tried to kill her in the spirit of hate that drove the Bergsbor to such violence, but she'd defended herself impassively, totally detached. This was a righteous kill.

Yet, how had this havtrol entered Teekwood Caverns? It must've followed her and Ruaidhri down from the beginning, somehow avoiding the detection of the subpar guards at the entrance. That was the only explanation. The coward probably waited and waited for a moment where Eilidh would separate from Ruaidhri just far enough for an easy kill. She regarded the slain berserker once more.

Not so easy, am I?

She beamed with pride and collected herself once more, ready to take on the world.

This foe had obviously been a novice like herself, and she'd dispatched it handily, but the next opponent could be far fiercer. Her smile faded and a grim resolution crossed her pale face. Too much time in the underground reaches of the Teekwood Caverns had faded her skin's sun-kissed hue. She deeply longed for the green grasses of Bristaen, but her mission in the depths required completion.

She had to find Ruaidhri.

Sword drawn and shield at the ready, Eilidh strode with purpose, navigating the intricately carved tunnels with superhuman clarity. The adrenaline-charged blood coursing through her whole being kept her mind sharp and her wits on edge. Two more bears fell to her blade, each more easily than the last. Her strength grew with each step in the dark recesses.

Eilidh stopped at the entrance of a dark tunnel. Her sense of direction indicated that she needed to head this way. She could feel that Ruaidhri lay beyond the utter darkness of the unlit passageway. Fear tried to edge its way into her mind, but sheer determination and desire forced the fright out. Eilidh grabbed one of the torches off of the wall and held it in her left hand, having mounted her shield on her back, under her brown cloak. The torch felt light in her grip compared to the mass of her wooden shield, but the lack of protection left Eilidh almost unbearably vulnerable.

Resolve took over. She marched into the darkness, torch leading the way, sword at the ready to offer a swift conclusion to any disagreements. Despite the blackness all around, her feet told her that the tunnel angled down further into the caverns under Teekwood. The silence loomed and pounded inside her head as she forced herself on, her stony gaze limited to only a few paces ahead.

Someone's boot scuffed the ground behind Eilidh. A tiny pebble skittered across the tunnel floor, skipping past her foot. The subsequent silence told her everything she needed to know.

She was not alone.

Chapter 3

The first arrow sailed towards Eilidh's back, but ricocheted harmlessly off the earthen wall thrown up subconsciously behind her. Before she could even think of summoning another buffer, a second arrow slammed into her wooden shield, still strapped firmly to her back. The impact knocked the breath from her, pitching her forward onto one knee and throwing the torch from her grasp.

Still gasping for precious air, Eilidh furiously pulled at her shield, trying to dislodge it. It wouldn't budge.

That second arrow must have pinned the shield to my cloak, Eilidh realized with horror.

Her dismay intensified when she caught a glimpse of her helmet lying on the ground next to the fallen torch. There was no time to retrieve it. She had to take the offensive quickly.

A third arrow rebounded off of a freshly summoned rock wall as Eilidh rose and rushed her shadowy enemy. With the light of the torch now lying behind her, Eilidh's own long shadow blocked her view of the assailant. Out of the darkness, pain erupted in Eilidh's left arm as an arrow found its mark, knocking her off balance.

The agony soared to heights Eilidh had never thought possible. The simple task of running became arduous to the point of hopelessness. She stumbled forward, still seeking the enemy ahead. Another arrow appeared from the gloom, barely missing Eilidh's cheek and sailing through her exposed red hair like a cool breeze. The missile's flights scratched at her ear on their way past.

The archer strode towards Eilidh, confident that she'd been sufficiently weakened. In truth, Eilidh felt miserable, leaning against the wall, breathing deeply, agony wrenching her lifeless arm. The enemy's lapse in professionalism cleared Eilidh's mind. The archer should've finished her off from a safe distance when they had the chance.

She dropped her sword to the ground with a clank. She reached up and yanked out the arrow from her arm in one sudden motion. The excruciating pain shocked her in its brutality. Her mind fought against the physical distress and released a calming sensation in defense. Eilidh felt oddly at peace.

Closing her eyes softly, Eilidh reached down through her feet into the ground, calling forth the Tree's healing powers. The earth's quick response flowed through her body like the warmth of a good bath.

Ethereal white vines wrapped around her arm and cinched tight, before fading inwards through her clothes and into her skin. Revitalized, Eilidh grabbed her sword off the ground and struck out at the cocky archer who now stood within her reach. The glint of two blades materialized from the darkness, illuminated by the torch down the hallway. The orange glow reflected wickedly against the swift steel, but the suddenness of Eilidh's attack had obviously caught her foe by surprise. The archer's weapons failed to catch Eilidh's sword in time, yet her blade infuriatingly missed its desired target in a sloppy uppercut motion.

Fortunately, Eilidh's fist, still wrapped around the sword, caught the archer directly under the chin. The gut-wrenching sound of shattering teeth resounded in the quiet tunnel, and a high-pitched, keening wail filled the air with pure suffering as the archer's mouth fell open once more. The impact knocked the poor archer's blades from their hands as they fell forward onto both knees, groping futilely at their destroyed mouth.

In the heat of the moment, Eilidh drove an armored punch into the side of the archer's head, sending a crimson spray of fragmented teeth to the ground. The emotional release of vengeance tingled in her bones, but Eilidh didn't think she should beat down a defeated opponent like she would a wild dog. It didn't seem right.

Eilidh loomed over her fallen adversary, her blunt sword pointed at the downcast head.

And she hesitated. What was she supposed to do? Execute the enemy? Leave them to wallow in their anguish? Provide a healing spell to ease their suffering?

The complexity of the decision increased tenfold when the archer's battered face finally lifted to Eilidh's.

An elf!

"Wha—? What are—?" Eilidh stammered, now taking a few steps back. There was no mistaking the telltale points of each ear, the alabaster skin hue, or the perfectly straight hair.

But why would an elf ever ambush her? They were both citizens of Andua together.

Obviously this Anduain sister of hers had mistaken her for an enemy. Eilidh could see how that mistake could happen, especially down in the depths where a person could hunt for days without encountering another soul. Paranoia would serve as an easy companion.

Upon closer inspection, Eilidh noted the dark green cloak, held together with an oval-shaped silver clasp depicting a soaring hawk. But that was impossible.

"Why did you attack me, tracker?" Eilidh yelled. Trackers served under King Darren, usually as scouts and snipers, and all wore the hawk emblem.

Embracing her anger, Eilidh approached, sword now directed at the tracker's exposed throat, the tip of the sword pushing on the pale skin, but not breaking it. Blood dripped from the elf's open mouth. The sight of the broken teeth turned Eilidh's stomach, but her fury remained in control.

"I could've killed you!"

Upon further reflection, Eilidh realized that the elf could've easily killed her, too.

But what happens next?

Something in the elf's clear blue eyes changed. The penetrating stare had picked up on Eilidh's indecision, her failure to act. Resolution filled those burning eyes. The elf slowly stood up. Eilidh held her sword uneasily against the tracker's throat. She gave up at least two hands' breadths in height to the slender elf, but that physical difference didn't concern Eilidh.

Her only concern was what this elf was thinking, and what she would do next.

Could she kill an ally, even one who'd attacked her first?

Her outstretched arm started to twinge under the sword's weight. She didn't know how much longer she could face this standoff, emotionally or physically.

Fatigued to failure, the sword arm dropped and the elf immediately grabbed at the weapon. Survival instincts kicked in for both fighters as the elf's hands gripped Eilidh's wrist. She twisted her arm back and forth, trying to break the vice-like grip of the elf, but the taller female held on for dear life. Knowing the fight was over if she lost her sword, Eilidh clamped her fingers around the handle with all her might.

The elf drove into Eilidh suddenly, forcing her up against the tunnel wall, where she smacked the back of her head. Stars bloomed before her eyes, obscuring her view of the tracker. Not knowing what else to do, Eilidh brought her knee up hard between the elf's legs. The result of this attack on a male would've been more effective, but the elf loosened her grip on Eilidh's wrist just enough for Eilidh to break free.

In one clumsy movement, Eilidh grabbed her hilt with both hands and drove the bottom of the sword's handle down onto the elf's forehead.

The tracker crumpled wordlessly. Eilidh breathed hard, hands on knees. The elf lay motionless, but Eilidh didn't have the heart to check for a pulse. If she'd just killed an Anduain, she didn't want to know about it.

Eilidh staggered towards the dimming torch and her helm, considered pressing on down into the pitch black tunnel, but then thought the better of it. The fierce struggle had left her feeling weak and drained, and her growling stomach reminded her that she hadn't eaten all day. Unfortunately, Ruaidhri carried the pack with all of their provisions.

I can't survive another attack like this, she thought hopelessly, still breathing hard. *I need to find Ruaidhri, but I can't do it alone.*

She resolved to head back up to the caverns' entrance, to find some allies in her journey to reunite with Ruaidhri. He would still be down there, searching tirelessly for her while she fearfully ran away to the surface, but what else could she do?

Surely it was better if she lived to find him later rather than getting herself killed searching for him alone.

Before leaving the downed elf, Eilidh managed to remove the arrow and shield from her back. The arrow had snapped near the tip, freeing her shield from her cloak. That must've happened when the elf threw her against the wall. In the firelight she could see the deep scar that the arrow had etched into her shield, leaving a sizeable gouge in the green paint. The next time she saw one of her brothers, they would have to fix it for her. She smiled as she thought about how impressed they'd both be with her stories of valor and bravery. Finally, she'd acted in a way that she could find pride in.

She worked her way quickly through the maze of the caverns, seeking the exit. The deserted corridors helped speed her progress. While jogging through yet another tunnel, she thought about how her brothers had never encouraged her in her desire to become a soldier. They both thought that she would fail miserably. How she'd proved them wrong.

Of course, here she was, running away from her mission.

As she left the depths of the caverns behind, Ruaidhri could be dead or dying, screaming for her to help him. The image brought a tear to Eilidh's eye, but there was no other option. She had to leave in order to return stronger, bolstered with the help of like-minded allies.

"Oh, Ruaidhri, please don't die," Eilidh prayed fervently.

She repeated the chant over and over, the repetition easing her mind's frantic worry. The mantra stopped when a tall figure in blue shot across the tunnel intersection ahead of her.

Could it be?

"Ruaidhri!" she yelled.

Eilidh ran down the gloomy tunnel faster than she'd ever thought possible. The air itself seemed to assist her, pushing her forward with supernatural speed. Rounding each corner brought a new pang of disappointment as her companion continued to evade her. Did he even know she was chasing him?

The sound of growling greeted Eilidh around one brightly lit corner. There she stood in great contrast to her surroundings, a small woman in a large hallway. Four giant bears now faced her, beating the ground with their paws, building up an unstoppable rage. Their eyes burned ferociously, their murderous intent blatantly apparent.

Frozen in time and space, Eilidh could swear that plumes of smoke flowed from the angered nostrils. The enraged creatures now moved as one, stampeding towards her.

Terror gave way to common sense as she turned on her heels and galloped back through the tunnels, her mind filled with visions of the bears catching her. Seeing her small body slashed to a bloody pulp forced her legs to pump harder. The deep roaring behind her invaded her body, more of a feeling than a sound. The ground beneath her feet rumbled under the weight of the stampede.

The tunnels passed by in a flurry and the irritated bears finally gave up their pursuit. But Eilidh didn't give up on her flight. She felt far more invigorated than ever before. Gravity struggled to keep her tethered to the ground as she flew down one tunnel after another.

The familiar sounds of Anduains fighting cave spiders floated down a tunnel towards her. Eilidh slowed to a careful walk. She yearned for friendly faces to assist in her mission, but a friendly face had just shot her in the back. She pulled up short at the intersection from where the cries and roars of battle resounded.

Did she dare step into the light, into the open for the Anduains to see? What if they no longer honored their allegiance to King Darren and the High Priestess? Had the elves deserted Andua? The unanswerable questions spiraled through her mind, adding and multiplying endlessly.

"Ruaidhri, I need you," she whispered.

Chapter 4

"Brian, stop flinging those swords around like floppy wet fish!"

Liam watched in horror as his new apprentice attempted to fend off a medium-sized cave spider in Teekwood Caverns. Thorns trained in the ways of fighting with a weapon in each hand, but Brian might as well have been poking at the spider with a pointy stick.

"Brian, you're trying to kill it, not trim its hair. Keep your wrists loose, but swing those arms with some machismo," Liam instructed, exasperated with the young firbolg.

In general, firbolgs made fantastic Thorns, so Liam had been overjoyed to finally receive one as a student. Brian was well over seven feet tall and boasted fantastically broad shoulders. At first glance, this trainee represented all the physical traits that formed one of the great Thorns, who killed seemingly limitless numbers of enemies with deft strokes of their swords and an air of well-earned self-confidence. The teacher of such a powerful Thorn would surely receive endless accolades and praise, quickly moving into the position of Master Trainer. Liam salivated at the thought of that prospect, despite his original reluctance in accepting his mandatory reassignment to the teaching corps.

Unfortunately, Liam's overhyped hopes faced a grim realization: Brian couldn't fight his way out of a damp wicker basket. The oaf would've had better luck just kicking the spider rather than flailing his arms around with all the grace and coordination of a three-legged dog learning to dance. Liam had hoped the trip out to the caverns would excite and inspire his young follower into revealing some hidden talent for extreme greatness, but the journey had proved fruitless thus far.

And, mercifully, the fight ended. The odds were good that swinging two large swords at a target long enough would eventually result in hitting and killing that target. When the target was a mostly decrepit and harmless spider, the odds increased dramatically for most people, but apparently not for poor Brian.

Liam's dreams of grandeur all but slipped away.

One look at the firbolg told Liam that reality had started to attack Brian's self-confidence: The slump of the gigantic shoulders, the sadness on his wide face. Firbolgs weren't known as a particularly happy race, but Brian looked that much glummer.

"Maybe I'm not a Thorn," he whined with the trademark deep bass voice of the firbolg race.

"With that kind of attitude you certainly aren't," Liam stated with perfectly choreographed hand gestures.

Brian's whole body seemed to implode even further.

"Yet," Liam added, marveling at his own timing.

The firbolg's face rose, his large eyes meeting Liam's.

"You have all the makings of a Thorn, Brian, but you've got to find that swashbuckling, adventurous spirit within you!"

For added emphasis, Liam bounded towards the tunnel wall and leapt into the air, performing a series of jumps and spins off of the stone surface.

"We are the proudest of all Andua's guardians," he yelled in mid-flight. "Some might say too proud, but I say 'too proud' does not exist!"

As with all of Liam's intense displays of physical prowess, Brian looked thoroughly impressed.

As he should be! Liam thought in the middle of an inverted spin.

Liam stuck the landing with a flourish and a flashy smile, his black cloak swirling epically behind him, only to see his trainee staring down towards the opposite end of the tunnel. The smile disintegrated. Why wasn't this peon worshipping his grand feats of agility?

"What's so interesting, Brian?" he asked politely. A gallant Thorn was always polite. Well, usually.

"Um . . . I think some nuathreens are in trouble down there," Brian said, a little unsure of himself. "Can't you hear it?" he added cautiously.

Despite hearing nothing of the sort, Liam couldn't help himself.

"Of course! Let's save the day, young one," he exclaimed, charging in the supposed direction of the supposed altercation.

The startled cries of a pair of nuathreens did indeed meet Liam's ears about halfway down the tunnel. So the student *did* have at least some small advantage over the teacher. Interesting, but of course superb hearing did nothing to increase proficiency with a pair of sharpened implements of death. *That* much was painfully apparent each time Brian tried to clobber an enemy.

The short and dainty nuathreens shrieked and danced around a wild pack of adolescent cave spiders that were intent on devouring the diminutive warriors. Liam immediately noticed that both screaming nuathreens wielded two swords, but he used the word *wielded* loosely. These were no Thorns. No, these were merely trackers, far inferior to the Thorn in blade skill, but at least they could dodge better than a three-legged dog with a cold.

In Liam's mind, one of the trademarks of any good melee fighter involved the correct and appropriate use of catchphrases. For example, to mark the occasion of charging into battle, Liam had coined the phrase, "I'm flyin' in!" Brian hadn't reached the stage in his training yet where he deserved the use of such exclamations of intent, at least, not in Liam's estimations. Of course, Liam already had a collection of suggestions for Brian to use, such as, "I'm going deep!" Yes, that was a solid suggestion.

With his well-practiced war cry and a totally unnecessary burst of speed, Liam roared through the cave spiders, hacking and slashing in a blur of motion usually reserved for humans running to the outhouse after a close encounter with firbolg cuisine. Within seconds, a gory mess of twitching spider remains lay strewn across

197

the tunnel floor, walls, and ceiling. The two blood-splattered nuathreens stood in what Liam assumed could only be complete and unadulterated awe.

Without waiting for the two to snap out of their worshipful trance, Liam sheathed one of his shiny blades and used the other to remove a few intact spider legs to sell to the witches back aboveground. Those crazy old hags were always looking for such ingredients to stir into those foul-smelling—and foul-tasting—stews of theirs.

A sharp object poked Liam in the buttocks. He turned to stare into the eyes of a bloodied and fuming nuathreen. Their physical appearance always put a smile on Liam's face. They had such small and fragile bodies that were topped off with a disproportionately large head. Sitting on his haunches, Liam stood eye-to-eye with the nuathreen, whose green cloak was secured around his scrawny neck by a hawk brooch, confirming his membership in King Darren's trackers.

"Just what in the bloody hell do you think you're doing, mate?" asked the scowling nuathreen.

Confused, the noble Thorn replied, "How do you do, nuathreen? I am Liam, and I am just collecting my fee."

The scowl turned furious.

"Your *fee*? Your *fee* for what exactly, mate?"

Liam didn't have much experience chatting with nuathreens, but he suspected that the tracker didn't mean *mate* in a literal sense, or in any positive sense for that matter. Confusing creature.

"For saving you and your companion, of course."

"You've lost the plot, you have!" exclaimed the nuathreen. "You believe this git, Gil? This bloke says he *saved* us. Like we needed savin'!"

"Aye, a right pile of shite that is, Bruce" added the second nuathreen, Gil apparently.

The pair continued to babble in increasingly quick language that Liam recognized less and less. Coming from a noble, southern birth had left the Thorn a bit out of touch with northern forest-folk like these, but no matter what, the protocol was clear: If no reward was offered for services rendered, then no reward would be taken. Also, Liam had to remain honorable and polite, despite the nuathreens' rudeness. Well, he suspected they were being rude; it was hard to tell at this point.

"Of course you are correct, little masters. We will be on our way now. Come, Brian."

Liam could hear the continued verbal foray as he and Brian wandered off back the way they had come.

"Who is he calling little masters? I've got a good mind to brain that eejit."

"Aye, right you are, Bruce."

"The pair on that bloke, thinking he can steal from us!"

"Aye, can't believe it myself, Bruce."

Their ungrateful animosity perplexed Liam. Surely they should appreciate his help. As far as he'd seen at the time, those spiders had held the upper hand against the outmatched and undersized nuathreens. The feisty little trackers certainly had heart, but they seemed to lack the necessary skills to succeed in close quarters combat. And despite having heart, the pair certainly lacked manners. Any rescued individual should always show their appreciation to the rescuer, preferably with money, but spider legs would also suffice. How would word of his altruistic exploits gain him fame if the recipients of his aid didn't praise his name from the rooftops, or at least yell his name throughout the tunnels of Teekwood Caverns?

"THORN! HELP!"

The high-pitched scream piqued Liam's curiosity. Obviously a damsel in distress had heard of his grand accomplishments, and in her darkest hour had called out his name. He stopped in the tunnel and looked around for connecting passageways. Now, where could she be?

"Liam, those nuathreens are coming," Brian said.

The interruption broke Liam from his search for his endangered fair maiden. Irritated at his presumptuous student, he looked back down the tunnel and saw the pair of trackers sprinting their big hearts out and screaming their little lungs out. So that at least explained the womanlike squeals for help. Liam was sorely disappointed. He hadn't rescued a lady in a while, and they *always* offered a reward, and not always in silver pieces.

Unfortunately, Liam had no time to reminisce about his female conquests. The nuathreens ran with good reason: A horde of bloodthirsty hulks stomped after them. Torchlight reflected off the scaly, armored hides as the monstrous creatures made up ground on the trackers, whose twig-like legs moved in a blur.

A less honorable man would've definitely yelled something along the lines of, "Wait, so *now* you need my help?"

Liam looked at Brian and smiled. Brian carefully smiled back, looking a bit confused. Ah, what a treat the young firbolg was in for. It wasn't every day that Liam encountered a mass of foes who would stress his fighting ability to its gloriously high limits. In preparation, Liam ran a hand slowly through his luxurious, wavy brown hair.

"Watch and learn, my young apprentice," Liam announced, drawing both of his swords from the sheaths that protected the rest of the world from them.

Legs pumping with reckless abandon, Liam charged directly towards his incoming victims, yelling, "I'm flyin' in!"

He leapt over the fleeing nuathreens, one of whom may have said, "What the bloody hell?"

All but one of the hulks slowed to a cautious lope at Liam's fearless approach, a little unsure what to make of this heroic human, Liam was sure. Only one, obviously the leader, continued its stampede towards the Anduains. The beast growled loudly and hefted a large, meaty fist over its head. The giant appendage didn't faze Liam; he'd fought larger and meatier fists in his time.

The two combatants closed in, and the hulk's gargantuan fist plummeted to the ground on which Liam stood. He gracefully evaded to the left and thrust a blade towards the hulk's exposed side.

The sword scratched harmlessly across thick armor, indicating to Liam that this foe wasn't the run-of-the-mill hulk that he'd fought in the past. Liam easily gave up at least one foot in height and one hundred and fifty pounds in weight to his furious adversary, whose raging red eyes now found their target.

The large arm moved sideways with amazing speed, performing a wicked cross-cut as Liam ducked and evaded once more. Parrying the blow seemed a bit out of the question considering the heft behind the fist. This creature had ludicrously stumpy legs but was all heft in the upper body department. As the hulk's flailing arm created a rush of air over his head, Liam looked up to see the hulk's legs open before him. A crease in the enemy's armor exposed flesh on the inner thigh. Liam's sword found the spot, slicing through the relatively soft piece of hide, right down to the bone.

Without waiting for the hulk's cry of panic to reach his ears, Liam jumped straight up and grabbed onto the back of the hulk's head-crest with his left hand. Pulling down hard enough on the boney ridge to keep his own feet floating off the ground, Liam sliced at the beast's stout, scaly neck.

The blade slid right off, not even causing a nick in the tough skin. A shake from the hulk's head sent Liam sprawling to the floor. The hulk's muscle-bound arm swung above its head once more, ready to finish its dazed opponent. Liam looked up in a haze, now a little worried about the outcome of the fight. Victory had seemed assured, but now he'd fallen behind.

Before the mighty fist could start its deadly descent, a pair of arrows ripped into the hulk's face, right between the eyes. The animal collapsed backwards immediately, a fountain of blood spraying the ceiling in a messy arc. Liam closed his eyes and leaned his head back, his nerves feeling a little shot by his brush with near-death.

"It's about time you moved your arse out of the way," declared a high voice behind Liam.

Liam rolled his eyes. *Such gentlemen.*

But they had saved him, so did that make them even? Did he owe them anything? Surely not. The thought of owing anyone anything made Liam's head hurt.

"Well, this can't get any worse," he muttered.

A small herd of hulks nearby seemed to believe otherwise.

Chapter 5

Life in the fire-lit tunnel stood still for a moment. The flickering light from the sporadically placed torches illuminated figures as stiff as statues. One body in particular lay more still than all the others. In fact, the only movement around the recently killed hulk chief was the pulsating flow of blood still pouring from its broken face.

Over his shoulder, Liam saw Bruce and Gil nock another arrow each. The ground trembled again and Liam's thoughts of the fight already being won left in a hurry. Some races gave up fighting as soon as their leader died; apparently hulks didn't ascribe to that school of combat.

Liam flipped off his back and onto his feet as a torrent of arrows passed by his head, hurtling towards the incoming stampede. Snarls and grunts echoed off the walls as Liam spun through his assailants, slashing out at any exposed weaknesses. A few of the lesser beasts fell quickly to his strikes, but the larger breed's hide kept Liam's blades at bay.

The hulks completely ignored the archers raining down pain upon them from afar. They'd just watched their chief die and apparently blamed Liam for it, because they spun around him in a circle of furious and untamed violence. That suited the brave Thorn just fine. He parried heroically, struck out forcefully, and then cocked his head to the side when he thought he heard a deep voice yell, "I'm flyin' in!"

He really hoped that he'd misheard and that Brian was not joining the fray. More importantly, that had better not have been Brian using Liam's signature battle cry!

Now completely surrounded by thrashing hulks, the dodging Thorn found himself in the deep shadow of unbridled rage. His blades glowed in a faint red as they sliced through the darkness, piercing their targets over and over. His magical sword ripped into the arm of one beast, unleashing the blade's power as a burning eruption. The resulting flame burned out quickly, but the panicked enemy toppled into one of its own, crashing both to the floor. Not one to wait for an invitation, Liam flipped forward and drove a blade into the throat of each hulk, ending their shrieks for help.

Liam felt the shadow around him deepen. He turned to see a dark form flying across the tunnel towards him. The collision pinned Liam to the wall, winding him momentarily. He freed one of his arms and raised a sword, ready to impale his assailant, but then saw Brian's enormous head in the dim light.

"Brian! Get off me! I must lay waste to these brigands!" Liam yelled, trying to wrestle his way out from underneath the large firbolg.

With a deep grunt, Brian rolled out of the way and Liam stood, collecting himself. After a quick check that his tattooed biceps looked impressive in the torchlight, Liam put up his blades and rushed the few hulks remaining on their feet. The closest beast rumbled towards Liam and abruptly crashed to the floor with a growl. Liam could see no less than fourteen arrows peppering the massive monster's back.

The last two enemies saw defeat and ran, stumbling over their fallen brothers in their haste. One dropped to a barrage of arrows from the nuathreens and the other escaped into the gloom, crying loudly. As much as Liam felt good about his performance in the battle, he would definitely appreciate the survivor not rounding up all of his friends and returning any time soon. Liam was fairly certain that his bark-skin armor was severely damaged in a few places, and he highly doubted he could find a smith in the caverns who could repair the bark of an ironbark tree. And even if he did find one, chances were the smith couldn't recreate the abyss black dye that permeated the armor. Any sane Thorn would rather wear no armor at all than armor that looked pieced together.

But more than just the chipped armor, if Liam was being perfectly honest, he was exhausted.

Such an admission of fatigue didn't come easily to the proud Thorn. The tales of old told of his legendary predecessors handling similar fights without the help of two little archers. Of course, it was Liam's extraordinary courage that had produced the victory. The trackers had run away from a fight that Liam had heartily embraced with gusto. As required, Liam struck a pose worthy of his triumph: hands on hips, elbows out, chest high, and one eyebrow arched up perfectly. He even thought about putting one of his black leather boots on top of a fallen foe. Where was a sketch artist when he needed one? He made a note to hire such an artist before his next expedition. Fame did not come to those who did not advertise.

"Oi, numpty!"

Disturbed from his celebration, Liam turned to the nuathreen called Bruce—or was it Booze?—with an appropriately irritated look.

"Aye, you," continued the tracker. "You're off in the clouds while your mate's lying here in a pile of his own guts. Shame on you!"

True enough, Brian lay on his side, where Liam had pushed him over, with a deep groove sliced into the chainmail armor covering his abdomen. The claws of a hulk had obviously raked him brutally. Now blood flowed from just under his ribs. As with most firbolgs, Brian's waist was the same size as Liam's, but overall the boy had the exaggerated hourglass shape of his people, resulting in oversized shoulders and stout legs. A firbolg's head matched its shoulders, resulting in a wide, flat face featuring almost no nose and long, narrow eyes. The boy's eyes were closed now, but not with the straining force of a mortally injured firbolg. If not for the growing stream of red staining Brian's grey cloak and the floor tiles beneath, Liam would've sworn the boy was merely asleep. Gil crouched next to Brian, checking for a pulse.

"Ghrian's calling him, Bruce," he reported gloomily.

Nuathreens fought angrily, spoke angrily, and drank angrily, but they had soft hearts for fallen friends. Even Liam could see the true sadness growing in both trackers at the sight of the dying firbolg that they'd not even officially met. Considering their innate empathy, it was strange that nuathreens were among the few races that had never mastered the healing arts of light magic.

Liam couldn't heal any more than the trackers could, but he was a valiant warrior. Surely they didn't expect him to masterfully inflict *and* repair wounds?

These distracting thoughts faded as panic set in. What if Brian really died? How would Liam tell Brian's parents? The boy was everything to them. How would Liam pay his rent? He hadn't had a student in a month before Brian showed up, having been cast aside by all the other trainers. The clumsy firbolg had happily followed along with the soon-to-be world-renowned Liam, but now he would die in the dirty depths of Teekwood Caverns.

It was a sad payment for the valor that Brian had finally shown in battle. Liam would never have guessed that the tall, muscular, and completely uncoordinated firbolg actually had such bravery to charge a mad herd of hulks. A smile spread across Liam's face. He alone had taken this boy that no one else could train. He alone had molded Brian into a true warrior, a true Thorn of Andua.

"Have you lost the plot, mate?" demanded Bruce, poking the distant Liam in the thigh with his curved sword. "Your boy is dying here! This is not a flippin' joke! You have to do something!"

Why did the nuathreen have to be so insistent and confrontational all the time? It was hardly the proper way to act, especially in the presence of a gentleman. Not quite sure what to do next, because he usually did the killing and not the reviving, Liam gazed down the tunnel with his best thinker's pose.

And he saw a pale apparition appear from the gloom. Before he could help himself, a small scream squeaked out from his lips, his hand belatedly cutting off the sound. Fighting hulks was one thing, but Liam had no desire to fight off a ghost. They were already dead and hence, unkillable!

Both nuathreens observed Liam with apparent confusion as he started to backpedal away from the latest player in the bizarre scene.

"Gil, what's his problem?" asked Bruce.

"I have no clue, Bruce."

To Liam's dismay, Bruce beckoned the ghost closer.

"Are you out of your mind, nuathreen?" he snapped in a harsh whisper, not wanting to displease the ghastly apparition.

"Are *you* out of your mind, you daft prat?" replied Bruce. Then to the pale, armored ghost, Bruce said, "Oi, are you a druid?"

Now panic-stricken, Liam said, "What difference does it make? It will devour all of our souls if we don't flee now!"

"Gil, he's completely off his flippin' rocker."

"Aye, he's a complete nutter, so he is, Bruce"

Liam fought to hold back the redness of embarrassment from his face as the apparition drew closer. This was no ghost, just a very, very pale woman in some of the worst fitting, and looking, armor Liam had ever seen. Now the scene made sense to the previously and unnecessarily perplexed Thorn.

The lady had been creeping cautiously down the tunnel, but now she started running, causing Liam to twitch involuntarily, despite knowing now that she was no ghost. Bruce shook his head.

"Flippin' ants in his pants, Gil."

"Aye, Bruce."

The woman knelt down over Brian, lifted his chainmail, and peeled up the shirt underneath, revealing three parallel crimson gashes. She started the familiar chant that Liam had heard many times after a battle. Her hands glowed with pure regenerative energy, the bluish white light casting a long shadow behind her. The gaping wounds sealed shut at her touch as the energy transferred from her healing hands to Brian's broken body. After three repetitions of this process, Liam started to wonder if she'd appeared too late. He deduced that she must be in the early stages of training, which also meant that her healing powers were far from perfect. Also, judging from the tacky state of her appearance, Brian's life didn't rest in the competent hands of an expert. Despite all of that, she wasn't giving up. She kept her hands on Brian's side, her eyes squeezed shut.

"Better to die gloriously in battle, than to live a peaceful life and die of old age," Liam said proudly.

Bruce shot a glance at him in response, and Liam could see the little archer shaking, veritably twitching all over. Had his profound phrase affected the tracker that much? When the tracker stomped towards him, Liam realized that perhaps he'd misjudged.

Perhaps the nuathreen was actually seething and boiling over with rage.

"WHAT'S WRONG WI' YOUR HEID, YOU GORMLESS TWIT?" Bruce screamed at a shockingly high volume for such a small creature.

Liam refused to answer such a ridiculous question. There was nothing wrong with his head.

"You just don't get it do you, mate?" Bruce continued, but before he could add anymore to his diatribe, Brian coughed and sat up like a shot. The young lady jerked away, let out a surprised squeal, fell on her rear, and then scooted back a few paces, her hand covering her mouth.

Liam had never seen such a novice. Shocked by her own abilities? Ridiculous. A Thorn *never* doubted himself, not for a second.

"Thank you, druid," Brian said weakly, panting to catch his breath. Running away from death could really take the wind out of a person.

"You're welcome," she stammered, staring at the space to the side of Brian.

"You see his darkness, don't you?" Bruce asked.

"Looks like it, Bruce," Gil added.

The young lady alternated staring at the nuathreens and back at Brian. Liam didn't see what all the fuss was about.

"What *is* that?" she asked, standing up slowly.

"It's a firbolg thing, lassie," Bruce said casually. "Something happens after they're brought back from the dead. I don't really know, because I can't see it."

"Aye, only druids can," added Gil.

"But I'm no druid."

Bruce smiled.

"You must be something, lass, because only druids trained in Arbreldin can see the darkness," he said.

"But I've never even been to—"

"This is all very interesting," Liam interrupted, bored out of his mind. Arbreldin was the holy seat of the druids, and therefore packed to the gills with crazed idiots who believed in magical trees and mystical sunrises. Bunch of damn tree huggers if you asked him. "Who are you, and what is a lovely girl like yourself doing down in a hellhole like this?"

The woman turned to him, as if seeing him for the first time. He had that effect on women. Only a true Thorn could take a woman's breath away every time they locked gazes.

"Just ignore him, lass," Bruce said. Liam threw his most outraged glare at the small creature, but the nuathreen didn't even possess the courage to acknowledge him.

"Aye, he's a twit," Gil added.

Before Liam could think of an appropriate way to express his displeasure, Bruce was already talking again.

"Does his darkness walk beside him?" he asked, somewhat tentatively.

"Uh, I'm not sure," the girl replied uneasily. "What does that mean?"

"I hoped you knew," Bruce said with a sigh. "It's just what people ask every time a firbolg's brought back to life."

"Aye, never knew what they were on about," added Gil.

Liam had never heard of this, but in fairness, he didn't really hang around the dead much. He was too busy trying to create *more* dead.

"Fair enough," Bruce said after an awkward silence. "So what *are* you doing down here, lass?"

"My name is Eilidh. I came down here with my friend Ruaidhri, and we got separated." Desperation flooded her voice. "You have to help me find him. Please."

"Sorry, lass," said Bruce. "We've got business in the forest to attend to."

Gil frowned slightly at his friend and then nodded in agreement.

Liam noted their leather armor and realized their true purpose in the caverns.

"Yes, dear Eilidh," he said very deliberately. "These trackers should probably return to their patrol through Teekwood, instead of sneaking off to make a few silver pieces hunting animal parts for witches."

The pair of trackers now stared at Liam, silent for the first time that he'd noticed. Andua relied on the likes of these to roam the border with Caldera, searching for signs of enemy troop

213

movements. Truce or no truce, the Reds couldn't be trusted as far as Liam could throw them, which was probably quite far actually. He made a note to find a better metaphor.

Liam examined the young woman. In the right light, she was actually very pretty. She'd spent far too much time in the dark halls of the caverns, but that was nothing some sunlight on the surface couldn't fix. Yes, she could be very beautiful if she had a few hearty meals and filled out a little. And she *needed* him. How could Liam possibly refuse such an offer from a potentially pretty girl? Although, he did wonder if this Ruaidhri was more than a friend. Well, that dalliance wouldn't last long after this Eilidh girl had spent some quality time in the presence of a courageous Thorn.

And to top it all, off-the-cuff adventuring always earned far greater notoriety than futilely educating a hopeless student. As far as Liam was concerned, his choice was as crystal clear as his own gorgeous eyes.

"Of course I will take you and rescue your fallen friend," Liam said. "Nuathreens, as payment for my spectacular fighting services, I require that you take Brian back to the surface. He's of no use on such a quest, as we saw in that recent skirmish. And the pair of you are borderline useless, running scared at the first signs of a stampeding gaggle of hulks."

Bruce and Gil looked at each other in disbelief. Liam saw their response and laughed heartily. Perhaps too heartily, but was there such a thing as having too much heart?

"Oh, come now, trackers. Don't get all bent out of shape. You use two blades in a similar, albeit inferior, fashion to a Thorn, so perhaps you can give Brian a few pointers on your way out of the caverns," Liam suggested.

He slapped Bruce on the back for good measure, showing the woman his good rapport with creatures big and small. After all, he'd already established dominance and leadership by delegating Brian's training to the nuathreens. Now he was showing his more personable side.

Bruce's face turned red in fury and Gil held the small archer at bay, whispering in his ear. Liam appreciated Gil protecting his friend from a hasty defeat at Liam's hand, should Bruce force a confrontation. The nuathreen's anger seemed to fade.

"Okay, Thorn. We'll take the boy off of your dainty wee hands so that you can help your wee damsel. But know this: He will learn more from us in an hour than he has learned from you in a month."

"I find that difficult to believe based upon your recent performances," Liam responded politely, smiling for effect.

Bruce ignored him. The pair of trackers pulled Brian to his unstable feet. Liam didn't appreciate the nuathreen's tone at all, especially not in front of a young lady. Brian had learned immense bravery, obviously all from Liam's instruction. A mere tracker couldn't teach this trait. Even two trackers couldn't, for that matter.

Brian, Bruce, and Gil started walking away from the new companions. Bruce said over his shoulder, "Miss, you'd be wise to keep an eye on this one. Don't let him get you killed."

Liam could hear Gil agree faintly, "Quite right, Bruce."

Eilidh turned to Liam with a look of concern. Liam welcomed the challenge that the nuathreen had set up for him. Now he was escorting a veritable damsel in distress who also didn't trust in his supreme melee skills. In due time, he would prove himself a master of the swords and win her over. He felt impressed with his abilities just thinking about them.

"Well, let's be off then, shall we?" Liam said.

Eilidh nodded slowly. The pair wandered after the trio before them, but didn't follow when the trackers turned off of the main path. What nerve these short people had! Liam had ordered them to take Brian straight to the surface. Why were they heading in *that* direction?

Eilidh looked a little unsure.

"Um, the trackers turned back there. We also need to head towards the surface to recruit more help. Do you know where you're going?"

Liam laughed, booming echoes off the walls.

"Of course, I do. Have no fear. *They* are the ones who have made the wrong turn."

Aren't they?

He quickly distracted himself from self-doubt by dismissing Eilidh's desire to find more adventurers. Liam the Thorn could handle this small quest all on his own.

Chapter 6

What had she gotten herself into now? Here she was, a young, relatively inexperienced woman, traipsing around in the dingy subterranean corridors of Teekwood Caverns with a man she'd just barely met. A man that she suspected might actually be crazy.

"Eilidh, have I told you about the time I saved two trackers from twenty murderous hulks?" Liam asked.

He'd insisted on walking ahead of Eilidh, leading her nowhere in particular as far as she could tell. Every now and then he would call back to her over his shoulder to recount some tale of his bravery and courage. With each entry into his verbal journey of achievements, Eilidh lost more and more respect for his credibility. She started to wonder if the trackers had in fact saved Liam in the fight that he'd now referenced for the third time.

"You told me about saving the trackers first from a group of eight, and then twelve hulks, Thorn," she said with a roll of her eyes.

Why, oh, why had she agreed to his help? Well, because no one else was around and the trackers both had business elsewhere. Also, seeing that dark, shimmering form come out of that firbolg had left her a bit uneasy. What had the nuathreen called it? His darkness? Eilidh could see where the name came from. Just thinking about it sent shivers down her spine.

Liam continued to prattle on about the fight from thirty minutes ago as if it was a historic and well-documented moment of fame for him. All Eilidh focused on was trying to place his accent. He was obviously from the south of Andua, most likely a big city like Casuuld. In ancient times it was a Thandaran fortress, but like the rest of that great empire, the only reminder of the occupation was a ruined fort. She didn't know much more about the place, because she'd never been farther south than Terlgow, but the stories of debauchery her brothers shared indicated the heathens there didn't care much for Ghrian.

Eilidh prayed that Liam would run them into some more Anduain folk to join their cause. She didn't think that she could handle much more of this man one-on-one. Also, the one tracker's warning still resounded loudly in her head. Don't let Liam get her killed. Perhaps easier said than done.

Ruaidhri spoke of great accomplishments, but Eilidh had seen him perform plenty of worthy feats to prove his valor. This Thorn just spoke and spoke and spoke. In all the stories told of fearless Thorns executing dangerous missions behind enemy lines, no one had ever mentioned they couldn't just shut up about those same missions afterwards.

"Please help me survive this man, Ruaidhri," she whispered quietly.

"What was that, Eilidh?" Liam called back.

How had he heard that?

"I was just muttering to myself, Thorn."

And this title business really irked Eilidh. He called her by name, yet insisted that she refer to him as Thorn, as if to constantly remind her of his profession. She got it alright. Liam was a cocky bastard who needed constant affirmation from those around him. Eilidh may not have been the greatest warrior or the best healer, but she had enough going on between her ears to see insecurity staring her in the face.

And that poor firbolg. The trainee had fallen in combat and his oblivious trainer had just stood over him. What if the firbolg's soul had actually passed on? What if Eilidh hadn't come at that exact moment to rescue him? It had taken every ounce of her power to retrieve his receding soul. She'd never done anything like it before, reaching deep inside the wounds of an injured ally to convince their spirit not to flee, not yet. She'd healed her own injuries in the past and once or twice fixed up a moderate cut or bruise on Ruaidhri, but she had no experience with fatal wounds.

Well, now she certainly did. The ordeal had left her physically exhausted, but at the same time had energized her spiritually. She had saved someone's life! How could her brothers remain unimpressed now? They'd never brought someone back from the brink of the deep abyss, she'd bet.

This Thorn definitely hadn't. No, Liam wouldn't have even deigned to carry his dead trainee back to the nearest rebirth stone. He would have done exactly what he did with the living Brian: pass him off to the trackers. Eilidh was sure that dragging Brian's body back up to the surface to reunite it with its soul would be far beneath Liam's deluded sense of grandeur and importance.

Even when she totally ignored his incessant storytelling, thoughts about him irritated the fire out of her. And the vain son of a bitch kept flexing and admiring his bare arms. She hadn't seen many Thorns before, but the regular soldiers she'd run into always wore some kind of arm protection, at least on their forearms if nothing else. This man wore only a black, sleeveless bark-skin hauberk, with matching bark-skin leggings and leather boots. On his back hung an impossibly black cloak that attached around his neck with interlocking thorny vines made of silver. The contrast between his attire and his pale arms was striking, and his intricate tattoos would've been intriguing if not for his total lack of amiability.

As they walked down yet another unfamiliar corridor, Eilidh saw a trickle of water forcing its way out from between two large bricks in the wall to her left. She didn't bother telling Mister Wonderful that she'd stopped to investigate. He would work it out soon enough. Or maybe he wouldn't. She didn't care at this point.

Yes, as she suspected, the water flowed down to the tunnel floor and then proceeded to carve a narrow canal in the same direction that Liam now walked. He was taking her deeper into the caverns, not up to the surface. Eilidh sat on her haunches, contemplating his actions. Either he thought he was heading towards the surface and was just incompetent, or he knew fine well that they were not heading to the surface and had an agenda of his own.

Eilidh looked up and down the tight corridor. She was alone with this man. Could he be luring her deep down to some secluded spot where he could do with her as he pleased? Eilidh had been around long enough to hear the terrible stories that circulated. Ruaidhri had explained to her in grave detail the consequences of falling into the hands of the Bergsbor or Calderans. She'd never heard of such atrocities before that. Did this Liam fellow think he could take advantage of a naive young woman?

Well if so, he'd chosen the wrong woman to ensnare in his web.

She stood and fell back into step behind the Thorn, who still babbled on endlessly, unaware that she'd ever stopped. Eilidh let the distance between them increase just a little. Thorns were renowned for their ability to charge with great speed into battle. If the need arose, she wanted time to brace herself. After all, Eilidh had already been attacked by one other Anduain today, so proceeding cautiously seemed prudent.

The tunnel walls in front of Liam appeared to flex slightly as the floor rumbled underfoot. Liam stopped and drew both of his blades, the metal glowing faintly red. His head darted back and forth, checking for incoming danger, his face a little confused, as if he expected such a tremor to be caused by stampeding hulks. But Eilidh had felt this before. This was no stampede.

"Watch out, Liam!" she yelled. "The ceiling's coming down."

Liam looked straight up and saw what Eilidh had noticed. With the corridor quaking more and more violently now, a deep crevasse etched its way across the ceiling above Liam's head. As the first sections collapsed, Liam shot backwards towards the wall and launched himself off of it, flipping through the air. Eilidh looked on in disbelief as he completed at least four back-flips with arms outstretched, still clutching his shining blades.

He hit the ground *behind* Eilidh and executed a perfect landing. With his swords now up, facing Eilidh, and with his face displaying a creepy grin, Liam didn't look particularly welcoming. She raised her shield in his direction and fumbled to release her blade from its sheath on her belt.

Liam approached Eilidh now, causing her to take a step back as her sword refused to cooperate. She started to panic as the dark images from Ruaidhri's story filled her mind. A deep-seated fear gripped her and she gave up on the sword and held her shield with both hands, ready to strike at the Thorn with all her might. He stepped closer still, his eyes staring straight through Eilidh with bewildering detachment.

As Liam drew within a couple of feet of Eilidh, he sheathed his swords and continued on his predetermined path. She carefully stepped out of his way, still holding the shield up, not trusting the man at all. Liam didn't even seem to notice her, or her fear of him.

What was going on here?

223

Now drenched with the salty sweat of fright, Eilidh watched Liam walk away, towards the cave-in. Now she could understand. Sort of.

The ceiling had given way to the tremor and formed a loose stairway into a dark space above. Apparently the brush with death and the idea of adventuring in a new area had captivated Liam to the point of scaring Eilidh half to death.

"What is wrong with you, Liam?" she demanded angrily.

All of her panic and fear and tension unraveled verbally as she lowered her shield. He paused and turned, looking confused.

"What do you mean?" he asked.

Eilidh stomped towards him and pulled out her blade, which now had suddenly decided to comply with her demands. To his credit, Liam didn't even flinch when she held the point to his throat. Worse, he smiled.

"Alright, Eilidh, can you explain what is going on, please?"

"You're the one with some explaining to do, Liam," she said, emphasizing the use of his name instead of his title. "You scared me witless and then just walked away."

Now the smile dropped and Liam looked incredibly concerned.

"Scared you? When? Just now? You were supposed to be highly impressed with my aerial acrobatics, not scared."

Now it was Eilidh's turn to be dumbfounded.

"No, you twit! Not the flips or whatever you did. Pulling your swords and walking towards me with a devilish look on your face scared me," she explained while slowly withdrawing her sword from his neck.

"Devilish look, you say? Well, we Thorns do train in the use of many excellent facial expressions, but I didn't realize I had a devilish look in my repertoire. Thank you for noticing," he said, smiling again.

"This isn't funny, Liam. I thought you were going to do something . . . horrible."

Eilidh blushed at the word, but not nearly as much as Liam did. He turned his face away quickly, trying to hide his shame at catching her meaning.

Still not facing her, he said, "I don't know what made you think of me as such a barbarian."

Now Eilidh looked down at her feet, his insult making her feel worse and worse. A hand gently touched her face and lifted her eyes to his.

"I am a Thorn of Andua. I pledged a solemn oath to protect and defend all Anduain people. We're a proud nation and we proudly stand on our integrity and principles. You have nothing to fear from me."

Were her brothers not defenders of Andua also? Why had they never shown her such respect?

"I didn't mean to offend you, but consider my situation, Liam. I don't think erring on the side of caution was a mistake."

A grand smile filled his whole face.

"Right you are, Eilidh. I appreciate your paranoia. 'Kill first and ask questions later' has always been my motto."

Eilidh frowned and looked away, once again a little bit confused by the Thorn's words. At least she was back to thinking the man was only crazy and not a vile predator.

"Well, let's head up through this gap in the ceiling. I do believe we now have an impromptu passage into the tunnel above. This is very exciting," he exclaimed as he bounded up the pile of rubble.

Eilidh shook her head at his sudden enthusiasm and tried to follow his path. His manic and careless approach to climbing sent small rockslides and debris flying down towards Eilidh. Twice she lost her footing and slid back a few feet, prompting a scream at least once. Okay, maybe twice.

The total climb was only thirty feet, and Eilidh quickly noticed a decrease in the number of stones hurtling towards her. Obviously Liam had already made it to the top of the pile. The climb drained the strength from Eilidh's muscles, hindering her progress. After what seemed like an eternity, she finally looked up and saw Liam standing just above her. Eilidh buckled down and dragged her ungainly armor through the last few lunges and collapsed on the floor at Liam's feet, which still stood on the pile of rocks and not on the new tunnel's floor.

Why hadn't he stepped into the tunnel yet?

In between breaths she sputtered, "Liam, I know that we just had a nice moment downstairs, and I don't really want to put a damper on that, but why didn't you help me up here?"

"Shut up, girl. And don't even think about moving."

This wasn't Liam's voice. This was a woman's voice, with a strong Anduain accent permeating each word. Fear infiltrated Eilidh's mind again. As instructed, she continued to hold still, staring at Liam's unmoving boots. Why wasn't he doing anything? If he truly wanted to impress her, now was definitely a good time to start.

Ruaidhri, why am I having such poor luck with my own people today?

Chapter 7

Two Anduain women stood in frozen awe as the large tunnel before them pitched and rolled like a ship battered in stormy seas. The tremors raged, spilling torches from the walls, punching cracks into the tall ceiling. One of the women gripped the hilt of a small, sheathed sword, seeking comfort in the grooves of the leather wrap. Her companion stood tall, gaining strength from the presence of the wolf at her side. She gently stroked the tense animal's bristling fur, assuring him that they were fine.

And as suddenly as the violent motion had started, the rumbling faded, leaving the walls intact, but crumbling slowly. A dusty breeze flowed through the expansive passageway, creating the only audible sound.

The women stood stalk-still, wide-eyed and shocked by Ghrian's fury. They'd both spent years studying the ways of nature, honing their skills by harnessing the Tree's deep magic, but never had they witnessed such raw power firsthand. Who could command such destruction other than the Sun Goddess herself?

Torches lay scattered across the tunnel floor now, burning their seemingly unquenchable flames, magically lit by the spells of Teekwood Caverns' early explorers. The rows of lights formed a walkway of fire, leading to a wide, dark spot in the ground. Even after taking just a few steps towards the spot, both women could see the large hole in the tile floor ahead. They continued forward slowly, curious, but guarded.

And both stopped in a heartbeat as a head appeared from the depths of the collapse. The bare head continued on its upward journey as an armored body and legs also rose from the gloom. Now was no time for hesitation.

"Stop right there," called out the first woman.

The newly arrived, much unwanted guest halted, facing away from them.

"And don't turn around, or I will kill you where you stand," she added.

Following the instructions well, the intruder resembled a statue. In the illumination of the fallen torches, another form appeared, this one lying down at the feet of the first. Red, flowing hair protruded from under a well-worn dome helmet. From the redhead, a female voice spoke in the Anduain tongue, but the two watching women had no patience even for their own kind today, and with good reason.

"Shut up, girl. And don't even think about moving," said the first woman. The wolf tamer had no issue allowing her companion to handle the talking for now.

The giant wolf accompanying the two women paced uneasily around them, its protective instincts peaking hyperactively. Kearney had a habit of guarding the sisters, and not just during cave-ins.

Once he'd bitten a chunk out of an overly forward male suitor who could now only sit on one cheek.

No matter where he moved in the tunnel, the wolf always kept an eye on the two newcomers, just as the sisters did. In the last few hours they'd learned to trust no one. Never before had they been attacked by other Anduains seemingly working in conjunction with the enemy, but there was apparently a first time for everything. One of the sisters still unconsciously poked at a fresh cut in her dark green armor, just over her left elbow. Even a slightly more powerful blow would've sheared her arm clean off.

"Shela, you're doing it again," said the other sister, still facing their newly encountered allies.

"So what?" Shela snapped, continuing to touch the rough edges of the damaged bark-skin sleeve. "You didn't just about lose an arm back there."

"Be nice, sister. If I recall correctly, I'm the one who prevented you from losing more than an arm."

Shela's glare could have melted stone. Fionn looked back with all the patience of an elder sibling.

"And if I recall correctly, I'm the one who got us away from that horde of traitors," Shela pointed out.

The woman lying on the ground coughed and both sisters snapped to attention. Shela started to shout for the woman to keep quiet, but stopped short. The man who'd stood next to the prostrate woman had disappeared. Fionn took a step back cautiously. If this man commanded knowledge in the ways of concealment, he could easily sneak up on them while they bickered.

"We might have a problem here," Fionn whispered.

Kearney picked up on his master's unease and stepped in front of her, sniffing the air menacingly, itching for a fight. Unfortunately, Shela doubted that even Kearney's acute senses could uncover a skilled master of hiding. Those damned tricksters could blend in anywhere and then strike without warning.

But, as usual, Shela didn't share her sister's concern.

"He can try whatever he wants. He won't be able to kill us."

Another cough resonated from the hole in the floor, where the girl, who the sisters had already identified as an Anduain like themselves, still lay flat. This cough sounded noticeably deeper than the last. Fionn and Shela exchanged a quick glance. Shela smiled and then slowly edged forward towards the opening in the ground. She stopped when Fionn hissed at her.

"If they were enemies, they wouldn't have stopped at the sight of two druids. We're hardly an imposing sight," Shela whispered adamantly, knowing their silver cloaks announced their identity to anyone who cared to notice.

In truth, neither of them had much combat training. Even Shela's short sword was just for show, a gift from her brother. Druids primarily studied the light magic of Ghrian, and during times of war they only fulfilled support roles for King Darren's soldiers. It was a difficult life, trying to keep those alive who seemed so desperate to die famously in battle.

"So?"

Shela shook her head in exasperation, her shoulder-length brown hair emphasizing the movement.

"So it means that they're friendly. And, if I'm not mistaken, I do believe my last comment upset that man," Shela explained quietly.

"Why's that?" Fionn asked.

"Just watch," Shela replied with a smile as she stepped towards the hole. Louder now, she said, "Sister, obviously the man has abandoned this girl, running for fear of the valiant and imposing duo before him."

Another deep cough flew out of the hole, a little angrier than the first. Shela stifled a laugh, and now Fionn understood the game. Shela was stepping on someone's pride. Fionn motioned for Kearney to stay put and then joined her sister, both very close to the hole now.

"That's right. He must be a very weak man and definitely not a warrior of any kind," Fionn said.

"A heinous lie," someone grumbled quietly inside the hole. "I'm the most valiant and superb Thorn ever!"

The whisper was followed by yet another cough in a bizarre attempt to cover up the involuntary rebuttal of slanderous words. The sisters doubled over laughing, having trodden on this poor man's ego to their satisfaction. The girl lying on the floor next to them now turned over and sat up, staring at the pair with a smile on her face. Apparently she knew the game as well.

Now the man leapt out of the hole and landed behind them, swords drawn. All three women regarded him with shock, not expecting such hostility. Kearney apparently had anticipated such a move and shot out from the shadows, tackling the man from behind. The red blades clanged across the floor as the man lay splayed out underneath the weight of the great black wolf. The animal's growling did little to silence the man's instant protests.

"Get this beast off of me!" he exclaimed. "I have done nothing wrong here. You have tarnished my good name with your lies!"

"It would appear that your dog has caught a mighty Thorn for dinner. Isn't that nice?" Shela said to her sister, grinning widely.

Thorns had a reputation for oversized and easily injured egos, a fact that Shela frequently enjoyed manipulating. She took great pleasure from the emotional discomfort of others, something most druids couldn't fathom. A heavily light-attuned druid such as Fionn could enjoy a good giggle, but any kind of harm to an ally moved them deeply, even if it was just the harm of embarrassment. Having said that, certain people, such as overzealous Thorns, deserved a good ribbing every now and then.

"Let him up, please," came a small voice from behind the sisters.

They turned to see a petite, redheaded soldier, and judging from her cheap and tattered equipment, not a very good one at that. Fionn whistled at Kearney, who quickly returned to her side, keeping his eyes on the befuddled Thorn.

"What are you doing with this blowhard, girl?" demanded Shela in her characteristic I-do-not-like-you-so-now-I-will-interrogate-you voice.

The tone seemed to surprise the young woman. She glanced at her recovering friend, who now was sheepishly retrieving his weapons. Without responding to the question, she got up and joined her companion. Shela just rolled her eyes.

"I asked you a question, dear," she said, and not nicely.

The girl continued to tend to her friend and answered without looking up at Shela.

"I'm Eilidh, and I'm searching for my lost friend, Ruaidhri. We were separated in a cave-in earlier," Eilidh explained, gaining a little confidence from her proximity to the Thorn, Shela sensed. The young woman looked over and continued, "This is Liam, a great Thorn who has chosen to help me find Ruaidhri."

Shela stifled a giggle as Liam's face turned red. This interesting encounter had taught Shela a lot about this man in a very short space of time. Obviously he didn't like his skills to be questioned, yet the affirmation from this pretty redhead made him blush. And from what Shela could tell, this naïve girl had no idea what effect she had on the man. She had a lot to learn about a lot of things from the looks of it.

Fionn jabbed Shela's side, probably in hopes of keeping her mouth in check. Fionn probably thought this was a cute love triangle of sorts, but she knew what Shela would think of such silliness. At the sound of Shela's patronizing laugh, Liam's face creased into a gallant smile and the red dissolved immediately.

"And what, may I ask, are you two doing here, druids of Andua? Taking a little break from your assignment to the king's army?" he asked pleasantly.

"Our rotation is over for now. We're on a mission of our own and encountered some opposition that decided to chase us for an age through these damn tunnels," Shela explained. "We ended up right here as the floor caved in, and then you two appeared."

Eilidh asked, "What is your mission?"

The sisters looked at each other. Communication didn't need words for the twins. Shela was mere hours younger than Fionn, but even from that moment, their mother knew that Shela would be the headstrong one.

"You weren't happy to be forced from the womb, my dear child," their mother would say. "Eventually the midwife resigned herself to waiting for you to come out in your own time. And that you did."

In Shela's mind, that first event summed her up perfectly to this day.

But now she nodded to Fionn, allowing the elder sibling to explain their situation. A grave countenance fell upon Fionn as she contemplated the dire business that had driven them into the caverns. Not every day did children search for the hope that their own father so desperately needed. Their failure to locate his prized possession could kill him, if the black depths of depression had not already claimed his fading life in their absence.

Shela could see the burden of their brother's disappearance pressing down on Fionn's spirit, physically compressing her body, it seemed. A gentle hand on the shoulder snapped away the miry daze clouding Fionn's eyes.

Watching them intently, Eilidh's gaze showed compassion beyond her knowledge. Fionn's shrunken appearance alone had moved the younger woman, who'd been but a girl only moments ago. Shela wondered if she had a druidic inkling or two.

Fionn opened her mouth to speak, but barely got one word out before Kearney growled deeply beside her. Her eyes followed his towards the darkness from where they had come, and her hand found his thick, black fur bristling sharply. The other three companions looked around, but saw and heard nothing.

"What is it?" asked Shela, a scowl preemptively forming on her face.

"They've found us."

Eilidh looked confused.

"Who's found us?" she asked.

Shela stepped forward and stared back up the immense tunnel. Now she could hear the faint cries and yelps approaching from an unseen passageway. The echoes haunted the hallway, prickling Shela's skin. She flexed her fingers, preparing for battle.

"*They* have found us," she growled.

Fionn rolled her shoulders under the weight of her green scale armor and then popped her neck to the left. They could try to escape down into the hole in the floor, but running away again was not really an option to either sister. Confrontation was inevitable.

So they would fight.

Chapter 8

T he screams and shouts resounded throughout the wide hallway, bombarding the four Anduains from seemingly all directions. The figures tensed as the cacophony reached its boiling point, flooding the expansive space with dread-inspiring noise. No enemies had rushed from the many side corridors spewing off of the main passageway, but their loud battle cries told that confrontation was imminent.

Eilidh looked at her three companions, four if she included the terrifying wolf. Ready for a fight, the large animal resembled a creature of nightmares, with enormous bared teeth snapping ferociously, claws like obsidian razors, and shoulder muscles bunched and twisted like thick ropes of iron. Despite knowing better, Eilidh took a step back, eyes wide and fixed on the seething furry fury.

"Don't worry about Kearney," Fionn said with the same calm anger that Eilidh recognized from being quietly scalded by her own father. The polite rage always frightened her the most.

"He's on our side," added Shela.

Shela stood holding no weapon other than visible obstinacy, but her armor was magnificent. In fact, Eilidh now noticed that all three human allies had similarly expensive-looking armor. She also shamefully noted that she didn't look the part at all, standing next to three confident warriors all decked out well beyond her means. Shela looked especially impressive, sporting figure-hugging, dark green bark-skin armor, whereas her sister had opted for heavier, scale armor that hung over a leather jerkin. Both druids wore silver cloaks, denoting their devotion to the Tree of Rebirth, whose bark was said to glow silver in the torchlight under Arbreldin. In the firelight of this tunnel, the tree emblem in the center of Fionn's cloak swayed gently, while Shela's tree seemed to suffer from swirling gales. The fantastic animations merely reinforced Eilidh's sense of inadequacy.

Eilidh's head barely had a chance to hang low when a gentle hand raised her face. Liam smiled at her, apparently oblivious to the sounds of chaos swiftly approaching. With a wink, he released her face and turned to address all three women.

"Hit me," he demanded.

Confused, Eilidh glanced over at the other two women. To her increased befuddlement, they both approached Liam, laid hands on him, and then chanted spells Eilidh didn't quite recognize. He closed his eyes and leaned his head back peacefully as the druids' magic flowed visibly across his body.

The chanting ceased, and Fionn walked towards Eilidh. When she hesitated at the druid's touch, Fionn smiled.

"Don't worry," she said. "The spell bolsters your body for a short time, granting you Ghrian's strength and agility temporarily."

Eilidh acquiesced and Fionn formulated the spell. Instantly, the Sun Goddess' power rushed through her entire being. She felt invincible, like she could drive a fist through a castle wall without straining. Never had she experienced anything like it, the extreme power and quickness that accompanied the druid's magic.

"The hounds of destruction are almost upon us," Liam began quite suddenly, and dramatically. He strutted back and forth before them, an arrogant swagger in his step. "Bard and druid, take up positions behind these pillars jutting out from the walls on either side of the tunnel. Eilidh, take a cover position behind the next pillar down, towards the approach of these dastardly devils. Wait for my signal, and then support me while I defeat all opposition."

Eilidh could tell that Shela wasn't used to taking orders. Her body was stiff as a board and her clenched fists showed bright white knuckles. Before the vengeful words could start, Fionn interrupted her.

"Sounds like a plan," she stated and then jogged to her position.

"Bard?" Shela growled. "I'm not some tavern-trawling, drunken lout struggling over some strings—"

"Stow it," Fionn snapped. "There's no time."

Shela glared at her sister, but Fionn just motioned for her to move over to the other pillar, against the opposite wall. Not happy, Shela stomped ungracefully to her place. Eilidh watched with worry, wondering why Fionn had agreed so easily to a plan that her sister disagreed with. Liam now stood in the middle of the tunnel, close to where Eilidh was supposed to be. The noisy din had increased in intensity once more, and Fionn had to shout to be heard.

"Eilidh, we don't have time to argue about this. Just get in position and do your best," she yelled from the shadows.

After hustling to her hiding spot, Eilidh peeked out to see Liam standing in the middle of the tunnel, all alone. His deep black cloak covered his lowered head and draped completely around his body, hiding his tattooed arms. In a slightly darker place, Eilidh could've easily walked right past the Thorn without even noticing him, but the torches lining the floor illuminated him eerily. Surely he knew that the enemy would see him? Was this just another foolhardy Thorn, or could he really save them all?

Ruaidhri, would you do this?

Her reverie ended abruptly as the hoots and cries suddenly ceased all around her. Another peek around the pillar revealed no enemies, but Liam remained as a statue. Sweat formed under Eilidh's ill-fitting helmet and ran in cold trickles down her neck, soaking the linens under her hideously adorned armor. A shiver gripped her as a cool draft of air kissed her exposed cheeks.

The silence felt like an unreachable itch, driving her mad with impatience. She feared the fierce enemy that threatened them, but she shook with the anticipation of letting her sword and shield speak freely amongst them. The shivering was constant now, the cool breeze assaulting the cracks and joints in her cheap armor.

She dared another look from her hiding spot and jumped back with her hand muffling a cry of surprise. At least eight foes had appeared silently in the hallway and were rushing noiselessly towards the isolated Liam. The confidence of having the druids' spells enhancing her combat abilities waned. Hardly daring to move, Eilidh forced her eyes to keep watch over Liam, anxiously awaiting his signal.

I can't do this, Ruaidhri. I can't do this. I'm not ready to die.

What was the signal? Liam had never said! How would she know when to attack? The questions shot through her mind, diverting her fearful worries into a lower priority. Now she concentrated on the mental task list that automatically materialized in her head. She focused on trying to create a magical earth barrier for Liam. With a few outlandishly dexterous movements of her hands, she drew on the power of the ground around her. Never had her hands moved so fluidly, so quickly, so accurately. Confidence welled up once more. The power of nature flowed through her body and radiated out to the ground around Liam.

Time slowed to a grinding halt. The enemies' faces held grim and wicked expressions, lit by the flickering of the flames on the tunnel floor. Eilidh steeled herself, her hands fervently willing the dirt to form Liam's defense, as it had done for her previously.

Now only a few strides separated the charging foes and the motionless Liam. Eilidh braced herself, fearing the worst as the pebbles at Liam's feet merely quivered under her intense concentration.

Liam is paralyzed with fear, and I can't make a wall to protect him.

A havtrol reached Liam first and hefted a monstrous hammer above its head. As the fire-engulfed head of the hammer began its downward stroke towards Liam's skull, his cloak billowed out away from his body and his hands produced his signature red blades.

Eilidh regarded the scene in awe as Liam's body twisted to avoid the enemy's blow, while he also managed to yell, "I'm flyin' in!"

The flaming hammer struck the floor with force enough to smash tiles and send a shockwave under Eilidh's boots. Through the fiery dust cloud created by the crushing weight of the hammer, she could make out a whirlwind of fury darting around shadowy enemies, unleashing disaster upon them. The sight froze her in place, but not with fear. It was like nothing she'd ever seen before, watching Liam dance through the blades and hammers of the enemy, lashing out elegant vengeance at will.

"That was the signal, idiot!" yelled a voice from behind.

Eilidh turned to see Shela rushing past her, bounding like a deer over the flaming torches, her silver cloak flowing out behind her. A single word from the druid's mouth had Eilidh's heart pounding uncontrollably and her muscles begging for use. Fionn stood in the middle of the tunnel, maintaining a safe distance as she chanted the healing spells keeping Liam seemingly immune to the crushing blows he sustained in his fighting. Old tales spoke of druids who could project their healing magic through the earth to nearby allies, but Eilidh had never seen such a thing in person.

Eilidh felt invigorated to a whole new level. She darted out from concealment and collided with a tall firbolg who must've been charging towards Fionn, trying to interrupt her healing spells. The pair crashed to the ground, but the veteran firbolg was on his feet in an instant, now eyeing the kill on the sprawled form of Eilidh. She looked up and saw the bemused look in his eyes as he made a move towards her.

The thought that a firbolg should never attack another Anduain didn't even enter Eilidh's mind. Her encounter with the elf earlier had thrown all preconceived notions of friend and foe to the wind. Now she scrambled backwards, scooting on her behind, trying to pull up her shield and sword to defend herself. If she took the time to stand in her clumsy armor, she would be struck down. The firbolg's swagger reminded her of Liam.

Well, not just like Liam. Liam didn't want to kill his own countrymen.

Before he got in range to swing, thick tree roots shot out through cracks in the floor and entwined themselves around the firbolg's thick legs. Eilidh quickly gained her feet while she watched the tall enemy fumble and struggle with the constricting vines.

Had she summoned these roots?

"He'll be stuck for a while. Go help Liam!" Fionn called from behind.

Apparently not.

The firbolg futilely struck out towards Eilidh as she ran past. She flinched instinctively, but kept moving, anxious to help out.

The scene before her was nothing less than absolute chaos. She'd never been involved in such a large fight before. Her hesitation held her feet in place, not quite sure what to do, how to help. Liam still moved ferociously and precisely around three enemies angrily wielding large weapons. Their inability to bring the man down fed their fury.

One roared inhumanly and rushed at Liam's exposed back. Eilidh jerked slightly as she felt an outpouring of magic. A dirt wall shot up behind Liam, thwarting his attacker long enough for Liam to turn and slash through the side of the man's armor. Eilidh staggered for a moment, still reeling from extending her power across such a distance. She hadn't even consciously thought to do it. It just happened.

Beyond the melee in front of her, Kearney pounced on a short, stout dwarf. The dwarf crashed to the ground and struggled feverishly with the much larger wolf.

Behind the raging wolf, a man appeared from the shadows and cast a spell that froze Kearney like a stone, jaws held agape in ferocity. The same man then chanted a spell that appeared to help the dwarf recover, because the next thing Eilidh knew, the sneering dwarf had broken free and called up a huge pile of rocks to unceremoniously dump on top of the helpless wolf. After being stunned, Kearney struggled frantically, but he couldn't budge the rocks with his broken body.

Shela rushed past in front of Eilidh with an enemy in tow. The long spear in the man's grip slashed endlessly at Shela's feet as she deftly leapt through the fallen flames and bounced off piles of rubble. The druid jumped high and landed with a great downward outtake of breath that burst a gust of wind in all directions, pushing her pursuer back a few paces as she started running again.

"Do something!" Shela yelped while dodging yet another attack from her assailant.

Shame cast a dark shadow over Eilidh. She'd been watching her companions fight on her behalf while she just looked on in confusion. Doing anything surely outweighed doing nothing at all. Her failure to act could've doomed them all.

Eilidh bodily tackled the man, who'd been totally oblivious to her presence. He went down hard with a grunt, and before he could recover, Eilidh drove the bottom edge of her shield solidly into the back of his head, cracking his face down onto the dirty tiles. Fueled by soaring adrenaline, she jumped up and rushed to Liam's aid, but her short sword couldn't even penetrate the exposed flanks of her enemies. Their armor rejected her blade as if it was a long piece of grass.

Liam poked his head out of the fray while still parrying the rain of blows effortlessly. "Go and get after that Calderan priest in the back. He's keeping these ruffians alive, and believe it or not, I cannot do this all day."

His smile worried Eilidh a little. Who could smile at a time like this?

She pressed on through the fight and found what she could only assume was a Calderan, based on his emblazoned jerkin. Despite the long war between Andua and Caldera, she'd never seen a Calderan in person, but she'd heard they put symbols on their armor and shields to represent their home region within Caldera.

This one stood perfectly still, with his eyes closed. Seeing her opportunity to prove herself, she charged and drew back her sword. Before she could strike the desired blow, a strong hand grabbed her wrist from behind. Eilidh twisted around and drove a knee into the gut of her attacker.

Shela gasped and let go of Eilidh's arm.

"I am so sorry, Shela," Eilidh called out, extending a hand to the woman.

Through wheezes, Shela slapped her hand away and replied, "Not now. Don't hit that priest. I put him to sleep. Go help Liam."

Thoroughly confused at being tossed from one end of the fight to the other, Eilidh sprinted back to Liam's side. With the Calderan's healing powers subdued, Liam had slain two of his opponents, leaving only the great havtrol standing, his fiery hammer casting wicked shadows as it sliced through the air in deadly arcs. Not taking his eyes from his most dangerous foe, Liam yelled for Eilidh to go take care of the nuathreen.

"What nuathreen?" she yelled back, feeling more useless than ever. Why wouldn't her own allies let her fight?

Shela materialized next to them both and called out, "I think he's on our side. He killed that dwarf, and he's chasing down that Movrisian."

These words flooded into the growing discombobulated mess within Eilidh's head. What nuathreen? What Movrisian? What *was* a Movrisian?

She scanned around and indeed saw the dwarf lying motionless, its skin charred black. Movement out of the corner of her eye attracted her attention, and she turned in time to see a dark-skinned man appear from behind a pillar and eye her intensely as he started drawing on unholy power, his hands glowing pink and red.

Eilidh ran towards the man, but knew that she could never reach her foe in time to stop his magic. She braced herself as his hands completed their motion. Eilidh squeezed her eyes shut, expecting the next few moments to hurt. A lot.

But she felt nothing.

She opened her eyes and saw the man sprawled before her, his staff strewn in smoking pieces around the lifeless body. Now disconcerted, Eilidh looked around, swiveling her head, trying to establish what had just happened. Why was she still alive?

Then she saw the small nuathreen appear from the shadows behind the dead man. The nuathreen's staff stood much taller than he did, and he radiated authority as he strode past her without even a glance. Eilidh watched in awe as the diminutive spell-caster created spheres of destructive light in his small hand and then launched the crackling spheres towards his enemies.

In short order, the powerful nuathreen dispatched the sleeping priest and the tangled firbolg. He then loomed over the man that Eilidh had failed to finish off in her hurry to help Liam. The man was on his hands and knees now, slowly getting to his feet. As the man's hand reached out for his spear, the nuathreen drew back his grey cloak over his shoulders, revealing a black robe underneath.

Bright white traces of light suddenly radiated all over the black robe, startling Eilidh in their intensity. The traces strobed and flashed chaotically, and in the uneven light, Eilidh caught glimpses of the spearman's face growing more and more enraged. He grabbed up his spear and leapt towards the nuathreen, but then explosive lightning burst out between them. The nuathreen channeled the lightning into the screaming human for a number of seconds before relenting. The entire tunnel faded to silent black in the aftermath of the dazzling display of Ghrian's raw power.

Eilidh's eyes adjusted slowly, and as horrified as she was at the spearman's death, she ignored his burned corpse and followed everyone's gaze towards the only living enemy remaining: the havtrol who still circled Liam in a terrible fury.

The Anduains closed in around the havtrol, who started to back up, taking a defensive stance. In a move displaying uncanny quickness for such a large being, the havtrol sheathed its enormous hammer and produced a shield the size of a cottage door. In its other hand glowed a smaller version of the larger hammer. It beat on the shield and roared furiously at the approaching Anduains.

A sharp whistle caught everyone's attention. Eilidh watched as Liam motioned with his hand for them to back off, to stay put. She hesitated, watching the others for a reaction. They all nodded and stopped, including their new companion, the nuathreen lightning mage. Kearney continued to growl from his master's side, but remained glued in place, unable to strike without Fionn's approval.

Eilidh edged closer to Fionn and drew a snap from the wolf. After emitting an awkward cough, trying to hide her overt flinch at the animal's aggression, Eilidh whispered to Fionn, "Why aren't we helping him?"

Fionn didn't break her gaze from the battle waiting to start, but she responded, "We don't interrupt duels, Eilidh. Just watch."

Aghast, Eilidh whispered back, "Just watch? But what if the havtrol wins?"

Now Shela joined the conversation and looked at Eilidh gravely.

"If the havtrol wins, we will reward it with a slow, painful death."

Chapter 9

S hela watched the duelers strafe each other, both searching for a solid opportunity to strike. The havtrol, despite being short for its kind, stood over a head taller than Liam, who was actually quite tall for a human. The armor of both combatants was dyed a deep black, and neither wore a helm of any kind. A ring of hair circled around the flat, bald area on top of the havtrol's head, while Liam possessed a light brown mane that drifted gracefully with each movement of his head. Shela observed the two shadowy forms shifting back and forth in the dim light, watching them edge closer and then away, immersed in the tide of battle. The deadly beauty of their seemingly choreographed movements captivated her.

Regarding the well-matched fighters vying for position disturbed an old and well-known disappointment for Shela. The Tree of Rebirth chose the path for druids following Ghrian's teachings, and rarely did the Tree bestow the exact same path to two individuals. As such, Shela was greatly skilled in the magical arts of voice and song, whereas Fionn commanded more traditional healing skills. Some called Shela a music druid, or worse, a bard, but music was far too vague of a description. Her true power resonated in her voice. With a sharp word, she could energize all allies around her, at least for a short time. When not running for her life, she could force even large numbers of the enemy into deep sleep with a gentle, yet powerful lullaby.

These support functions were all well and good, but where was the glory in them? She spent most of her time in fights just trying not to get killed.

The havtrol of Bergmark darted forward, its shield blocking a cross cut from Liam. The Bergsbor's great hammer swung from out wide, barely missing Liam's exposed thigh. The havtrol's reach advantage required the lithe Thorn to evade perfectly in order to draw in close enough to attack. Liam moved easily and swiftly, but had a hard time getting either of his blades past the berserker's great shield.

Shela continued to watch, but her thoughts drifted. What could *she* do to kill those who deserved her vengeance? Yell at them melodically?

All she'd ever wanted was to swing a weapon as Liam did so effortlessly. Her songs inspired others to fight, but did little to help her own awkwardness with a blade. In battle, Shela's job consisted of suppressing and distracting the enemy while her allies did all of the real work, the rewarding work.

Shela looked at her sister, deep in hushed conversation with the completely helpless redhead they'd picked up. How could Fionn stand it, being in the backlines of every fight, keeping others alive, but never dealing out her own wrath? In truth, Shela's twin sister had never been quick to anger. The Tree had dealt *that* card to Shela, her short fuse well-known in their hometown of Rubha.

Perhaps helping others gave Fionn all the reward that she needed, but Shela wanted more. She had always wanted more, wanted to not be so vulnerable by herself. Relying on others was a sign of great weakness.

After a quick feint to the havtrol's left, Liam drove forward with both swords flashing straight ahead, but the Bergsbor countered brilliantly, not biting on the fake. The enormous shield thrust straight down, pinning one of Liam's red blades to the ground. Shela heard Eilidh gasp. The havtrol's other hand brought the hammer down onto the top of Liam's left shoulder with a sickening thump, flattening him.

With a deft lunge, the Bergsbor's foot shot out towards Liam's injured shoulder, but the Thorn had sensed the move and rolled away to his right. The havtrol's stomp echoed in the quiet hallway and left a deep imprint in the stone floor. Now on his feet, Liam stood with his left arm hanging limp, yet still his left hand gripped his sword. The havtrol grunted and squared up against Liam again.

Now Shela saw, as she had done many times in the past, her reason for being. She could easily help Liam defeat the berserker, if she so desired. Or in this case, if Liam so desired, but the Thorns were a stubborn crew who were far too proud to back out of a losing battle. With a few words and a wave of her hand, she could heal his broken shoulder. Not as efficiently as Fionn, but she *could* do it. She wouldn't, though. She had to respect the rules of the duel.

Looking to her sister, Shela saw Fionn fidgeting listlessly with Kearney's fur, grinding her fingers into the animal's tough hide. The wolf growled deeply and continuously at an incredibly low note, the sound reverberating in Shela's bones. Both Fionn and the wolf desperately wanted to intercede. Druids typically couldn't stand the sight of a brother or sister dying in combat, and Fionn was no exception.

The havtrol circled Liam, sensing the end to be near, but maintaining a safe distance to let the pain seep into the Anduain's core, to destabilize the still dangerous Thorn. Before the havtrol could maneuver to stop him, Liam sheathed his right sword and produced a glass vial from his belt. Shela recognized the potion as Liam chugged the fluid down in a single gulp. Aggravated to no end, the havtrol rushed forward, hammer reaching to pummel him, but the potion had worked its magic quickly, returning the feeling to Liam's deadened arm. Now the two struggled in their most intense exchange of blows yet, clashing weapons and smashing armor in a whirlwind of movement. Liam felt no pain now, but if he lived through the next few minutes, that shoulder would scream with the fury of a thousand banshees.

And the Thorn would gladly accept that agony if the sweet taste of victory followed close on its heels. Men like Liam lusted after the recognition and fame of a battle won, something Shela could only envy in vain.

The fiery hammer flew down from high above the havtrol's head, intent on smashing Liam's, but he raised both blades in a cross

254

to catch the blow. The force of the collision dropped Liam to one knee, but with a twist of his wrists, the havtrol's weapon flew free and dashed against the tiled floor. With a great roar, the havtrol smashed forward with its shield and knocked Liam onto his back. While Liam regained his footing, the berserker produced its two-handed hammer once more.

Barely on his feet, Liam had no way to block the incoming blow. Eilidh screamed in warning, but her cry only distracted Liam more. The fiery hammer struck him square in the chest and sent him flying down the hallway. He careened into the wall and lay in a crumpled pile at the far end of the tunnel, away from his allies.

If the havtrol wins, we will reward it with a slow, painful death.

Those words were still true. Shela thought about them as the havtrol slowly, methodically approached Liam. Even with victory so close, the havtrol showed its extreme level of discipline, not rushing into any potential traps.

Well, if it wins, the nuathreen will have to kill it, because the rest of us can't.

Shela and Fionn, both lacking in combat skills, would never have come all the way to the caverns by themselves, but other matters had complicated their rescue effort. Their father was dying. Gower, once an honored soldier of Andua, was now succumbing to an incurable illness that had ravaged his once perfect body. He had insisted that his daughters seek out the fate of his only son, because he couldn't rest in death without knowing whether King Darren's mysterious errand had killed Gavin.

As the havtrol pulled up next to the battered and unconscious Thorn, Shela feared the worst. Time crawled by as the Bergsbor towered over Liam, hammer held high.

But then it lowered its weapon and looked to its left, ignoring Liam. As Shela still assumed the worst for the Thorn, Eilidh broke the solemn silence.

"What's it doing?"

Shela had no idea, but didn't respond to the girl's stupid question. It annoyed Shela to no end that even a novice like Eilidh could still do something that she never had: Kill an enemy of Andua.

With a great yell, the havtrol sprinted into a side passage leading from the main hallway. The Anduains all charged after it together, not sure whether to expect friend or foe approaching. When they reached the small passage, the sight shocked them.

The havtrol lay dead at the feet of a young female elf, dressed in the flashy robes of a wealthy mage. Shela had a hard time believing that such a young spell-caster could be so powerful, but then again, elves rarely showed their true age in their appearance. Before she could inquire about how the elf had managed to fell a mighty havtrol, the nuathreen stomped up to the elf in a tizzy, waving his tall staff in her face.

"What is wrong with you, Aelfraed? You just interrupted a duel!" he cried in a high-pitched voice.

"I saved that injured human, Bob, which is more than I can say that you did," replied the elf evenly.

"He told us not to help. That's the whole point of a duel," the nuathreen pointed out.

"That havtrol would have killed the human, and then what? Who would have killed the havtrol as retribution?" The elf paused before looking down her nose at Shela. "The bard, perhaps? Ha. I think not."

Bard?

Now Shela was not amused.

"Who do you think you are? Keep your opinions to yourself, elf."

The elf regarded Shela with the patronizing disdain that elves commanded so well.

"Hush, human."

Seething now, Shela stepped forward, but the nuathreen called Bob motioned her back.

"If he'd lost, I would've killed the havtrol, Aelfraed, and you know it," he said.

"I think not. You would have killed him already if you thought that you could," the elf responded.

Apparently the two spell-casters knew one another. Bob wielded the staff of a wraith, a mage loyal to the High Priestess, trained in Arbreldin to rein in wayward dominators who'd taken to abusing their immense powers for personal gain. Shela regarded Aelfraed more warily, suddenly suspecting she may in fact be a

257

dominator, a mage who could literally destroy an enemy's mind. But if the elf had indeed embraced the darker side of her arts and given in to mind-lust, Bob would've already executed her, or at the very least taken her soul hostage with his staff. In any case, Shela tired of watching the pointless argument. She looked around, instinctively scanning her surroundings for any potential threats. That was when she saw it. Or at least, she thought she saw it.

Yes! She definitely saw the tell-tale shimmery form of a magically concealed tracker creeping through the shadows of a dark recess of the tunnel. Another shape caught her eye and when she glanced towards it, she could've sworn that she saw the large head of a firbolg disappear around the far corner. Now she couldn't find the shadowy movements of the tracker, but she suspected that this elf hadn't slain the havtrol alone. Still ignoring the pair of bickering mages, Shela crouched down next to the dead havtrol to investigate.

And sure enough, Anduain arrows peppered the corpse.

Apparently a friendly tracker or two had helped kill the havtrol, sticking to the shadows to avoid detection. Shela had greatly doubted that even the greatest dominator could defeat a havtrol berserker like this so quickly one-on-one, but the broken arrows protruding from under the fallen havtrol confirmed that the elf had received some welcome assistance. Perhaps if the nuathreen could get over his pride for a few moments, he too would notice the evidence and cease the fruitless debate.

But why would our hidden allies not reveal themselves after the fight?

The question hung in her mind restlessly, seeking an answer that she couldn't yet provide. Shela stood, turned her back on the embattled mages, and instead headed back to where Liam now sat up against the far wall, eyes open, but without an arrogant smile plastered across his face. He actually looked concerned.

"Thank you for restoring me, Fionn," he said evenly. "But I had that havtrol exactly where I wanted him. That elf had no right to steal my kill."

Shela and Fionn exchanged a wry look of doubt, but Eilidh marveled at the man's confidence.

Oh good, now Eilidh is impressed with a guy who just got belted a field's length through the air.

Eilidh's naivety made Shela laugh. The girl had surprised Shela by calling up an earth-shield for Liam, but her control over her power was simply terrible. Hopefully Fionn could teach the poor girl a few things, because all Shela knew was that *she* wouldn't be teaching her a damned thing. She had enough to deal with.

"Okay, Liam. That's enough time on your arse. Up you get," Shela said as she grabbed him by the wrists and yanked him up.

"Thank you, bard, but I could've done that myself," he said, dusting himself off, his expensive black armor now coated in dust.

Shela slammed Liam bodily against the wall, her forearm pressed against his throat.

"What is the meaning of this—" he stammered.

"Shut up," Shela snapped. "I'm not a pathetic loser who strolls into taverns looking for a-drink-for-a-song. By the Tree, I'm a druid, and you best remember that."

Liam smiled, and in a flash rolled around to her back and let her fall face-first into the wall. Kearney growled as Shela twisted to face Liam.

"Easy, boy," Liam said playfully as he backed away from Shela. "We're all Anduains here. Isn't that right, *druid?*"

Shela felt her cheeks redden, but said nothing. Liam took that as an indication to keep talking.

"As you can see, I'm a perfectly capable fighter and was in no danger of dying to that berserker," he said. "And did anyone see how brilliantly fantastic my cloak looked when I burst out with my swords? I've been working on that for weeks."

Shela stroked her bruised cheek and rolled her eyes at the man as he ran off to retrieve said cloak. In truth, even if Liam had died, Fionn or Shela, or even Eilidh probably, could've rescued his soul from death and repaired his broken body. Of course, that arduous process took time and concentration, two things that the havtrol would not have afforded them. Either way, she was glad to have the impetuous Thorn with them, because all things considered, Liam had bravery and some skill with his showy red swords. They would need that if they were to find Gavin. Also, hadn't Eilidh mentioned something earlier about looking for her lost love down deeper in the caverns?

Mulling these thoughts over and thinking about how to combine their quests, Shela wandered back over to the elf and nuathreen who were still going at it tooth and nail.

Maybe they would stop pestering each other long enough to help the humans complete their quests. Shela certainly hoped so.

Chapter 10

T he vast, labyrinthine pathways appeared endless, yet Shela still insisted that she knew where to go. Eilidh had explained as accurately as possible where the cave-in had occurred that had separated her from Ruaidhri. Quickly claiming superior knowledge of the caverns' layout, Shela had taken the lead.

In fact, even before that conversation, Shela had automatically assumed command. Eilidh hadn't spent much time fighting alongside other Anduains, but was confused why the weakest member of the group would lead them. Surely Bob or Liam would've been a better choice. Nobody seemed to object, so perhaps druids often navigated for others. In any case, the whole group followed Shela through the silent, unending passages, winding around blind corners cautiously, and trying to avoid committing any crime grand enough to deserve a scowl from Shela.

Fionn was the polar opposite to her brash and assertive twin. Fionn spent most of the time walking beside Eilidh, talking about the Tree and Ghrian, how long had she known Ruaidhri, and when did she plan on taking her pilgrimage to Tan Arbrel, and to Arbreldin beyond that? Eilidh had politely replied that she hadn't heard the Tree's call yet, and Fionn had smiled and suggested Eilidh wasn't listening very hard then.

The druid also taught Eilidh an unbelievable catalogue of spells. Of course, Eilidh appreciated the advice and lessons, but the sheer volume of the ancient knowledge was far too great to absorb all at once.

"Repeat back to me the spell for curing a poisonous affliction," Fionn whispered. Shela had ordered everyone to keep quiet in order to avoid as much needless confrontation with enemies as possible, but Eilidh hadn't noticed any signs of life on this leg of their journey.

"Alright," replied Eilidh, who then fumbled the curing words out.

Despite Eilidh's difficulty with the wording of the spell, Fionn smiled in that ever-present supportive fashion. "Very good. Now try to cure Kearney."

The wolf shot a quick glance at Fionn upon hearing his name. Eilidh then saw the large animal stare at her, as if begging her not to accidentally do something terrible to him, like drop a pile of rocks on him like the dwarf had done earlier.

But of course he didn't know what they were talking about. Or did he?

Still mildly perplexed by that idea, Eilidh stood still and focused on the wolf, reaching out to connect their spirits. His fur bristled under her tentative touch. Never before had she sought to make such a union with a beast, but he shared the spirit of Andua with her, and she found the intersection of their souls far easier than she would've imagined.

The feeling of his unease was painfully apparent, but Eilidh felt fairly confident that she could squeeze the words out correctly. What was the worst that she could do anyway?

She avoided that thought, not sure what a mispronounced word could do to the poor animal.

In that space, everything around them faded from her perspective. Only Eilidh and Kearney existed. The spell rolled off her tongue quietly and far more fluently than before. The tingling sensation of the transfer of power between them broke her concentration and she lost the connection with the wolf. She opened her eyes to see that she had held onto Kearney for long enough. Ripples of the druid magic twisted softly around the wolf, who'd probably felt their healing effects many times before.

But that was when his master, Fionn, had cured him, not some random girl. A smile broke across her face as she and Fionn now trotted to catch up with the rest of their party. What an amazing feeling this was! To think, she had just cured an affliction. Well, if Kearney had actually been poisoned, she would've cured him, but still, she had seen the magic float around him and then dissipate, taking any maladies with it.

"You did well, Eilidh," whispered her proud teacher with a grin.

"Thank you."

Shela stopped ahead and glowered at the pair of giggly women.

"Are you two done trying to bring every damn enemy in the caverns after us?" she snapped quietly.

Despite the low volume of the words, they slapped Eilidh in the face with a tone of authority that she'd never heard before. She stood stunned for a moment before recalling that Ruaidhri had once explained that those blessed with an attunement to vocal magic could scream with enough intensity to disorient and confuse the enemy. Now Eilidh believed it, still waiting for the stars to clear from her vision.

Common sense fought to keep her mind in a positive light, but images of her lost Ruaidhri sought to drag her down into deep, dark recesses of her memory. Her recent magical success now already forgotten, Eilidh wallowed in a sudden sadness.

Will I ever find you, Ruaidhri? What will I do without you?

Shela continued on, pushing the group into a new area of the caverns. The style of the construction of the walls changed abruptly. The carvings etched into the stone conjured more memories from the last few days with Ruaidhri. Déjà vu forcefully struck Eilidh, visions of the cave collapse appearing far too real. The pain of separation welled up, renewed in its vigor by her weakened state of mind.

"What's wrong?" asked Fionn.

The druid put a comforting hand on Eilidh's trembling shoulder, but she felt no respite.

"This is where I lost him," she mumbled.

"We're close to one of the old shrines. It's at a major intersection, so maybe you'll remember the way that you went from there?" asked Shela indifferently.

Eilidh glared at her leader, but said nothing. Shela turned her hands up in a surrendering gesture.

"Look, we all have a stake in this. We're trying to find *your* friend, and we're trying to locate *my* brother. Help me out here," Shela said.

Eilidh looked to Fionn, and then to Liam. Both returned her gaze with sympathy. The elf, Aelfraed, stood behind the group, seemingly apathetic. Bob shuffled his feet across the dusty floor, his eyes finding the cracks in the ground quite intriguing.

"I'm not sure," Eilidh finally admitted.

The realization hurt to vocalize. What was she doing? She had no idea where Ruaidhri could be. He was almost certainly dead, lying under a pile of collapsed stone. Alone.

Shela walked off, not looking back to offer a kind word.

Fionn produced a piece of scented cloth and wiped away the tears forming in Eilidh's agonized eyes. Slight reassurance eked through the darkness fogging her mind. They silently fell into step behind the more assertive druid sister.

They reached a large crossroads, one great hallway terminating into the middle of another. In the center of the junction stood a pillar of polished stone, glinting in the uneven light of the torches. It was barely taller than Eilidh. She peered closely at the series of intricate runes carved into the crafted rock. Fionn lowered her head and whispered into Eilidh's ear.

"We call these markers, but we're not sure what they do." Eilidh looked at her as Fionn ran her fingers across the stone's markings. "They could've been magical once, but not anymore."

Moving past the small stone pillar, Eilidh looked up into the great space attached to the crossroads. On the left wall stood what she was sure was once a great monument to a god of some kind, but none that she recognized. Now all that remained were ancient scorch marks where someone had presumably burned everything associated with the religious site.

"So now that we're here at the shrine, and we don't have a clear path to take, how deep do you want to go?" asked Bob, speaking up for what seemed like the first time.

"What do you mean?" replied Shela, exasperated.

"I mean that we are looking for two people who could be anywhere in this damned place. I'm not sure how far you've really gone to explore here, Shela, but I can assure you that we will not just randomly run into your brother, or her friend," he said, sticking a thumb in Eilidh's direction.

Shela now looked troubled and Eilidh sensed an irritation growing in the woman. Shela spoke through clenched teeth.

"So what do you suggest?"

"I suggest that we skip this level of the maze altogether and drop down towards the submerged sections."

"Why would going deeper get us any closer to locating our lost ones?" asked Fionn.

Bob turned to her and explained, "We know the general area that Eilidh lost Roory or Rory or—"

"It's Ruaidhri," Eilidh interjected.

"Yes, right, Ruaidhri. If our young friend followed her path back out towards the higher levels of the caverns, then that means that her companion had to delve deeper into the darker sections."

Now a deep silence covered the party as they each thought about the nuathreen's suggestion.

"I agree."

Everyone turned to face the elf.

"Had he survived the ceiling collapse, he would have been forced downward. That is where we should now go," Aelfraed stated.

"And I suppose you know a shortcut, Bob?" Shela asked.

"Yes, as a matter of fact, I do," he replied smugly. "Follow me, please."

Eilidh could see the fire in Shela's eyes, but the druid fell into step behind the nuathreen as he approached a large cylindrical pillar of stone that supported the high ceiling.

"You see, there's a crack under this support," Bob said, pointing at the base of the pillar. "We can slide right down through this section of the floor and jump down into the level below us."

"How far of a fall is that going to be?" asked Fionn.

"Nothing that you cannot fix, good druid," Bob said with a reassuring smile.

That didn't sit well with Eilidh.

"Hold on a minute. You want us to jump down and what, break our legs?" she asked.

Bob kept smiling, but had a truly inquisitive look on his face, with no hint of condescension.

"You have the makings of a true druid, my dear. You're more than capable of healing yourself afterwards."

Could she hold her concentration long enough to perform a healing spell if she had two broken legs? This didn't seem like a good idea at all.

The group clambered up onto the square base of the gigantic pillar and edged around to the backside, hidden from view from the main chamber. Eilidh followed close behind Bob as he easily slunk into a fissure formed between the back wall and the base of the pillar. He paused in the gap for a moment and turned back to Eilidh.

"Just watch your step here. It's a bit slippery."

Before Eilidh could respond, he took a single step and disappeared from view with a shout of what sounded like genuine excitement. The noise of sliding gravel echoed out of the slim space and then she thought she heard a sharp cry of profanity.

"Get on with it, Eilidh," Shela urged.

Eilidh stepped down into the crack and saw utter darkness inside. She couldn't tell how steep the decline was, even when she slipped on her first step and slid uncontrollably down into the dark hole. She screamed and reached out her hands and feet, desperately seeking purchase, but the crack widened dramatically as she fell. Looking down at her useless feet, Eilidh saw a dim, bluish light growing beneath her quickly until she was enveloped in it and freefalling through the air.

Her body rotated of its own accord as she looked down and saw the watery floor rushing up towards her. She must've fallen from a height at least ten times her own. No air left in her lungs, she panicked and tried to scream once more, but failed. She righted herself as her feet crashed into a shallow stream of water, barely a hand's breadth deep.

Pain rocketed through her legs and she cried out, her face partially submerged in the dirty water. Powerful hands gripped her shoulders and pulled her up. Her vision filled with a terrible sight as she saw her battered legs dragging behind her, shattered and bleeding everywhere. Bone protruded in every direction as she screamed fearfully, her mind completely blank with terror.

While she watched, her legs glowed brightly, covered in ribbons of white and blue light, and she could feel the soothing words of Fionn nearby. She closed her eyes and listened as Shela's quiet song joined her sister's calm voice. The sounds faded away and all she could hear were feet sloshing and people talking.

"She'll be fine," she heard Shela say, a bit indignantly.

"Shut up, druid. What are you doing down here with such an inexperienced girl?" demanded a new, unknown voice.

Eilidh opened her eyes and stood up to find a giant of a firbolg towering over Shela's defiant form. Shela's eyes shifted for a moment to look at Eilidh and the firbolg followed her gaze.

"I mean no disrespect, girl, but this is a dangerous place for you," he said.

Despite not appreciating the contents of his words, Eilidh could sense genuine concern in his deep voice. Why did he care if she suffered? Even Eilidh could see that this firbolg stood amongst the strongest of King Darren's soldiers, and his scratched and dinged armor was nothing short of spectacular. Only his eyes and chin were visible behind his dark blue helm. A matching tunic displaying the silver tree of Andua covered layers of scale-mail and chainmail, and a blue cloak draped majestically across his broad shoulders, also emblazoned with the Tree of Rebirth. An enormous two-handed broadsword protruded from a sheath on his back and just the sight of it both terrified and intrigued Eilidh. Who could effectively wield such a weapon?

"I'll be fine, thank you," she replied uneasily. After taking a moment to right herself, she added, "We're searching for my—"

The words caught in her throat as she realized the dark shape looming next to the firbolg wasn't just a trick of the poor lighting.

"—lost friend."

The firbolg squared his shoulders towards Eilidh, giving her his full attention. Eilidh retreated a few steps as the solid shadow glided around to stay by his side. She hoped the look on her face didn't betray her fear.

271

"I can only tell you that I've been here a couple of hours, and I've not seen any other Anduains. Only the guardians of the dracolich roam these halls," he explained.

Timid, but determined to find Ruaidhri, Eilidh asked, "Will you help us?"

Without skipping a beat, the mighty firbolg responded flatly, "No. I have other business here."

"And exactly what might that be, Captain?" demanded Shela. "Sparring with yourself?"

Eilidh guessed that the druid could also see the strange shadow standing by the firbolg, but she didn't seem worried at all, so Eilidh forced herself into a calm state. She wondered if Shela had overstepped her bounds, because the soldier was visibly irritated by her question.

"My business is my own, druid," he stated. He pointed a large hand at Liam. "This man looks like a decent enough Thorn, so you'll be fine." Liam's face lit up with abject smugness at the partial compliment.

The firbolg carefully examined each of the group members and seemed satisfied with his decision to leave them to their own devices. Eilidh once more considered why this firbolg even cared to justify his actions in this case.

When his eyes reached Bob, his gaze narrowed, but the firbolg said nothing. Once more, the nuathreen was shuffling his feet and staring at the waterlogged ground.

A high-pitched scream pierced the air from downstream. The firbolg immediately sprinted in that direction. He moved with incredible litheness for such a large fellow. Over his shoulder, he yelled back at them, "I'll handle this." After a pause, he slowed and faced them for a moment, the strange darkness swirling by his side to keep up with the sudden turn. "You should leave. Now."

Eilidh and the others exchanged confused expressions as the firbolg charged off without them. Shela climbed up out of the shallow stream and pointed at a gouge in the blue-green tunnel walls. The floating reflection of the dingy water on the walls captivated Eilidh as she followed Shela.

Shela paused at the opening to the crack in the wall and turned to address the group.

"Forget about him. We'll move on with our quest, and we'll be fine."

Fionn and Eilidh shared a worried glance as the group moved into the fissure behind Shela.

Liam pulled up behind Eilidh and whispered, "Is she trying to reassure us? Or just convince herself?"

Eilidh's eyes widened at the Thorn's strangely sage words, but Liam quickly smiled in that overly charming way of his and added, "Do not fear, Eilidh. I shall protect you."

She nodded and followed him into the dark.

Chapter 11

T he weary Anduains rested in the shadow of the narrow slice in the thick wall. Inexorable sounds of ceaselessly dripping water grated on nerves as they sat in silence. Eilidh wanted nothing more than to find sleep behind her tired eyelids, but closing her eyes caused the awful thoughts of Ruaidhri's fate to intensify. They'd had no real direction to begin with, but now thanks to Bob, they'd traveled far too deep into Teekwood Caverns.

Ruaidhri, why did we listen to him? Will I ever escape this place?

A frail sense of peace settled over Eilidh. The feeling proved short-lived as sudden nightmares jolted her awake.

"I see that Eilidh has decided to join the rest of us in the land of the conscious," Shela quipped irritably.

Eilidh frowned. "What? I just closed my eyes for a moment."

Most of the members of the group stifled a chuckle at this. Eilidh stood up frantically.

"What's so funny?" she demanded, her face reddening.

Liam placed a hand on her shoulder, but she shrugged his gesture away. He shrugged in return and backed off. Bob's voice echoed quietly in the dark space that the group occupied.

"Your snores could wake the dead, my dear child."

Now her face turned the color of beetroot as the group laughed quietly. Why hadn't they woken her up?

With a smile, Fionn reassured the poor girl and passed her a piece of dried meat. "Don't worry, Eilidh. We didn't want to wake you since you've been down here longer than any of us. You needed the rest."

Eilidh didn't even sniff the mystery meat. She'd been famished for hours, so she ripped it apart in seconds.

"How long did I sleep?" she asked through a mouthful of food.

The druid looked around dramatically at their surroundings with a smile. "Well, I can't see the sun from here, but I would guess that you slept about an hour."

Eilidh nodded and sat down once more. A quick glance at the group revealed a missing person. "Where's Aelfraed?" she asked.

After a moment of silence, Bob spoke up. "That is a very good question, young one."

He wandered to the edge of Eilidh's vision and peered farther down the small passage. Despite his apparent dislike for the pompous elf, Bob's face showed concern at her unexplained absence. For all of his flowery and borderline condescending speech, the powerful nuathreen spell-caster did seem genuinely worried about the wellbeing of his companions.

Shela plonked her athletic frame down nearby and Eilidh could have sworn she heard the druid mutter, "Just who does he think he is? Not helping us."

The quiet rant continued, but Eilidh could only hear muted and garbled sounds. Bob on the other hand seemed to have no problem hearing the diatribe. He spoke without turning away from his vigil at the mouth of the small space formed by the crack in the wall. "His name is Cadman, Shela. And he is possibly the greatest soldier to ever fight against Caldera and Bergmark. King Darren doesn't promote just anyone to captain."

Shela merely grunted in response.

"I've never seen a shade so well tethered," Fionn said. Bob nodded his assent knowingly.

"Is that the shadow standing next to him?" Eilidh asked tentatively.

All eyes turned to her, and she really wished she'd kept her mouth shut.

"Even *you* can see it?" Shela demanded in tones of disbelief. When Eilidh nodded, Shela huffed and turned away from her.

"You have a strong bond with the Tree if you can see a firbolg's shade, my dear," Bob said approvingly. He looked to Shela. "Some druids can't even see the curse." Shela ignored him.

"The curse?" Eilidh asked.

"Ancient lore states the firbolgs were brought into this world before your kind, Eilidh, but they lost the favor of their creator, who we now call Ghrian," Bob explained. "So now after they're brought back from the dead just once, their dark spirit follows them back into this world, seeking to overcome them in an emotionally weak state, in order to drag them back to the afterlife. Most call this their shade, but an ancient firbolg saying calls it their darkness."

Now that he had everyone's attention, he faced the group before continuing. "Cadman is a great soldier, or at least he was," Bob said cautiously.

"And what does that mean?" Shela asked.

"I've heard rumors, but that's mere hearsay," Bob answered. "But no matter what, he should have come to our aid. Letting us delve so far into the depths of the caverns is downright irresponsible on his part."

Confused faces showed a failure to grasp his meaning.

"Friends, he is a captain of the king's army! His every instinct should be to drop whatever task he is currently engaged in and help those in need. Something is amiss here."

Fionn spoke up. "Why is he here in the first place? This place is a very remote area for a lone soldier to hunt in. And what did he say he was hunting? The guardians of the dracolich? I don't even know what those are."

"All good questions, dear druid," Bob replied. "I suspect that the captain has an ulterior motive for his presence here. It would appear that someone like Cadman would have no use for hunting such monsters as the dracolich's minions. I have fought with them on occasion. They are strong and exceedingly vicious—"

"And they closely resemble the brood that you people seem so intent on alerting to our untenable position," announced Aelfraed quietly, stepping silently from behind Bob.

The group jumped in fright and Kearney barked in surprise and agitation. Bob grasped his chest and faced the elf.

"Thank you for trying to stop my heart with fright, elf, but your plan has failed. I still live!"

Liam laughed, but the rest of the group sat on pins and needles, waiting for the elegant Aelfraed to explain herself. She glared dismissively at the nuathreen, who added, "And you know you're not supposed to stray that far from my side, Aelfraed."

The elf's glare intensified for a moment. After a painfully long and deliberate delay, she proceeded in the calm, unhurried manner of the elves, for whom time never seemed a pertinent issue. "This passage opens into a vast cavern not far from here. The mouth of the tunnel is about forty feet above the cavern floor, so in order to cross the cavern, we will need to traverse a series of natural bridges formed by some interesting rock formations."

Liam piped up, "That doesn't sound too difficult."

"What's the problem here, Aelfraed?" Shela asked with her usual brusqueness.

"The problem, young druid, is the garrison of the dracolich's guards marching on the cavern floor," the elf explained sharply.

Eilidh could see Shela's mouth twitch in frustration, probably with the condescension lacing the word *young*. To the woman's credit, she didn't rise to the elf's abrasive tone. To the elf's credit, despite not looking a day over twenty in the years of a human, she could very well have been double or triple Shela's age.

"I'm surprised that none of them heard the racket that *you* people produced," Aelfraed added, veritably spitting out the end of the statement.

An uncomfortable silence befell the group, but Aelfraed simply stood there, tall and elegant, exuding the perfect confidence of her ancient people. She wore the robes of a mage, but if the design or pattern revealed a specific attunement, Eilidh didn't recognize it. The group had yet to actually witness her perform any kind of magic. Was the elf in fact as powerful as she led them to believe?

All at once, Eilidh's vision filled with a fiery image of Aelfraed's furious face. Eilidh's head shot back in recoil, smacking her helmet against the tunnel wall.

And then the moment passed. The hellish face had disappeared as quickly as it had appeared. Aelfraed stood still as a statue, looking off away from Eilidh. Bewildered, Eilidh looked around at the rest of her companions, all of whom, except the elf, now regarded her with slight concern.

"Nodding off again?" Shela asked with an unkind smirk.

A stern warning voiced itself inside her head. "Tell them nothing."

Definitely Aelfraed's voice, but the elf had yet to even physically look at Eilidh. The rumors in Andua told of domination magic attacking the mind of the enemy, either causing them to fight amongst themselves or withering their conscious self to the point of complete uselessness. A nightmarish death awaited those who suffered at the hands of such a spell-caster.

Was the elf's display some cheap parlor trick or was Aelfraed really a powerful dominator? Eilidh didn't care to find out and simply shrugged at the group, not needing to feign the embarrassment glowing on her cheeks.

Liam stood up.

"Right. Well, I like the sound of these dracolich guardians, so let's go find some, shall we?"

Now Aelfraed turned to face him. "I would urge you to keep quiet in the cavern and just cross the bridges with as little chance of confrontation as possible," she said. Liam raised an eyebrow and gave a dashing smile, but Aelfraed cut him off. "I am serious, Thorn. Do not get us all killed in there."

Liam's face scrunched up at the implication. Upon realizing that Eilidh was watching him, the man's ever-present ego recovered quickly enough to flash a dastardly grin. She just rolled her eyes in response. This Thorn was unbelievable!

The group shuffled quietly through the remainder of the narrow tunnel and quickly found themselves in the great space described very accurately by the elf. An enormous cavern opened before them, with great twisting bridges of rock spanning a deep trench. Giant glowing rocks, the likes of which Eilidh had never seen before, provided illumination for the large space. The light revealed a few strange creatures milling around in the trench floor.

Their height was indeterminable from her vantage point, but their appearance scared her half to death. They were mostly grey all over, mostly humanoid in shape, and mostly terrifying in nature. A pair of tattered wings stood out from their backs, and the light glinted off of jagged talons and claws. A large head with a long beak-like mouth snapped constantly as the guardians traversed the trench aimlessly.

"There were far more only moments ago," Aelfraed insisted quietly.

"We should still be quiet in crossing the bridges to that plateau on the other side," added Bob. "These creatures may not look like much, but those mouths contain rows of razor-sharp teeth, and they never surrender once provoked."

The small nuathreen eyed Liam in particular as he warned the group. The Thorn grinned in return. Eilidh could tell the young man was itching for a more direct solution to their problem.

Aelfraed stepped out onto the ledge and cautiously approached the first bridge. The elf paused and slowly turned to the group, a finger to her mouth, reminding them yet again of the danger. A few of the evil-looking guards roamed in the space below, also reminding the group to watch their step.

Eilidh followed closely behind Liam, feeling no comfort from the Thorn's overconfident attitude. What was a dracolich anyway? And so what if they could cross the chasm? They wouldn't be any closer to recovering Ruaidhri. The sadness weighed down on her as she turned to find Fionn and Shela physically urging Bob towards the bridge. Eilidh saw the small nuathreen at first resist their persistence, looking around the great space frantically.

All at once, the mage gathered himself and strode quietly past Eilidh and inserted himself between her and Liam. As he passed, Eilidh could see rivulets of sweat on the nuathreen's face and neck. The temperature this deep underground lacked the soothing effects of nature's breeze, yet Eilidh wouldn't have called it stiflingly hot. Bob walked on in front of her, very close behind Liam, staring straight into the man's lower back.

Odd.

The troop continued in single file, only stopping when Aelfraed paused and ducked, intensely examining the lie of the land before her. Before long, the group crested the first part of the stone bridge and encountered an unforeseen junction.

The bridge didn't travel straight over to the other side of the cavern.

The left fork of the split seemed to curve away from their destination, terminating in the ground below. The right path led straight to what Eilidh now recognized as an ancient marker, like the one Fionn had told her about earlier.

Following their new leader, the Anduains slowly edged their way down the narrowing path, careful not to disturb loose rocks in the process. In plain view below them, a handful of the vicious creatures still milled around, oblivious to the potential meal sneaking above them.

Before reaching the stone marker, which stood near the side wall of the cavern, Aelfraed halted once more and peered over the edge of the rock bridge. After a moment of contemplation, she motioned for the group to follow as she deftly threw her legs over the side of their walkway, her robes flaring gracefully, and then disappeared from view. Eilidh had worn a dress on a few occasions and had absolutely no idea how the elf managed the feat so elegantly in her long robes. Eilidh had shown less gentile agility when clambering into the back of a horse-drawn carriage in a dress.

One by one, the group crept over the edge and discovered the sloping column of rock heading to the cavern floor. Eilidh carefully placed each hand and foot, desperately not wanting to be the novice who slipped and crashed into her friends below. She paused for a moment when she noticed that she was essentially dangling out in open air, twenty-five feet from the floor below. A look down revealed a very pale nuathreen gripping the natural pillar with white knuckles.

Liam apparently had picked up on Bob's hesitation and climbed back up to the poor mage. After some increasingly severe prodding, the nuathreen slid cautiously onto the man's back and wrapped his small arms around Liam's throat in an unintentional death grip. Eilidh stifled a smile as Liam's eyes bulged in surprise. After a few moments of reassurance, Bob loosened his grip enough that his rescuer could breathe again.

The rock column twisted out as the decline became less severe, making traversing the pillar much easier. At the bottom,

Eilidh stepped onto the cavern floor and froze. A snarling chattering of teeth reverberated from every direction. Despite her earlier feelings on the temperature, sweat streaked down the back of her neck. She dared not move, yet she knew that she was standing out in the open.

She closed her eyes, not knowing what else to do. Those vicious creatures were swarming and would tear her apart at any moment. A strong grip latched onto the shoulder of her cloak and almost lifted her off her feet. She stumbled in that direction and opened her eyes to find Liam forging ahead with her in tow, half-stumbling along behind him. She slapped his hand away and they both moved forward to a series of switchbacks etched into the rock of the far wall.

Only in the relative safety of her group did she turn and look back for the hordes of guards pursuing them, their snarls still filling her ears.

But she saw nothing.

Aelfraed saw the look of confusion on the young woman's face and the elf's voice rang clear as a bell inside Eilidh's head. "Their foul noises echo off of the cavern floor and walls, creating a sensation of the animals being all around you. Do not fear this."

With a nod, Eilidh turned back to the open space, reassuring herself that none of the beasts had followed them. In fact, only a handful of the dracolich's guards roamed the area, and they'd all congregated at the opposite end of the great hall. Aelfraed signaled for the group to march quietly once more and followed the winding switchbacks up the wall.

At the top, Aelfraed put up a hand and lay down flat on the dusty floor. Eilidh initially appreciated the elf's disregard for her own appearance, but then recanted this thought when the elf stood once more without a speck of dust sticking to her fantastically adorned outer robe. The mage gestured for none to follow and disappeared over the lip of the path.

Time passed painfully. The tension built in Eilidh's aching muscles, the pause allowing her body to emphasize its displeasure at her most recent exploits. She would have time to rest fully when they all died to whatever calamity awaited them next. The dire thoughts of Ruaidhri now played constantly through her mind. Even gazing upon Bob's terrified face brought no distraction to the dismayed woman. In fact, his fear didn't concern her at all, one way or the other.

Aelfraed reappeared and gathered the group together.

She whispered, "It seems that we have made a slight miscalculation."

"*We* have made a miscalculation? You—" interrupted Shela.

"This is no time for semantics, human," snapped the elf. "The ruler of these abominations is resting about fifty yards from our position."

Liam grinned.

"So what's the problem? Let's start at the top of the food chain," he declared, already rising and unsheathing his red blades.

Aelfraed grabbed him, and with surprising strength thrust him back down.

"You do not comprehend my words, naïve Thorn. We alone cannot win that fight. The dracolich is one of the ancient dragons and is a ferocious beast unlike any you have ever encountered. Attacking with anything less than twenty-five or thirty would be nothing short of suicide."

Something tapped gently on Eilidh's foot. She turned away from the elf and found a grim-faced Bob looking at her, his eyes pleading for help. Unfortunately for him, she had no reassurance to give. Eilidh turned back to the conversation at hand.

"Can we sneak past the dragon?" asked Fionn, her voice not nearly as steady as usual.

"No, I do not believe so. There are minions nearby watching the path approaching the dragon's lair," explained Aelfraed.

Once again the tapping started on Eilidh's boot. She turned and saw Bob's pathetic face once more, but this time his arm was outstretched away, pointing over the edge of the switchback. The fear on his face didn't match her expectations of a mighty spell-caster.

She once more turned away from him, but almost immediately he shifted up behind her. His small hands gripped her head suddenly, and she could feel his anxiety through his clammy palms. Eilidh struggled at first, but he gently moved her head to the edge of the cliff, giving her a view of the cavern floor and the bridges above.

A scream broached her lips before Bob stifled her with his slender hands. The group immediately joined her at the edge of the cliff. Fionn gasped and Shela groaned.

The dracolich's forces had quietly formed ranks on the cavern floor. The silent monsters observed the stranded Anduains with an eerie calm that Eilidh judged unnatural for their kind. She didn't know much about these vicious creatures, but their poise seemed all wrong.

Bob finally spoke.

"Look! The marker!"

Their heads followed his outstretched arm in unison, to the stone marker they'd passed on the bridge. Apparently the small pillars weren't as benign as Fionn had claimed. A constant stream of Anduains, Calderans, and Bergsbor materialized and flowed out of the marker, filling the bridge with a screaming horde of violence.

The dracolich's army below loosed a terrifying battle cry before charging the bottom of the switchbacks.

Instinctively, the Anduain group took a collective step back, but then remembered that the mighty dracolich and his guardians lurked in the shadows behind them. To Eilidh's increasing dismay, these guards now poured out of small caves along the cliff wall, screaming and loping towards them, their ratty wings unable to carry them more than a couple of strides at a time. She sank to her knees and bowed her head.

Finally the time has arrived, Ruaidhri. I will soon meet you in the afterlife.

Chapter 12

C adman strode through waterlogged passages in search of his prey. Making no effort to hide his presence or intentions, the giant firbolg waded noisily through rank water that rose almost as high as the tops of his boots. His trusty two-handed sword led the way. Sometimes he swore the weapon had a mind of its own, a mind that constantly sought a new home inside anyone near at hand.

The halls resounded with the echoes of his feet splashing in the dirty water, yet he'd encountered no dracolich spawn. When those Anduains had dropped from the ceiling, and almost crushed him, he'd suspected that the dragon's guards would infuriatingly go into hiding. At least, of course, until they'd sent scouts to spy on the Anduain strength, of which there was little in that group. The scouts' unintelligible cries that had beckoned Cadman away from those weak Anduains could easily have been a call to retreat, or just a diversion.

All Cadman knew for sure was now the bastards were nowhere to be found.

Once again he found himself sloshing through the greenish blue soup where the other Anduains had appeared. Before their interruption, he'd discovered a convenient loop of tunnels that had offered plenty of willing victims to slay in his quest to hone his skills. Now the halls stood still and quiet, other than the incessant dripping of water from every crack in every wall. Cadman's arms tensed, not so much under the weight of his giant sword, but more from anticipating some deadly ambush.

When none came, Cadman lowered his guard, but never stopped listening.

Taking full advantage of the sudden idle time, Cadman sat and rested his large frame on a slightly elevated step of blue stone that ran along the length of the foot of the wall. Leaning back against the moss-covered wall, a sudden weariness descended over his mind, clouding his senses. His monumental head slowly nodded forward as long-ignored fatigue imposed its will, despite his protests.

Cadman jerked awake and glanced around anxiously. How long had he been out?

It was impossible to tell the time in the dank reaches of Teekwood Caverns, but he suspected his eyes had only closed for a moment. Looking around again, Cadman noticed for the first time that the passageway streaming along in front of him appeared to have no definitive light sources, yet there was an ambient glow. Other tunnels at this level featured grand magical torches, or even just regular torches, placed by more recent explorers.

A memory flowed smoothly through his groggy brain.

About one year ago, Cadman had led a handful of elite soldiers through Teekwood Caverns. They'd received word that a contingent of Calderans had broken through the defenses at the caverns' only known entrance. The Reds had been spotted entering a new passage, apparently with the intent of raiding the Anduain archaeologists working diligently to loot some grave site. Cadman's crew had held no interest in the moral or ethical issues brought up by assisting Anduains engaged in illegal activities, but they did enjoy a good scrap with the Reds.

Cadman's group had walked brazenly down the tunnel, dousing all of the flames hung on the walls by the explorers below. Nearing the grave site in question, Cadman had observed a scene that would have turned the stomachs of most. In his mind's eye, he could still see it all so clearly, and the emotions returned just as strongly as ever.

Blood of fallen Anduains coated the walls of the small crypt in gory splatters. Beyond the mutilated corpses littering the floor, seven or eight Calderans taunted and beat a small, bloodied female elf. She refused to give them the satisfaction of a scream as they maliciously stripped her down. Cadman didn't need his imagination to ascertain their grim intentions.

With a cry of raw rage, he'd launched himself and his small band down the tunnel, charging with weapons drawn. They continued to toss down the torches, darkening the space around them, hiding their numbers. Cadman still smiled at what the Calderans must've felt, staring up the passageway and seeing ghostly forms screaming towards them, the tunnel closing around them as darkness rushed with the incoming Anduains.

As any good soldier would, Cadman reveled in the action of saving the poor elf from a fate worse than death. Those supposedly holy priests and palatines of Caldera had deserved an end far more painful than the prompt dispatch given by Cadman's companions, but at the end of the day, one Anduain life had been spared.

If only I was strong enough to save them all.

The vision of the past faded from view and Cadman now more closely examined the slime coating the walls of the wet, expansive tunnel. Was he imagining things, or did the green muck itself emit a slight glow? Cadman knew little about plants, but this growth fascinated him. How could a plant, if that was really what this was, grow in the absence of sunlight, yet also generate its own light? The idle questions mounted up and up, leading nowhere.

Cadman thought about the Anduains who'd passed through the tunnel earlier. What had they said they were doing? Searching for some friends? Stupid. None of those Anduains had the experience or know-how to successfully navigate the caverns this far down. A year ago, Cadman would've felt obligated to lead the band of novices around and perhaps teach them some useful lessons in survival. He sighed deeply. A lot had happened since then, since his final mission.

His eyes started to droop once more as he sat and listened to the quiet lapping of the murky water around his boots. With his eyes closed, he could almost imagine sitting in a glade, hearing the soothing murmurs of a crystal-clear stream.

Very quickly, Cadman was fording a small river east of Teekwood, seven young soldiers splashing along with him, well behind the relative safety of the Anduain strongholds in western Astrovia. The fresh recruits had recently graduated from their respective training schools and then transferred into the care of Cadman, a captain in the Anduain army. He would've much rather remained on the frontlines of the war with Bergmark and Caldera, but he always bowed to the wisdom of King Darren. Experienced soldiers and leaders needed to introduce the most promising recruits to the defense of Andua. These students had been entrusted to Cadman to get them operating at a high level as quickly as possible. Lesser students went to lesser teachers.

This simple reconnaissance mission should've provided no challenge for even the least of Cadman's charges. Each had proven very capable in training, and Cadman had to fight to contain a smile as they worked so hard to impress him with their abilities. He would've never guessed that teaching would bring him any joy, but he had to admit that seeing the fruits of his labor growing before his eyes had a certain attraction.

Watching his understudies cross the river, Cadman noticed the sky darken severely. Within moments, he found himself totally immersed in a dense, thick fog. The sudden sounds of battle roared around him, but he couldn't see anything. Running in every direction revealed nothing. His own hand wasn't even visible right in front of his face. The solid darkness gripped him bodily and weighed him down, forcing him to his knees.

The battle now whispered, fading away into the distance. His cries went unanswered. Where were his companions? What was happening?

Kill me! Come back here and kill me!

Where did those words come from? Did he say them?

Now only the bubbling flow of the stream remained, a relative silence compared to the violent trauma that had passed.

Cadman's eyes shot open and he leapt to his feet. Cold sweat poured over his entire body. Swinging his sword around in a circle, the soldier searched for his assailants.

Only the gentle sounds of the caverns' waters greeted him.

With a weary sigh, Cadman sheathed his weapon and placed a hand against the slime-covered wall. He leaned forward, head bowed, frustration washing over him anew. The nightmares visited his sleep more and more these days. The druids had said his pain would ease with time, but there was no escape from the constant mental reminders of his failure.

Mercifully, the humiliating feelings of defeat and loss passed quickly. Cadman stood up straight and reconsidered his situation. A deep-seated resolve wormed its way up, a resolve that couldn't be held in check by failure alone. The determination that had made Cadman one of the great soldiers of his time now squashed the petty emotions eating at his spirit.

A mission had effectively fallen into his lap and he, in his preoccupation and self-pity, had missed a redemptive opportunity.

What kind of soldier would possibly leave the fate of such an inexperienced group in the hands of a low-ranking Thorn and a—

A nuathreen mage wielding the staff of a wraith and possessing the bearing of real experience.

Cadman slapped himself on the forehead as his memory finally engaged and he recalled the identity of that nuathreen accompanying the group. Upon seeing the wraith, Cadman had felt suspicious. A spell-caster like that diving around in the dangerous reaches of the caverns with a group of novices hadn't made much sense, but that meant little now.

Frantic to redeem yet another mistake, Cadman rushed after the group, splashing through the shallow water, retracing the steps of those he'd abandoned to the wraith.

To the traitor.

Grim adrenaline drove him through the crack in the wall that he believed the young group had taken. His heart sank as he realized the destination awaiting him at the end of the passageway.

The lair of the dracolich.

No noise echoed through the narrow tunnel, so his hopes rose slightly. Perhaps there was still time to save them, time to save himself. If he could reach them before the guardians of the dracolich awoke their undead master—

He erupted into the gigantic cavern as a wall of sound hit him bodily. Undaunted by the terrible battle cries and ear-piercing screams of the dracolich's army below, Cadman raced across the first section of the natural rock pathway suspended above the cavern floor. He rounded a curve in the elevated bridge and found himself staring at a stream of warriors from every nation, all rushing in the direction that he wished to go. A mixture of Bergsbor, Anduains, and Calderans all flowed in a chaotic procession down a ramp to the cavern floor, intermingling with the dracolich's minions below, but not engaging them.

How had this many Bergsbor and Calderans gotten down here? The only entrance to the caverns Cadman had ever heard of was the main Teekwood Forest entrance that was guarded by Anduain soldiers, albeit a little lightly for Cadman's taste, despite the ceasefire.

And why would all these sworn enemies move together like this? And with creatures of darkness in tow?

It didn't make any sense. It was as if all these parties had one goal in common. Cadman paused to take stock of the situation. From his high vantage point, he could see the conglomeration of supposed enemies all funneling into a series of switchback ramps leading up to the dracolich's lair at the far end of the cavern. And at the top of this path stood a Thorn and some other small warrior, holding their ground as best they could. Maybe they weren't as dumb as they looked. These young Anduains were taking advantage of a bottleneck to reduce the power of the enemy's sheer strength of numbers.

Cadman knew that he should be up there with them. Hopefully the rest of their group was up on the ledge behind them and not dead under the trampling feet of the enemy, an enemy made up of four different groups that should be fighting each other and not together. In fact, he found it very odd that none of the enemies running past him had noticed him nor deemed him a threat.

"No matter. I'll make them regret this mistake," Cadman said aloud with a grin, his words lost in the continuous racket of the frenzied army all around him.

He wasted no time and darted forward towards the enemy, his weapon ready to slice a path through the torrent of targets before him. As he ran, another thought occurred to him. Instead of gouging his way through the vast numbers, he instead inserted himself into the wave rushing down towards the cavern floor.

And they completely ignored him. The mindless herd swarmed chaotically and Cadman had to vie for his position, forcing others out of his way to maintain a place on the edge of the pack. Funneling down the ramp, Cadman observed the same glazed look on all the faces of those around him, their eyes all set on the poor Anduains fighting above.

Halfway down the ramp, some loose gravel caused Cadman to slip, and the oversized firbolg fell against a dwarf in front of him. The squat Bergsbor fell flailing off the edge of the descending path. His cry of surprise was cut short after falling twenty feet onto his head. Despite his scream being lost in the din all around, the dwarf's absence apparently drew some attention from those around Cadman. A look into the glaring faces surrounding him hinted that the jig was up.

Without waiting for their response, Cadman preemptively swung his great sword in a wide frontal arc, cleaving some space to work in. The hordes collapsed upon him, but he pressed forward, ignoring the dings and smacks of various weapons on his armor and on the giant shield covering his back. Cadman figured that his main goal was to make it up the switchback ramps ahead. Failing that, he would take down as many enemies with him as possible.

All before him fell in droves as he continued to swing his weapon powerfully back and forth. The punishment soaked up by his armor started to take its toll, but he had a trick or two up his sleeve. Cries of defeat around Cadman intensified when he allowed his shade to soak into his body, just enough to take the edge off the pain.

The enemy looked on in dismay as Cadman pushed on with renewed vigor, now oblivious to the injuries inflicted by only the relatively few brave enemies who dared attack him. Terrified warriors broke away, and those remaining felt the wrath of Cadman's enormous blade. He quickly reached the bottom of the path leading up to his goal. Lowering his head, Cadman drove upwards, battering a torrent of enemies over the edge of the inclined pathway.

Rampaging through the opposition, he felt his shade edging further into him than was safe. Resisting the strong urge to embrace the power of pure, unbridled rage, Cadman broke the bond and focused on pushing the shade back out. He hesitated a second to make sure it had fully released its talons from his soul. The consequences of leaving the shade's hooks unchecked could be dire, but Cadman sensed the presence was completely gone.

My darkness walks beside me.

A lone dracolich guardian leapt onto his back, clawing and slashing at his helm. Now separated from his shade, Cadman felt the stabs and scratches intensely, but the pain only drove his fury. With a snarl, and without breaking his stride, Cadman reached back and gripped the monster by the neck. In a sudden and shocking movement, he ripped out the beast's throat and tossed it aside as a bloodied shriek erupted and the mutilated guardian fell to the floor.

Slashing and crashing through enemies, Cadman burst from the masses and finally found himself facing the group of Anduains that he'd abandoned what seemed like only moments ago. Exhaustion threatened to slow him down, but the adrenaline flowed when the Thorn spiraled towards him with red blades lashing out. Confused, but not stupid, Cadman parried the attack away and yelled at the Thorn to stop.

The human looked confused for only a moment before recognizing him. After all, Cadman didn't look much like the mangy mob of enemies enveloping the Anduains. One glance at him was enough for the average foe to think twice, and usually thrice, about attacking. Using this to his advantage, Cadman loosed a battle roar that eclipsed the screams and cries of the enemy. The opposing frontline hesitated and took a decided step back.

"We need to push them back to get out," he yelled at his new companions, instinctively taking the lead. "We need to move before they wake up the dracoli—"

He was interrupted by an ear-piercing shriek of unimaginable proportions. Initially both sides of the fight paused and glanced around anxiously. The cavern grew deathly quiet for a moment. Cadman's weary muscles would've appreciated the small break, but he couldn't bring himself to relax. He could see all of his Anduains were still in one piece, but he suspected that might change on the way out if the dracolich had just risen.

A second terrifying shriek reverberated around the cavern and the enemy hordes roared in celebration as the monstrous dracolich ambled onto the wide ledge behind the Anduains. The ground shook violently under the weight of the enormous undead dragon. Red eyes glowed inside a skull missing large portions of its decaying, grey flesh. The skeletal structure of enormous wings arched out from its back, skin and flesh completely absent. Cadman's new companions looked to him with genuine fear plastered across their faces, except for the Thorn. A cocky smile hung confidently on the man's face.

A third shriek forced Cadman into action.

"Let's move," he said.

Nobody moved.

"Now!"

The enemy ranks had reformed after Cadman's barrage, and they started to push up the switchbacks again. With the slow-moving dracolich pounding along the ledge behind them, the Anduains followed Cadman headlong into the waiting jaws of the enemy.

Dracolich guards snapped and clawed at Cadman as he led the way, forming a void around himself with his giant sword. Beside him, the Thorn spun through attacks and separated heads from shoulders in spectacular showers of blood. Just behind Cadman, a girl darted to and fro, careening into enemies with her shield, knocking them flat for the druid's wolf to finish off.

The sudden surge of coordination impressed Cadman as he plowed through foe after foe, not taking the time to worry about killing fellow Anduains in the enemy army. As far as he was concerned, they'd abandoned Andua when they joined up with these creatures.

Rocks from above started to fall as the dragon marched right above the escaping Anduains. Fireballs shot from its mouth, barely missing Cadman multiple times. He pushed on, unaffected. The group reached the cavern floor and ran straight into another wave of winged guardians. Cadman ducked instinctively as a shower of purple orbs blazed over his head from behind. The swirling orbs penetrated the skulls of the enemy, who suddenly grabbed at their own heads and writhed around on the ground, screaming horribly.

He turned just briefly to see an elf holding her arms outstretched in the shape of a cross, an ancient spell flowing from her mouth, her domination magic executing its wrath on their enemies. Without more time to observe the elegant dominator, Cadman pressed on.

The wretches around him scratched at their heads feverishly enough to break their own skulls, making Cadman's job far easier as he trampled over them, heading towards the ramp leading back up to the bridge they needed to reach. Pushing forward through the droves of attackers, Cadman only paused when the ground under his feet shook so hard that he flipped onto his back. Glancing back he saw the dracolich had leapt from the top of the ledge straight down to the cavern floor.

Bolts of energy erupted from the dragon, scattering death in every direction. Searing pain darted through Cadman's entire body as the evil energy assaulted him. Through barely open eyes, he could see the enemy ranks regaining their feet and forming up to finish off the incapacitated Anduains.

"So this is how I die," he mumbled as he feebly raised himself into a crawling position, still unable to give up, despite his current state.

The enemy army must have assembled themselves in suitable numbers, because then Cadman heard a terrible battle cry ring out all around. The ground trembled now with the charging feet of a hundred hell-bent enemies. It would all be over soon.

A soft voice pierced the dark, tumultuous noise all around. Cadman turned to see a druid standing amongst her fallen friends, chanting out what he recognized as the most powerful healing spell known in Andua. Knowing that he would be fully recovered in about two seconds, Cadman prepared himself for a final confrontation with the incoming enemy. They would not take him without obscene losses on their part.

The soothing words of the spell hit him like a mule kick to the backside. The entire group of Anduains leapt up and charged the enemy, engaging them in a last stand for the bards to sing of for years to come.

As long as one of us lives to tell the tale.

Cadman fought valiantly, slashing enemies in two as they came at him three or four at a time. Their blood now layered his armor in crimson streaks. He looked to his left and saw the young girl with the shield charging through a crowd of the enemy untouched. She was yelling something unintelligible. That stupid girl! It was only a matter of time before they noticed her and killed her.

The soldier in Cadman automatically drove him in her direction, but the enemy swarmed him incessantly, halting his progress. Despite his cries for her to stop, she just kept running, screaming the name Ruaidhri. Cadman didn't understand, but he couldn't dwell on it. The enemy had them surrounded again and the undead dragon now approached, thumping the ground so heavily that Cadman could hardly remain upright.

He looked over the enemy army one more time and saw the girl slip through a crack in the wall, apparently unharmed.

"Perhaps I've saved one," he muttered to himself as he watched his death approach once more.

But yet again, I couldn't save them all.

Bergmark

Chapter 1

Gruesome dug his thick claws into the rough bark of the tree and craned his neck to look at the clearing below him. Well below him...for he was over three times his own great height above the solid ground. *If the gods wanted havtrols to be so high above the earth, glorious Fjur would have given us wings,* he grimaced to himself. He watched Pjodarr as he knelt in the snow. The old shaman was odd, given to amusing himself in all manner of ways, but Gruesome had learned to trust the slave's instincts. If Pjodarr said frost wyverns now hunted this forest, the havtrol believed him. But he didn't have to like the old man's improvised method of hunting, which brought him so high in this tree.

The little old man below raised his tattooed arms above his head, the steel of a knife's blade glinting in his right hand. In one smooth gesture, he sliced the palm of his left, and pushed both arms upwards. Snow swirled toward the sky. Gruesome's keen nose caught a faint whiff of blood on the shaman's wind.

A raspy screech echoed from above. Gruesome hadn't heard the call of the wyverns in over ten seasons, but he knew it well. The carrion beasts were ever present on battlefields in the highlands of the Bergmark. He never expected to see them here, across the sea. A chill ran up his spine. Was the dwarf homeland so desolate now that

305

even the vermin of the sky had left it?

A soft *whoosh* signaled the first wyvern's glide toward its prey. The havtrol knew another would follow. As the second beast passed him, he steeled his nerves. He'd hunted the great leviathans of the sea, so why would he dare be afraid to jump from a simple tree? He aimed for his target and launched himself into the air with a grunt. His full weight smashed into the second wyvern's back, and he clawed desperately at the creature's furred body to find a grip. It wailed and flapped its leathery wings, but the scavenger was unable to protect itself from an attack from above. The pair plummeted into the first wyvern. Gruesome briefly hoped the shaman had time to get out of the way before all three bodies smashed into the frozen ground. His bones jarred on impact, and he heard a gushing crunch from one of the beasts below him. The wyvern directly under him thrashed weakly. Warrior instincts took over; in a daze, the havtrol found the thing's long neck and easily crushed it.

Another screech brought him to his senses. Pain rocked his massive body as he rolled onto his back to face his attacker. He heard the creak and groan of ancient wood and the panicked cries of a wyvern above him. A large clump of snow fell on his face. When Gruesome opened his eyes again, the shaman's silver mask filled his vision. The old slave grinned mischievously beneath it.

"How does it feel?"

The big warrior groaned as he sat up. "Ice giants do not hit as hard as this cursed ground."

"No, no. How does it feel to be the first havtrol to ever fly?

First Bergsbor, really. I'm sure some elf has done it at some point or other. But you should be proud."

Gruesome growled at the little man and pulled himself to his full height, almost half again taller than the thin shaman...and three times as wide. He looked up to see a third wyvern trying desperately to free itself from a prison of large tree limbs.

Pjodarr looked toward his captive. "I love these trees here, so old and mighty. If we'd had these in the Mark, I would never need dwarf or havtrol. Just an army of roots and limbs." He raised his hand and made a motion as if pushing something down. The great tree shook and the last wyvern was thrown to the ground. The havtrol pounced on the creature and broke its neck before it could even attempt to defend itself. These beasts were completely helpless on the ground, and never much of a threat to live prey without greater numbers, despite their large size. They could easily carry a man or a skinny dwarf, but only a dead havtrol had anything to fear from them.

The shaman gave a long whistle and then went to work with a small axe. He began cutting the wings off one of the wyverns while Gruesome lumbered to where his armor and weapons were piled under the base of one of the huge trees. Pjodarr was right to tell him to leave it all below; the extra weight probably would have killed him along with the beasts. A large var bounded into the clearing, in answer to the shaman's call. The female snuffed excitedly at the carcasses. She clamped her powerful jaws around the neck of the last wyvern and shook it violently.

"NO!" Gruesome roared at her and cuffed her on the snout. Her hackles rose as she growled at him. He returned her snarl with a rumble from his own throat. No stupid var could back down a mighty havtrol warrior. He didn't even like riding the beasts, much less sharing the bounties of his kills with them.

"Oh, for the love of Berta," the shaman groaned. "Mila!" He called as he chopped off the head of the wyvern he was busy preparing for travel and tossed it to the var. She dropped the other and snatched her prize in her wide jaws. She crunched the entire head in her mouth twice before swallowing it whole. "That's a good girl," Pjodarr cooed as he went about his work. Gruesome shook his head and went back to donning his gear. The chainmail shirt went on easily, but he had to have the shaman help him cinch the steel plates on his upper and lower arms. Like most havtrols, he did not wear gauntlets. He did not want to deprive himself of the natural weapon of his thick claws. The last piece to go on was his most cherished. A black steel helm in the shape of a snarling bear's head, the gaping maw framing Gruesome's own fearsome face. It marked him as a proud warrior of Clan Beartooth, given only to those that proved themselves in great battle. The helm was a symbol of the respect his people held for him. Even after he'd stained his own honor, they had not taken it from him. He placed it on his head and felt almost complete.

But only the warrior's true treasures could make that so. He bent down and lifted the large hammer and double-bladed axe from the ground. Forged from solid Thurin steel, they gleamed in the sunlight. The thick leather wrapped around their hafts kept his grip firm. The weight of them brought him great comfort. High King Henrik had presented them to Gruesome as gifts on the day he'd pledged his clan's loyalty to the dwarf's cause. Where most weapons of power were covered in runes, only a single one graced each side of these. It represented the bond between their peoples, and havtrols did not take oaths lightly. With a rumble of satisfaction, he slid the hilts into the big loops at his hips.

By that time, Pjodarr had the wyverns ready for travel. Sweat beaded on the shaman's bare arms, even in the crisp winter air. The man was slim, but wiry. The tattoos that covered most of his skin depicted various parts of nature: a mountain here, a tree there. Fire, clouds and waves cascaded down his arms, interspersed with animals of all sorts. The havtrol knew that they were all things the shaman had used as weapons. All battle-tested shamen had similar markings, given to them by other shamen. It was how they showed each other respect. But Pjodarr was the only one to have a certain type of tattoo; no other could boast the lightning bolts that covered the backs of each hand. All of the inkings were smooth and clear, as if the slave had just gotten them recently. A shaman trick, just like they never showed their age. Such magic was beyond the mind of a warrior, so Gruesome did not wonder about it. One other spot, high on the old man's right arm held a different mark than any other shaman as well: a brand in the shape of a serpent twined around a column. It was the symbol of his eternal bond to his master. Few slaves were given such an honor.

In contrast to his markings, the old man's attire was mostly nondescript: sleeveless chain shirt over a plain tunic, worn brown pants and a thick brown cloak. Only one thing stood out, the silver mask that left only his mouth and beard visible. Most shamen wore masks of carved wood; Pjodarr was the only one Gruesome had ever seen with one of pure silver. The old man's stringy hair hung under the mask's leather cap, tufts of silver-streaked red blowing in the cold breeze. The slave did not normally carry himself with the weight of the power he truly bore, but the big havtrol knew that the shaman could command as much authority as a dwarf king if he desired. None from the Mark doubted his bond with Fjur.

Gruesome strapped the wyverns and their wings to the var's back, and they all began the short trek east to their camp. They'd taken shelter in a cave in the foothills of the Deerleg Mountains. Over the past five seasons spent with Pjodarr and his master, Gruesome had learned the southern part of the mountain range well. Due to the war, the area was less inhabited than most of Caldera. There were a few small villages, but they were more likely to see a dwarf patrol than anyone else. The dwarves did not trust the Calderans to maintain the terms of the recent treaty, and Gruesome did not blame them. Human nations were not known for their honor.

Pjodarr talked for the whole journey, mostly to the var. The shaman seemed to enjoy talking simply for talking's sake. Well, maybe the var enjoyed it, too. But something bothered Gruesome, so he finally decided to ask the old man the question that burned in his gut.

"Pjodarr, when will we find their trail again?"

The slave was silent for a moment, then his shoulders slumped slightly. "Give me tomorrow to prepare these wyverns, then we will continue. These will keep us fed for a few days, and we can trade the wings. Folks here have never known leather like wyvern leather."

"Eight nights have passed, are you sure you can find them?"

Pjodarr chortled. "Your folk aren't known for their subtlety, my friend. Especially not after they go wild."

"Do not mistake Honorless for wild," Gruesome rumbled. He wondered more and more about the shaman. Perhaps age was making the slave weak, but recently he seemed to be trying to avoid battle. Gruesome was on a mission, and he now felt the shaman was keeping him from it. He knew Pjodarr was not afraid to fight, nor afraid to die. He'd seen the man give all of himself in battle. No, Gruesome was sure it had something to do with Blade. Did the shaman sense some change in his master? The havtrol continued the rest of the journey in silence.

"Master," Pjodarr greeted the dwarf joyfully as he entered the cave. "We've had quite the bounty. And you missed a most glorious spectacle. The mighty Gruesome flew through the air with the grace of a stone butterfly!"

Of course, the old dwarf did not answer. Gruesome did not have to look to know exactly what the honorable general was doing. He knew he stood in the same place from when they left that morning. He knew that Pjodarr would now be giving his master water to drink and a bit of food. Because the once great Blade would do nothing but stand as still as a statue unless the shaman told him otherwise. Gruesome pushed one of the other var away as he untied the carcasses from the big female. The shaman named them all, but the warrior never cared to learn which was which. They were simply "var" to him. He left Pjodarr to care for his master in peace.

"And we will have quite the treat tonight for dinner. I'll make you my famous wyvern stew. Or infamous, as you like to call it, Master."

Chapter 2

Pjodarr knelt in the snow by the dead havtrol, its bones picked clean of meat. "They are definitely hungry. They killed their own and ate him." He poked at the corpse. "I wonder if he was already wounded. There had to be some reason they picked him as the weakest."

"Does it matter?" Gruesome grumbled, shielding his eyes from a beam of the midday sun that poked through the canopy of leaves above them. "One less to kill."

The shaman sighed and rose to his feet. "It might not matter. They've picked up more." He walked around the corpse and studied the ground.

"How many?"

"Four, maybe five."

Gruesome roared at the sky. "This is what happens when you do not hunt them, shaman! Instead of three, we now must face eight! Are those odds more to your liking?"

Pjodarr spun to face him, sunlight glinting off his mask. "What are you accusing me of, mighty Gruesome?"

The warrior fixed the old man with a stare. "We will do what must be done."

"I have never done less." The shaman returned his attention to the area around the dead havtrol. Gruesome never knew if he used

313

his magic or just his eyes, but Pjodarr had amazing tracking skills. "Yes, they exhausted all their food supplies in the mountains. That's why they are here in the middle of winter. There wasn't much fighting amongst them."

"That means one of them is very strong. Very strong indeed to keep so many in line. Honorless do not get along so easily."

The old man nodded and moved towards an ancient oak. "They head west." He paused, face to the sky. Then spun around, eyes wide. "Toward Willowbrook!"

They ran back to the var. Pjodarr leapt upon a small male with the grace of a much younger man, while Gruesome wrestled his bulk atop the unappreciative female. On another male sat Blade in full armor, with only the right side of his face visible above his beard. Whatever injury befell the glorious dwarf when the Great City fell, his shaman went to great lengths to conceal it. The general's shiny helm was made to completely hide the left side of his head down to his cheek. Dragon wings flared from either side, matching the ornate carvings on his armor and the golden crest on the large shield now strapped to his back. A dragon wrapped around a white tower, the dragon the symbol of House Thurin, the tower for Blade's family. As general of the First Army, the dwarf had the crucial duty of protecting Northwatch and the rich mines north of it, the source of the dwarf kingdom's power. Or it had been, before the Great Mountain burned and took all of that away. Blade was now the only member of House Thurin, all other survivors of the cataclysm having joined other Houses. Upon his shield and the shaman's arm were the last symbols of the noble family, whom most say were brought down by the gods themselves. The old dwarf's gray beard was split down his chest in two braids, and his hair hung wild from beneath his helm. The bone handle of glorious Tremble, the wide-bladed sjalsword of House Thurin, peered over Blade's right shoulder, a final reminder of his greatness.

Together with a fourth var carrying their sundry equipment, the trio raced west toward Willowbrook. It was a small village nestled within the Brinnoch Forest, just a day's ride from its western edge. It was a favorite of the shaman's and they visited at least once every new moon. Gruesome judged that it would be a few hours before they reached the village and doubted the sunlight would hold. Pjodarr wove them through the thick trees of Brinnoch with ease, the other var simply following him with no guidance needed from their riders. It was one of many traits of the var that Bergsbor found appealing over the horses preferred by Calderans and Anduains. Var ran as a pack. With the shaman as their pack leader, the rest would follow with no need for steering. Even the var carrying goods did not need to be tied to another. The massive hounds were also fierce in battle, usually from being starved for a day or two beforehand. After a victory, they were allowed to eat their fill from the battlefield. Var fared much better in the snowy mountains of Bergmark, and were much lower to the ground than horses. The latter was probably most important to dwarves. Still, var as big as the female could easily carry a havtrol into battle, though most of Gruesome's people chose to run on their own legs toward their enemies. Var just got in their way.

As they approached the village, their mounts became uneasy. Pjodarr's male whined, and the havtrol could feel the female growling under him. "There, there, Furgi. What's the matter, boy?" The shaman patted and scratched his ride's thick neck. He looked back toward Gruesome and his master. "Something is wrong. Let's leave them here for now. Help me get their kit off." With practiced ease, the two removed the gear from all four var. Pjodarr held his hand on each of the furred heads and whispered soothing words into their ears, then nodded at the big warrior. "Do not worry, they will come when called."

The slave led them through the dimly lit forest, the trees blocking most of the orange light of dusk. He dropped to a knee suddenly. "Look here," he whispered. "The Honorless were here. All of them, close to this spot." He stood and fixed his gaze toward the village. It was close, though Gruesome could see no fires through the trees. He knew what lay beyond. A village of only two or three hundred, hunters and gatherers, against eight or nine hungry havtrols? Only the slaughtered remains of men, women and children would they see. Maybe one or two of the havtrols, if the men of Willowbrook were tenacious enough. Gruesome did not remember any being such.

"But," the shaman said, drawing the word out. "They went no further. They turned north." He pointed west. "The village is right there, just a few steps away. And they did not go. They would have smelled the flesh of man, of goat and pig. But they did not go."

316

Gruesome squinted through the darkness, but Pjodarr's eyes were much keener than his own. He sniffed the air. There was emptiness to it. The shaman was right; the stench of man saturated the air where humans lived. Even in a village this small, the mix of leather, flesh, oils, steel and sweat should fill his nose. Some of that was in the air, but not the flesh and sweat. Not the smell of life.

"There are no people there, shaman. I do not even smell blood."

"You mean they are all gone?"

The havtrol shrugged his wide shoulders.

"Could they have known about the Honorless, Gruesome? Could they have fled to safety?" The old man was genuinely concerned about these simple people. "There are no fires, no smell of ash. The havtrols would have gone in there like rampaging beasts and set the whole place ablaze, wouldn't they?"

The big warrior had no answers for him. Pjodarr walked toward the village and Gruesome followed. He heard the crunch of Blade's steel-covered steps behind him. "It is so still and cold." The shaman's clear voice floated back to them.

When they stepped past the first hut, they saw Willowbrook as it was created by its founders. The natives of Sudmark, or Grunland as the humans called it, were simple folk, their homes little more than shelter from the elements. In the plains, they would actually dig a hole in the ground and build stone or wood walls around it to hold a roof, with fur curtains to hide the dwellers. They only slept there, their lives spent outside mostly. Here, in the forest,

317

they built lean-tos against the wide trunks of the great oaks, but still arranged them in the circular pattern of their people. In the center would be a large hall, where the village would congregate and share meals. The havtrol understood their desire for community, his own people being similar. But this land was a stark contrast to the massive stone cities built by the dwarves, each building a testament to its architect's glory. Already, the dwarves had transformed the northern ranges of the Deerleg Mountains to resemble their once great empire.

But Willowbrook seemed completely deserted. Nothing moved. No cat prowled the night, no fire peeked from the cracks of the little huts. Not a single snore, grunt of human mating or whisper of voice, all the sounds Gruesome associated with a human village at night. The air was still as death. Only a faint musty smell caught his nose.

Pjodarr pulled back the curtain of animal furs and stepped into the hut. He poked his head out and waved Gruesome in. The big havtrol had to squat to get through the low opening. An old woman lay peacefully on a bed of blankets.

"Does she sleep?"

The shaman shook his head and knelt by the still form. He touched his fingers to her breast and pulled them away, rubbing them together. "Blood. She was stabbed through while she slept."

"I do not smell it. She must have died some time ago."

Pjodarr shrugged. "I cannot tell. But if she died some days ago, why has no animal claimed her? No sign of worm or maggot?"

"Was she a witch? Killed by the villagers and left here? No beast of Fjur would dare eat the corrupted corpse of a witch."

The old man shook his head. "She just looks like an old woman. Dark magic deforms the body and soul, true. But they leave their marks long before death. No, she was killed while she slept, and her fire stepped out with care."

Gruesome looked at the small circle of stones in the middle of the hut. True to the shaman's words, the fire was deliberately stamped out.

Blade grunted in anger behind them. The dwarf never made a sound, unless while fighting. The slave jumped to his feet and bolted past the havtrol. The big warrior followed, to a most disturbing sight.

Blue lightning crackled from Blade's sword as the old Warshield called upon the power of Bodr, the glorious war god. It arced around him, charring half a dozen tiny white bodies. They looked like hairless rats, eyes pale as if blind. They swarmed from some of the other huts toward the dwarf.

"Master!" Pjodarr called and thrust his arms forward. Wind rushed past him, hurling some of the creatures through the air. They simply righted themselves and charged toward Blade again. The dwarf hacked at them with his sword. Gruesome roared and leapt onto a mass of the hideous beasts. He stamped them underfoot and smashed their little bodies with his hands. But the rest of the vermin simply ignored him and continued toward the general. Sharp roots poked from the dirt at the shaman's beckoning, stabbing a few of the albino rats, but many just squeezed past them. None of the things made a sound, even as they died. They continued their onslaught of the dwarf, climbing up his armored legs. A dozen of the creatures crawled around on him. Flailing shield and sword wildly, Blade fell on his back and a dozen more covered him.

Pjodarr rushed to his master, but fell back with a cry as the Warshield unleashed a spray of lightning from his entire body. The slave held his right hand painfully and looked at Gruesome. "Help him!" The havtrol scrambled to the dwarf's side, clawing little bodies off him. Lightning flashed again, but Gruesome snarled back the pain. As many as the dwarf killed, double that number took their place. His arms swung in a panic. The edge of the great sword sliced easily into the havtrol's unprotected left hand. Gruesome rolled backwards and watched in horror as Blade became a mass of writhing, pale flesh. The things completely covered the dwarf.

"Master!" Pjodarr shouted to the night. "Master!"

Soft, blue light cascaded over them, coming from the village's center. There, just a few yards away stood two figures, one tall and lean, draped in chain armor from head to toe, a large sword held in both hands in a warrior's stance. The other was only a few inches shorter and leaner still. The clothes weren't visible under a dark cloak, but the face was that of a young man. His eyes squinted in concentration as his mouth moved in a rush of whispered words. In his right hand, he held a staff of black wood. The blue light emanated from something set atop it.

As one, the white rats stopped moving. Blade lay motionless

beneath their still bodies. Then their noses all twitched in the air, and every one of the vermin moved slowly toward the young man, until they completely encircled him and his friend. Gruesome moved his hand to the hammer on his right hip. He looked to Pjodarr. The shaman was crouched just a step away, singed hands trembling. The sorcerer waved his left hand over the ugly creatures, and then whipped the staff over his head in a flash. Gruesome started as all of the tiny, white forms exploded in a small shower of dark blood. Not a one of them even twitched afterwards.

The young man looked down at his clothes, as if to make sure none of the blood spattered his own dress, before walking toward the three of them. The light from his staff dimmed and vanished. His armored companion followed diligently, weapon at the ready.

"Hello," the young man said softly in norovid, the language of humans from Bergmark. His accent was sharp, unlike any Gruesome had heard from Calderan or Anduain folk. He held his left palm out, and Gruesome could now see that his hair was short and blond. The thing on his staff was some sort of cloudy-blue quartz, carved in the shape of a skull. The wizard nodded to each of them and fixed them with a wide smile. "I am Tarac. It is a pleasure to meet you."

Chapter 3

"This is my guardian, Folik, please forgive his silence. He is not rude; he simply has no tongue to be able to speak."

Gruesome and Pjodarr stared at the young man. Never had the havtrol witnessed such magic as this Tarac performed. And now he spoke to them as if they were simply travelers meeting in the commons of some great hall.

"I am Pjodarr," the shaman returned in norovid, never at a loss for words, although his usual greeting was far more blustering. "Yon is my master Blade of House Thurin, General of the First Army, Lord of Northwatch. This is Gruesome," he waved his shaking left hand in the big brute's direction. "Mighty warrior of Clan Beartooth."

"Ah, I see the helm," Tarac said gleefully. "How remarkable." He bowed low, Folik doing the same. "T'would seem I am in honored company. I beg your forgiveness beforehand, but I am not experienced with the customs of dwarf and havtrol. We have traveled most of this way alone, following the river."

"Yes, well, would you mind if we get ourselves somewhat settled then, sir Tarac? I would see to all of our wounds."

"Oh, you are a shaman! How delightful! Of course, tend to your companions. Folik and I will await you here."

With a grimace, Pjodarr spoke soft words. His body shook as white magic flowed out from him. He sighed in relief and shook his now-healed hands, then rubbed them together. He walked over to where Gruesome still knelt on the ground and placed both hands on the havtrol's thick chest. With more ease he cast the spell that sent a wave of healing magic through the warrior's body. Gruesome felt the sting of mending flesh as the cut on his hand closed and the small burns under his armor washed away under the shaman's spell. The slave shared an odd stare with the havtrol before moving on to Blade.

"Master," he soothed and helped the dwarf to his feet. "Let us see how you fare." He walked Blade behind the hut that held the old woman's corpse.

"Is there a problem?" Tarac's face showed real concern.

"He lets no one see his master out of his armor," Gruesome rumbled.

The pair returned shortly. "Not a mark on him," the shaman said quizzically, in the language of dwarves.

"I would suspect as much," the young sorcerer said, again using norovid.

"You speak dvarid?" Pjodarr asked in the human tongue.

"Speak, no. Understand, some. I read it better."

"And trolvid?" The shaman inquired, somewhat bemused.

Tarac bowed to Gruesome. "Alas, no. My people have no dealing with your own. So there was no one to teach me."

The havtrol merely shrugged his shoulders.

"Well, perhaps, we would all be content with using norovid, then, Tarac." Pjodarr bowed his own head to the much younger man.

"I would greatly appreciate that, and again apologize for the inconvenience."

The wizard's politeness was...unnerving...to Gruesome. He'd met with all manner of folk, from lowly slave to noble king, and none displayed such bizarre manners. The shaman was better at dealing with people, so he decided to hold his tongue. Pjodarr walked to another hut and pulled back the flap. He stared for a moment, then stepped back and moved the silver mask to the top of his head. He looked at the havtrol with sad eyes, his tattooed face unreadable in the dark.

"They are all dead, good shaman. All those that remain here, anyways."

The old slave nodded slowly. "Gruesome, would you mind starting a fire for us while I retrieve the var?" He then walked further into the village, and the warrior knew what hut he sought. With his stomach in knots, Gruesome drew flint and steel and bent over a large circle of stones set amid several of the huts. Central fire pits like this were set throughout the village to be lit in the coldest parts of winter.

It was quite a while before Pjodarr returned with the var. He'd taken his time putting the kits back on them. Gruesome knew why. Humans and dwarves went to great lengths to hide their grief and fear from others, where havtrols celebrated their emotions. Not that a havtrol knew fear. But rage at your enemies, joy at the birth of your son, sadness at the loss of a loved one, these were what defined each soul. Sadness. This thought brought emptiness to Gruesome. Sadness filled him now. For the past five years. Sadness for his own actions. But his honor would be reborn.

The five sat quiet around the fire for some time. Well, three sat. Folik and Blade both stood, as if on guard.

"Have you eaten?" Pjodarr asked solemnly.

"Not since yesterday." Tarac shrugged. "I am not the best hunter."

"We will all eat, and talk. I'm sure we all have questions." The shaman then busied himself preparing a stew of the tough wyvern meat he'd dried out.

They ate in silence. Blade shoveled deliberate spoonfuls of the awful stew into his mouth, and then dropped the spoon and bowl to the ground. He drank deep from a water skin when Pjodarr offered it to him. Folik took no sustenance, nor did Tarac offer him any. Gruesome and the slave exchanged glances at this, but said nothing. Finally, the shaman leaned his back against a large stump and fixed his cool, gray eyes on the young wizard.

"What happened here, Tarac? Who killed these people?"

"I-I cannot say," the sorcerer shrugged. He sat with his hands clasped over his belly. Gruesome had time to study the man more during their meal. The boy, for he was truly more boy than man, was tall for his age. But his face gave it away: innocent eyes, energetic smile, and the smooth skin of the privileged. His clothes were of deep purple, plain but finely woven. His thick, black cloak was lined with dark fur. His leather boots were dyed the same purple and also lined with fur, and as well-cared for as the rest of his attire. He wore no charms or trinkets, as most wizards were apt to do. Even Pjodarr had a necklace of small skulls and other items under his armor. The wizard's staff was another matter. It was of ornately carved wood, painted such a deep black that it looked to be the natural color. The crystal skull on top was unremarkable; the moonlight did not even shine off it. But Gruesome remembered the soft glow from before, and Tarac kept the staff close at hand at all times.

"Do you not know, or do not wish to tell?"

"Oh, I do not know at all, good shaman," Tarac stammered. "I only know that no one living was left here."

"How do you know?"

"I was searching the other side of the village when you all arrived. I went through many of the other huts." He shifted his wide eyes to the ground and scraped at something with his foot. "I went through more than enough of them."

Pjodarr's eyes never left Tarac's face. Gruesome watched the shaman intently, and wondered what worked in the man's mind. Havtrols never shared humans' curiosity.

"Were they all killed the same? A single blade through the heart?"

Tarac nodded. "They went peacefully, in their sleep, at least."

"Small consolation for a young life cut short by murder." Masked grief tinted his words.

"When Drogu calls, all must answer." The death god. Gruesome's chest tightened. He met the shaman's eyes. Pjodarr leaned forward.

"Where are you and Folik from, Tarac?"

The boy raised his head to meet the old man's gaze. "I am Tarac, High Priest of Drogu, and Shepherd of the Souls of Durum Tai."

Durum Tai! City of the dead!

Gruesome rose slowly to his feet and pointed his finger at Folik. "What is that thing, boy?" The armored figure stepped between Tarac and the havtrol, sword held up. Gruesome's hands caressed the hammer and axe at his hips.

Tarac held out his left palm. "Peace, good warrior, we wish no fight." Gruesome growled. "Folik is my guardian. He will only fight to protect me." The sorcerer stood up and exchanged long looks with both the havtrol and the shaman. Only Pjodarr remained seated. "It was only for that purpose that I raised him."

The old slave hissed and spat into the fire. Gruesome's body tensed. Necromancer. Folik was a walking corpse, obeying the unnatural commands of its evil master. All of the big warrior's misgivings about the young man were more than founded.

"Gruesome," the shaman said calmly. "Please sit. I'm sure young Tarac here means us no harm. Or else why break bread with us? Why save Master Blade from those...*things*?" He heard the wisdom of Pjodarr's words, but this necromancer...

He gritted his teeth and choked down his bitter disgust, and slowly lowered himself to his haunches. The undead abomination relaxed slightly, but stood even closer to its master. The necromancer stood still, eyes to the ground.

"Please, Tarac, sit. I'm sure we can all be reasonable here, now can't we?"

"Of course," the boy's voice was barely a whisper. He returned to his seat, his head down and back straight. He gripped his staff tightly.

"Thank you, by the way, for saving my master. I have no idea what we would have done." Tarac raised his head to look at the shaman and gave him a meek smile. "Which raises more questions. What were those things, and what did you do to them?"

"Hmm," the necromancer thought. "Well, while I've never seen them before today, they reminded me of the little creatures from the legends. *Kriote*...soul scavengers. I saw them feeding on some of the dead here, so I'm sure that's what they were. Why they attacked your friend-"

"Master," Pjodarr corrected him.

"Hmm?"

"He is my master, I am his servant. It would be improper for you to call him my friend to others."

"Oh, yes, sorry. We do not have slaves in Durum Tai."

"No, I don't suppose you would. Now what do you mean by legends? And soul scavengers?"

"Well, the legends of the Hungry Gods, of course." Gruesome and Pjodarr stared at him, confused. "You do not know the legends of the Hungry Gods?" They both shook their heads. "I see. Well, long ago the Hungry Gods came from the depths of hell to steal-"

Pjodarr interrupted him with a wave of his hand. "Tarac, Tarac, hold on. Let's do one thing at a time here. Tell us about the soul scavengers first. What are they?"

The necromancer shrugged. "Just that. They are soul scavengers. They feed on the dead as their souls make the journey to the other side."

What skin was visible on the shaman's face went pale. "Why would they attack my master?"

Tarac shrugged again and stared at Blade for a moment. "That is a mystery to me as well. According to the legends, if they find a fresh corpse, they can drain the soul from it like *that*!" He snapped his fingers. "But nothing in the tales told of them attacking the living. That's why I had to help your frie-...master."

"Yes, that. What did you do to them?"

The conjuror beamed. "Quite clever, if I do say so myself. I did not even know if it would work!" He leaned forward with eager eyes. Gruesome found himself crouching forward as well. "I made an aura of my own energy, and shaped it into a soul. A strong soul. Once they surrounded me, I lifted it above their heads, just out of reach to hold them in place." He spread his palms to the sky. "Then I killed them." He leaned back. "Mindless beasts do not take precedence over living souls. So, I was obligated to save the good dwarf."

The shaman gaped at the young man. "Amazing."

"Oh, not really. High Priest Brodjak has done much more amazing things. He is incredibly old and wise."

"Why are you here, Tarac?" The shaman's words came out with deliberate slowness. The younger man's face turned red and he averted his eyes from the slave's.

"Destiny, good shaman. Why are any of us here?"

Chapter 4

The old man watched the full moon through the trees. Fjur's night eye was high overhead, but Pjodarr knew sleep would not come to any of them tonight. The havtrol stared at the Folik creature with open disgust, his clawed hands never far from the hammer and axe at his sides. If the dead man made a move toward them, the shaman had no doubt it would be just a pile of bones again before it took two steps. Gruesome was stronger and faster than any being he'd seen in his long years. Well, long years for a human. He was a fraction of his master's age and still twenty years the junior of the Beartooth warrior, but he felt every bit of his sixty-plus years.

He turned his attention to Master Blade, the quiet statue standing just inside the fire's light. The dwarf's one eye stared blankly ahead. *What hell did I put you in, Master?* The shaman thought of the kriote things and how Tarac had said they only attacked the dead. His master ate, drank, bled; why did they think him dead? Guilt crushed Pjodarr's heart. Had he taken his oath too far? He missed his master, even though he hadn't left his side in seventeen years.

He moved his thoughts from the dwarf. Only sadness grew there. But the boy…

The old slave eyed Tarac carefully. The necromancer hadn't

said a word in hours now. None of them had. The tension was thicker than flies on a dung heap, but what could be done? Gruesome's honor would not allow him to simply murder the boy unless Tarac attacked them first. Pjodarr had no idea what the boy and his pet were capable of, and he had no intention of attacking them without knowing their abilities.

Tarac was young, unsure of himself. He had difficulty making eye contact and was afraid of unknowingly insulting Gruesome and Blade, yet he trafficked with the dead. Did he not think robbing graves upset anybody? Pjodarr knew nothing of Durum Tai and its people, save the stories told around fires at night. Any outsiders that sought the city out were skinned alive and raised from the dead to work the salt mines. The only evidence that the city existed were the caravans that brought their precious salt and the bitter winterberry wine loved by dwarves. No one dared travel to the city of the dead.

Still, the necromancer seemed polite enough, and Pjodarr certainly didn't want Tarac suspecting he'd spent the past few hours thinking of ways to kill him. So, he figured he might as well make the boy feel more comfortable.

"You said you were a high priest, Tarac?"

The young man looked shocked that one of them spoke to him. "Y-yes, sir."

"Don't call me 'sir'. I am only the servant of my master." Tarac nodded with a small smile. "I asked because I wonder if all high priests are as young as you. You can't be more than seventeen or eighteen."

"I just turned eighteen this year, good shaman. But no, it takes a long time for most to rise to the rank of High Priest. There are only twelve of us. I am considered a special case."

"Aren't we all," Pjodarr gave the young man his most affable smile. To his satisfaction, Tarac returned it. "You are eighteen, so you were born in the year of the Century Star?"

"Yes, on the last night of its passing. The priests took it as a sign. I was raised to be a High Priest, taught everything about our people. I learned our entire history, from the time of the prophet Mephraim to High Priest Hyrgdaal, who discovered the power of the blood. I am practiced in all of our magic, not just soul-walking." The necromancer talked as if Pjodarr had any idea of what he spoke. The old man decided to let him continue rambling and save his questions for later. "When I turned fifteen, I was raised to the rank of High Priest when good Dorid passed into Drogu's arms. As customary, I walked him to the other side. It was my first time to do so." Tarac stared into the fire. "I was so nervous, but he helped show me the way. Such a kind man; I'll never forget his soul. It was beautiful." A sad smile spread across his face; then he shook his head and looked at Pjodarr.

"Tarac," the shaman said softly as he looked into the man's eyes. They were wide and green. "Tell me about Folik." Gruesome shifted in his seat, but Pjodarr held the necromancer's gaze. "Ease an old man's mind."

"I am sorry; I know you people are not used to our

guardians. But he is such a part of me that I forget how upsetting he might be to those that do not understand." He took a deep breath then smiled again. "I raised him when I was eight, the youngest to ever do so. It was a test, to see if I might truly be the prophet reborn." Another question for later. "Folik was a mighty Bloodguard. I remembered his story well from reading it a few years earlier. He was a true hero." Tarac looked at the dead man with unmasked awe. "A group of children were picking winterberries in the vineyard, and Folik was there watching over them. One of them was his son, Dravel." He turned back to the old man, his young face solemn. "Three trolls ran at them from the forest. Folik called for the children to run back to the city and threw himself between them and the monsters. How he fought off three full-grown trolls, no one knows. But when the other Bloodguards arrived, good Folik lay dead along with two of the trolls. They killed the last and carried Folik's body back to the temple. The whole city celebrated him as a hero, and he was immediately named a future guardian. When it came time for me to choose, his was the only name that passed my lips." He bowed his head. "I only hope to honor his mortal remains as his soul deserves."

Pjodarr stared at him. "You mean you dug him up because he was your hero?" Gruesome grunted in disgust.

"What? No!" Tarac looked aghast. "What do you mean 'dug up'?"

"Where did you get his body?"

"At his death, his body was embalmed and placed in the

vault!"

"And what about his family?" The shaman felt his anger rise. "Why did they not get to see him to his final resting place?"

"Why would they go against his wishes?"

Pjodarr shook his head. "He wished to be-," he waved his hand at the corpse standing by Tarac's side. "-*this?*"

"Of course, all Bloodguard do!" The necromancer was incredulous. "It is the goal of all Bloodguard to become a guardian for a High Priest. It is a great honor for them and their family. That is why it is only given to those who perform extraordinary feats."

"This is a reward?" Gruesome was shocked. Pjodarr was almost as shocked to hear the havtrol speak.

"Of course. It was only in the War of the Free that the priests raised the dead to fight the dwarves. Then it was proclaimed that only High Priests could raise a guardian, and they could only raise those that gave their remains willingly. It is custom to wait several decades to raise them." Tarac raised a finger as if he talked to children. "Some souls linger longer than others, and we do not want to take any chances."

The old slave sat in disbelief. The boy spoke as if this were completely normal. As if they should all have been aware of the rules for raising the dead. In the face of such madness what could you do?

Pjodarr laughed. He laughed heartily, such as he had not in seventeen years. He did not care if Gruesome and Tarac stared at him, for the absurdity was too comical for him to hold it in.

The havtrol growled. "What is wrong with you, shaman?"

The slave patted himself on the chest and tried to regain his composure. "Nothing, mighty Gruesome." He pointed at Folik. "I just don't know if we should build him a pyre, or give him a medal!" None of the others shared his mirth.

"A pyre would not be appropriate. We bury our dead; we do not burn them." Tarac's tone was almost chiding. Pjodarr feared he had upset the nice boy.

"I'm sorry, friend Tarac. I meant no disrespect. It is simply that you have no idea how odd you are to us." The necromancer looked hurt, and shied from the shaman's gaze. "I do not mean that as an insult, son, but none of us have ever met anyone like you. Or Folik, for that matter. And that is saying a lot. Master Blade is over three hundred years old and has never met one of your folk. The only things the other Bergsbor know of Durum Tai is that you trade salt cheaply, brew the bitterest wine in all the lands to the delight of dwarves everywhere, and no army that marched against you has ever returned."

Tarac's eyes went wider than the full moon above. "That is true. We shut ourselves off to keep the dwarves from attacking us. The prophet Mephraim decided that they would not bother us if we did not bother them. And so it was. We were not threatened again until Freemark attacked us." The fire danced in his bright green eyes. "By then, we'd learned the power of the blood."

There it was again. Power of the blood? Pjodarr had heard rumors. Among the undead that walked Durum Tai, were creatures that drank the blood of their victims. Could they be the Bloodguard that Tarac mentioned? He could talk to the boy for a fortnight and not exhaust his own curiosity, but Gruesome had business to attend. The great warrior was bound by oath to kill the Honorless, only their blood would cleanse his. Pjodarr knew the havtrol was anxious to be on the hunt.

"You are fascinating, Tarac." The shaman stretched his back and legs. "But dawn comes soon, and we've more immediate things to discuss."

The young man nodded.

"First, how did you come to Willowbrook at this time?"

"Willowbrook, good shaman?"

Pjodarr gestured at the huts around them. "This village. How is it you are here? And all these people are dead?"

"Surely you don't think I had anything to do with this!" Pjodarr saw the hurt in the boy's eyes, and felt a pang of guilt. "I would never harm a child. I have only committed violence in defense of myself." He pointed at Blade. "Or others."

"I did not say that. But these are odd circumstances, aren't they?"

"Indeed." Gruesome's deep voice dripped with menace.

The necromancer looked from one to the other; his eyes settled on the fire. "I am on a pilgrimage, of sorts. My birth was deemed a sign. Then the Great City fell, and the world was plunged into war. It was decided that I would be trained and sent here, to the southern continent. With only Folik to accompany me, I was my own guide." He blushed and gave a weak smile. "Once I arrived at Blackgate to the north, I kept to the river."

"Why did you choose Blackgate? Why not the human cities? It must have been a treacherous journey east to the dwarf ports."

"It was," Tarac nodded. "But I wanted to see it."

Pjodarr smiled bitterly. "It was beautiful. The greatest city the world has ever known, all carved stone and worked gold. A monument to the gods that slept beneath it." He shook his head. "Now it is nothing but ash and the smoldered wreckage of nobility."

"Yes," Tarac agreed. "The Great Mountain still belches black smoke into the air. Words cannot describe it." They all sat silent for a moment before he continued. "Besides, I was told that dwarves are less troublesome to deal with than the free cities. 'Be nice, and pay with gold,' they told me."

"My master's people do like to keep things simple. But why are you *here*? In all of Caldera, why Willowbrook?"

The young man wrung his hands and bit his lower lip. "I-I do not know exactly. I was drawn here." He finally looked up at the old man. "And not just here. There was another village to the west."

"What do you mean?"

"I found it, just like this one. Everyone that died was killed in their sleep."

Pjodarr leaned forward. He thought he knew the little village Tarac talked about, just on the edge of Brinnoch. "Everyone that died?"

"Oh, yes, I forgot. You have seen very little of what

happened here." He clasped his hands against his chest and bowed his head. "Only the very old and very young were killed. The rest are simply… gone. Men, women, older children, all gone, and the livestock taken too. Only the dead and the kriotes remained." He frowned. "And the smell of dark magic."

"You think these people killed their own and left with their animals?" Villages in the forest didn't keep more than a few chickens and goats for eggs and milk. They relied on hunting and foraging to survive. But why would they kill their elders, their own children? The little girl's angelic face filled the shaman's thoughts and he swallowed hard.

"No, good shaman, that doesn't seem reasonable at all. I have nothing but suspicions right now. And remorse."

"Remorse for what, necromancer?"

Tarac sighed and seemed to take no notice of Gruesome's accusation. "For the souls of these dear people. I fear what happens when the kriote have their way with them. I walked at the other village, and saw them as they fed." He shuddered. "It was horrifying." He grabbed a water skin from his belt and took a long draught. "I followed them here. I arrived a while before you all. I did not need to watch while they fed. Then I destroyed them all when they attacked your master." He looked at Pjodarr with sad eyes. "I'm not sure what to do now."

The old slave felt sympathy for the odd boy. "This is your destiny, Tarac? You think you were sent here to avenge these good people?"

"Avenge? I do not know about that. I would not know how to begin to avenge them. But I believe I was sent to discover what happened to them." He pursed his lips. "I have had dreams in this land. They have guided me here. They have led me to this place, at this time. Perhaps I am meant to meet you."

Gruesome grunted and Pjodarr chuckled. "I cannot imagine what answers you hope to find from three old warriors. We know less about what happened here than you." He looked over at the havtrol. "And we have matters of our own."

"What could be more important than discovering the fate of the ones that left here?"

"We are hunters," Gruesome rumbled.

"Yes, I saw the wyverns on your var."

"No, necromancer, we hunt a much more dangerous prey. The Honorless have come here from the mountains. They will kill everything in their path."

"Honorless?" Tarac cocked his head at the big warrior.

Pjodarr cleared his throat. "Havtrols who have forsaken their oaths. Gruesome is sworn to spill their blood. Master Blade and I have promised to help him. We tracked them here, then they went north. We are within a day or so of them. If we do not catch them, who knows what carnage they will unleash. There are other settlements, more innocents."

"And they are in danger of this as well!" Tarac motioned around them. "Would these Honorless destroy an entire village?"

Gruesome jumped to his feet. Folik raised his sword in

defense. "Nine havtrol warriors that did not hold themselves to honorable combat would lay waste to this village. They would commit horrors you cannot imagine!"

"Yet the three of you would face them? Where three hundred souls would die, you would not?" The young man looked from the havtrol to the shaman.

Pjodarr smiled and winked at Tarac. The fire flashed and a man of flame stood before the boy. Tarac fumbled backwards, grasping for his staff. Folik took one quick step and slashed through the fiery figure. His sword passed through the flames harmlessly. The old shaman waved his hand and the fire crackled and popped as if it had never changed. The necromancer held his hand up and the dead man relaxed his stance.

"You're not the only one with tricks, boy."

Chapter 5

Gruesome clawed the earth. The cold ground did not give itself easily, but he did not need a big hole. The shaman would do the rest. The necromancer stood nearby, as silent as the abomination that followed him. The havtrol did not share Pjodarr's apparent tolerance of the boy and was thankful their paths were about to part. He stood and inspected his work. It would do.

Pjodarr carried the small form wrapped in a blanket in both arms. Gruesome knew the slave's silver mask hid the tears. The slave was soft-hearted; his master's mute existence was proof of that. But Gruesome understood. Though he did not have tears to shed for the little girl, he knew the shaman held her dear to his heart. The old man nodded his head at him as he approached.

"Thank you, friend Gruesome. That does make it easier." Pjodarr stared at the shallow grave. The earth trembled slightly as the hole deepened and the walls became smooth. Piles of dirt grew around the edges. Once satisfied with his work, the shaman gently laid the girl in the ground. He stood and spread his arms wide. "Fjur, we offer you this gift," he said in dvarid. "Though her soul has left this vessel, we commend her body back to you, Great Giver. For it was with her actions that she showed the beauty of all life. From hands that crafted with care to a smile that gave joy to all, she was one of your true blessings. And for this we thank you, and return her to your embrace."

With that, the old man slowly brought his hands to his chest. The dirt poured into the grave until only a perfectly smooth mound remained. Pjodarr stretched his left hand toward the village, and made a motion as if grasping something. The rounded white stones of a fire pit rolled and tumbled in a line then encircled the little girl's resting place. The shaman held his right hand over the grave and whispered to himself. Nothing stirred around them, but the slave's hand began to tremble. He stayed that way for some moments before finally making a fist. He lightly shook his hand, and then smiled at his master.

"She liked daisies. Now they will forever grow over her, Master." The old dwarf just looked ahead, his mind unreadable to Gruesome. Did he even know the shaman's words?

Tarac swallowed hard. "That was beautiful, Pjodarr." The havtrol was shocked to see tears flow freely down the conjurer's face. "Who was she?"

Pjodarr stared at the girl's grave. "Just some much needed light in the darkest of times."

Silence reigned in the early morning hours as they prepared to leave. The necromancer watched them pack the var, and Gruesome wondered why the boy just didn't leave them. Although sleep never came for any of them, the big warrior did not feel tired. Of course, a havtrol's stamina was legendary. A fully armored war pack could run for two days straight without rest if need be. But the boy and his undead pet had him on edge. His heart ached for the fates of the people of Willowbrook, but his duty came first. He was sworn to rid the land of his own people that had forsaken their oaths to the gods. They killed innocents, for sport. They partook of the flesh of havtrol, dwarf and man. They turned their backs on their honor and gave up all reasoning. He had to spill their blood to end their wretchedness.

Pjodarr helped his master atop a var, and then turned to the boy. "I consider it an honor to meet you, Tarac. I wish you well in your journey and hope you find the answers you seek."

The necromancer worked his fingers along the etchings in his staff. "I-umm," he trailed off, eyes on his feet. "I don't know exactly what to do now. I don't know where to go."

The shaman fixed him with a stare. "You said the rest of the village might have left with the animals. Follow their trail."

"I don't know how to do that," the boy blushed. "I am not a tracker."

"It won't be hard to follow a couple hundred folk and their livestock, trust me." Pjodarr shook his head.

"I was actually wondering," Tarac stopped and cleared his throat. "I was actually wondering if I could join you."

"What?!" Gruesome growled.

The shaman stared at the young man. "Join us? But your destiny lies elsewhere. Would you risk it all fighting a pack of savage havtrols with three old men?"

"I have thought about it." Tarac raised his head and

straightened his back. He looked the havtrol in the eyes, and then focused on Pjodarr. "I am not helpless. I have power. I could help you kill these Honorless. I could join you on your quest, then you could join me on mine."

Gruesome growled.

The old slave cocked his head. "And why would we do that?"

"Because," he gestured to the girl's grave. "You cared for her. She was taken from you, and you want to know why. You have all shown me kindness, even if you do not approve of what I am." He nodded to the thing at his side. The havtrol felt his lip curl in a snarl. Tarac bowed his head to him. "Sometimes the kindest thing is to remain silent when all you have are harsh words. And I appreciate that, good warrior."

Gruesome was taken aback. What manner of person was this boy?

"It appears I have much to learn. I am lost in these lands. And, though I did not say it before, you have been the only folk to offer me simple conversation. I am alone, and I do not wish to be. Is that wrong of me?"

"No, boy, of course not," Pjodarr said softly. "But I don't think you truly understand the danger of what we face. The Honorless are not like Gruesome. They won't have *any* words for you. They kill all but each other without question. And this group is larger than any we've seen before."

"Some have taken the fall of the Great Mountain to mean

their oaths to the gods are forfeit," Gruesome offered. "My people have tremendous rage in battle. But we save it for battle. These live with it always."

Tarac's face hardened. It was almost a comical sight on the young man. "Then who's to say you don't need me? Folik and I have seen battle. We are not strangers to violence. And I share your desire to protect the weak from such as the Honorless. I also wish to never see a village like this one again." He waved his hand at Willowbrook. "Do you feel the same?"

Gruesome looked at the quiet remains of the hunting village. They had visited it often. At first, the people were afraid of him and mistrustful of the dwarf. But the old slave had a way about him, and the folk of Wilowbrook had warmed to them. The villagers were simple and hard-working, like havtrols. They were not like the lazy humans of the big cities. They soon welcomed the three warriors, trading readily with them and sharing news from other travelers. The men marveled at his weapons and armor, and showed him great respect. The children wanted to ride his back more than they wanted to sit on the var! He had begun to look forward to visiting the village at every new moon.

Sorrow darkened his heart. The boy was correct. It was not right what happened here. Gruesome growled low and met Tarac's eyes.

"We do not promise your safety. Your people might call you High Priest, but that means nothing here."

Pjodarr looked at the havtrol in shock.

"You do whatever we say," Gruesome continued. He pointed a thick finger at the dead man. "And you keep that *thing* away from me. Whatever power you use to make the dead walk, will not touch me!" He cocked a thumb at the shaman and Blade. "Or them! If I feel for a moment that you cannot be trusted, I will rip you apart."

Tarac gulped and nodded. "I wish no harm to any of you. Indeed, I will do all I can to protect you from it."

Gruesome chuckled deep in his chest. "You think to protect me, little one?"

"I thought you said all must answer to Drogu, Tarac?"

"So, I did, good shaman." The necromancer lowered his head to Pjodarr. "But that does not mean that I would stand by while others would do harm. It is not the strength of another's arms that should decide our fate. Murder and violence are tools of other gods, or the choice of man. Drogu would have us pass peacefully into his realm."

"I never heard that before."

"My people believe that harmony is the providence of Drogu. Why would he wish unsettled souls in his care? Why would he wish a child such as this one," he waved to the ring of stones, "to come to him before their earthly purpose was fulfilled? I said what I said earlier because I wished to ease your mind. As a shepherd of my people, I have learned that sometimes you must say things you don't necessarily believe to bring peace to others."

Pjodarr paused. "So you think her soul 'unsettled'?"

"You must have known her well enough, good shaman. Do

you think she was ready to die, or did she still have the love and fire of life inside her?"

The slave looked at his master. Gruesome wondered what went on behind the mask. Finally, the old man faced Tarac again. "I think I would show whoever killed her the wrath of Fjur's favorite son."

"We have other business first." Gruesome hauled himself atop the female var.

Pjodarr leapt onto the small male. "Have you ever ridden a var, friend Tarac?"

The boy gritted his teeth in a forced smile.

~~~~~

The var did not take kindly to Folik. Gruesome was not surprised. The shaman led them at a fast pace through the forest, first north, then slightly west. The Honorless did not linger at Willowbrook, as if they wished to put distance between themselves and the village. The warrior wondered what they had seen. Tarac rode behind Pjodarr. He had apparently never ridden anything before, not even a horse. His dead man was far behind them. The necromancer seemed more nervous without his "guardian", but swore that Folik would catch up to them eventually when asked.

What bond did the boy share with the corpse?

Pjodarr stopped them just after midday. He studied the ground carefully before remounting his var.

"We are getting closer. And the wind comes from the north. That's good."

"Can they smell us?"

"Not us, Tarac. The var. And var would mean a dwarf patrol to them." He grinned back at the necromancer. "The one thing we don't want is a pack of hungry havtrols on edge. Stealth is going to be our key." He urged the var on.

The hours passed quickly. Gruesome's stomach tightened as he knew they drew ever nearer to battle. His arms longed to swing his hammer and axe again, to feel the crush of his foe's bones beneath their weight. But he knew this would be no simple fight. Eight or nine of the beasts. It would be a struggle. But he had honor and friends at his side. He looked back at Tarac. And whatever he was.

The shaman halted them again as the sky above turned orange with the waning sun. The var were restless. "We'll lose the light soon; I'd rather not go rushing right into them." He scratched his mount behind one big ear. "What's got you so, boy?"

Gruesome took a deep drag of the wind. The smells of winter entered his senses. Dried leaves, the crispness of snow-filled air, and something else...

"Blood."

Pjodarr's masked face spun around. "You smell it?"

"Faint, but it is there. Must be fresh."

"Then they are close indeed." The old man dismounted and began helping his master down. "We will leave the var here for now."

Tarac fumbled his way off the smaller var. "We will attack them now? Can't we wait for Folik? We'll need his sword!"

"We're not going to just walk up and challenge them, boy! I will go and get a look at them. We don't know if they've found someone or killed another of their own. But you all must stay here. I can't have the rest of you trampling about like a herd of bison!"

The boy nodded. He was afraid. Gruesome doubted the young necromancer had the strength to survive the Honorless; but they needed to fight them *now*, before they moved on. Pjodarr wasted no time and left while Gruesome tended to the var. Tarac paced back and forth while the havtrol removed the kits from the raucous animals. He was not gentle with them like the shaman and they nipped and growled at him. When he was done, he faced the necromancer.

"If your pet is not back before Pjodarr, we will not wait for it. Every moment we let them live is a blight on my oath to Jaga."

Tarac said nothing.

They waited in silence. The night grew dark. Gruesome knew the shaman was clever and did not fear for the man's life, but each moment saw the boy becoming more fidgety. A true warrior had to be calm before battle. There was no time for short nerves when your enemy was upon you. The female perked up her ears before Pjodarr stepped from behind a tree.

"There are eight of them," he spoke quickly. "Another died and one of the eight looks badly wounded."

Gruesome felt relieved. "So, they fought amongst themselves then."

"No." The shaman did not look at him. "They found a party of humans, a small caravan of some sort. The men were able to kill one and hurt another, but they stood no chance. Couldn't have been more than thirty in their group."

"Eight havtrols killed thirty men?" Tarac's eyes were wider than a dwarf's shield.

"Some of them were women." He looked up through the thick net of limbs. "The men's fates were kinder." The old man turned to Gruesome. "They feast now. With their bellies full, they will want sleep. They will be slower."

The var all jumped to their feet and faced the way they'd come, hackles raised. Gruesome's weapons were in his hands before any of the big hounds could snarl.

The Folik creature raced between two trees, sword on its back. It sprinted in full armor, and then came to an abrupt stop at Tarac's side. The necromancer pressed his left hand against the things chest and sighed. He smiled at Gruesome, and the havtrol saw him fully composed. So, it was not the shaman that bothered him.

"Good," Pjodarr spoke low. "We're all here. Let's prepare."

Chapter 6

"Y ou have all forsaken your oaths!" Gruesome roared at the top of his lungs. Blade held shield and sword high beside him.

Sixteen rage-filled eyes glared at him. They snarled and growled through blood-drenched lips. He took in the sight of them, the horror of them. Dead bodies lay strewn about. Three horses were on their sides with their bellies and throats ripped open. They were still attached to a small cart. The dead men were mostly armored, maybe guards of some sort. The women were naked, ravaged and broken. Gruesome felt his blood rise.

"You have unwritten your honor in the blood of the innocent! You have turned your back on your people and your gods!"

An old havtrol spat blood at him. His warrior's braid unkempt, the savage's white hair hung loose behind him. The pale-skinned Honorless rose to his feet.

"The gods are dead, fool. Your oaths mean nothing."

"You would give your honor so easily for folly?" Gruesome had heard the line before. Did they truly think the sleeping gods died beneath the Great Mountain?

"Is it folly to take what we can with the strength given to us by your *gods*? Surely they meant us to be better than these weak bags of flesh!"

So, this was their leader. He was a big brute; Gruesome guessed he'd seen thirty seasons or more than himself. Two of the havtrols were completely bald. The rest were like the old one, a ring of hair above their ears only and long in the back. No hair grew on the top of any havtrol's head. Some of them wore scraps of ill-kept armor, but none held weapons of steel. The metal of the dwarves was not suited to life in the mountains. It needed care the Honorless could not provide. But their teeth and claws were weapon enough.

"You mistake your purpose, coward." They were all on their feet now. Blade did not twitch beside him. The old general would hold fast. Gruesome's own hands rested on the heads of his great weapons. These base creatures would soon feel the full weight of them.

The old havtrol smiled. "The two of you think you can take us? You think your honor will make you stronger?" The rest laughed. The leader reached to his feet and picked up a woman's limp body and shook it. She screamed. She was alive! Her clothes were ripped, and claw marks marred her flesh. "I was saving this one for later. But I will make you a bargain. Throw down that pretty steel of yours, and you may have her." He sniffed her hair and moaned. "Young and fresh!"

"You mistake *my* purpose now!" Gruesome hefted the hammer and axe. "You have all forgotten the names of your fathers. Your mothers shed tears for their lost sons." The Honorless stamped the ground and roared at him. "You have chosen your fates, and only your blood will make amends! Oblivion take you!"

He charged the leader. Blade moved with him. One havtrol threw itself at them, and the dwarf slammed his shield into its side. Glorious Tremble flashed and black blood flew. A club swung at Gruesome. He caught it with his axe-head and spun his feet. The great mallet in his right hand crushed into the brute's head. Its jaw cracked, and teeth and blood spilled out. Lightning crackled behind him.

Two more of the animals rushed Gruesome. Before they were a step away, giant roots sprang from the ground and wove themselves around their legs. The shaman held them in place while the warrior swung both arms. His hammer broke the collarbone of one, and his axe cut deep into the other's chest. Death would come later; he needed to weaken them all first. Snow rose up around him, and turned into huge slabs of ice. Two more havtrols slammed into them and the frozen walls shattered. But Gruesome was already past them. He was surrounded now by Honorless. This would keep them focused on him.

Something tackled him from behind. He fell to the ground, arms swinging. The old havtrol leaped onto his chest. The air rushed from his lungs, and he felt a rib crack. The old beast grasped his right arm with both hands and held it down. Another coward held his left arm. Their claws dug into his flesh where the steel plates of his armor did not cover.

"Hold him!" their leader screamed. A third fell on his right arm and sank teeth into chain mail on his right shoulder. Gruesome kicked his knee into the old one's gut. It grunted and wrapped rough hands around his neck. Spittle and blood fell on his face as the bastard leaned over him. "Join your gods in hell!"

The dark of night turned blacker as something rushed over them. With a growl, the female var slammed into the old havtrol. Sharp claws tore at Gruesome's neck as the hands were ripped from his throat. He hadn't even heard the shaman whistle for the var!

The creature on his left arm let go suddenly. It howled and scratched at its face. Gruesome and the other havtrol watched in horror as the thing's eyes, lips and tongue bulged and exploded in a shower of hot blood. It sizzled and steamed in the snow. Gruesome reacted first. He grabbed the Honorless on his right by the neck and lifted with both arms. It flailed as he raised himself to his feet and slammed the massive body onto the ground. He smashed his fists into the thick body again and again. He felt bones crack, but he did not stop until the beast's torso turned to mush.

Blood rushed in his ears, the rage was well upon him. The thing beneath him gurgled and coughed up black blood. Gruesome stood and looked around. One of the Honorless nearly ripped Folik's arm off. The dead man swung the big sword in one hand without as much as a flinch. The blade cut deep into its throat, and the godless havtrol fell to its knees. Folik twirled the hilt of his weapon in his hand until the blade pointed down and drove it through the havtrol's neck. Another Honorless was being torn apart by two var. The dwarf stood over the body of yet another.

"They're getting away!" Tarac's voice cut through the night. Gruesome spun around to see two of the havtrols running into the forest. He leapt after them.

"Gruesome, no!" The shaman beseeched him. The big warrior stopped in his tracks and looked at the old man.

"What?!" he roared.

"They are wounded; they will not get far! Tend to the living!" Pjodarr stood over the still form of a woman. She was naked and bleeding. The shaman threw off his cloak and draped it over her.

Gruesome roared after the Honorless. "You will not live another day! I will have your blood!" His breath steamed from his body. His heart pounded in his chest. He took a deep breath and offered a silent prayer to Jaga. He felt the rage leave him in a wave. The cuts and bruises he ignored earlier now ached.

He walked over to the shaman. The woman still did not move. Was she even alive?

"Carry her, please, Gruesome. We need to get her away from all this."

The havtrol bent to pick her up. She screamed in terror. She wrapped her arms about her legs and shook like a leaf. Her head moved back and forth as she wailed gibberish at them. Gruesome looked at Pjodarr. The old man waved him back and motioned to the necromancer. "Tarac, here, help me." Together they managed to lift the girl to her feet. She continued to sob as they carried her away from the carnage.

Gruesome picked up his weapons from the frozen ground.

The var fought over two of the havtrols. *Let them have them.* The Honorless gave up all they were when they broke covenant with the gods. It did not bother him for the var to eat their flesh. Blade still waited over his fallen adversary, sword and shield at the ready. The havtrol he'd beaten with his fists moved and vomited blood. Gruesome shifted the wide hammer in his hand, stepped over to the dying beast and smashed its head in with casual ease.

"You think this brings you peace, Beartooth?"

Gruesome realized the old Honorless still lived. He regarded it with disdain. "Peace for me? No. But peace to those you might slaughter."

The villain laughed and coughed up blood. The var had torn into its shoulder then ripped open its belly. The Honorless lifted a bit of its guts and waved them weakly at Gruesome. "Bags of flesh, that is all we are. All we ever were." Its eyes were wild and bloodshot. The pale skin of its face was whiter from loss of blood.

"You would deny the gods' reason?"

"Reason?!" It coughed again. "The gods are dead, fool." One eye closed as it shuddered in pain. "At least they had the comfort of dying in their sleep. My sons burned. Burned in the river of fire. My strong, glorious sons!" Tears flowed down its cheeks. "Tell me the gods' reason for that!"

"Ours is not to question the will of the gods."

"Ours is only to lose the prides of our heart to their whims?"

"We all lost loves in the Burning. Only the weak lost their honor with them."

"I know you, Beartooth. You were chief, now you hunt us. Your honor is tarnished, just like mine."

"NO!" The var jumped at the warrior's voice. "Not like you, never like you. My honor will be reborn in your blood."

The old havtrol smiled grimly at him through its tears. "Then take it. Choke on it and die. The gods are dead and oblivion waits for us all. You will never again see the face of whoever you killed, and I will never again see my sons."

"If the gods are dead, what kept you from the village?" Gruesome stepped toward the wretch. "If you are the strongest, why would you fear a village of hunters?"

Its dark eyes widened, then lowered to the ground. "Worse than me walks these woods, Beartooth. The devils have come, and they reap the souls forgotten by the dead gods."

Gruesome stood in front of the dying Honorless. "What did you see?"

Yellow teeth dripping with blood showed in a grim smile. "The end of all things. I was a blessing, fool; I only brought them death." It spit at Gruesome's boot. "You've saved no one."

"I would be rid of the stink of your breath, mad beast." He raised his hammer and felt the weight as it plunged downward and crushed the left side of the monster's head. The thing twitched, but its right eye still stared at him, full of murder and contempt. Even this close to death, the old outcast had no honor within it. With a final blow, Gruesome ended its miserable existence.

He looked one more time at the wreckage of life around him. No, killing these beasts did not bring him peace. Peace was not something he desired anymore. Now there was only honor and duty.

Chapter 7

The old shaman whispered soothing words to the girl. And a girl she was, for she could not be as old as Tarac.

"Do you have a torch, boy?"

"Yes, sir!"

"Light it, quickly!"

The necromancer fumbled flint and steel from a pouch at his side while Pjodarr pulled out his water skin. He offered it to the girl, but she only sobbed again. He knew she needed water because no tears fell as she cried. Her face was streaked with mud and blood, and he could not tell if the latter was all hers. He could heal her, but it would be more dangerous for her if she was dehydrated. Part of the magic relied on the body's ability to heal itself.

"Drink, girl, you are safe. No one will hurt you here," he whispered in dvarid. Her eyes were closed tight as her body shook and spasmed. He needed her to be calm if he was to tend to her. The cold night and terror of what she'd witnessed worked against him. Finally orange light bathed them. He did not look; he simply reached his left hand back and called the fire to him. He breathed more life into it as it floated above his palm. "Bring wood!" he called back to Tarac.

The boy was smart. Folik threw two large limbs down beside

the girl almost as soon as the words left his mouth. Pjodarr briefly mused how useful such a creature must be. He threw the flames on the wood and caused them to blaze with a wave of his hand. The girl's shivering subsided as the warmth washed over her. He poured water over her lips. She gasped and licked them with a swollen tongue. He offered her the skin again and this time she drank. He quickly pulled it away, and she coughed. He let her drink a little more, then a little more after that. He did not want her taking too much at once.

"I mean you no harm, dear. I must heal you." He pulled the cloak from her thin body to see the extent of her wounds. He shushed her as she cried out. She was naked but for a slave collar around her neck. A metal tag dangled from the thick leather. The old slave knew it held the crest of her master's family. Dried blood was smeared over her flesh, but she seemed to only suffer from a few scratches and some bruising. One of the scratches was deeper than the rest where the havtrols tore her clothes from her back. Pjodarr placed his hand over it and cast a spell. He pushed his will into the thin girl. Her breath caught as Fjur's gift flowed into her. Flesh mended and bruises lightened. At last she opened her eyes and looked up at the shaman. They were blue, with flecks of gold. Beautiful eyes that had seen things none should witness. The contact was brief, but he sensed some measure of relief from her. At least from her physical pain. He covered her again and leaned back.

"Is she...alright?" Tarac seemed anxious. Pjodarr was proud of the boy. He'd been calm before and during the fight, and Folik was amazing. Stronger and quicker than any man the shaman had ever seen. The fight only lasted a few moments, and the necromancer had shown great efficiency. Master Blade would have been impressed. But Pjodarr still wondered about the nature of the boy's magic.

"She's fine. Her wounds were minor. Now she just needs rest." He stood up. "And clothes. Could I trouble you to go back and find some? Search the cart. Make sure they're clean, please."

"Of course, whatever we can do."

Pjodarr looked at Folik. His left arm hung limp; the havtrol had almost ripped it from the socket. "Wait. Do you want me to see to Folik?" He thought for a second. "*Can* I see to Folik? Can he be healed?"

"I can see to him," Tarac gave a small grin. "I'll need to do it where we fought though."

Pjodarr was confused as he watched the boy go. He wondered if the folk of Durum Tai found Tarac so odd as well.

The shaman focused on making the girl more comfortable again. He spread the snow away from her and the fire. He gave her more water and left the skin beside her. He was using his power to soften the ground beneath her when Gruesome joined them with Blade in tow. The havtrol's neck still bled. Pjodarr walked over to the warrior; he pressed his palm into Gruesome's chest and removed the wounds. He went to his master. It appeared the dwarf's armor wasn't even touched. Pjodarr figured the havtrols would focus on Gruesome and he was right. He slapped his master's shoulders and smiled.

"You win again, old goat," he whispered.

Gruesome stood over the girl. "I left the var to feed. They will not touch the others, right?"

"No, they will only eat the havtrols. I was clear with them."

"Thank you, shaman." The big warrior nodded to him. "Your var saved me. But what did you do to the other one?"

"The other one?"

"The Honorless. How did you do that to his eyes?"

Pjodarr gave the havtrol a wry smile. "That wasn't me, my friend. That was the boy."

The warrior's dark eyes widened. "What did he do?"

"I have no idea," the old man shook his head. "But it was quick. He and Folik killed two of them. It looked easy."

"The girl will live?"

"She will. She needs food and sleep right now, but I do not think she will take either readily."

Gruesome knelt behind her. "I am sorry, girl." He placed one massive hand on her. She cringed and cried out. Her whole body shook in terror. The big havtrol pulled his hand away as if she burned him.

"I do not think she is ready to be touched by one of your people just yet."

The warrior nodded and stood. "I will leave her and retrieve your var's saddles."

"Be careful, those other two are still out there," Pjodarr

cautioned.

"They will not stop running for some time. They will stay together, but we cannot tarry long."

The shaman watched him go. How difficult the havtrol's life must be. His battle was never over.

Tarac returned. Folik carried a large leather bag full of items. His left arm seemed back to normal. Or what passed for normal for a corpse.

"I found many things on the cart. I think a woman would use them."

"Set the bag by her." The necromancer pointed his fingers at the girl and Folik laid the bag behind her. Pjodarr finally realized that she was a human slave. He cursed himself for speaking dvarid to her earlier. It was too easy to slip into his native tongue after a battle. "She needs to be cleaned and dressed, but I do not think she wants a man to touch her right now."

"I could have Folik-"

The shaman silenced him with a raised hand. "Something tells me that would not be an improvement. We will make camp a bit away and give her privacy."

"But what if they come back for her?" Tarac whispered.

Pjodarr spread his arms and made a motion as if covering something with both hands. The trees closest to the girl bent to the earth, shrouding her in a veil of thick limbs. "You will be safe," he said loud enough for her to hear. "When you feel well enough for food, we will be close. I have left an opening for you. We hope you

Kramer/McIntyre/Underhill

join us soon."

He waved for Tarac to follow him. He took them far enough that they could still be heard as they talked and began making a fire.

"Why don't you just call one up?"

"Call what up, boy?"

"A fire," Tarac said simply.

"Just snap my fingers and conjure fire? Do I look like a wizard to you?" He raised the silver mask from his face and grinned at the necromancer through his tattoo-covered face.

"No, I don't suppose you do." Tarac thought a moment. "But what you did back there, and with the campfire last night."

"That? Simple enough." Pjodarr sat back and looked at the sky. "Through communion with Fjur, I can control all of his elements. I can affect the bodies of his children, and have a great bond with his beasts. He shares with us shamen all of his gifts save one. He will not let us create."

"Create?"

"Wizards make fire and ice and wind and rock. But we have governance of these. A battle shaman will best a wizard any day."

"You are a battle shaman?"

Pjodarr waved his hand. A fist of snow rose from the ground and hit Tarac in the stomach. He winked at the boy. "What do you think?"

Gruesome joined them eventually. He sat silent while Pjodarr melted snow in a pot.

"Why do you go to such trouble tonight, shaman? We have

dried meat."

"The girl needs hot food, therefore it is no trouble."

The warrior grunted. "You will see her safe?"

"Wouldn't we all?" He did not look at the havtrol. He knew what thoughts lay in the big brute's mind.

"We will lose them. More people will suffer."

"The two Honorless?" Tarac interjected.

"Yes, they will move faster now. And they have eaten."

"But they are wounded."

"Pain does not matter to my people."

"No, good warrior, I mean they must be bleeding."

"And when the snow covers their blood?" Pjodarr knew the havtrol was losing patience with Tarac from his tone.

"But I can still follow them!"

The old warriors both looked at the necromancer. "You said you were not a good tracker."

"I'm not. Well, not in the sense of a hunter. Like you, I may not be able to create, but I can control."

"Control what, Tarac?"

"Blood, of course. I told you before."

"The power of the blood...," Pjodarr whispered under his breath. "You can *control blood*?"

"Well, yes, like the Bloodguard. Surely you know of High Priest Hyrgdaal and his work?"

"Tarac, how is this possible?"

The boy thought for a moment. "Well, you have to....hmm,

it is difficult to explain, I suppose. Took me years to learn, but I never had to teach anyone else."

"I don't want to learn it, boy." Pjodarr took a deep breath. "Tell me how you killed the havtrol back there, the one that was attacking Gruesome."

"Oh, well, I tried several things. But havtrols have thick muscles and flesh. So, I had to think of something else. Then it came to me!" The boy looked quite proud of himself. "I-," he closed his fist sharply. "-pushed his blood to his head. It was too much, even for his thick skull!"

Gruesome gaped at the necromancer. "You can do this?"

"That and more, let me show you!"

The warrior's big hands went for his weapons. Tarac raised his hands and bowed his head. This time Folik did not make a move to defend his master. "Peace, friend Gruesome. I wish to show you an aspect of the power, not attack you. Did you strike the two that fled?"

The havtrol relaxed somewhat. "One with hammer, one with axe."

"Excellent, have you cleaned your blade yet?"

"Not yet, but soon."

"Show me, please."

Pjodarr watched with rapt attention as Gruesome pulled the axe from his hip. He pointed the double-bladed head at Tarac. The boy rose carefully and peered at its edge. He bent the tip of his staff to it, whispering words of power. Blue light spread over the two figures. The hair on the back of the shaman's head stood on end as the night went silent. Tiny bits of dried blood flaked off the shiny steel. They followed the necromancer's staff and floated in the air, then crashed together in a splash as the blood turned to liquid again.

"Yes," Tarac moaned, his voice husky. "He still lives." He cast his big green eyes up to Gruesome. "And wherever he goes, the blood will follow."

The havtrol took two steps backwards. With great deliberation he returned the axe to the strap on his side. Eyes never leaving the young man's face, he squat down on the ground. Then his eyes narrowed and he nodded slowly. "So be it, boy."

For the first time in his life, Pjodarr found himself utterly speechless.

Chapter 8

ruesome contemplated the boy conjurer. Blood magic. Necromancy. Of what depravity did the people of Durum Tai not partake? And what did that make him? Tarac saved his life, and now he would allow blood magic to lead him to his prey. Did this stain his honor? The Honorless were beyond the reach of the gods, and their bodies were food for var and worm. Their souls would be shattered upon the rocks of oblivion. Nothing of them and their broken oaths would remain, so why not use their blood? Do they deserve no less than to be tools for the boy's dark magic?

All these thoughts passed through his mind as his hands worked. He sat by the dwarf, putting oil to armor and weapon. Blade's hands worked absent his eye, for the old general stared ever forward. Gruesome wondered for not the first time what magic ailed the glorious Lord of Northwatch. In five seasons the dwarf had never spoken, never slept. He fought, but not with the gusto of a proud Warshield. It was as if he walked in his sleep. He knew the shaman's voice it seemed, but the havtrol had to push or nudge him to get his attention.

The shaman sat by the fire and moved the pot of meatless broth he cooked in the embers. He still thought the girl would come to them. Gruesome admired the man's heart. It held much kindness and love, and might be all that kept the dwarf alive.

Snow crunched and all eyes turned toward the slim figure in a plain dress. Her long blonde hair fell over her face as she stared down. Pjodarr scooped some of the broth into a bowl and set it by the side of the fire away from everyone else.

"It is not much, but it is hot. It will help."

She picked up the bowl and sipped tentatively. Her face was cleaner, but still streaked with mud and blood. Her hair was matted and wild. She lifted her face to drain the bowl and the collar around her neck jingled. Slave. There were no human lords this deep in the forest, so why would she be here?

"I am Pjodarr, shaman to Master Blade." He pointed to the dwarf. "This is Gruesome, warrior of Clan Beartooth." Her gaze sunk deeper into the ground. Gruesome felt renewed outrage at the Honorless, that they would cause her to fear him as them. "That is High Priest Tarac and his companion Folik."

Pjodarr traded glances with the rest and leaned toward the girl. "What is your name, child?"

She set the bowl beside the fire, and then lay on her side. She curled her knees to her chest and wrapped her arms around her shins, then buried her chin into her chest. The shaman pursed his lips and nodded. They sat in silence. Pjodarr crossed his legs under him and placed a hand on each knee.

"You are well learned, right, Tarac?"

The boy cleared his throat. "Well, I suppose. I know the history of my people, but I am not so clear on the rest of the

Bergsbor."

"Do you even know how the world came to be?"

"Came to be? Well, the gods created the world, of course."

"That sounds a bit simple, doesn't it?" The old slave arched an eyebrow at the younger man.

Tarac smiled. "I would never call the gods simple, good shaman."

Pjodarr laughed and slapped his knee. "Neither would I, but I'm in the mood for a story. Would you like to hear how the world began?"

"I would!" Tarac's face was childlike.

The shaman stretched his arms to either side and lowered his head. Snow surrounded him in a great drift and flowed around the fire to settle as a pile before each of them. The necromancer clasped his hands together.

"First, and always, there was Fjur, greatest of the gods." A thick man-like figure formed in the snow before Pjodarr. "So mighty was he that he carried all the heavens on his back." The man crawled on all fours, and a large dome appeared on his broad back. "Then the other gods came. They lived in the emptiness of the heavens." Tiny people popped up on the dome. "The lesser gods fought amongst themselves." One of the tiny snow gods punched another. Tarac laughed with glee. The girl's eyes shifted to the shaman.

"Fjur grew weary of the gods' petty squabbles. They argued and fought and then argued about why they fought! Wise Fjur knew their problem. They were bored! He had the whole weight of the heavens upon him, but if he did not hold them in place, they would twirl madly. What could he do to help the other gods? The answer came to him. He would give himself, and watch over the heavens to make sure they did not tumble into oblivion."

The fire flashed and a huge ball of flame hung in the air. "His right eye became the sun. Fjur's morning eye brings us the day." Snow flew from the ground and formed a crescent. "His left eye became the moon, to watch over the night." Gruesome looked at the shaman's face. The old man's right eye was surrounded by a black sun, his left framed by a crescent moon.

The Fjur puppet spread itself flat. "His body became the earth. But he knew that was not enough. The gods needed others to rule over, or they would continue fighting amongst themselves. First, he created dwarf and elf." A snowy dwarf formed in front of Blade, followed by an elf. "He told dwarf to build the mountains, and gave elf dominion over the forests and its creatures. Dwarf was clever and knew the ways of stone. But his arms were short, and he could not reach the top of the mountain!" A mound of snow rose up and the snow dwarf tried in vain to grab the tip. Tarac clapped his hands, and Gruesome could not stifle a laugh. "So, Fjur made the giants and trolls. Tall and strong they were, but not very bright. They tried to eat dwarf!" A larger snowman bit the dwarf's head off. "Dwarf said to Fjur, 'Why do you give us such a task, then make these monsters to eat us?' Fjur knew they were right, so he made havtrol." A bulky figure popped up in front of Gruesome. "They were also strong, and also not too bright."

Gruesome grunted and slapped the little havtrol apart. Tarac was beside himself with joy.

"But there was still a problem. Dwarf and elf and havtrol performed their tasks too well. The mountains grew tall, the forests thrived. All was peaceful. And Fjur knew what the gods did when things were peaceful. He needed something to keep them busy. What could he create that would upset the beautiful balance of his world, his body, his very being? No more monsters. Something with the ability to create and destroy; a being that he would allow to make its own choices." Pjodarr snapped his fingers. "He created man." Snow people formed in front of Tarac and the girl. The boy rubbed his finger on its head. The slave girl moved her hand, as if to reach out, and then drew it back to her body.

"Now, he was ready for the gods. The three brothers Mobin, Mani and Drogu were the strongest. Then there was Lyndaa, wife of Mobin, mother to Bodr and the bear god Jaga. Berta was the last." Seven forms appeared before the shaman.

"To Mobin, he gave the rule of the other gods. He would watch them, and see that they oversaw their realms justly. Mani was given the vast seas and all the great beasts within. Drogu was given reign over the souls of Fjur's children. He would see that they passed to the other side." A small, cloaked figure rose in front of Tarac. It held a basket, the symbol of Drogu gathering souls.

"Lyndaa became goddess of wisdom, for a mother always knows best. Bodr, Mobin's strongest son, became the god of thunder and war. He would decide which side was right when two nations fought." An armored man grew before Blade, with snowy shield and sword.

"But wars are not won in a day. Fjur knew they would depend on many contests. So he made the angry Jaga god of battles. He would give the fight to those who fought with the most honor and ferocity." A little snow bear swiped a claw at Gruesome. The havtrol smiled and bowed his head to it.

"And to Berta, most beautiful of the gods, he gave dominion over all that grew. She became the goddess of love and fertility." A snowy bulb pushed its way through the mound in front of the girl. It opened and blossomed into a flower with a winding stem and long petals. As it bloomed, it crystallized into pure ice. The slave girl gasped and placed one finger on the edge of a single petal. The fire danced in her eyes.

"Have you ever seen one of those, my dear?"

She shook her head weakly. Her finger never left the icy blossom.

"They used to grow on the side of the Great Mountain. They bloomed only one week out of the year, right after the snow melted. There was a festival every year. The Winter Lily Fair. That's what they were called: winter lilies. Every flower is a beautiful gift from Fjur, which is why we name them."

The slave girl looked at Pjodarr. Gruesome could see the pain in her eyes. Where there was pain, there was a wish for relief. Her face softened.

"Erliga," she all but whispered.

The shaman smiled. "A pleasure, Erliga." He pointed at the flower. "Take it; it will not melt for some time."

Erliga plucked the flower with a hiss from the cold. She turned her back to the fire and them, and drew herself tight. Pjodarr leaned back and smiled at Tarac.

"Eons passed, and the nations of the world flourished under the watchful gods. Peace reigned. Mobin decided that they had learned great Fjur's lessons well. Together, the gods built the Golden Table under the earth's highest peak, the Great Mountain. They tasked the dwarves with protecting the land over the Golden Table until the end of all time. And there they sit, and there they sleep...until the Dragon of the Heavens comes to swallow the world."

Gruesome stared into the fire. The night air grew colder with the shaman's last words.

Chapter 9

Pjodarr spread a thick blanket over the girl, not knowing if she slept or not. Her eyes remained closed. She was a very beautiful young woman. She had the fine features of the Bergsbor, but blonde hair like most of the Grunlanders. She was probably enslaved with her family when the men of Freemark invaded. The dwarves and freemen took many slaves. *Freemen.* The shaman held back a chuckle at the thought. The lords of Freemark were far more likely to take slaves than the Great Houses. And they were more barbarous than any dwarf ever thought to be. A pretty girl like Erliga? He could only imagine how she was treated. He hoped she felt well enough to talk in the morning. There were many things he needed to ask her.

If the Honorless had any compassion in their hearts, it was that they didn't leave survivors. They did not give Erliga even that little charity.

He turned around and regarded Gruesome and the boy. They sat quietly on opposite sides of the fire. Pjodarr's master stood just within the fire's warmth, and would for the entire night. The old slave had grown used to Blade standing silent guard. Folik was behind Tarac's right shoulder, as if in mock exaggeration of the dwarf's condition. But Pjodarr knew his master was not dead. He sighed to himself and willed sad thoughts away. He walked towards the var and waved the havtrol and necromancer to join him. Gruesome rose without issue. Tarac looked at both of them then followed with some hesitation. The shaman took them out of earshot of the girl, but still kept his voice low.

"Well, I never planned on this."

Gruesome nodded.

"Planned on what?" Tarac was confused.

"The girl. Why they kept her alive is beyond me, but they did." He set his gaze on the big warrior. "And now we have to make sure she's taken care of."

"We cannot leave the other two, shaman."

Pjodarr bowed to Gruesome. "I know, friend, but we have a duty to get her back to her family."

"And if her master died with the others? Will the boy claim her?" They both looked at Tarac. The necromancer's eyes were wide with fear.

"Claim her? But no High Priest has ever taken a wife! And who knows if she would even have me?"

The old shaman stared at him. "Wife? What in Drogu's name are you talking about, son?"

"But you said-,"

Pjodarr placed a hand on his shoulder. "Not claim her for wife. Claim her as your slave."

Tarac's face showed an odd mix of relief and confusion. "Oh, well, that would be impossible. We do not have slaves."

"I understand. Neither do havtrols." Pjodarr cocked a thumb

at Gruesome. "I, of course, am not allowed to take a slave, and dwarves only take what they need to run their households. Since my master no longer has a house, I am all he needs."

"What do we do then, shaman? We cannot leave her out here alone. And who knows what villages are left near to us?"

The havtrol was right. It would all be made easier if they could find another group of humans or dwarves. They could leave Erliga with them, and she would be returned to her rightful lord's home. However, if her lord died to the Honorless, Blade or Tarac could claim her by law because they defeated her captors. Pjodarr rubbed his neck and sighed. The humans' form of slavery was such a tricky business. At least dwarves kept it simple. Unless sold, a slave belonged to his master until he or his master died. Given that dwarves outlived humans by a century or more, it was rarely a topic for debate. Havtrols, of course, found the notion of having anyone perform any task for them preposterous. Their women maintained fierce households. Any female that bore children was responsible for the welfare of their village. While the bulls hunted or, more often as not, fought, the cows worked the small farms and fished. One out of ten females was barren. While this placed them in positions of lesser respect than the mothers, they still had vital roles within the clan. They would be blacksmiths, boat builders and any other craftsman needed. Havtrols did not believe in laziness.

"She must come with us for now. We'll keep her by Master Blade. He will protect her while we deal with those other two. Then we'll have to find out who her master is and return her."

"If her master is dead, couldn't we just free her?" The boy's face was so innocent. Pjodarr was struck by how someone so powerful could be so naïve. Tarac raised a dead man from the grave when he was a boy, but had no idea how dark the world truly was.

"Where would she go, boy? What would she do? A slave has no family. A young girl like her probably has no skills to make her way, save the one her master probably uses her for now."

The necromancer frowned. "What do you mean?"

"She's a pretty little thing, Tarac. I've spent a good bit of time in Freemark with my family and rarely did I see a pretty girl cooking or cleaning. They are generally saved for...*other* things."

Tarac pursed his lips in thought. Then his eyes went wide and his face turned bright red. "Oh, my, I had no idea. That's quite horrendous, isn't it?" Now it was Pjodarr's turn to be confused. A practitioner of blood magic disgusted by something?

"I have found that humans do not hold honor as dearly as the rest of us, necromancer."

The boy shot Gruesome a look. "I know you do not approve of me for some reason, but I wish you would not call me that!" His voice was almost a hiss.

"You consort with the dead. You are what you are."

"I do not! I honor the remains of a great hero! His soul passed long ago, and I do not ask anything of Folik the flesh to which Folik the man would not have agreed! It was *your* people that ate human flesh and raped women!"

"They were not my people!" Gruesome roared at the boy and

towered over him. To his credit, the boy did not flinch, although Folik suddenly had hand on sword. "They were Honorless! Havtrol no more! They broke covenant and gave their souls to the abyss. Their bodies will return to dust, and no one will sing their songs! Their names will be stricken from our hearts and they will have never existed!"

Pjodarr moved between the two, but he had no idea what he would do if they came to blows. Tarac drew himself to his full height and the shaman was keenly aware of just how much smaller he was than either of them.

"No High Priest has ever broken their sacred vows. We spend our lives praying for the souls of our flock, and we honor the chosen by raising their bodies. They protect us, and are revered by the people. When you call me necromancer, you blaspheme the memory of this great man." He waved his hand to Folik. The dead man dropped his arms to his sides and stood still. "While I do not care what you think of me, I will not have you insult *his* honor." The young man lifted his chin and regarded the havtrol coolly. "Quite frankly, for one that speaks of honor, you do your own ill justice when you cast aspersions on us both because our culture is different than yours. My people find slavery detestable, but I refuse to think poorly of good Pjodarr and his master until they give me reason. Have I given you reason to hate me, good warrior?"

Gruesome looked like he'd been slapped. The anger left his face, and his lower jaw jutted out in serious contemplation. Finally, he met the boy's eyes again. His massive head bowed.

"I cannot say you have. I have wronged you, little man. What would you have of me?" Pjodarr was shocked. Havtrols did not ask this question in such a manner lightly. He doubted Tarac understood the significance.

The young man smiled. "I would only ask your respect, that you call me Tarac. Or priest." He moved the staff to his left hand and offered his right to the warrior. "And the hope that we might try to become friends. I apologize to you for misinterpreting the Honorless. It seems we both have much to learn."

Gruesome's thick paw covered the boy's forearm. "And what would you have me call him?"

"Folik, if you must."

The havtrol bowed to the dead man. "I am sorry, Folik." Tarac laughed as they ended their grasp.

"It's not necessary to speak to him, though. He cannot hear you, as such."

Pjodarr was impressed by the younger man's ability to defuse the warrior's rage. "What do you mean, Tarac?"

The young man's smile softened. "Nothing of the man Folik was remains in his body, save a shadow of the warrior. My will sustains him."

"Your will?"

"Yes, all of his actions are guided by my thoughts."

"You mean you learned how to use a sword as well?"

"Oh, no," the boy chuckled. "Like I said, that is the warrior's shadow." When both Gruesome and Pjodarr stared at him, he continued. "Well, Gruesome, when you fight, do you have to tell your arm how to swing your hammer, your legs how to avoid your opponent's blow?"

"No, we train at an early age to fight."

"Like all great warriors, you trained your body to react. The Bloodguard are the best of our people." He shrugged his slim shoulders. "Simply enough, the body remembers. At least it remembers enough. Folik is not capable of any real strategy, but he will swing his sword to kill. And I can command him with a thought to do other things because his body is infused with my will."

The shaman reached a hand out and touched Folik's arm. "By all the gods, that is astounding…" He looked at Tarac. "So you could put your will into anything? I can shape the elements into man-shapes, but it is only for a short time. Wizards are better at it, but their constructs do not last either."

"No, it only works on the flesh of the dead. Priests have tried in the past with no success. And the guardians only came about after the power of the blood was discovered."

"Is that how you healed his arm?"

"Hmm," the young man thought. "Of sorts. I can heal myself with the blood of others, but only the blood of the dead can heal Folik."

Gruesome eyed him. "You healed him with blood?"

"Yes, from one of the havtrols." Tarac bowed his head to the warrior. "I would never use the blood of an innocent."

Pjodarr grinned in amazement. The boy was right; they all

had much to learn. "And you can track the one with its own blood?"

"Yes, as long as he lives."

"It was not a mortal wound. Havtrols are incredibly hard to kill." The shaman nodded at Gruesome. "They are resistant to disease and poison, and heal much quicker than humans or dwarves. Your best bet is massive amounts of violence." He turned his gaze toward the firelight and clenched his fist. "If only my master had his senses. He would have called the thunder down on them, and we would not have to deal with this."

"He is what they call a Warshield, yes? I have seen him use the lightning."

"Aaah, boy, he was so much more." Pjodarr closed his eyes and bowed his head. "*Is*. He *is* so much more, the finest of his House."

"What ails your master, good shaman? Why does he not speak?"

Gruesome turned his attention to the old man as well. The great havtrol never asked about his master, and never would, but Pjodarr knew he had to wonder about the general. The former clan chief knew Master Blade before the Great City fell. He knew the warrior the dwarf had been. The shaman was torn. It had been so long since he'd shared his burden with anyone else. But how could he betray the honor of his master? How could he expose a weakness that he did not even understand himself? He shook his head.

"Nothing ails him, Tarac. His body is as strong as it ever was. Please, excuse the ramblings of an old man." He turned his back to them and walked toward the camp. "We will head out as soon as the girl is able tomorrow. I suggest we all get some rest for now."

Chapter 10

Erliga kept her head down as she rode behind the dwarf. The var wasn't uncomfortable, like she thought it might be. The young wizard had awkwardly given her a pair of breeches to wear as they rode. They must have belonged to one of her lord's guards because she had to cinch them up tight and roll up the legs. The boots were a little too big, but at least they covered her feet. The shirt and coat fit though. She knew they belonged to Freda, but that sweet girl didn't need them anymore.

She was dirty and unkempt, her hair matted. She was unfit to be presented to any court, let alone her lord's. Those monsters. They attacked so fast, like nightmares given flesh. The guards were some of her lord's best, and they never stood a chance. All she remembered were screams and blood. So much blood.

But they didn't kill her or the other girls. Not at first. They threw them in a pile. Then made them watch. Watch as they ate. Then they…

She shuddered and clutched the dwarf tighter. He did not look back at her. In fact, he did not move at all. She found that somewhat comforting. She just wanted to be left alone.

The old man asked too many questions. He was a shaman, but he wore a silver mask. He must have thought himself pretty important. He reminded her of another shaman that spoke polite words and held himself in high regard. The tall young wizard was odd. She knew he stole glances at her, knew what they meant. Then there was the havtrol. He wasn't like the ones that killed everybody. He had the bearing of a great man, and not the savage eyes of those others. But he was so huge. Did the rest really trust him? And the other man, the armored one. He was like the dwarf, completely silent.

And they had just left him behind when they started off. Just got on the big wolves and left him there without a word. What kind of men were these? None of them had touched her since the shaman healed her, even given her privacy to change again. But how long would that last? Were they waiting for her to get her strength back? Maybe they wanted her clean. They all seemed more like the men of her lord's court than a roaming band of brigands, but what else would they be doing out here?

The old man, Pjodarr he called himself, he knew her lord's crest and name. He'd asked her after she woke if her master had died to the havtrols. She said nothing, but did not lie. She had just shaken her head. He asked her where they were going, why they were in Brinnoch Forest. She answered nothing else, though. What was she supposed to tell them?

Now the shaman escorted them through the trees while he followed some red bead. The wizard made it float in the air. Erliga had no idea where they were going. They were fond of not talking in front of her and she wasn't sure how to feel about that. She was usually ignored by men until they were done talking. She didn't know what these men had planned for her. They didn't seem to want to kill her. If she said nothing, maybe they would tire of her sooner than later.

~~~~~

They made camp early that day, even with the late start. Tarac thought Pjodarr was keeping a slower pace for the girl's sake. She hadn't said anything since she told them her name the night before. The shaman knew her master was a man named Ranagol. He was apparently the lord of something called the Sky Palace. Poor girl. It was an awful thing she witnessed. Tarac had seen more than enough of the scene while he looked for clothes. They had decided to not bury any of the dead. Pjodarr said they would tell someone what happened.

He felt so sad. They had left so many dead behind in the last two days. His life with the priests had not really prepared him for all of this. He thanked Drogu for Folik. His guardian was a great source of strength. All Tarac had to do was think of the hero, and his own courage was fortified.

He looked at Erliga. She sat staring at the fire. She had cleaned her face more and pulled her hair back. She was quite possibly the most beautiful woman he had ever seen. Her skin was smooth and clear of any blemishes, her hair long and a darker blonde than his. She had full lips and a thin neck that begged him to look lower. He closed his eyes and lowered his face. How dare he have such thoughts about a victim of such unspeakable cruelty? And he didn't necessarily mean the Honorless.

Her eyes. They were the most intriguing aspect of her. Deep blue, but something in them made the fire dance. The sadness in them did nothing to lessen her beauty; rather it gave her a depth that he felt could only be bridged by kindness and respect. He so wanted to see her smile.

Tarac chastised himself and apologized to Drogu. He was a High Priest, and should be above such base thoughts. She was a soul to be cherished, not flesh to be coveted.

He returned his thoughts to his new friends. At least he felt they might truly become friends. Mighty Gruesome had only kind words for him after their discussion last night. And Pjodarr had so many questions about his life in Durum Tai and his abilities. The young priest's heart swelled with pride. He believed he was representing his people well and had found his purpose here in the south. What happened in those villages was not natural, of that he was sure. He felt confident that Gruesome, Pjodarr and the dwarf would help him seek the truth of the events.

The dwarf filled his mind for not the first time that day. The shaman said his body was strong, but Blade neither spoke nor slept. Tarac had never heard of such a condition. Pjodarr was a healer of flesh, but perhaps the good dwarf needed a healer of souls…

He waited until they all lay down to sleep. He needed time to perform the ritual. He crossed his arms over his chest and began the process of slowing his heart. He took long, deep breaths and focused all of his will. Entering the world between worlds required all of his concentration, and he had to block out all sounds and smells around him. He pooled all of his thoughts into a single essence, like a lone star shining in the night. He moved toward it. Everything around his body lost all meaning, and he no longer felt his arms or legs. The star grew brighter. It rushed toward him, white light filling every part of his being.

He stood in the darkness of the world between worlds. Tarac felt completely himself. There was no awkwardness of the flesh. Here, he was confident, sure of what he was. But he had to be careful. The souls around him were fully alive, and what he saw here could not be unseen.

He drew himself together and strengthened his will. This was a dangerous place, not meant for travelers. He could get lost here, and his soul might never find its way to the other side if he did. He felt the other souls around him, but had no idea which might be Blade's. He focused on one. It was not like turning his head, more like pulling something into view.

It was Erliga! The form of a naked woman, glowing white stood before him. Her face was that of the girl's, but scarred. In fact, black scars marred the purity of her soul across her entire body. He knew that if he wanted he could brush the marks from her. All he had to do was reach out…

Her eyes flashed at him. Red eyes, full of anger and hate. He pushed the whole of her away.

He felt another presence and drew it into focus. Gruesome, the mighty warrior. A great, red bear slept before him. It was massive, and bound by chains of thick iron. Huge muscles flexed and strained the shackles. Tarac pushed himself back. He dared not try to touch the rage-filled warrior.

He floated toward another, massive soul. A large oak formed, with leaves of flame. The roots sank deep beneath it and the trunk pulsed as if the tree breathed. The priest marveled at the shaman's soul. He had never felt one so powerful, so certain of purpose. The shaman was life. With every bit of his being, Pjodarr displayed the very essence of his god. Tarac wanted nothing more than to rush to the shelter of the shaman's limbs. He knew the bark would be warm and soft.

He steeled himself and let himself drift away. The next soul would have taken his breath away if he had it in this place. A small ball of light stood before him. Stretching from it, from all sides were strands of pure white. He made out the faint outline of a squat man around the ball. The dwarf's soul was being pulled apart. How did this happen? Blade could barely be considered alive. Is this why the kriotes attacked him? Did they mistake the dwarf for a dying man? Tarac could see why.

He studied the man's soul. What the other priests would give to see this! Nothing of this sort had ever been discussed among them. But there had to be something he could do. If he was truly Mephraim reborn, he would find a way to repair the dwarf. He would give him back to the shaman.

He reached forward. He needed to be delicate. Despite the appearance, this was still a living soul. He needed to bring it back to itself, not change it. It was easy to affect souls here, and doing so changed the fiber of the person. Such a thing was forbidden to the priests. Their place was not to judge, but to shepherd.

He touched one of the strands. The dwarf's soul flowed into him. He placed a wall between himself and it. He could not have the dwarf changing him either. He pulled the strand, fitting it around the ball of light. It was an arduous task, like rewinding a ball of yarn while putting the pieces of a puzzle together. He had to place it exactly as it was before Blade came to this. Time had no meaning in this place, so he had no idea how long each strand took him. As he progressed, the outline became bolder. It was a dwarf, with strong features. The eyes were sharp, the bearing regal. The skin was not the texture of flesh, but stone rather. Running through the stone were veins of deep power. Something unnatural coursed through the dwarf. It was old and embedded. It was a part of him now.

The stone figure's eyes narrowed at him. The dwarf knew what he was doing! He gently pushed a sense of patience at the soul. Blade looked around at the rest of his being. Tiny strands still stretched out to forever. The general nodded at him. Tarac focused on the strands. At some point, the stone dwarf began to help. He took the strands from the priest and pressed them to his chest. Blade's spirit was strong. Like the shaman's, it was solid, complete. These two never doubted their places in the world. Soon, the dwarf was able to pull himself together alone. Tarac found it difficult to let go. It was comforting to be so close, but he drew himself away.

Something pressed into him, another presence. He touched it, tentatively.

A great cloud rushed into him. The face of a bearded man, contorted in pain, appeared to him. The eyes were pained, almost manic, and they peered into the bottom of him. Fear threatened to break him apart. Never had a soul invaded him like this. The man's mouth opened, like a chasm that threatened to swallow him whole.

COME TO ME!

Tarac drew his own spirit to itself. With much strain, he solidified himself. He pushed the being away. It scratched and clawed at him. He raised a barrier between them and shoved with all the focus he could muster. He reached for his body, out of this realm. It was like swimming through molasses.

The priest awoke with a gasp. His senses were flooded. The smell of ash from the fire, the crispness of winter air filled his nose. Loud voices roared in his ears as someone yelled, the words made no sense to him. Tarac struggled to rise to his feet. Folik grasped his arm and helped him.

Blade was on the ground, coughing and sputtering. Pjodarr was at his master's side, screaming in dvarid. The young man could not make out the words. Gruesome stood tensed, as if ready to attack. Erliga was on her feet staring at the dwarf and shaman; her eyes were full of fear. Slowly, things began to make sense to the priest.

"Master!" the old slave screamed. "What…wrong…hurt?"

Finally, Blade calmed his shaman with a hand. "Water…need…water…" His voice was hoarse, the words broken.

The havtrol was quick; he grabbed a water skin and threw it to the pair. Pjodarr held it to his master's lips and the dwarf drank. He drank as one deprived. When he finished his hands fumbled with his helm.

"…take…helm…"

"No, Master," the shaman grasped the thick fingers. "Come…will help…" He pulled the dwarf to his feet and led him away from the fire.

Tarac shivered. He had sweat profusely, and now the cold air surrounded him. His muscles were sore, as if he'd strained them. He looked at Gruesome and Erliga. She opened her mouth to speak, but instead shuddered and closed her full lips. A question loomed in the depths of her blue eyes. Tarac thought of the tortured soul he'd seen and tried to reach out to her. The earth hurtled toward him and everything went black.

Chapter 11

His master could barely walk. He was so heavy, and Pjodarr was not a strong man. As soon as they were out of sight of the others, he pulled the helm off the dwarf's head and dropped it on the ground. He was used to Blade's ravaged face after so many years, but not like this. There was life in his right eye. His bearded mouth gaped open as he struggled for breath.

"Where are we?" his master croaked.

"Shh, Master, don't speak."

"So tired. Are we in battle?"

"No, Master."

"Then get this armor off me." He pulled at one of his gauntlets and it clattered to the ground. Pjodarr sat him by a tree and began unstrapping the plate that covered the great dwarf. The back plate came off with Tremble still hooked to it. Blade grasped for the handle, and sighed in relief when he gripped it. He looked around as the shaman continued removing the armor. "I don't know these trees. Where's my tower?"

"Master, what do you remember?"

"Fire. And ash." His wide shoulders slumped. "So tired."

The old slave choked, but did not try to stop his tears. "Sleep, Master. Please, sleep." The dwarf nodded and his head dropped. His eye closed. Pjodarr's stomach tightened until he saw the rise and fall of his master's chest. He finished taking off the plate armor, then buried his face in his arms and wept. He whispered a prayer to Fjur.

When he'd composed himself, he went back to the fire. Gruesome and Erliga stood in their same spots. The girl had her arms wrapped around her body. Pjodarr did not meet their gazes. He rummaged through a pack until he found a small blanket. As he left he saw that Tarac slept while Folik stood over him. He ripped off strips of the old blanket on his way back to the sleeping dwarf. The slave gently wrapped them around the left side of his master's head. He was careful to leave his right eye, nose and mouth uncovered. The great general did not stir.

Once satisfied his master's scars were sufficiently concealed, he gathered up the armor and returned it to the camp. When he had all settled, he bowed his head to the havtrol and slave girl.

"He sleeps for now."

"Pjodarr," Gruesome held up a hand. "What happened here? What happened to them?" He pointed to the boy.

The shaman shook his head. "I don't know. I just don't know." He looked at the sky. "The sun will rise soon. I suggest you all try to get a little more sleep." He bowed to Gruesome again. "I am sorry, but we may be delayed from your quest yet again."

The warrior nodded. "All is well, shaman. Care for your master."

Pjodarr returned to the dwarf's side. He knelt beside him and waited.

Fjur's morning eye sat high above them before his master lifted his head. He stretched his thick arms and groaned. The slave sat silent. Blade yawned and coughed, and Pjodarr offered him the water skin again.

He drank and leaned his head against the tree. "Did we fight ice giants?"

"No, Master."

"Then why do I feel like they've been beating on me?"

"I don't know, Master."

The dwarf grunted and coughed, then drank again. "By the gods my throat hurts." He shook his head and looked around. "I've had such a dream...," he trailed off as his right eye cleared. He lifted a hand to the left side of his face. "What is this, am I injured?"

"Not anymore, Master."

The red-rimmed eye settled on Pjodarr's face. "Bodr's beard, boy, what happened to ye? Ye look so old."

The shaman smiled sadly. "You've missed so much, Master. Where have you been?"

Blade stared into the distance. His hand began to shake. "I remember drums. And the voices of my fathers. They called me to them." He shook his head. "Where are we, boy?"

"The Sudmark, Master."

"What in Drogu's ass is the Sudmark?" He shivered and grunted again. "I feel like my bones are all cracked. Help me up, boy, and make a fire."

"We have a fire, Master. Come, there are others with us."

Blade grumbled. "If we have a fire, why am I sitting here in the cold? Fool boy." He groaned as he rose to his feet. "Or fool old man, whatever ye be now."

"I am a great-grandfather three times over now, Master."

He grasped his master's arm and led him toward the fire. "I am sorry, but I did not want the others to see your scars. And forgive the lack of a fire. My mind was not focused."

The others watched with rapt attention as they entered the camp. Even the girl was wide-eyed as they approached. Gruesome promptly stood and bowed to the dwarf. Tarac sat with a blanket wrapped around him, sipping at a steaming bowl. He gave them a small smile.

"My master wakes," Pjodarr announced in norovid. "But he still needs to gather his strength."

"Why do ye speak the human tongue, boy?"

The shaman waved to the priest and Erliga. "They do not speak dvarid. I would not want to insult your guests."

Blade grunted. "As this is not my tower, they are not my guests." He spoke the words in norovid, and Tarac blushed. The dwarf settled himself by the fire and reached his hands to it. Pjodarr saw a pot of broth and poured some for his master. He took it and sipped. "Is there no meat in this place?"

The old slave chuckled. "We have some dried wyvern, if you want."

"I'm not starving yet, boy." He cast his eye around the fire.

Upon seeing the havtrol, he bowed his head. "Chief Gruesome, 'tis good to see ye again. I'd rise and bow, but this is neither my land nor ye own."

The big warrior was taken aback. "My general, we have traveled together for some time now. At least five seasons."

Pjodarr held his breath while Blade took in the havtrol's words. He stared ahead. "We have fought together? We have fought havtrols."

Gruesome nodded. "You help me hunt the Honorless in this land."

The dwarf took a long sip. "Ye fell to the rage then? I am sorry to hear that. I know ye honor is strong, though."

"Thank you, general."

Blade took in the others. He gave Tarac a long look. "I know ye, boy. I don't know ye name, but I know ye."

"Yes, good dwarf, I think you would."

The dwarf motioned to Folik and Erliga. "Who are these?"

Erliga looked up at the shaman. Pjodarr nodded to her. "My name is Erliga, my lord. I am-," she stammered. "You saved me from-," her head bowed. "You all saved my life."

"Hmm," the general grunted then swallowed. "Well, I reckon ye are welcome then. Do ye belong to one of these?" He waved at Tarac and Folik.

"No, my lord," her head stayed down, like a dutiful slave. "I belong to Lord Ranagol."

"I don't know him." He looked at Pjodarr. "Should I know

him?"

The old shaman shrugged. "Not really, Master."

"Fine then. Don't call me 'Lord'; Blade is my first title, ye may call me that."

"Yes, Lord Blade."

"It's just 'Blade', my dear. There's no need to use two of his titles."

"Blade," she said, as if testing the word. She was clearly not used to a dwarf's bluntness. Pjodarr worried how his master would react to the priest.

"What's ye name, lad?" He pointed a thick finger at Folik.

Tarac rose gently to his feet. "He is Folik, my guardian."

"And ye?"

The young man took a deep breath. "I am Tarac, High Priest of Drogu, and Shepherd of the Souls of Durum Tai."

Blade cursed and spat, then threw his bowl on the ground. He put a sharp eye on Pjodarr. "Is that where we are, boy? Are we by that gods-forsaken city? Why in Mobin's name would ye bring me here?"

Tarac was quicker than the old man. "Good dwarf! I will not have you disparaging my home. The city of Durum Tai is an important part of the Bergmark, and has certainly *not* been forsaken by the gods!"

"Easy, son," Pjodarr raised a hand to ease the boy. "He means no harm. Do you, Master?"

"That remains to be seen, shaman." He gave the boy his full

attention. "I'm not sure how it is, but I know ye, lad. I know the very heart of ye."

The priest immediately lost his reserve. "That will be difficult to explain."

Pjodarr stared at the boy. "You did this, Tarac?" He shook his head. "*How* did you do this?"

The young man sighed and lowered himself to the ground. "I did, good shaman. I do not know how to tell you."

Blade held up his hand. "Not now, boy. I am tired, and my bones ache. I'd have more sleep."

"Of course, Master. We still have a journey ahead of us. You must get your rest."

The dwarf settled himself and lay down. "When I wake, ye can tell me about this 'journey'."

They all watched as the dwarf promptly drifted off to sleep. Pjodarr grinned. It was just like his master. In and out like the winter wind. The shaman's heart almost burst to think of him back to his old self.

Chapter 12

Gruesome would have been impatient if the reason for their delay had been any one but the glorious general. The dwarf commanded much respect. Blade slept most of the day. The young priest looked like he was sick, but his spirits were up. The boy had shown his honor when he confronted the havtrol about calling him a necromancer. He had been right, after all. Gruesome only knew the rumors of Durum Tai, how could he judge their people? He knew what humans said about havtrols.

Raising the dead did not sit well with him, but the boy said it was done to honor them. That confused the warrior. His people burned their honored dead on a pyre. They sent their souls and bodies to the gods. Dwarves carved the likenesses of their cherished ones in stone or gold, like they might forget their faces. The freemen of the Mark had no end of rituals for the dead. They might burn them *and* build a statue of them. So why not turn their hero's bones into a puppet for their highest office?

They spent the day in relative quiet. Pjodarr stayed by his master's side. The girl stole glances at the priest, who tried his best to avoid looking at her. Gruesome was unsure if this was some form of human courtship or not. Most men were more aggressive in the presence of one such as Erliga. He assumed from the shaman's words that she was a consort for her lord.

Blade awoke as night began to fall. Pjodarr gave him plenty of water, more broth and some of the wyvern meat to chew.

"Now, boy," the dwarf said as he tossed aside the last bit of meat. "Ye have much to tell me."

"It seems I do, Master." Pjodarr gestured at the rest of them. "Do you wish privacy?"

"What, are ye going to tell me a secret?"

The shaman shook his head sadly. "Hardly, Master."

"Then talk. Tell me about this," Blade indicated the left side of his face. Only a hint of pink scars showed under the makeshift bandages.

"You said you remembered the fire. And ash, yes?"

The dwarf thought for a moment. "There is something else. Roaring, like a dragon. The whole world shook."

"Yes, yes it did."

Gruesome knew what the shaman had to tell his master. The destruction of his home. Tarac and the girl leaned in, for they were too young to remember the day the Great Mountain burned.

Pjodarr closed his eyes. "I was in the var pens that night. You know how much I love being with them. My stomach had been bothering me for days, and I thought it was just some passing ailment. But they were upset, and I could not calm them. I think now they knew what Fjur had tried to warn me about.

"Suddenly, the ground beneath my feet began to tremble. The walls of Northwatch cracked and the very earth bubbled. I ran to your chamber as fast as I could, and tried to keep the ground still. It was a futile effort, of course. By the time I reached your tower, fire was spewing from fissures. Black smoke choked the air. I bounded up the steps and crushed the wood of your doors. Part of the wall had caved in, and hit you on the head. You were bleeding and unconscious."

The shaman took a deep breath. "I healed you and led you to the door. That was when the tower fell. I could feel the fire all around us. I was hurt from the fall, but nothing too serious. I healed myself-," he stopped as tears ran in rivers down his cheeks. "If I hadn't done that, I would have gotten to you sooner, Master."

Blade held up a hand. "Or we both may have died. Continue."

"Your body was broken, but you still breathed. I pulled bricks and stone off you, then the fire came." The old slave stared into the flames with bitter enmity; flames that brought warmth to them all and pushed the night's darkness away, but also brought terrible memories to him. "I cannot call it fire, though. It was liquid and burned hotter than the forges of the Great City. When it ran over your face, it took all of my power to pull it from you. You screamed. I tried to heal you, but...I have never been the best." He looked into the dwarf's one eye. "Do you remember what you told me, Master?"

The Lord of Northwatch's coal-black eye never left his servant. "'This is not my death.'"

Pjodarr nodded. "I knew it was a command. But you did die. In my arms, who swore to perish before you. It took me several hours to drag you to the soulstone."

Soulstones were powerful artifacts. Few existed in the Bergmark. Gruesome knew the dwarves held all but one of them in their great keeps, the last belonging to the High Lord of Freemark. They were deep magic, stolen from the Calderans and their goddess. The soulstones had the power to resurrect the dead, as long as their bodies were brought to it before the next dawn. Havtrols did not care for the things. What is the point of killing your enemy, only to fight him again?

"I brought you back, and healed what I could. But your wounds were great, and you died again. So, I brought you back and healed you more."

"How did the soulstone escape the fire, good shaman?" Tarac's eyes were wide. Gruesome shared the boy's curiosity. Few survived the Burning. Most of those were in much worse shape than the dwarf and shaman.

"I protected it, Tarac. I used every gift Fjur had ever given me." He turned his attention back to the dwarf. "This went on for some time, Master."

"How long, boy?" Blade's voice did not even crack.

"Almost three days." The priest and girl gasped. "You died nine times in all. Each time you lived a bit longer and suffered more. I exhausted myself keeping you alive through the second dawn. All the while, smoke and ash and fire threatened us." He smiled grimly. "But you were right; the gods did not want that to be your death.

"On the third day, you stood. But you would not speak. You

asked for no food, no water. I gave them to you when I ate or drank. You responded when I talked. When I told you to do something, you would do it."

"What happened to Northwatch, boy?"

The shaman shook his head. "Gone, Master, turned to rubble and ash. The Great Mountain drowned it in fire."

Blade gritted his teeth. "What else?"

Pjodarr bowed his head. "The Great City met the same fate. Everything was destroyed, the palace, the library, the forges...everything."

"What became of my House?"

"You, Master. You are all that remains of House Thurin. What few survived were forced to swear fealty to one of the other Houses."

Blade's eye bore a hole in the old slave. "Who rules the Mark now?"

"House Darvos."

The dwarf snorted.

"There is more." Pjodarr raised his eyes to his master. "That was seventeen years ago. They say the Great Mountain still bellows out black smoke. All of the land around the Great City is deserted. No one lives there, nothing grows. Two other great cities fell to the smoke and ash in the year that followed. Vrolldag and Stromheim. The dwarves were in crisis, and had to do something. They had to find new farmland to feed the people. At first, it was said some suggested taking the free cities, and even attacking the havtrols."

Blade laughed at this. He met Gruesome's eyes. "Can ye imagine? Invade ye people, and give them a reason to all fight together. The gods give each of us a fool."

"Luckily," the shaman continued, "cooler heads prevailed. They decided to retake the northern lands of Caldera. Some two years later, they invaded Grunland and renamed it Sudmark. The Calderans were none too happy about it, but they were already at war with the Fain. Of course, the elves didn't want to let the humans be the only ones fighting two wars, so they attacked the dwarves as well."

"Fools, they probably could have crushed the humans."

Pjodarr shrugged at the dwarf's words. "Do not underestimate the Calderans, Master. They have some good leaders, and their people still fight for their homes." He made a dismissive gesture. "But none of that matters for now. There's been peace for a couple of years. If you can call this peace."

"And why did ye bring me here?"

The shaman smiled wistfully. "I didn't at first, Master. I took you to my family's home in Freemark."

Blade's belly shook as he laughed heartily. "I bet Aela loved that! No wonder we're so far away now!"

"She did not mind, Master," Pjodarr shook his head sadly. "But she passed some years ago. She did not share my bond with Fjur, and it was her time to go."

The dwarf sobered. The fire danced in his eye as it moistened. "Ye lost ye sweet bride, boy? I am sorry."

The shaman bowed his head. "She lived a good life, Master. She lived to see her first great-grandchild. When she went, her whole family was there. *You* were there. She was grateful for us all."

"She meant the world to me, Pjodarr. For all the happiness she brought ye." Something passed between the two, and Gruesome felt as if he intruded on them. He lowered his eyes to the ground.

The rest of the night passed in somber silence. The general slept again and was ready to travel the next morning, though his mood was somewhat mournful. He did not argue when the girl asked if she could ride behind him again, and only raised an eyebrow when they left Folik behind. Pjodarr promised to explain it to him later.

They followed the havtrol's blood at a much quicker pace. When Tarac mentioned that it felt like the Honorless was close, Pjodarr jumped from his var to scout ahead. He returned with a very casual demeanor, but his face was unreadable behind the silver mask.

"You might want to take the lead, Master."

"Why would a general attack an Honorless havtrol first?" the dwarf asked, bemused.

"No, there's a troop of dwarves not forty yards ahead. They appear to be guarding some sort of cave."

Blade grunted. "A cave, in a forest? Are ye mad?" He stroked his long beard. "Who are these dwarves?"

"House Darvos, although their men don't usually patrol this far south."

"No," the dwarf sounded thoughtful. "Ye make the introductions. Ye know more of what goes on here than me."

Pjodarr bowed. "I will represent my master well." The old general grunted again. The shaman turned to Tarac. "Don't say a word, unless asked a question directly. Which will be unlikely, since they won't speak norovid to us." He paused. "Perhaps it's best if we wait for Folik. His sudden entrance might spark a new war."

They gave the var a rest until the dead man came crashing through the forest. Gruesome had to marvel at the pace he kept. A havtrol could sprint almost as fast as one of the big wolves, but he had never seen a human move so quickly. Especially while wearing armor.

They made their way steadily to the northwest again. A whistle went out long before they saw any sign of the dwarves. The shaman's craftiness never ceased to amaze Gruesome. How could he travel without being seen by a trained scout? There was commotion ahead of them, and they were soon met by four dwarves atop their var. A large dwarf with a thick brown beard walked his mount forward. Pjodarr ruffled his var's neck and brought the pack to a stop. The big wolves' noses all sniffed the air.

Gruesome saw four vertical stripes painted on the dwarf's armor to signify his rank as a sergeant. His helm bore the stag, the crest of House Darvos. He looked a bit young to the havtrol. The Burning and the war had taken a hard toll on the dwarves' numbers. Before, they would not allow one of their own to ride to war until they had seen at least thirty seasons. Martial training was important to the rulers of Bergmark. They taught their soldiers tactics before they ever held a sword. The large shield strapped to the man's back meant he was a Warshield. That meant even more training. This dwarf was already a sergeant, meaning he'd proven himself in battle, and he couldn't be more than forty. These terrible times had changed everything for the stout men of the mountains.

"I am Vordin, First Sergeant of the Ninth Army of House Darvos. Name your purpose in these woods."

Pjodarr bowed as deeply as he could from the var's back. "We are hunters, Sergeant. We come to you on the way to our quarry."

"You bear the crest of House Thurin. A House that is no more."

Blade's breath hissed between his teeth, but the general said nothing. "You speak wrongly, Sergeant, but not of your own determination. My master will give you the right of it."

The dwarf held up a hand. "Your master will give me nothing. This would be a matter for my captain. You two and the havtrol do not worry me." He pointed to Tarac and Folik. "But you travel with a human wizard and a mercenary. I would know why before I let you go any further."

Gruesome tensed. How would they take the boy, a High Priest of Durum Tai and his undead companion?

"He is not a wizard, First Sergeant. He is Tarac, a priest of Drogu; and this is Folik, his guardian."

Damn the shaman's craftiness. He did not lie, but he

managed to keep the young man's secret. Priests of Drogu took vows of poverty, they wore simple clothes. And it was not unheard of for a priest of any god to travel with a bodyguard.

The young dwarf nodded and turned his var around. They followed without a word. The dwarves were in the process of setting up tents. There were perhaps thirty of them, along with a half dozen shamans. They all looked far too young to the warrior. One bearded figure separated himself from the rest. He was short, even for a dwarf, but thick. Gruesome could tell this one was a seasoned veteran, and clearly the captain of this troop. The sergeant spurred his var forward and quickly dismounted. After a sharp rap of his fist on his chest he spoke to his captain in a hushed tone. The older dwarf looked at the newcomers with narrowed eyes and strutted toward them.

"Who comes here, claiming to be of House Thurin?" he demanded in a booming voice.

Pjodarr jumped from his var. "My master claims nothing. He only asserts what is!" The shaman's words were carried on the wind to every ear. All eyes focused on him. Gruesome had never known another slave that could command such authority. "He is the Blade of House Thurin, Lord of Northwatch, General of the First Army! The enemies of the realm shrivel when his name is spoken! Any that draw arms against him weep at his gaze! For his are the strength of the mountain and the heart of all the land!"

A few of the dwarves gasped at the shaman's proclamation. The captain's face remained stern.

"And who would speak for such a man?"

The old slave crossed his arms and held his head high. The wind swirled around him, blowing leaves and snow. But his voice only grew louder. "I am Pjodarr, my master's humble servant. By his will do I commune with Fjur. By his grace do I command the very bonds of the earth." The fires spread throughout the camp blazed in a flash. "The wind is my breath, the rivers my blood. In my very footsteps are the seas born. At my master's command, I have stood on the dragon's wing and kissed both of Fjur's eyes."

And just like that, the world was quiet. Gruesome grinned. Tarac stared at the shaman in wonder, while Erliga huddled against the general's back. The other shamans peered at Pjodarr with mouths agape and the younger dwarves held hands over their weapons with nervous apprehension. The captain took a deep breath.

Then burst out in raucous laughter. "By the gods, I have not heard such a greeting in too long, Stormbreaker!" He bowed so low to Blade that his head almost touched the ground. "It is truly you, General. I admit I did not know you without your usual armor." He gave the havtrol a bow. "It is an honor, glorious Gruesome. I have heard that you hunted Honorless in the mountains. Have they really come this far down?"

The big warrior slid off his mount and returned the bow. "We killed six a few days ago, but two escaped." Tarac whispered something to Pjodarr, and the old man nodded. The boy was anxious.

"Eight Honorless were together? That is ill news."

"It is why we are here, Captain Kinar," Pjodarr walked up to the stout dwarf. "We have chased them here, to this cave." He pointed to the rocky opening.

The captain shook his head. "No havtrols have come here today save for Gruesome Beartooth. We have ridden fast from the north by command of the High King himself."

"They may have made it here before you." The shaman looked back at Tarac. "We are quite certain they are in that cave."

The dwarf's eyes narrowed again. "Take a look at that cave, shaman. What do you see?"

Pjodarr let out a long breath and stared at the grass-covered mound. His eyes went wide, and he turned to the captain. "That is not natural."

"So my shaman tells me, too. We're not sure how long ago it appeared, but there has been strange things occurring north of here. We are here to secure this area until further investigations can be made."

Gruesome looked at Tarac. "Did they truly go in there, priest?" he said in norovid.

The young man nodded. "Yes, good warrior."

The havtrol nodded and addressed the dwarf captain again. "Then I must go there. My honor demands they die."

Kinar grumbled to himself. "I have much respect for the three of you, but I was told to let no man pass that was not of my king's realm. Gruesome, you are outcast of your people. And the general has sworn no fealty to a king. Though it pains me, I cannot count you as my allies."

"I swore fealty to one king and one king only. He was not proven unworthy to rule by right of arms, or by a vote of his own people. I call no other High King except him." Everyone stared at Blade.

"He died, Blade. He died when the Great City fell. You belong to a House that has no home."

"Tribute," the old dwarf countered.

Pjodarr smiled. "My master is right. If we pay tribute to your king, we will be allies."

The captain's eyebrows rose. "Aye, that is true, if you want to be like the freemen. What would you pay?"

Pjodarr waved behind him. "The var," he said sadly. "They are good beasts, and war-hardened. We have wyvern leather." The shaman shrugged. "We have nothing else."

Kinar looked at Blade. "You have one other thing." Gruesome felt the old shaman tense. "The gods only know what lies in that cave. It would be a shame to see Tremble lost in such a place." The other dwarf soldiers around the captain became more attentive. The havtrol lowered his hands to his weapons.

"That is a sjalsword, Captain Kinar. It holds the lifeline of its House. It is not given or taken lightly."

"I know what it is, shaman. What good does it do a dead House?" He eyed the old dwarf. "What say you, Blade?"

The general growled deep in his chest, then fixed his eye on Kinar. His voice came out like gravel. "Any of ye with the stone to take this sword from my dead hand, best draw steel now. Twenty-seven of my own kin have tried. Men of honor, heroes of wars. But a fool's pride only leads to one outcome."

"It was said you died when Northwatch fell, Blade. You haven't been seen in several years. Could be that you were hurt." He strutted past the shaman. "Just how close did you come to the fire that swallowed the Great City?"

Blade lowered his head. His right hand rose to his helm. Pjodarr opened his mouth, as if to speak, and stopped himself. Slowly, the general pulled the winged steel from his head.

His right eye glared at the captain, but that was not what Gruesome saw. The top left side of Blade's head was a mass of pink scars. The flesh had melted over his left eye, and the ear was gone. The havtrol had seen people burned before, but none that died from it and were brought back. The old dwarf only said two words before he covered his grotesque face.

"Close enough."

Kinar was shaken. Dwarves did not show such a thing easily. His voice had lost its boldness. "And what would I tell my king if it were lost?"

"Ye tell him that something lives down there that killed the Blade of House Thurin, and he should make his prayers to every god he holds dear. 'Cause there'll be no hope for the rest of ye."

The captain chuckled. "You haven't changed, General. I'll let you pass. And gods have mercy on whoever you find."

The old slave sighed, almost imperceptibly. "We have

information for you as well, and would ask a boon."

"A boon?"

"The girl," Pjodarr pointed at Erliga. "She will need an escort home."

"And where is her home?"

"The Sky Palace."

Kinar looked at the girl with suspicion. "What is one of Ranagol's slaves doing in my king's forest?"

The shaman shook his head. "I'm not sure, but it's one of the things we would discuss with you."

Erliga whispered something in Blade's ear. "They'll take ye home," he told her over his shoulder in norovid.

"What?" she screamed. Everyone looked at her. "But I am yours, you saved me from them. I'm yours now!"

"I never claimed ye, girl!"

She jumped off the var and ran toward Pjodarr. "You'll take me, won't you? I'll be a good servant!"

"A slave taking a slave?"

The girl looked at him with panicked eyes. She spun around until she saw Tarac. She ran to the boy like a mad woman. "Claim me. I'll be good to you. Don't make me go back!" She put her hands on the young man's chest and whispered something to him. His face turned bright red, and then he grabbed her hands and lowered them to her sides.

"I can't command you, Erliga. You may go wherever you wish."

"I want to stay with you. Please, let me stay."

The priest gave Pjodarr a pleading look. The shaman shook his head. "I guess she stays with us."

"Does he claim her as spoils?" the dwarf captain asked the old slave.

"So it seems."

Gruesome stared at the little girl. Why would she choose to stay with them, when she knew they still hunted the fiends that killed her other companions? Erliga clutched the priest's arm as she huddled behind him. Tarac seemed to almost fear the girl's touch. Kinar gave them a skeptical glare.

"The day grows late. Will you stay the night, or do you plan on sleeping in the unknown?"

Blade slipped from his perch atop the var. "We will accept ye hospitality, so long as it doesn't come with more threats."

"Are you saying the Lord of Northwatch felt threatened by me?" There were some chuckles from the captain's men.

In a flash, the general pulled the large sword from his back and pointed it at Pjodarr. "Shaman!" he shouted and lightning shot down the blade toward the old slave. Without turning his attention from Kinar, the shaman reached his right hand toward the blue arc. It bounced from his palm to land squarely in the middle of the closest fire. Kinar's face sobered. Blade returned the bone-handled sword to its hook with a flourish and winked at the younger dwarf.

"I think I'll sleep the peace of the gods tonight. How about ye?"

#####

Note from the Author

If you enjoyed reading *The Chosen*, please let us know. Remember to support all your favorite authors by taking a couple of minutes to write reviews on websites like Amazon or Goodreads.com.

Also, please visit http://www.the4threalm.com and sign up for The 4th Realm newsletter to keep up with all the latest releases from our talented crew! Check out the next page of this book for a listing of other works from all of us at The 4th Realm.

Thanks for reading.

Other Works by Authors From The4thRealm

The Chosen

The first book in our epic fantasy series, The Rise of Cithria. Written by Kris Kramer, Alistair McIntyre, and Patrick Underhill

"I loved This Book and can't wait to read the rest of the series." (Amazon.com review)

The Extraction

Some over-the-top crime fiction fun from Kris Kramer. Book 1 of The Organization

"If the author's other works are anything like this one I will be purchasing and reading all of his work." (Amazon.com review)

Phalanx Alpha

An expansive sci-fi thriller from Alistair McIntyre

"...would recommend it for anyone, not just science fiction fans." (Amazon.com review)

Sanctuary

A dark, historical fantasy novel by Kris Kramer. First in the Dominion Series

"Not only could I not put this book down, I want more!" (Amazon.com review)

Shallow Creek

A West Texas Thriller written by our resident Scot, Alistair McIntyre

"The mysteries and twists made me not want to stop reading." (Amazon.com review)

The Wind Riders

A new young adult fantasy from Kris Kramer. First in the Tales of the Lore Valley series.

22557121R00230

Made in the USA
Charleston, SC
23 September 2013